Brand of the Black Bat *and* Murder Calls the Black Bat

TWO CLASSIC ADVENTURES OF

THE BLACK-BAT

by Norman Daniels
writing as "G. Wayman Jones"

plus **THE MASK STRIKES by Raymond Thayer**
a rare classic from the Golden Age of Comics

and a new historical essay
by Will Murray

SANCTUM BOOKS

International Standard Book Number:
978-1-60877-183-7

First printing: August 2015

Series editor/publisher: Anthony Tollin
anthonytollin@shadowsanctum.com

Consulting editor: Will Murray

Copy editor: Joseph Wrzos

Proofreader: Carl Gafford

Cover restoration: Michael Piper

OCR text reconstruction: Richard Harvey and Audrey Parente

The editors gratefully acknowledge the assistance of Chuck Juzek, Michelle Nolan, Bob Carter, Rebecca Searson and John Gunnison in the preparation of this volume.

Published by Sanctum Books
P.O. Box 761474, San Antonio, TX 78245-1474

Visit the Black Bat at www.shadowsanctum.com.

THE BLACK·BAT

Volume 1

Presenting TWO Complete Book-length novels from the files of Tony Quinn, Nemesis of Crime, as originally edited by Leo Margulies, Mort Weisinger and Jack Schiff

Thrilling Tales and Features

Front cover art by Rudolph Belarski
Back cover by Rudolph Belarski, Emery Clarke and Raymond Thayer
Interior illustrations by Harry Parkhurst

BRAND OF THE BLACK BAT

A Complete Book-Length Novel
Introducing Tony Quinn,
the Nemesis of Crime

By
G. WAYMAN JONES

*Author of "Alias Mr. Death," "The Murder
Club," etc.*

*Walker closed his
fingers around the
gun (Chap. VI)*

CHAPTER I
VISIT BY NIGHT

TONY QUINN stirred restlessly in his sleep as a man's form moved silently across the room. The intruder was in a hurry, but he made not the slightest sound. Moonlight brought him into relief a moment, showing him to be about forty with a high, bald forehead, pointed, narrow nose and a small mouth. While there was nothing sinister or evil looking about him, he did exude one specific quality—that of being slippery.

He touched the sleeping man's shoulder and shook him slightly. In a flash, Tony Quinn was awake. His brain oriented itself immediately and one hand darted beneath his pillow to come forth with a .38 automatic.

"Wait, sir," the intruder whispered. "I'm doing you a great favor. Hear me out—please."

"Go ahead," Tony Quinn said softly. "Explain what you're doing in the house of the District Attorney."

"Are you the D.A.?" the intruder gasped. Then, without waiting for an answer, he went on. "That settles a lot of things. I'm not the only man in this house, sir. There's another, searching the rooms, and he's carrying a gun. Oh, I admit I came here to rob, but I don't relish being made a part of murder, sir."

"In the closet with you," Quinn said quickly. "Close the door and make no sound. If you're telling the truth, you won't be sorry. If this should be a trick, I'll riddle that closet door with slugs."

A MYSTERIOUS AVENGER IS BORN!

The intruder seemed to float across the room, so little noise did he make. Quinn lay down again, shoved the gun beneath the covers and slowly released the safety. His mind was fully awake now. He even grinned a little.

Then, through slitted eyes, he saw his bedroom door open. A man's chunky frame was silhouetted against the moonlight for a second. Lights flashed on. Quinn turned nervously, sat up and blinked. The man who had entered held a gun pointed straight at Quinn's chest and he was not more than ten feet from the bed.

"Take it easy, D.A.," the second intruder warned. Quinn studied him. He saw a short, pudgy man with a wide, cruel face and eyes that were narrowed tensely.

"All I want to do is talk," the man said. "You're alone in the house so I know I won't be interrupted. Just don't make any fast moves because I don't want to kill you."

"Now just a moment," Tony Quinn said calmly. "Who are you and why did Oliver Snate send you here?"

The intruder grinned. "You guessed it. Smart—ain't you? That's right—Snate sent me. Never mind who I am. Now listen, today court was adjourned to give you time to produce a surprise witness against Snate. He's on trial for intimidation and conspiracy. So far he's way ahead, according to the way we look at it, but you said something about a witness and recordings of Snate's voice. I came to make a deal."

Quinn never moved a muscle. "My life—against the recordings and the name of the witness—so you can murder said witness. Don't bother to tell me—I know. The answer is—nothing doing."

THE killer made a wry face. "You're making it tough, D.A. I got my orders—either the recordings and the witness' name, or I put a slug in you where it'll do the most good. Think it over—for five minutes. Don't do anything rash because I've got the drop and I'm ready to shoot."

Tony Quinn glanced at the closet door and wondered if this stealthy intruder who had warned him was no more than an agent of Snate's also. Mentally he damned himself for being so cocksure. Police Commissioner Warner had wanted to provide a guard, but Quinn had laughed that off. Now he seemed to be in a spot with death as the only exit.

True, with the automatic concealed beneath the bed covers, Quinn had a trump card to play, but he shuddered as he thought of what his predicament might have been if he hadn't been warned.

His finger tightened against the trigger of his gun. He looked squarely at the killer.

"I want this clearly established in my mind," he said slowly. "Snate sent you here with orders to get the recordings I mentioned—and also the name of my witness. Unless I produce them, I die. Is that correct?"

"You heard me the first time," the killer rasped. He was getting a bit jittery. A man in Quinn's precarious position should be trembling, quaking under the threat of sudden death. Yet Quinn was as cool as though he were addressing a jury on an open and shut case. It wasn't natural and the killer sensed that Quinn had something up his sleeve.

The killer licked his lips and primed himself for the murder. If he killed Quinn, Snate couldn't complain. Maybe the witness wouldn't dare come forward then—and the recordings might be in the house and easily found. The killer's finger tightened on the trigger.

Quinn saw the gleam in the man's eyes. He prepared to raise his own gun, still beneath the covers. It all depended upon who could shoot the fastest now. Then Quinn's heart stopped beating a moment. The gun was caught in the covers—

At that moment, the closet door opened and a shoe came hurtling out, straight for the gunman. He turned his head, swept the gun toward the closet and fired once. Quinn's automatic came free and the bang of his shot almost merged with that of the killer.

For a second or two, the thug stood perfectly still, gun still pointed at the closet. Then he gave a long sigh, his body sagged, hit the floor and rolled over into a heap. Quinn was out of the bed in a flash. On his way to the closet, he kicked the gun out of the thug's hand.

The intruder who had warned him was holding onto a hook with one hand while blood streamed down his face. He attempted a grin, but it failed because he was on the verge of unconsciousness. Quinn seized him just as he was about to take a header to the floor. He carried the man to the bed, placed him on it and then secured towels from the bathroom. He hastily wiped the blood from the man's face and saw that the bullet had inflicted only a scalp wound. Unless there was a concussion, the intruder would be on his feet within ten minutes.

QUINN poured raw brandy down the man's throat and nodded in satisfaction when the eyelids fluttered. Quinn left him for a moment and examined the gunman. He was quite dead.

"You—you're all right, sir?" the man on the bed asked. Quinn straightened up from his grim task, walked over to the bed and sat down.

"Thanks to you, I'm quite all right," he said. "You have a scalp wound that doesn't look serious. Can you talk now?"

"Yes, sir, I can talk all right, but there isn't much

Doomed to Darkness by a Murder Monger,

to say. I—I entered your house with full intentions of robbing you. I—I have a police record and—well—I suppose it's all up with me now."

Quinn poured another pony of brandy and helped the man prop himself up against the pillows. "Not by any means," he said. "You saved my life. Your act of burglary is wiped out by your act of courage. You practically gave yourself up to warn me and then you deliberately brought down that killer's bullets on yourself so I'd have a chance to shoot. Tell me more about yourself."

"My name is Kirby—Norton Kirby. I—I'm known on the records as Silk Kirby. I'm a confidence man. Burglary is out of my line, but I was hungry and desperate. I opened your front door with a master key and got inside just in time to see this other man open a window and crawl in. I knew he wasn't on the prowl and I figured he intended to murder you, sir. I reached you first—that's all."

"Silk Kirby," Quinn smiled a little. "I've never heard of you. I'm going to get you some food and coffee—if you can stand the stuff I call coffee."

"Let me, sir." Kirby raised himself and swung both feet to the floor. "I used to be a valet, sir. I can do it."

Quinn believed him, twenty minutes later, while he sipped some of the coffee Silk had made. The confidence man talked eagerly, as if he wanted to get things off his chest.

"I've never been vicious, sir. Whatever I did was against people who deserved to be—ah—clipped. Breaking into your home was the first act of violence I've ever attempted."

"It will be your last," Quinn said, and then as Silk grew pale he added hastily, "I'm not going to turn you in, Silk. You see, I need a man like you. I'm not married, I've plenty of money and I am also the District Attorney with any number of enemies. One in particular would like to see me wiped off the Earth. He sent the thug I killed. How would you like to work for me—act as sort of a bodyguard?"

Silk's eyes lighted up with an eagerness that couldn't have been assumed. "I'd like it, sir," he said simply. "I won't be so much of a bodyguard, but I could help you, sir."

Quinn grinned. "You're hired. I can judge men and I know you'll be honest with me. Now about this attempt at murder. You see, I'm trying Oliver Snate—a racketeer—for conspiracy. As with every other one of his tribe, it looked like a farce with witnesses who became tongue-tied, alibis for Snate that cropped up and couldn't be broken down by

any amount of questioning. Snate thought he'd be free soon, but—I had a trump card.

"A LITTLE old man named Brophy who runs a store on the West Side. He refused to knuckle under to Snate's men and Snate himself paid Brophy a visit. Brophy was no fool. He knew Snate would come so he arranged to have their conversation recorded. He turned the records over to me and they are in my safe now. Tomorrow Brophy will mount the witness stand, testify and the recordings will break Snate's alibis and protests of innocence wide open. I've got him on the run."

"I have heard of Snate, sir," Silk said and tried desperately not to wolf the sandwich he had made. "He's a dangerous man and I don't think he's finished yet. I'll remain up the rest of the night, sir, and guard the safe. You get some sleep. You'll need to be refreshed in the morning, sir."

Quinn walked over to a wall phone in the kitchen and dialed a number.

"You forget, Silk, there's a dead man in my bedroom. Even a District Attorney has to report sudden and violent death. Now remember, you're my valet. I hired you yesterday. No one will ask questions because the only servant I have had is a woman who cleans during the day."

Silk filled up on sandwiches while Quinn talked over the phone. Twenty minutes later a coroner's assistant appeared on the heels of a score of police. The body was removed. Silk prepared another room and Quinn retired. Silk found a gun in a library table drawer, sat down on a straight backed chair, tilted it against the wall safe and sat there until morning.

When Quinn came down, breakfast was ready.

CHAPTER II
SEARING ACID

 PROBABLY the tensest man in the courtroom was Oliver Snate. Attired in a two hundred dollar suit and a twenty dollar shirt with accessories to match, he sat on the edge of his chair and nervously chewed on the tips of his fingers. He knew that Quinn was the ablest District Attorney to operate in years and he knew also that the man he had sent to kill Quinn had himself died. Snate was scared and dangerously desperate.

He looked over his shoulder and some measure of confidence returned. Mingled with the onlookers

the Black Bat Makes Darkness His Weapon!

in the courtroom were five men, imported from a distant city so that detectives on guard wouldn't know them. These men had specific instructions. If they failed, Snate was doomed—not to a term in prison but to the electric chair. He didn't know these men either for an assistant had hired them, but he was a judge of such things and could pick them out.

Quinn entered the courtroom followed by Silk, who carried a bulging briefcase and two heavy law books. Silk set these down, whispered to Quinn and then took a seat at the reporter's table.

Court opened. Quinn addressed the judge and jury briefly. "Your Honor and Gentlemen of the jury, court was adjourned yesterday in order that I might produce irrefutable evidence that Oliver Snate is guilty of intimidation and conspiracy. My witness has been carefully hidden. Recordings that will prove Snate's guilt have been kept in my own home. I alone know exactly what those records will reveal and to what my witness will testify. These precautions are necessary because Oliver Snate is a ruthless, vicious beast. He—"

"I object," Snate's lawyer howled. "Bring on the evidence. Never mind the accusations. The District Attorney is trying to defame my client before the jury. My client, who is innocent and happens to be as upright a man as the eminent District Attorney himself."

Quinn faced Snate and inquired mildly, "Would an innocent man send one of his paid assassins to murder me during the night?" Snate turned his head away quickly. His lawyer gulped and sat down. Quinn stepped up to the witness stand, turned and motioned to a white haired old man who sat in the front row of the gallery. "I call Joseph Brophy to the stand," Quinn said. Brophy got up, looked around and all but tottered to the witness chair. He was sworn in and sat down, tapping his fingertips together nervously. Quinn opened his briefcase, drew out two recording disks and placed them on the table. Then he faced the witness.

"You will tell, in your own words, exactly how you met the accused. You will point him out and testify to everything you know concerning him. When you have finished, I will play back the recordings you took and then allow the learned counsel for the defense to see if he can discredit cold, mechanical testimony from a phonograph."

BROPHY began talking.

"It was three months ago tomorrow. Two of Snate's men came into my store and told me I had to buy insurance. I didn't need any and I told them so. Then they broke my showcase. Two days later they came back and assaulted me. I—I had to go to the hospital for a week. They came again and I told them to get out. This time they smashed my plate glass window. After that I got ready for the next visit. I prepared a recording machine with a sensitive microphone. I was in luck, because Snate himself came. I let him think I was ready to knuckle under and he talked. Every word is inscribed on those records."

"Tell us what he said," Quinn asked and watched the jury lean forward. These twelve men were eager to convict Snate. The super-racketeer had gotten away with every crime from murder down to simple assault and battery. All the jury needed was evidence enough.

Snate saw the jury, too. He nervously drew a silk handkerchief from his pocket and wiped his forehead. Behind him, five men tensed. It was the signal. One casually dropped a hand into his pocket, yanked the pin on a specially created smoke bomb and suddenly he jumped up, hurled the missile and then whipped out a gun. His four companions followed. The bomb burst the moment it landed just outside the jury box. The courtroom was thrown into an almost impenetrable fog. Working in unison, the five men pushed their way through the gates. Two of them jumped for the recordings on the table. One held a bottle of powerful acid in his hand. He dumped part of the contents on the disks.

Quinn, fighting his way to the table, saw the act. He lunged for the man with the acid. He drove a hard blow to the face, missed and stumbled. He fell heavily, but was up in an instant. The courtroom was in a frenzy. Women screamed and men cursed. Police and guards tried to distinguish the men who had started the riot, but the smoke fumes were too thick.

Quinn spotted the man with the acid and this time he wound both arms around him, trying to pin him down to the floor for a knockout blow. The thug, realizing his danger, used the only weapon handy. He hurled the remaining contents of the acid bottle over his shoulder. The searing liquid struck Quinn full in the face. He felt it bite into his flesh; felt it burn his eyes until the white fog was displaced by an inky blackness. He stumbled around, clawing at his face. Tears ran down his cheeks. The agony was almost more than human nerves could stand.

He reeled, clutched at the table, dabbed his eyes again and as the acid bit deeper and deeper he gave vent to a scream. Someone took his arm. Dimly he heard two quick shots and then blessed unconsciousness wiped out the torture that throbbed through his body.

Silk was at Quinn's side. A gun gleamed in his hand. Someone stepped up beside Quinn. Silk peered through the haze, raised his gun and fired once. A man, with an automatic in his fist, toppled to the floor, shot through the center of his forehead.

THAT shot seemed to be a signal. More guns barked. Someone smashed windows and air rushed in to displace the smoke. As the fog gradually cleared away, two men were seen elbowing their way through the milling crowd in the courtroom. They reached the heavy swinging doors.

Someone shouted, "Stop them! Stop those killers!"

The gunmen whirled and pumped half a dozen bullets in the direction of the bench. Then they burst into the corridor to be met by a hail of hot lead from a rapid-fire rifle in the hands of a policeman. The two men went down, riddled.

It was almost half an hour later before a semblance of order was restored. Ambulances and squad cars packed the curb in front of the court building. A horde of police filled the corridors, searching and questioning everyone. Snate sat between two guards, both wrists cuffed. Doctors worked frantically over half a dozen men.

Police Commissioner Jerome Warner came in. He surveyed the courtroom and swore softly. Outside, in the corridor, lay two gunmen, killed by a score of bullets. Within the courtroom itself lay the other three men who had been hired by Snate. All three were dead. One, accounted for by Silk, the other two killed under a withering fire from a dozen policemen's guns.

Brophy, the sole witness to Snate's act of conspiracy, still sat in the witness chair, but his body sagged forward and a knife was driven to the hilt in his chest. Quinn lay on one of the long tables while two doctors swabbed his eyes. He knew nothing of what went on. Silk hovered nearby, sweat running down his cheeks.

The commissioner mounted the bench and sat down beside the still pale jurist.

"An act which should make the people of this country blush with shame," the judge said, his voice trembling. "Despite all the precautions which I ordered, this ghastly thing has happened. The witness is dead, his recordings are destroyed by acid and the District Attorney probably blinded for life. Mr. Commissioner—why can't you do something about this?"

The commissioner mopped his perspiring face. "What can I do that I haven't already tried? If we can pin this on Snate—we'll send him to the chair, but don't be too certain that we can. Snate has been in jail and has a perfect alibi. Unless we can establish the identity of these five killers—who can't talk—we're licked. We must tie them up with Snate and his mob or there is no evidence."

"I'll hold Snate," the judge snapped. "I'll hold him just as long as I can. Get your men to work, Commissioner. Tie those five killers to Snate's gang and you'll have him. Show the public we have a police force—not a bunch of blue uniformed morons."

But Commissioner Warner soon learned that this was impossible. The five dead thugs were identified by fingerprints. They were strangers in town and in no way could be linked to either Snate or even the most obscure member of his gang. It was the old story of the ruthless destruction of evidence and witnesses that couldn't be otherwise suppressed. The case against Snate had collapsed. What people thought, or assumed, had no material effect on the letter of the law. There was absolutely no evidence against the sneering racketeer.

THREE hundred especially picked detectives worked frantically, night and day, to uncover some scrap of evidence which might hold Snate, but no such piece of evidence existed. Snate's attorneys were clever, too. They protested that their client could never have conceived this hideous plan. They proved that he had been allowed no visitors and could in no way send out word to his men. Whatever had happened was not of his doing, Snate's high-priced attorneys protested cynically.

They spoke of theories by which some man whom Tony Quinn had sent away had exacted his vengeance. The theory was plausible for Quinn had made many enemies during his three years' term as a crimebuster. Theories, conjectures and suppositions filled the air, but there was no meat to them. In the end, Snate was released by the same judge who had been forced to duck bullets dealt out by Snate's hirelings. Not even the intruder who had been killed by Quinn could be connected with Snate's mob. In fact, the dead killer had been identified as a man with good cause to hate Quinn. His brother had died in the electric chair as a result of Quinn's work.

Newspapers took up the challenge. They called for everything from a complete change of administration to the arrest of Snate on no charges at all. Commissioner Warner lost fifteen pounds in two weeks. His face grew haggard, his eyes became puffed and bloodshot from lack of sleep and physical exhaustion.

Only one man offered no suggestions, made no statements. Tony Quinn lay on a davenport in the library of his home. He spoke rarely and to no one but faithful Silk, and then only when necessary.

For Tony Quinn's heart was filled with a rage. His mind sought vainly to find some solution to it all, but there seemed to be none. And what sent Quinn deep into the blackness of despair was a new affliction which filled every waking hour with agony.

Tony Quinn was stone blind!

CHAPTER III
GIRL OF MYSTERY

TONY QUINN, no longer district attorney, lived on in darkness. The days grew into weeks, the weeks into months. "I'm blind, Silk," he said for the thousandth time.

"Blind as a bat, Silk. I'm doomed to live the rest of my life in a world of darkness so that an inhuman monster like Snate can flourish. What are the latest reports about him?"

Silk shook his head slowly. "I won't hold back anything, sir. You're clever enough to know when I do. Snate is back where he was before you arrested him a year ago. He's growing more powerful than ever. I—I didn't tell you this before, sir. Snate sent a box of flowers to the hospital when you were there—with a note of sympathy. I threw them into the trash can, sir."

Quinn laughed hollowly. "You did quite right. I only wish it had been Snate himself. Well, Silk, I don't suppose you'll be around much longer. I've recovered as much as I ever will. My face is scarred for life, I'm blind with absolutely no hope of recovery according to the best doctors that money can hire. I'm washed up and above all I want no sympathy, so if you wish to leave—it's all right with me."

Silk straightened out the covers on Quinn's shoulders. "If you don't mind, sir, I'll stay on. You need me now and I—I've grown to need you, sir. Perhaps one day we will meet a doctor—one who may give us some hope. As for your scars—they are hardly worth mentioning. One can scarcely notice them, sir."

Quinn laughed again cynically.

"You're a cheerful liar, Silk. Why, I can even feel them with my hands. Odd, Silk, how strange my sense of touch has become. It's a year since I became blind, yet already I can distinguish things by merely passing my hands over them. A recompense, in part, for my lack of sight. What about some of that good coffee, Silk? In one thing at least I'm fortunate—having you."

Silk swallowed hard. "I'll make the coffee, sir. It won't take but a few moments. Don't try to move."

Quinn arose, threw off the blanket about his shoulders and walked rapidly toward a table in one corner of the room. He sidestepped a chair, stopped an inch from the table and put his hands on it.

"No need to worry about me, Silk," he said with a smile. "That's another thing I've learned. Objects I cannot see tend to warn me in some way. I know they are in front of me and I can avoid them. I'm quite all right. Get busy with the coffee."

Silk moved to the door. "It's almost midnight, sir. I'll have it ready at a quarter after."

HE HURRIED to the kitchen with a slow shaking of his head. Silk was grateful that Quinn couldn't see the livid scars that made a mockery of a face once handsome. The acid had eaten deeply, etching a hideous mask around Quinn's eyes that now were dead and blank.

Quinn made his way back to the davenport and sat down. His mind was spinning. What could he do? He couldn't even read. The radio had long since grown to be a bore and Quinn refused to see any of his friends with the exception of Police Commissioner Warner.

Quinn's fingers worked in and out, as though he had Snate's fat neck between them. Once Quinn had even considered sending for Snate and shooting him down. He gave up that idea when he went looking for a gun. Silk had removed every weapon —to guard against suicide.

Suddenly Quinn raised his head and turned it to one side, like a listening dog. He reached out and curled his hand around a heavy cigarette container.

"Who is there?" he demanded in a whisper. "Speak up. I know there is someone in this room. I can hear the wind rustling through the curtains and every window was closed when Silk left me."

There was no reply but Quinn's highly sensitive ears caught the rustle of silk and his nostrils dilated as they sniffed a perfume. Then a cool, soft hand touched his wrist.

"Please," a woman's voice said softly, "I'm here to help you, Tony Quinn. I'm sorry I had to do it this way, but it was necessary."

"Who are you?" Quinn's hands rose and touched her face. Eagerly the fingers traced every curve and outline. "You're pretty," he went on. "Very pretty. Your hair is soft and silken. You have warm, well shaped lips and I'm betting your eyes are blue."

"You win the bet," the girl said softly and sat down beside him. "What I have to say will not take long, Tony Quinn. I know how you lost your eyesight—I know everything about you. The doctors all said there was no hope, but I am here to give you that hope. Will you accept my suggestions no matter how strange they may seem?"

"Who are you?" Quinn asked. "And how can you give me hope?"

"You will wait exactly three days," the girl said, paying no heed to his questions. "Then go to a little town in Illinois—Springville by name. You will consult a doctor named Harrington. Everyone knows him in Springville. He knows you are coming and he is ready. He alone can cure you."

"How?" Quinn demanded in a hoarse whisper. "How can some country doctor do what world famous surgeons say is impossible? Why are you so interested?"

"I'll tell you… someday," the girl said. "You will do this for me, Tony Quinn? For yourself?"

He nodded and tried to find her hand. She pulled them both out of his reach and arose.

"Come back." Quinn was on his feet. "Come back—please."

But there was no answer. Silk ran into the room with a broad bladed kitchen knife in his hand.

"What is it, sir? Was there someone here?"

Quinn sat down slowly. "An angel, Silk. She must have been an angel because she has given me hope."

Silk gaped and edged toward the phone. What he had so long feared was now an actuality. Quinn's tortured mind had snapped.

"No," Quinn laughed, sensing Silk's actions. "I'm quite sane. There was a girl here. She came through one of the French windows and she told me where to go and get my sight back again. In three days, Silk, we leave for Springville, Illinois. No one is to know where we have gone. No one, understand, Silk?"

"Yes, sir, but—"

"NO BUTS. If you so much as whisper this to the canary, I'll skin you alive. Look here, Silk, I've got faith. I have visions of a new life beginning for me. I know that someday I'll see again and when that day comes, Oliver Snate is going to wish he had never been born. He's going to be broken—mentally and financially. I'll wear him down until he's on his knees. And I won't use the weapons I had at my command as District Attorney. I'll use highly unorthodox ones. I'll fight him with his own methods. I'll—"

"*We* will do that," Silk put in. "We, sir."

Quinn smiled. "Right. In my enthusiasm I forgot you, Silk. You'll be of tremendous help to me. Together we'll twist the coyote's tail until he howls. Perhaps all this is false hope, but that girl sounded so real, so sincere. Find out where Springville is, Silk. We won't charter a plane because I want this whole affair kept a secret. Make reservations on a train, under assumed names."

The buzz of the doorbell put an end to further conversation. Silk escorted three men into the room. Quinn nodded in their direction.

"I can't say the usual thing—that I'm glad to see you, Commissioner Warner, because I can't see. Rather, I'll say I'm happy you're here. You and your friends."

Commissioner Warner sat down and twirled his hat. His iron grey hair and mustache seemed to have taken on a lighter shade recently. The lines of worry under his eyes had become permanent. His companions ranged themselves on either side of him.

Warner introduced them. Paul Stewart was a robust type with a short, fat neck and squinty little eyes. He was nonetheless Commissioner of Correction for the entire State. The second man was Otto Fox, head of the nation's largest armored car service. He was thin, mild looking and even more nervous than Warner.

The Commissioner said: "We've come to you for advice. When you were District Attorney, you could place your finger on the authors of crime faster than any dozen detectives. I wonder if that trait still holds good?"

"It's about armored cars, Commissioner?" Quinn asked. "Go ahead, fire away. If I can help you, I certainly will."

Warner looked a little startled. "I suppose you guess it was armored cars because Otto Fox is with me. You're right. We've run up against the strangest thing, Quinn. Armored cars are sent out over their routes. They start with a full crew of men known to be perfectly honest. They make their regular calls and then drop off the face of the Earth. Somehow they are being spirited away with their entire crews and, of course, every cent they've picked up along their route."

"They vanish like some of the things a magician waves his wand over," Otto Fox broke in with a reedy voice. "I tell you it's supernatural. How could anybody steal an armored car full of armed guards with orders to shoot? It can't be done, I tell you. It's not possible."

"How many have vanished?" Quinn asked.

"Three—so far," Warner said. "There isn't a trace of them. I've a hunch your friend Oliver Snate might be secretly behind this little plan. Does this look like his work?"

QUINN shook his head. "It may be his work, but not his brains. Snate couldn't think that deeply. I'm sorry, gentlemen—I can't help you. A year ago I'd have joined in as eagerly as possible, but—I'm a blind man. I can no longer move without a man at my side. I stumble over things and I can't step outside my home except for a short breath of air."

Warner put a hand on Quinn's shoulder. "I know that, old man, but your brain isn't impaired. I thought, perhaps, you might recognize the methods behind this new racket. I'll tell you what, Tony: if there are any new developments, I'll drop in again. You might solve the whole problem for us."

Otto Fox, faintly drumming his fingertips on the arm of his chair, nodded assent. Paul Stewart looked a little bored. Quinn shook hands with them and Silk ushered them to the door.

Silk returned, frowning. "I don't understand it, sir. The Commissioner comes out here with his problems and expects you to solve them instantly—without even an investigation."

Quinn laughed. "He's not fooling me, Silk. Warner only drops in to pretend he needs my help. That serves to give me an idea I'm still in the running. It's a colossal bluff and I might seem to fall for it, but there's only Commissioner Warner's good heart in all this. Mind you now—not a word of our intended trip."

Silk served the coffee and sat down to drink a cup with Quinn. The blind man stared straight ahead.

"You know, Silk, Warner had an interesting problem. Imagine, three armored cars, staffed by reliable men, disappearing in broad daylight? In the face of that this enforced inactivity is enough to drive a man mad."

In the following four months, eleven more armored cars vanished from sight while police ran themselves ragged striving to uncover the slightest clue. Commissioner Warner listened to frantic appeals for help. The relatives of the armored car guards clamored for some news of their loved ones. Newspapers took up the cry.

Commissioner Warner listened to the frantic appeal.

And all the while Tony Quinn sat in a darkened room with bandages across his eyes. His visit to the little rural town in Illinois had been brief—barely two weeks. He had undergone an operation, the nature of which an old, brittle-tongued, family doctor had refused to discuss, but Tony Quinn knew one thing—he could see.

True, there had been only vague shadows, but those were sufficient to bring his courage and hope up to a maximum. As to the girl, he had learned absolutely nothing. The one stipulation under which the doctor had consented to treat him was that he must ask no questions.

Silk finished reading the latest newspaper and threw it on a table. Quinn leaned back in his chair, gently massaging his eyes.

"In a few days, Silk, I'll see again. I know I will. I must because there is so much work to do. You and I are going to find out what has happened to those armored cars. We're going to pin something on Oliver Snate and see that he pays a suitable penalty for the suffering he has caused."

"I don't see how you'll be able to do it, sir," Silk put in. "You're well known. Of course everyone thinks you are blind and there is no hope of ever recovering your sight. You could wander around without arousing suspicion."

"SILK, what do you suppose I've been planning all this time?" Quinn spoke passionately and exultantly. "Wander around?" Quinn laughed and there was no longer a hollow tone to his laughter. "We won't wander, Silk. We'll go out—with smoking guns in our hands if necessary. We'll use whatever means we think best in our fight against Snate and others of his kind. We'll fight them with their own weapons—with treachery, intimidation, theft—and draw the line only at murder. If we kill, it will be in self-defense. We'll take every nickel of their stolen loot. We'll worry them until they are as jittery as a one legged man on a tightrope. We'll work with the police or against them if need be. We'll make our own laws and we'll enact our own judgments. Silk—this is the opportunity I've waited for during long weeks of darkness. Every moment when I was blind, Silk, I planned for this."

Silk's eyes flashed eagerly. "So have I, sir. I've hoped—almost as strongly as you. I've even thought of quitting your service and going after Snate myself. I can still see him, so smug and domineering, in a courtroom filled with man-made fog and spitting guns. I wanted to shoot him that day. I almost did."

"Good," Quinn approved. "Not about shooting Snate. That's too easy for him. It's your attitude I like. You see—I'll need a man like you—one who knows the underworld and has a few connections."

"But how are you going to handle it, sir?" Silk wanted to know. "Your face, if you'll pardon me, is disfigured. It won't be a pleasant sight when you first see it. You'll be recognized."

"My face?" Quinn leaned back and compressed his lips. "That can be taken care of. Plastic surgery can make it over. But not now, Silk. Not now! I want people to think I'm helpless and that I haven't enough interest in life to even have my features mended. We'll operate anonymously. No one must know who we are. I'll have to wear a mask, of course—a complete hood, I suppose, if my features are as bad as that doctor said they were."

"Yes, sir," Silk nodded, "it will have to be a hood. I'll make one, sir, of silk. Black silk, that can't be seen in the night. You can dress in black also and be nothing more than a dim shadow in the darkness."

"But there must be some means of identification," Quinn pursed his lips. "Something by which men can recognize me. An insignia—a name, Silk—I have it! I've been blind—as blind as a bat. I still am so far as anyone knows. I shall prowl during the night. Bats are blind and fly by night, also. I'll be the bat, Silk. The Black Bat!"

CHAPTER IV
THE LIGHT AGAIN

 EACH day Silk read the newspapers aloud while Quinn mentally filed away whatever information they offered. Another armored car had vanished. Even the increased staff of guards hadn't prevented it from disappearing.

The papers traced it carefully. Under sealed orders, the contents of which were known only to a trusted employee, the car had first visited two big banks and carried away heavy payrolls. Then they had picked up more money at busy department stores and restaurants. The previous day's receipts of prominent theatres were collected until it was estimated that two hundred thousand dollars rested within its steel-lined walls.

It had visited a small manufacturing plant where ten thousand dollars was dispensed to meet a payroll. After that the car had been seen heading north along a busy boulevard and from that moment on it had never been seen again. Somewhere, along an important street where thousands of people walked and rode, where police cars and patrolmen were on active duty, the car had vanished as completely as if swallowed up in the middle of the road.

There was other news, too—of Oliver Snate. His connections had grown during the months of Quinn's blindness. He was now the recognized overlord of crime. His influence reached into political offices, delved deeply into private businesses and touched the very bottom of the underworld. No crook, no matter how big or small, would dare to operate without sharing a portion of his profits with Snate. His power had increased until even the newspapers were afraid of him. Only one dared print the real truth, and that paper had suffered a bomb explosion in its linotyping rooms.

"Peter Gage is trying to do his job," Quinn told Silk. "He owns the *News-Record* and he's certainly thrown down the gauntlet to Snate. But there is someone else behind Snate. He's just a front—a man to take the rap if anything happens. Snate is ruthless, but he can't think. There are brains behind all this and I'm banking that those same brains have concocted a way to make armored cars vanish from the face of the Earth. One of these days we'll know, Silk. We'll know and Snate will be unpleasantly surprised."

"You'll remove the bandages tomorrow, sir?" Silk asked.

"Tomorrow," Quinn repeated. "Yes, Silk. Then I must remain in a darkened room for thirty days. They'll be the longest thirty days of my life, even though I shall be able to see a little. That's all, Silk. I won't require anything more tonight."

Silk withdrew silently, his lean face aglow with enthusiasm. Quinn wanted to be alone—in these last few hours of his blindness—for with the morning he would know whether or not he might really see again.

Oddly enough, Quinn's mind wasn't on his affliction or the possibility of its cure. As he sat before a glowing fireplace he thought of the soft spoken girl with the silken hair and the blue eyes, hair and eyes he hadn't been able to see. Yet somehow he felt as though she was always near him, watching over him much as Silk did. A clock intoned midnight. Quinn raised his hands to the bandage around his eyes. Slowly he began unwinding it and he knew that his heart never missed a beat.

The confidence which the country doctor had exuded served to give Quinn part of its measure. The last folds of the gauze fell away and two thick pads dropped from his eyes.

THERE was a searing flash of light and Quinn uttered a cry of pain. He turned away swiftly. He had been facing the fireplace and had forgotten that its light might harm his vision.

One thing he did know. His eyes reacted! There had been a flash of light! He could see! How much, he didn't know—yet. But he was satisfied. He could really see. A hymn of thanksgiving rose in his soul. He turned his back on the fire and then slowly and carefully opened his eyes again.

There was a chair. Dim, yes, but still a chair. He could see it! A mirror on the further wall reflected some of the light from the fireplace. Quinn gasped. He could see that.

Then he stiffened. There was something else. A dim shape—there in the dark corner of the room. It was moving. Moving out toward him, like a grim spectre. Quinn blinked and tried to penetrate the haze. He moved his head to one side and closed his eyes tightly. There was a pad of feet, a swish of silk. And Quinn knew. The girl of mystery had returned.

"You," he cried. "You!"

"Yes, Tony Quinn. I knew that when midnight passed, you'd no longer be able to restrain yourself. But you must not expose your eyes to light—not yet. It might harm them. Walk into the next room and I shall follow. It is darker there—and better for your eyes."

Quinn obeyed, keeping his lids tightly closed as he passed the fireplace, but basking in the knowledge that some of the light penetrated the lids. He was going to see again!

He sat down and opened his eyes. Faint moonlight streamed in through the tall French windows. Then he saw the girl move across his range of vision and to his amazement he could see her plainly. Far more clearly than it had been possible before he had been blinded. Even the colors of her face, her hair and her eyes were visible to him in this room of almost absolute darkness. He started up, involuntarily, with one hand reached out toward her.

"No," she said sternly. "You must remain just where you are, Tony Quinn. I have come to talk and ask a favor."

"Favor?" Quinn said. "All the favors within my power could never fill the appreciation I feel for you. And you are lovely—your hair is so golden, your cheeks so red and your eyes so blue."

"You—can—see that?" she asked incredulously.

"I can. Somehow that operation has given me hyper-sensitive eyes enabling me to see in the darkness. You're as clear to me as if the lights were on. I—I hardly understand it myself."

"I do," the girl said quickly, breathlessly. "I know the anatomy of the human eye, Tony Quinn. Within the cornea are the aqueous humor and the iris. The iris is a colored muscular membrane with the pupil in the center. The pupil is, actually, a hole for the transmission of light and in your eyes this pupil is exceptionally large and therefore much more sensitive. A cat's eyes are the same. Just behind the pupil lies a crystalline lens which acts the same as the lens of a camera. Yours is much larger than that of a normal eye because of the enlarged pupil. Your range as well as your sharpness of vision is greater and—you are enabled to see in darkness. I tell you this, Tony Quinn, so you will know for yourself. I won't talk about it again until you hear my complete story."

SHE sat down, ten feet across the room from him. "I did all this for you with one idea in mind, Tony Quinn. Now that you can see again, you are ready to fight back against the forces that blinded you. I want to join that fight."

"You?" Quinn gasped. "But how did you know that? No one knows—except Silk, and he certainly hasn't talked."

"He hasn't," the girl answered. "Yet I do know that you plan to fight evil and crime with their own weapons. That you hope to force Oliver Snate to pay for his crimes. Don't ask me how I know. The fact that I do will suffice for the moment. You will let me help you?"

Quinn shook his head. "No. That is one thing I cannot do. From tonight on I am no longer Tony Quinn but the Black Bat! There will be danger where I go—and sudden death. It is no place for a girl."

"That is final?" she asked.

"It is final," Quinn answered. "Anything else in the world I will more than gladly do. I owe you the return of my sight, but I can't repay that debt by exposing you to death. There is no place for a girl in my operations. I tell you all this because I know you are to be trusted. But—why not tell me who you are? Why you did this and what lies behind your request to join the forces of the Black Bat?"

"Close your eyes, Tony Quinn," she said with something that sounded like a choked sob. "You must not keep them open more than a few moments at a time until several days have passed."

Quinn closed his eyes slowly. It seemed a very natural thing to obey the girl. He heard a rustling sound, the click of a window lock and she was gone. He started up, walking rapidly toward the window through which she had escaped. A light laugh came from the darkness outside.

"Tony Quinn," her voice drifted in to him, "I'll join your forces whether you like it or not, and one day you'll ask me to work with you. No—don't interrupt me. I have one thing more to say. On the first of next month—after your eyes are quite recovered—Oliver Snate plans to start a campaign of bank robbery. You must prevent it."

Then she was gone. Dimly, Quinn heard a car's motor whine into life. He walked slowly back to his chair and sat down to think. How had this girl learned of his plans to rid the city of crime in all its vicious forms? Silk hadn't talked. Quinn knew him too well to suspect that. Yet not another soul knew of these plans. Her mysterious knowledge spelled clairvoyancy, even though Quinn believed in none of the occult sciences.

It was daybreak when he went to bed—with his eyes covered by pads and adhesive.

The days passed quickly after that. By night, Quinn worked furiously. A soundproofed target range in the cellar of his spacious home echoed to the roar of exploding guns. Targets that were mere blobs in the darkness were shattered by Quinn's expert marksmanship. Not until he could hit a playing card, tossed into the air by Silk, did he cease his pistol practice. And that card had been used as the target in a range as dark as pitch.

"IT'S A sort of payment for the months you couldn't see at all," Silk offered happily. "I can't even see a regulation size target three feet away, but you put two bullets through the deuce of spades at thirty feet."

"Darkness is almost like daylight to me," Quinn said. "But there is no time for talk. In two days I can face daylight. When that happens, Silk, we shall begin to create furrows of worry on Snate's placid brow. Is everything lined up?"

"Yes sir. Two or three of Snate's men have been systematically robbing jewelry houses and the loot runs into many thousands of dollars. They haven't fenced it yet because none of the local fences will handle the stuff. It's too hot."

"So?" Tony Quinn pursed his lips. "You have something else on your mind, Silk?"

Silk parted his lips in a cold grin. "Yes sir. A new fence—with plenty of money—might suddenly appear and be willing to buy up all kinds of hot goods. I think it could be arranged, sir."

"It is arranged," Quinn said happily. "Draw enough money, Silk. Work quickly and get things all set. Have every bit of that stolen jewelry concentrated in one spot.

"Begin—now!"

CHAPTER V
VOICE ON THE WIRE

 ILK KIRBY presented a wholly new appearance when he walked into the expensive cafe ten hours later. He couldn't disguise his narrow face, nor the thin nose and slanting forehead, but he looked anything but a valet. His clothing was obviously expensive and loud. He smoked dollar cigars and kept his vest pocket stuffed with them. A two carat diamond flashed iridescent rays from the ring finger of his right hand and he wore a diamond-studded watch low on his wrist where it was constantly in sight.

"Brandy," he informed the bartender. "The very best—Napoleon '96."

There were half a dozen men at the bar and they

eyed Silk with interest. That interest grew when he paid the dollar and a half check for the sip of brandy. Silk's purse was crammed with bills of big denomination. He drank slowly, relishing each drop. Then he went out.

One man followed him very carefully, but Silk was aware of that. The men at the bar had been of Snate's tribe and they accepted him immediately as either a positive sucker—or a man who might be valuable to Snate. Silk didn't care which idea they assumed.

He took no pains to conceal his movements and once he stopped at a jewelry store where he had a whispered consultation with the manager. Watching eyes saw the manager shake his head violently and Silk put something back into his pocket. When he had gone, the man who had followed him entered the store.

He flashed a badge, stolen from a detective many months before. "That guy who was just in here. What did he want?"

The store manager looked around quickly and dropped his voice to a whisper. "He had an emerald—a perfect specimen—and he wanted to sell it. Somehow that stone looked familiar. I don't want anything to do with crooks. I put him out."

"You should have called headquarters," the pseudo-detective growled.

He left and headed up the street in the direction Silk had taken. Much to his surprise, Silk was loitering along the avenue, gazing into store windows. When Silk turned into a swanky hotel, his shadow heaved a sigh of relief. Snate would pay well for this information. His organization allowed no poaching and this flashily dressed man was definitely engaged in some kind of crooked work, else where had he secured a valuable emerald—and the wad of cash that filled his purse?

A discreet question to a bell captain and Snate's man had everything he needed.

"That man?" the bell captain slipped the two dollar bill into his pocket. "His name is Alexander Green, sir. He came here from Los Angeles. A perfect gentleman, sir."

Upstairs Silk watched through parted curtains as his shadow stepped into a taxi. He grinned, stripped off his loud suit and donned a bathrobe. Then he placed two guns in different parts of the room, both of them concealed, yet quickly accessible. After that he read newspapers for the better part of two hours. When his phone rang, he betrayed no surprise. A Mr. Walker wanted to see him. Silk had Mr. Walker sent up.

WHEN he opened the door, two men stepped in. One closed the door, put his back against it and kept one hand deep in his coat pocket. The other, who had been Silk's shadow, sat down and offered Silk a cigarette.

"Being a stranger here," he began, "I suppose you are surprised to receive visitors. I'll be perfectly frank with you. A few hours ago you tried to pass a certain kind of rock in a certain kind of store. Maybe you could interest me in it."

"Could I?" Silk asked mildly. "Perhaps if you asked that gorilla by the door to let go of his gun, I might feel more in the mood. Personally, I hate guns. They have no place in my business."

"Okay, Joe," Walker said. "You can relax."

The gunman eyed Silk fishily, but he sat down and folded his arms. Silk had a notion that a second gun rested only a few inches from the thug's right hand.

"That's better," Silk grinned. "Now, Mr. Walker, I'm listening most intently. By way of introduction my name is—"

"Green," Walker put in. "From Los Angeles. We've checked, you see. First of all I want to warn you. Taking it for granted that you are a right guy, get this straight: nobody operates in this town without permission from a certain man. This town is all sewed up. You either work with the organization—or you don't work at all."

Silk puffed contentedly on his cigarette and crossed his legs. "I see," he said quietly. "You're a bit off the trail, though. I'm no hood. My specialty is the discreet handling of gems. I'm an artist when it comes to jewels. I feel the warmth of them, glory in their allure and sparkle and, very incidentally, I like the profits they sometimes produce."

"That rock you showed a jeweler downtown," Walker narrowed his eyes. "Where'd you get it?"

Silk looked into space. "I don't violate confidences. Enough that I paid a fancy price for it and I expect to get about fifty thousand for the gem. It's quite perfect. Here—look for yourself."

He reached into his pocket and the thug instantly moved to action. His right hand vanished under his coat and half pulled a gun from a spring holster. Silk regarded him with a mild grin and dropped the flashing emerald on the table top. Walker scooped it up and whistled.

"Some rock! Sure you can get rid of this?"

"I certainly would not have purchased it if I thought I might have a white elephant on my hands. Don't be a fool—of course I can sell it. Why?"

"Would about fifty or sixty stones like this interest you?" Walker asked cautiously. "Not all emeralds, of course. There are diamonds, a matched string of pearls and a few other doodads. You know what I mean."

"How hot?" Silk arose and walked the floor, hands clasped behind his back. He paused at the side of the thug and put a hand on his shoulder. "Please don't bother with the cannons. You'll tire your shooting hand always keeping it tense."

The thug scowled and muttered something, but he did relax. Silk faced Walker again.

"I asked you—how hot are those rocks?"

WALKER shrugged. "Not very. They've been out of circulation about three months. Maybe you'd like to see them, huh?"

"Perhaps. Will you bring them here?"

"Smart, aren't you?" Walker laughed. "We're no saps, Green. No—you'll come with us, and blindfolded at that. You'll see a few samples and we'll dicker."

"I'll get my hat," Silk suggested. "We'll go at once."

Ten minutes later, Silk was inside a sedan. He felt a gun shoved into his side and Walker pressed adhesive over his eyes. They rode that way for almost an hour. Then Silk was led out of the car, across a cement driveway and up five steps. He sat down when a chair was shoved under him and blinked when the blindfolds were removed.

He found himself in an expensively furnished library. There were four men lined up against the wall and they wore the surly looks of professional killers. Behind a huge desk sat Oliver Snate. He hadn't changed much during the months since Silk had seen him in court. He was still tall, angular and his patent leather hair was slicked down on his scalp. His closely cropped mustache was jet black and he kept rubbing his hands together.

But Snate's eyes were narrow. "I've seen you somewhere before," he said suspiciously. "I rarely forget a face."

Silk's lips parted in a smile. "I heard that of you, Mr. Snate. You did see me. Once, three years ago, you came to Folsom Prison to visit a man named Mandell who was doing the book. You were trying to spring him, but the screws caught on. Mandell was transferred to Alcatraz. I was the trusty who led Mandell into the visitors' room. He told me about your plan after you had gone. We were pals."

Snate nodded. "You must be on the level or you wouldn't have known that. All right, I'm convinced, although I might warn you that if I'm crossed you'll join a lot of other saps at the bottom of the bay where they're resting in a bed of cement. Now, what's your racket?"

"I buy—and I sell," Silk answered readily. "Which means we can help one another and I'm in no way infringing on your own rackets, Snate. I've got cash and I'm ready to buy."

"To the tune of a hundred and fifty grand?" Snate asked.

Silk nodded. "I'll give you an even hundred thousand for the stuff you say is worth a hundred and fifty grand. Don't play me for a sucker, Snate. I know what hot stuff is worth."

"Okay," Snate grinned. "We understand one another, I see. You'll be taken back to your hotel. Wait there. Tonight some of my men will show. Look over the stuff they offer and give them your best price.They'll phone me and if it's all right, we trade. You might also give me the name of one or two right guys on the coast. I'll phone them and get an okay on you—just to be sure."

"Of course," Silk agreed. "Call Jerry Monohan—at the Club Elite. You know Monohan even if you are three thousand miles away. Ask him about Alex Green. That's the name I went under out there."

An hour later, Silk was escorted into his hotel suite by Walker and the same pug who had acted as guard.

"You," Silk indicated the pug, "come here." He dropped a hand into his pocket and withdrew a short barreled pistol. With a grin he passed it over, butt first, to the gunman. "I took this out of your pocket before we went to Snate's place. Take my advice and always keep your guns in holsters. And beware of pickpockets."

THE thug took the gun with a stunned look. Walker guffawed.

"You must be okay," he said. "Imagine—seeing Snate with a gun in your pocket! That never happened before. We'll see you about ten-thirty tonight. Have the dough ready."

Silk waited more than an hour after they had departed. Then he went down to the lobby, studied the faces of the men and women who lounged there and entered a phone booth. He dialed a number.

"This is Green," he reported. "At ten-thirty tonight we do business. Everything looks okay."

Then he hung up and went back to his room. He felt confident that he had put the deal across nicely. If Snate did contact the coast, Jerry Monohan would identify Alexander Green. Silk had once deemed it wise to assume another identity now and then.

But Silk might not have been so sure of himself had he been able to listen to a conversation in a taxi just outside the hotel. While Silk surveyed the people in the lobby, an ugly face was almost pressed against one of the big plate glass windows that overlooked the entire lounge of the hotel. The man who watched nodded his head emphatically, as if to emphasize to his own mind that he had been right.

Walker was in the taxi. "Well," he asked eagerly, "were you right?"

The thug grimaced, "Was I? Say—that guy is made up plenty and he dresses different, but take it from me—that's the same mug who followed Quinn, the old D.A., into the courtroom the day he got the acid in the face. I know because I was close to him. He came outta the same car with Quinn and carried his briefcase and books. Then, later on, this same mug bumped one of them hoods Snate hired to take care of things in court. We gotta see Snate—quick."

Walker shook his head and smiled wisely. "Not so fast. Look—if this guy is really a stooge, we'll make him talk so we can prove it to Snate later on. But what nobody but you and I will know is where that hundred grand has gone. We'll give the jewels back to Snate, tell him it was a plant and this guy didn't bring any dough."

"Okay," the other man growled, "but how do we work this?"

"Snate doesn't know that Green is a stooge of Quinn. He wouldn't even know the guy was in court that day because Snate wasn't watching anybody but himself. So what do we do? We take Green for a little buggy ride and see if he's got a tongue in his head. I know treatments to make stubborn men talk. What's more, we don't tell anybody else because if we do, they'll try to horn in. Soon as this punk tells us enough to convince Snate, we bump him. I'll have the dough and the boys who are to help us won't know it."

The cab drove away quickly and Walker plotted the procedure of the evening.

Snate, meanwhile, waited until he was alone in the study. Then he carefully locked each door, pulled open the lower drawer of his desk and removed a telephone. He simply lifted the receiver and the connection was automatically completed.

"I GOT something," Snate reported without the preamble of introducing himself. "A guy blew in here from the coast. Says his name is Green and he's looking for rocks. How about getting rid of that stuff? I can get a hundred grand for it—in cash."

The voice that answered him was steady, monotonous and obviously disguised by turning the tonal qualities into a hiss.

"Be sure you're right, Snate. The price seems too good to be true. Have you checked up on him?"

Snate answered, "I'm trying to now. But he must be okay because one of the boys saw him try to get rid of a nice big rock just a couple of hours ago."

"Very well," the hissing voice agreed. "Do business with him and keep him handy for more. Just be certain he's no police spy."

"You bet," Snate answered cheerfully. "I'll take care of things."

"Yes," the voice purred, "you will, Snate—or I'll take care of you. Oh—one more thing. Tony Quinn, the ex-D.A., is getting active. I want to be positive he is really blind. See to it."

Snate hung up and shivered. Odd how that voice affected him. Snate possessed no doubts as to the caliber of this man who directed his every move. There was cold-blooded murder in that voice and a ruthlessness which even surpassed that which Snate packed in his so-called heart.

Snate tapped the top of his desk a moment, replaced the phone and then growled. Why should he waste his time trying to contact the coast for confirmation? If this Green was a stool, he'd pay for it!

CHAPTER VI
BRAND OF THE BLACK BAT

AT TEN-THIRTY Silk opened the door to let Walker and his pug into the hotel room. Instantly, Silk sensed danger. Walker was too smug, his gunman too eager.

"You have the stuff?" Silk inquired and edged over toward a chair under the cushion of which he had a gun concealed.

"What kind of a sap do you think I am?" Walker demanded irascibly. "Show us the dough and I'll take you to where the stuff is waiting. We don't take chances, see?"

Silk shrugged, removed a wallet from his pocket and threw it on the table. Walker flipped over the sheaf of big denomination notes, closed the wallet and nodded.

"It's okay. Now just come with us. It's about a ten minute ride and we'll turn over the stuff to you."

Silk started to rise, but the gunman shoved him back on the chair and carefully searched him. "This time," he said flatly, "you ain't gonna pack no rod and don't try grabbing mine because I'll bust you one in the jaw if you do."

He stepped back. Silk put his hands against the chair to arise. Neither man saw the small gun moved from the chair into Silk's pocket. He felt better with it, for more and more Silk sensed the fact that things weren't going just right.

He preceded the two men out of the hotel and into a car driven by a third thug who leered openly at him. No blindfold was placed over his eyes and Silk felt a sinking sensation in his stomach. Was Quinn's plan to fail when it was only beginning? Would Snate get the upper hand at once?

The car headed due east toward the river and stopped in front of a darkened warehouse. Silk climbed out and now the gunman deliberately shoved an exposed automatic into the small of his back. Silk marched into the warehouse, through its damp, spacious interior until he reached a small office where two more men were waiting. Five against one! He wondered just what he could do about it, but he savagely determined to take as many of them in death with him as possible.

"Sit down, Green," Walker motioned to a rickety chair. "Take a load off your feet and off your mind, too. Before you get the rocks, we want to know something."

"Yes?" Silk sat down warily. Two men stood directly behind him. Out of the corner of his eye he saw a blowtorch resting on the top of the scarred old desk in a corner. A blowtorch had no business here—not a shiny new one.

"We checked with the coast," Walker explained suavely. "Everything is okay, but there's just one thing we don't understand. What were you doing in the courtroom the day that Tony Quinn got his?"

Silk's face never moved a muscle. He sighed and folded his arms across his chest. "Sorry—I don't know anyone named Tony Quinn and I've never been in a courtroom in this city—yet."

Walker stepped close and slapped him across the face. "You're a damned liar. You even plugged one of the hoods who started the rumpus there. Tell the truth."

"I don't know what you're talking about," Silk insisted and while he spoke, little beads of perspiration formed on the back of his neck.

WALKER gestured and one of the men picked up the blowtorch. He pumped air into it, primed it and then applied a match. He turned the flame down until it was light blue and almost invisible. He stepped up to Silk and ripped his vest and shirt open. Silk felt the heat of the torch and shuddered.

Walker said, "Going to talk—or do you want to be roasted alive? The torch will make you open up eventually. Why not save yourself a lot of worry and pain by talking now?"

Silk averted his eyes from the stabbing flame. He looked directly over Walker's shoulder and, for a moment, doubted his own senses. Just inside the door he saw a black object pasted against the wall.

It was the figure of a Black Bat with wings outspread!

"What do you want to know?" he asked stonily, and then delivered a message to whoever had applied that eerie sticker to the wall. "There are five of you—all armed. I don't see how I can fight that many. Not even if I had help."

"You're getting smart," Walker said. "Tony Quinn hired you, didn't he? He paid you to set a trap for us so you could lay your hooks on the rocks we lifted. Didn't he?"

Silk made no reply. He didn't know what to say. If he admitted it, Quinn would be given away. If he didn't speak, that damned torch would sear his flesh. The thug who held it seemed to relish his job. There would be no mercy from this quintet of killers.

The torch advanced a couple of inches and Silk winced at the terrific heat. Walker slapped him again and motioned to the torch bearer. "Give him a good taste of it."

The torch moved forward again and then the two lights in the room went out. Walker yelled an imprecation. The thug who held the torch decided to go through with his deed anyway. He pressed the flame closer and closer, but now Silk was able to move without being seen. His hand darted into his pocket and came away with the gun. He fired once. The man with the torch lost the sadistic grin around his face and doubled up like a small boy who had eaten too many green apples.

That happened in a split second and then hell really broke loose. Walker yelled orders to shoot. Silk was out of his chair in a flash. A bullet smashed into the wall beside his head. He snapped two quick shots in the direction from which the flash of gunfire had originated and he heard a man sigh deeply, as if exhaling a long breath of despair. There was a crash as a chair smashed to bits.

"Stand where you are!" The voice was low, ominous. It came from the direction of the doorway. "The first one of you who moves will die. Walker—you're leaning back against the desk. Stay there! Your two men are lined up by the east wall. All of you are covered."

Walker gasped. "How—how did you know that? I can't see you. You're guessing. Take him!"

THE last two words were directed at his men. They jumped forward, guns racking the vicinity of the doorway. Mingled with the roar of their weapons came two quick blasts of powerful automatics. The two gunmen stopped in their tracks. Their weapons dangled from lifeless fingers and they slowly sagged toward the floor.

Walker was smarter. As his men acted, he leaped in the direction where he figured Silk would be standing. Silk fired at the dark blob that loomed up, but he delayed a fraction of a second too long. Silk wasn't entirely sure of the identity of this figure that came for him.

Walker luckily found Silk's gun hand and turned the wrist cruelly. The gun banged against the floor. Walker seized Silk, whirled him around and held him as a shield.

"Okay, wise guy," he snarled. "If you can see so damned good in this darkness, maybe you'll know the spot your stooge is in."

"He is no stooge of mine," the voice had absolutely no expression. "You are holding him as a shield and your gun is thrust out ready to shoot. Walker, you have one last chance for your life. Drop the gun and let him go."

For an answer, Walker fired two rapid shots in the direction of the voice. He heard the bullets crash into the wall and a shiver racked his body. What manner of man could move so fast? What sort of a devil could penetrate inky darkness and know the instant when his finger tightened against the trigger?

Suddenly Silk moved. His right foot kicked out

and rapped against Walker's shin. Walker howled in pain and his grip loosened a trifle. With a lurch, Silk pulled himself free, but he faced a new menace now for he was very close to Walker and the gun covered him. Silk didn't hesitate. With one hand outstretched, he leaped straight toward Walker. The extended hand reached his throat and closed around it. At the same time Silk threw his body sideways and the bullet only ripped through the tail of his coat. Walker stumbled and fell heavily. Like a flash, Silk was upon him. Walker nudged his gun up until it covered Silk—the muzzle resting against his side.

THE BLACK BAT

which he held behind him was his own and there were bullets in the firing chamber. He knew this.

"Racket?" the Black Bat asked and behind the mask lips smiled grimly. "The extermination of rats. My methods are as ruthless as yours, Walker. Not many minutes ago you threatened a man with a hideous death unless he talked. Now, perhaps you face the same fate. A blowtorch can be a ghastly means of killing a man and you ought to know it. Snate is planning to start a campaign of bank robberies. Which bank is he starting with?"

Walker gasped. Only two or three men knew of that intended

Something slapped against Walker's skull and he vaguely felt the muzzle of his gun turned forcibly outward as he pressed the trigger. After that Walker lost all interest in things.

When he opened his eyes, the office was flooded with light. Silk sat on the edge of the desk, but Walker didn't see him. His eyes were riveted upon a weird form that loomed up half a dozen feet away. The man was tall, very well built and there was a shining black hood and winglike cape encasing his head and shoulders. Merciless eyes watched Walker's movements. The killer shivered. Those eyes got him. With an effort he tore his gaze away. He saw the four men who had been a part of his trap. They were lying side by side and the floor around them was smeared with blood. Upon the forehead of each man was the insignia of a tiny black bat.

"Who—who are you?" Walker found his voice after a moment. He sat up, bracing himself with his hands. As he did so, he felt the cool butt of a pistol beneath him. Walker closed his fingers around the gun and confidence surged through him once more.

THE eerie figure, dressed entirely in black, moved like some grim shadow. The voice made Walker shiver again.

"I am new to men like you," the voice intoned. "You might call me the Black Bat. Fools like you have brought me into existence. So long as your breed lives, the Black Bat will work to crush you. No—don't move!"

"What's your racket?" Walker asked. Inwardly he forced himself to remain calm. He wanted to know all this hooded creature had to offer. Snate would pay plenty for the information and Walker had few doubts but that he could deliver it. The gun

campaign. Yet this hooded man knew it, also. Walker decided this had to end swiftly. His eyes narrowed and his crafty brain formulated a plan. If he could get the Black Bat close enough, he could fire quickly and be protected by The Bat's own body. Then, before Silk could swing into action, Walker would have a bead on him.

"I'll talk," he declared sullenly. "Only I ain't going to yell the news. Come closer and I'll whisper it. If Snate ever finds out I sang, he'll tear me apart. You got to promise you won't spill this to anybody else."

The Bat made a surreptitious motion with his left hand. Silk saw it and thrust one hand into his coat pocket where his fingers curled around a gun. He pointed the weapon at Walker and half pulled the trigger.

The Bat moved toward Walker. He held no gun, but Walker saw the butt of an automatic protruding from The Bat's belt.

In his mad desire to wreak vengeance upon this man, Walker lost his head for a moment. He told the truth, figuring it would sound more authentic than some trumped up story and, anyway, The Bat would never live to repeat it.

"He's going to tackle the Security National," he said hoarsely. "It's all set for tomorrow morning at ten o'clock sharp. This is the way it's to be worked."

Walker's voice dropped to a mumble and The Bat stepped closer, bending down to hear better. At that moment Walker twisted his body, brought the gun into view and compressed the trigger. Something smashed into his shoulder, sending him sprawling. He knew he had missed The Bat, but Walker was on his feet and shooting again.

This time he saw The Bat's gun come up. With a yell of terror Walker lunged for him, gun extended.

The Bat's gun barked. The bullet, ranging upward, smashed a button on Walker's coat, ricocheted and ended by crashing full into his face. Walker swayed drunkenly, fell to his knees and tried to speak. Words turned into a bubbling scream as he fell forward.

THE Black Bat rubbed a hand over his forehead. Silk was at his side in a second.

"You hurt?" he asked.

The Bat shook his head. "He missed me—by a fraction of an inch the last time. I knew Walker had that gun and I gave him a chance—to talk and surrender, or fight—and die. When I followed him here, saw him and his men carry a blowtorch inside, I knew he planned to bring you here and apply his own brand of torture. I know why, too. You were recognized. Some of Snate's men watched everyone who entered court the day his hirelings threw the acid around. They remembered you. I hadn't planned on that. So I slipped into this warehouse and arranged things. I cut the electric light wires at the crucial moment."

"Then we're sunk," Silk said sadly. "They'll know I work for you—Quinn the lawyer. They'll connect me with The Bat, too."

But The Bat shook his head. "Every man who could have known is dead. I slipped into Walker's so-called office and overheard a brilliant conversation. Snate didn't recognize you and he doesn't know you are working for me—either as Tony Quinn—or the Black Bat. These pleasant mugs were set to take your money and double-cross Snate. They told him nothing."

"But we didn't get the jewels," Silk groaned. "I figured we could lay our hands on them."

The Black Bat laughed and threw a chamois sack on the table. "I said I watched Walker all day. The jewels were kept in that office where I was hiding. Getting them out of the safe was very simple, Silk. I've studied a few things about safes and Walker's was no treasury vault by any means. You take charge of the gems. Send them back to the insurance company that paid the losses on them. There's a reward for almost every one. Drop them an anonymous note saying that the reward is to be paid to a good charitable organization. Sign it with one of my stickers—the image of a Black Bat."

"Yes, sir," Silk agreed. "That's a good idea."

"And now," The Bat went on, "this is only the beginning. I'm certain Walker told the truth about the bank holdups because what he said compares favorably with scraps of conversation I overheard in his office. Tomorrow we'll stick our heads into danger. We'll try to stop the holdup by calling the police in. If that doesn't work, we'll stop it ourselves. Now one more thing. I want Snate to have a shock tonight. It's bad for his nerves."

CHAPTER VII
THE TEST

 LIVER SNATE, attired in pajamas and bath robe, heard the doorbell buzz. He yanked open a drawer, thrust a gun into the pocket of his robe and hurried to the door, motioning a stolid faced servant away. This should be Walker, with news. Snate yanked the door open. There was no one on the porch. He frowned and tightened his grip on the gun. Then he shrugged and turned back. Something squeaked. He glanced down the length of the porch and saw a rocking chair, back toward him, rocking slowly. Snate stepped back, turned on the porch light and cautiously made his way along the porch.

"Don't move," he called softly. "You're covered! Stand up!"

But the chair only kept on rocking. Snate made a lunge along the rail until he was in front of the chair. His gun hand sagged and his eyes grew wide in horror and amazement.

Walker sat in the chair. His head hung down over a bloody chest, his arms rested against the arms of the rocker. Snate raised the head and then stepped back with a yelp.

In the middle of the forehead was the image of a Black Bat!

With a supreme effort, Snate recovered his wits. He dashed back into the house and made two hasty phone calls. First, a light delivery truck pulled up in the driveway and Walker's corpse was transferred into it. Then a car, filled with armed men, appeared. Snate got into that himself. He was driven far outside the city limits, directly to the house which he had made his headquarters. Assembled in the big library were Snate's lieutenants—ten in number.

Snate sat down importantly.

"Now listen, every one of you. Walker is dead. I don't know what happened to the four boys who went along to dicker with this fence, Alex Green. I checked on Green by calling the coast and he is okay. I think he's dead, along with everybody else who was in on the deal. I found Walker on my porch with some silly piece of paper pasted on his forehead. It looks like a bat with wings spread way out. The guy who pasted that on Walker also killed him, killed Alex Green and the men I sent with Walker. He hijacked the stuff Green was going to buy. I don't know who this guy is or what his racket can be, but you men get out and find him. Contact everybody you know. Put out a dragnet for this killer who pastes a bat on his victims. Find out who he is and why he's bucking me. Then kill him! Pump him so full of lead they'll need a wrecker to lift his body. Smash him—do you hear me?"

"What's he look like?" one of the men asked.

Snate made an impatient gesture. "How do I know? But you mugs find him. And another thing— tomorrow morning the job at the Security National goes through an hour earlier at nine instead of ten. You've studied the blueprints, you know the whole layout of the bank. You who have been assigned, be there when the doors open and the timelock goes off. Have your guns ready and shoot down any fool who tries to resist. Be sure all of you are masked. That's all—except for Grogan. He is to remain."

The others filed out. Grogan lit a cigarette and dropped into a chair. Snate leaned across his desk and spoke very earnestly.

"YOUR job is to check on that ex-D.A., Tony Quinn. Find out if he's blind. You're not known, so go right into his house. Fake some papers so you'll seem to represent a home for the blind. Tell him he's a rich man and you want a donation. All the while watch him—test him—and be damned sure he can't see. Report back the minute you know one way or the other."

Grogan arose. "As good as done, boss. What about the armored cars?"

"You'll get your orders," Snate snapped. "Now get busy with Quinn."

Grogan drove directly to Quinn's house, walked boldly to the door and rang the bell. He heard slow, faltering steps move across the hallway and the door was opened. Grogan winced at the sight of the man who stood before him. The deep, acid burned scars were vividly clear. Quinn's eyes stared blankly ahead, seeing nothing.

"Mr. Quinn?" Grogan asked. "My name is Blackwell—from the Home for the Aged Blind. May I come in?"

"Of course," Quinn answered. "Follow me."

Quinn became tangled in heavy drapes that hung across one doorway. He extricated himself, smiled in an embarrassed way and then stumbled over a footstool.

"Careless of my servant to leave that stool around," he said. "Of course you know how dangerous such things can be to a blind man. Won't you find yourself a chair?"

Grogan pushed a chair toward Quinn and as the blind man began to sit down, he threw his hat on the seat. Grogan knew that if a man was only pretending to be blind, he would hesitate the barest fraction of a second if there was something on his chair. But Quinn sat down heavily and the hat flattened while Grogan groaned. That hat cost him sixteen bucks and he liked it.

Quinn half arose, fumbled beneath him and extricated the hat, "Is this yours?" he asked. "I'm so sorry. I didn't know it was on the chair."

"It's okay," Grogan fumbled. "My fault. Now—

we'd like a little donation, Mr. Quinn. You know how dependent blind people can be and you are independently wealthy."

"Of course," Quinn said. "Just leave me your card and I'll be happy to send something. I'll even run up and talk to your directors. Being blind is a terrible calamity, Mr. Blackwell, but if one is blind and destitute also—that must be infinitely worse."

Grogan stuck a cigarette into his mouth, struck a match and then leaned forward very silently. He brought the match closer and closer to Quinn's eyes, but they never flickered. Yet inwardly, Quinn's nerves shrieked aloud. It took every ounce of will power he possessed not to blink. The slowly approaching light was bright enough to hurt and had his visitor made any quick movements with the flaming match, Quinn would certainly have blinked despite himself. But the match moved forward slowly enough not to induce winking. Suddenly Quinn jumped.

"What was that?" he asked. "It felt as though fire was brought toward me. I distinctly felt heat."

GROGAN made a clucking sound with his tongue. "Sorry—I just lit a cigarette and I guess I got the match too close to you. I'll be going now. Be as generous as you can, Mr. Quinn. You, of all people, must know how it feels to be blind."

Quinn fumbled around until he found a cane. He accompanied his visitor to the door, opened it for him and, as Grogan stepped out, Quinn's cane flicked sideways. Grogan tripped over it and went sprawling on the porch. He emitted a curse that didn't jibe with his alleged profession of seeking funds for the blind. But he recovered his wits quickly enough and got up.

Quinn was apologetic. "I'm terribly sorry. My cane must have tripped you. You're not hurt?"

"I'm okay," Grogan snapped as he brushed himself off. "Maybe I'll see you again, Mr. Quinn. Next year, shall we say?"

"Shall we?" Quinn asked innocently.

Grogan jammed on his battered hat and hurried to his car. He stepped on the starter with an oath.

"He's blind as a bat. Snate must be going nuts if he thinks that guy is trying to muscle in."

But as the front door closed, Silk stepped out of the dining room. He stowed away the gun he held and grinned at Quinn.

"Perfect, sir. I couldn't have done it better myself."

Quinn threw his cane across a chair and frowned. "He came from Snate all right. The fool didn't even leave a card to back up his statements. What worried me is this—who in the world would suspect I'm not blind? Who would want my sight tested? Snate couldn't possibly know, so there must be someone who suspects. Someone who is the real power behind Snate and gives him his orders. Silk— three men visited me this morning. Otto Fox, Stewart and Commissioner Warner. I offered my services and one of those three men believes I may take a more active part in the game than I pretend. One of those men, or somebody very closely connected with them, is the real leader of Snate's mob."

"Yes, sir," Silk was worried, too. "It would seem that way. This man knows your record as a prosecutor, sir, and he fears you. He knows that if you could see, he'd never get away with it."

Quinn nodded. "Right. We've learned to be careful, Silk—and to suspect Stewart, Fox or Warner. Now to work. Run outside and take a quick look around. There may be another man watching and we can't take chances."

Silk drove Quinn's car out of the garage. To all appearances he was alone at the wheel. But deep within the shadowy tonneau another figure was hunched up against the corner. There was an ebony black hood over his head and his clothes were jet black. A pair of rubber soled shoes covered his feet and deadly automatics hung from shoulder holsters concealed beneath his coat.

The car pulled up to the curb directly across the street from the Security National Bank. It was almost two in the morning and except for a private patrolman, the street was deserted. From the parked car, a shadowy form flitted toward an alley and vanished the moment darkness closed around him.

THE Black Bat had a bulky object under his arm and he moved deftly through the inky night until he stood in front of the rear entrance to the big office building. He laid his burden down carefully, drew a small leather kit from his pocket and went to work on the lock. In less than a moment the door swung open and he stepped inside. He closed and locked the door again and then moved noiselessly along the corridor until he was in the lobby.

He found the superintendent's office, let himself in by the use of the same kit of thin tools. He examined the register of the building, consulted floor plans pinned to the wall and found that one front office was vacant. He slipped back to the lobby, climbed the stairs to the third floor and entered the office designated. He peered out of the window and nodded in satisfaction. The entire front of the Security National Bank was before his gaze.

Working with amazing speed, yet making not the slightest sound, he set up an automatic motion picture camera equipped with a long range lens. He sighted it, arranged a time clock so that the shutters would begin clicking at five minutes of nine the next morning and then he departed. Three watchmen in the building had no inkling of his presence.

"That's taken care of," he said from the depths of the car. "The next job is yours, Silk. You know what to do."

CHAPTER VIII
BANK ROBBERY

AT EIGHT-FORTY the next morning, a heavy sedan pulled up to the curb directly in front of the bank. Silk climbed out, left the keys in the switch and only partly closed the door of the car.

He walked hurriedly up the street and turned into a doorway of a store not yet opened for business. After a two minute wait he saw another sedan roll slowly along and stop. Quinn was behind the wheel with a slouch hat pulled very low and his coat collar turned up around his face. Silk approached the car, slid behind the wheel abandoned by Quinn and then parked across the street from the bank.

"Everything set, Silk?" Quinn asked from the folds of his coat collar.

"All set, sir," Silk replied. "You don't think you're biting off too big a chunk this time, do you? You'll appear in broad daylight."

"The mask will take care of everything," Quinn answered. "I'm climbing into the back of the car. You duck beneath the dash and stay there. This car must appear empty. I'll pull down the curtains in back."

"Will the police be here?" Silk asked anxiously.

Quinn shrugged. "I don't know. They have an hour yet and they probably will appear by ten, but I talked to some stupid, pigheaded fool called Sergeant McGrath. Commissioner Warner wasn't to be found. McGrath, first of all, said he wasn't in the habit of accepting anonymous tips. I told him the bank would be held up at ten o'clock, but to get his men here before nine—just in case the bandits changed their minds and decided to strike earlier. I have no hunches about the matter, but it seems to me that the minute the bank opens its doors is the best time to stage a robbery."

"Yes, sir," Silk replied quickly. "I've talked to a dozen bank robbers and they all say the same thing. No customers to fool with then and the dough is all in one place—not scattered around to a dozen tellers."

They were silent for a moment, but The Bat was alert.

Eyes, framed behind a black hood, watched another car draw up as a clock struck nine. The bank guard swung the doors wide, tested the revolving doors and then walked back into the building. From the car that stopped and double parked in front of the bank stepped six men, all masked and openly armed with submachine guns. They worked with the precision born of long practice. So quickly were they inside that not one of the bank employees, nor the few clients, knew where they had come from.

One man raised his gun and yanked the trigger. A clerk went down with his face a blob of blood.

"That's a sample," the killer yelled. "Open the vaults and haul out the cash. Snap to it before my finger gets itchy again."

The bank guard had more courage than sense. All his mind clicked on was the fact that he was paid to protect the bank. He reached for his gun. The blast from two Tommy guns almost cut him in half. Tellers had the big door open and under the menacing muzzles of the machine guns they hauled out thousands of dollars in currency. These were stowed into a big sack, slung over one man's shoulder and the bandits backed out of the bank.

Outside, two others stood guard with Tommy guns at a ready position, a third with a menacing revolver. The latter suddenly dropped and triggered. An advancing plainclothes man fired a single shot before his life was blasted away. The four men inside emerged and raced for the parked car.

AT THAT moment things happened. From another sedan, across the street, stepped an eerie figure. The bandits had struck an hour earlier than expected and The Bat was being forced to show his hand. There were no signs of the police yet, but The Bat, taking no chances, was fully prepared.

Under one arm The Bat held a long barreled rapid-fire rifle. It sang a deadly song and the slugs smashed into the hood of the bandits' getaway car. The driver shoved a gun through the open window. The rapid-fire rifle raised its curtain of fire and the driver slumped over the wheel.

But The Bat was handicapped. Crowds packed the streets at this hour. They stood in a dense throng, held by fear and the threat of flying bullets. The escaping bandits were directly in front of a score of pedestrians. The Bat couldn't shoot or he'd mow down innocent people.

"Grab another car," one of the masked bandits shouted when he saw the driver of their own sedan dead at the wheel and the motor stalled. A group of stunned pedestrians were in the way. One of the thugs snarled a curse and raised his automatic rifle to clear a path. Berserk with rage, he was ready to slaughter any number of them so long as his own warped life would be saved. In another second a score of people would go down under the curtain of lead.

But before that second had elapsed, one man made a wild dive out of the crowd. He was poorly dressed and his hat was knocked off as he moved. His skull was smooth shaven and he had a stumpy, muscular neck. His features were crude and wide; his jaw undershot and aggressive.

He reached the killer before the spattering rifle could get working right. One hand ripped off the mask from the gunman's face and revealed him as a pimply, pasty-faced thug.

At that moment the crowd sensed the danger and scampered for safety. It left a clear path for The Bat's gun. He raised it, but the unmasked thug saw him and acted quickly. He slugged the husky looking man who had prevented the wholesale slaughter, wound his arms around him and with the strength born of desperation, pulled and pushed his human shield toward the getaway car. Eager hands pulled them both inside. The Bat lowered his gun, backed up and suddenly darted away. No one in the crowd saw where he went.

The bandits sent a warning hail of lead over the heads of the crowd and the car started away from the curb. A radio car shrieked toward them and the Tommy guns went to work again. The radio car piled up against a wall, its driver dead and the second patrolman badly wounded.

Someone in the crowd shrieked and pointed to the spot where the Black Bat had been standing. "There's another one of them over there."

But there was no sign of The Bat. Police arrived in droves and began a methodical search of the neighborhood. Commissioner Warner appeared, shouting orders and paling as he saw the havoc wrought inside the bank. Four men were dead, several others badly wounded. Outside, a traffic cop lay in a welter of his own blood and a radio patrolman was crushed behind the wheel of his wrecked car.

"THERE were seven of them—and another at the wheel of the getaway car," one of the bank officials told Warner excitedly. "The seventh man stood across the street. He was a weird looking figure—all dressed in black and he had a hood over his face—not just a simple mask. And he did a very strange thing. As the bandits raced for their car, he opened fire, riddled the getaway car and killed the driver. If there hadn't been another car parked at the curb, God knows what would have happened. The bandits appropriated it and ran."

"What's this about one of them being unmasked?" Warner queried.

A detective hove into sight with a frightened young man at his side. The young man talked—a rush of words that fell over one another.

"Big guy—grabbed one of them crooks—just in time or we'd all have been shot—pulled mask off one man's face. They cracked him—with gun—flung him in car before they ran—"

"What did the unmasked man look like?" Warner asked.

The young man gulped. "I—I dunno. Honest, I was so excited he coulda been colored pink for all I know. Say—that guy was ready to mow all of us down."

"Who is the man behind the wheel of the stalled car?" Warner asked.

A uniformed sergeant answered that one. "We don't know, sir. His prints are on their way to headquarters now. Looks to me like that hooded man we've heard so much about wasn't a member of this outfit. He tried to prevent the bandits from getting away as I see it."

"You're right," Warner agreed. "But we'll go into that later on. Call headquarters and broadcast an order for all suspicious cars to be stopped. Cover every road, even the country lanes. How much did those rats get?"

"Almost half a million," a bank official proclaimed sadly. "But the money is nothing. They killed half a dozen people. Shot them down ruthlessly. Commissioner, why isn't this sort of thing stopped? The entire city is seething with crime. No man or woman is safe on the streets. Not even a great bank such as this can open its doors in the morning without a prayer that none of these killers will appear."

"We're doing all we can," Warner replied. "I"—he was looking through the big plate glass windows—"Stop him, somebody! Quinn—look out!"

For Tony Quinn, tapping his cane, progressed slowly across the road. A car was bearing down on him. The driver swerved the wheel crazily, cursed and rammed into a parked truck. Warner raced out of the bank, elbowed his way to Quinn's side and took his arm.

"What's happened?" Quinn asked blankly. "There are many people around. I can hear them. And sirens!"

"You gave me an awful scare," Warner exhaled violently. "This is Warner, Tony. There's been a bank robbery with several people murdered. You blundered across the street and the fool drivers traveling along had their heads stuck out looking at the bank. One of them almost knocked you over."

QUINN shrugged his dropped shoulders. "Would there have been much lost, Commissioner? No—I'm sorry I said that. You've tried to help me, saved my life just now, in fact. I'm very grateful."

"Get into my car," Warner suggested. "I've got to go to headquarters for a few minutes and then I'll have you driven home."

Quinn was assisted into the big police car and he relaxed against the cushions. His stony eyes stared straight ahead, but something of a smile crossed his lips. Silk was elbowing his way through the crowd. Under his arm he held a bulky package.

Commissioner Warner gave further orders and the crowd was pushed back. Warner walked toward the getaway car, looked at the dead man behind the wheel and then casually raised his eyes. They jerked wide open. Plastered against the windshield was the image of a Black Bat with wings outspread.

"That wasn't there five minutes ago," Warner yelled. "Who put it on the windshield?"

No one seemed to know, but inside Warner's car, Quinn idly rubbed his gloved hands until a smear of glue vanished from the tip of the right index finger.

Warner piled into the car beside Quinn and the driver headed back toward the office. Warner pushed his hat to the back of his head and swore.

"Those damned black bats," he said aloud. "I don't understand them. We found four dead men in an abandoned warehouse this morning and each one had a black bat pasted to his forehead. Now another of those

The third gunman suddenly dropped and triggered.

insignias has appeared—on the windshield of the getaway car that the bandits left. I can't understand it."

"Probably one of Snate's pleasant gestures," Quinn offered without enthusiasm. "He might be putting those things on the men he kills."

"Would he paste one on a car his men intended to use in getting clear?" Warner asked irritably. "No, Tony—there's someone else operating recently. I can't make up my mind whether he's on the side of the law or against it. Those four mugs were of Snate's tribe. We can't find a possible motivation for their deaths. Only the Black Bat insignias. I wouldn't be surprised if such a creature existed. The Black Bat! I only hope, if it's true, that he's working against Snate. We can't do a thing to him legally."

"Why?" Quinn asked, but there was no particular interest in his tone.

"Why? Because he's become clever lately. Devilishly clever—almost as if he possessed a new set of brains. He sits back like an octopus and flings out his tentacles, but not once does he show himself. He has every crook from shop lifter to murderer lined up behind him as solidly as an attacking army. Snate does nothing but plan and give the orders. We can't pin a thing on him. Damn it, Tony—if you were the D.A., we'd get some action. You never did bother much with technicalities."

"But I'm not," Quinn said sadly. "I'm just a helpless, blind man. I wish I could be of assistance, Commissioner. I'll tell you what. Perhaps I can't see, but—I can think. The acid didn't sear into my brain. Sometimes a blind man can think even deeper than one with healthy sight. If I mull these things over long enough, I might reach some kind of a logical conclusion. At least it will give me something to do—make me think I'm of some little use in the world."

"EXCELLENT," Warner cried. "I've been trying to get you to do just that for weeks. You always had a knack for thinking out puzzles. See what you can do with this one. Explain the Black Bat business. Tell me how I can corner Snate. Tell me just how eleven armored cars, filled with cash, can vanish in broad daylight."

"You're asking for a lot," Quinn seemed to have acquired a new interest in life. "But I'll do my best. When you have a spare moment, drop into my home and tell me all you know. I've an idea I might be of help."

The radio under the dashboard squealed.

"Calling Commissioner Warner. Commissioner Warner. Getaway car used in Security National stickup found abandoned fifteen miles north on Route 4. Waiting your orders. Please contact dispatcher."

Quinn said, "You can let me out here, Commissioner. I'll only be in the way. Just call me a taxi."

The police car's siren shrilled and a taxi pulled up at the command of the police driver. Quinn was helped into it by Warner. They clasped hands a moment and Warner was off. Quinn settled back.

"Drive me to the park," he told the chauffeur. "I need more exercise."

When the taxi stopped at the entrance to the park, another car pulled up behind it. Silk raised a newspaper to cover his features, but he watched Quinn alight clumsily, pay off the driver and then head for the park.

Once the taxi was gone, Quinn turned, tapped his stick and approached the curb. Silk jumped out and helped him into the tonneau. Then he got behind the wheel and headed north.

"I caught the broadcast, too," he said excitedly. "We're going after the bus, eh?"

"Right," Quinn said from the back seat. "And you'll have to lay on the whip, Silk, old man. Fifty police cars will head there within three minutes."

Quinn was busy as he talked. He removed his topcoat and grey suit. In their place he donned a black outfit. He covered his white shirt front with a piece of black silk, pulled his hood over his head and from a specially constructed compartment in the tonneau removed two automatics. He gloved his hands again and leaned back.

"We're making headway, Silk," he said. "You got the camera safely, I see. Now to reach the car before the police. Then we'll know our bandits and be in a position to deal out some rather high handed justice. They'll hole up for days before they dare show their faces again."

"Did you see that little episode where a man jumped out of the crowd and tackled that killer?" Silk asked.

"I saw," Quinn answered. "That man would be a decided asset to our little group, Silk. But I suppose he's been thrown into some ditch by now. Can't you make this car roll faster?"

SILK hunched over the wheel and brought his foot down hard. The sedan raced at ninety along the highway, guided by Silk's expert hands.

Then Silk suddenly slowed up. Ahead of them they could see two cars pulled off the highway and a uniformed man standing on the shoulders of the road. One car was a State Police patrol, the other a city detective cruiser.

"Someone came out without waiting for Warner's orders," Quinn said. "I hope there's not too many there. Slow up, Silk. You turn around and run for it. I'll handle the police. Meet me back on the fourth lane to your right."

CHAPTER IX
The Trap

ETECTIVE SERGEANT MCGRATH had one foot on the running board of the car which Snate's men had stolen for their getaway. He wore a puzzled frown on his face.

"It's so damned odd it can't be coincidence," he maintained to his driver and the two State Troopers who listened silently. "This bus was stolen last night. It was left in front of the Security National with the door half open and the keys in the ignition. Nobody can tell me it wasn't planted just in case something happened. Those killers were smarter than usual by having two cars ready."

One of the State Troopers walked over to the sedan and peered through the window into the tonneau. He nudged Sergeant McGrath.

"Take a look at the upholstery—along the back seat I mean. Looks like part of it had been cut out and then sewed back. Now, why would anybody want to carve a chunk out of the seat?"

McGrath looked too and grunted. "I know what it means," he said. "That seat was carved up and there's a sort of hidden compartment behind it. See how that spot is directly over the trunk at the rear? Maybe those hoods passed their guns into the trunk—or got them by shoving their arms through the hole in the seat. In case of a quick frisk the roscoes wouldn't be found."

McGrath was chunky, beefy-faced and he had been a policeman for more years than he liked to brag about. He had risen to his present position by hard, long hours of work. There wasn't a spark of mercy in his makeup. If a crime was committed, someone had to pay and McGrath didn't give a hoot if that person happened to be his brother, the mayor or even the governor of the state. Thoroughly honest, no criticism had ever come his way and his record stood positively clean.

McGrath turned away from the car and jerked erect. Ten feet behind the car stood a lone figure of a man dressed entirely in black with a hood covering his head and neck. There were two automatics in his hands and by the way this masked man held them, McGrath got the idea he knew how to shoot.

"Gentlemen," the hooded figure spoke politely enough, "you've examined that car sufficiently for the present. Will you stand away from it now—with your hands up?"

Slowly the four men obeyed. "Just keep right on backing up," the Black Bat said cheerfully. "And don't become so foolish as to think you might reach those holstered guns before I can open fire.

I'm rather good with a thirty-eight automatic, but I'd hate to prove it—right now."

McGrath leaned forward slightly. "You're the masked man who polished off the bandits' driver this morning. You're the mug who pastes black bats all over the victims you leave behind."

"Not all over them, Sergeant," The Bat said. "Just upon their foreheads. I have two reasons for doing that. I don't want the crime pinned on anyone else—nor do I wish to have the friends of those men who shoot it out with me kept in the dark as to who was the victor. Killing those four men in the warehouse simply saved the state the expense of four executions later on."

"You can brag now," McGrath snapped, "but someday I'll do the bragging. You're a murderer and you'll pay the penalty, even if the men you killed deserved to die."

"MY," THE BAT said laughingly, "you do have a sense of duty. But you really ought to exercise more, Sergeant. When the day comes that you will find the chance of chasing me, I'm afraid you wouldn't run far. Anyway, it's bad for the heart. Now there are all sorts of contrivances to help you thin down that waistline. I could name them—"

"Shut up," McGrath yelled, for the Black Bat had touched a sore spot. "And how long do we stand here with our hands in the air, listening to your crazy jabbering?"

"Turn around—all of you," The Bat warned. "I want this car. I have a liking for it. You see—I stole it last night."

The Bat climbed behind the wheel, stepped on the starter and slowly backed up. Every moment, one gun covered the quartet. He had no doubts as to what would happen the moment he drove onto the highway. Bullets would fly fast and thick. Furthermore, the State Troopers had a reputation for accurate shooting. Yet The Bat had no time to disarm them. By now a dozen police cars would be racing from the city toward this spot.

The rear wheels rolled to the pavement. The Bat straightened the car out, raised his gun a few inches and yanked the trigger four times. The bullets whined over the heads of the four men and they dropped quickly. The Bat tramped on the gas pedal and shot away.

McGrath didn't stop to shoot. Instead he ran over to the detective cruiser and jumped into it. The troopers stepped into the road and emptied their guns at the speeding sedan. Then they raced for their own car. Two minutes later, four disgruntled men stared at the motors of the two cars. The wires had been ripped away so that there was no spark.

"That guy," McGrath said, "thinks of everything, but someday he'll slip and that same day I'll slip—cuffs on his wrists."

The Bat turned off the road four miles from the spot where McGrath worked on the cruiser. Halfway up a lane he saw Silk waiting. He stopped and instantly Silk flung himself into the tonneau. He ripped away the sewed portion of the seat and extracted a heavy recording machine. He stowed this into the other car and jumped in to find The Bat already at the wheel.

They left the stolen car parked across the lane so that no pursuit was possible until after it was moved. There would be some difficulty there, too, for The Bat had ripped wires away again and tall trees on either side of the lane prevented any attempts at pushing the car off the road.

They struck another highway two miles east. The Bat stopped, turned the wheel over to Silk and got into the tonneau. He worked quickly now. He changed his black clothing for the conservative grey suit that he wore as Tony Quinn, the blind man. The black outfit, hood, guns and all went into a hidden compartment which locked securely and gave no evidence of its existence.

When they reached the State Police barrier, Silk Kirby, gentleman's gentleman, was taking his blind master for a ride. The State Police all knew Quinn. They called greetings to him and passed the car along.

"Neat, Silk," Quinn grinned. "Now back to the house as fast as possible. I want to develop the films and run off the recordings I hope we picked up."

THERE were recordings, all right. Plenty of them inscribed on the thin disk. Quinn could identify the men only by their voices. Two men took up the brunt of the conversations and they were apparently the leaders. One had a hoarse bellow of a voice, the other a reedy tone.

The hoarse voice came through clearly. "I just slugged this bozo who pulled the mask offa Whitey. What're we gonna do with the guy?"

"Bump him—whaddya think?" Reedy Voice snapped. "Only we gotta wait until we get the orders from the big boy. Anyway, I think this guy was planted an' maybe he knows somethin'."

"Okay," the first man agreed. "I hope he knows about that Black Bat guy. Did you see him mow down Joey? I still wonder why he didn't turn that gat on us. Hey, Slim, you know the way okay?"

A third voice, muffled, came through. It was the driver. "Yeah—ditch the bus and pick up the other buggy. Then about four miles north, right turn, second left and first left after that, until we hit a red farmhouse. Think I'm so dumb I can't remember them directions?"

Gruff Voice snarled a curse. "You wasn't supposed to drive, so I figured maybe you forgot where the hideout is. Don't get wise, Slim. It don't pay with guys like me."

There was more conversation but nothing of interest. Quinn turned off the playback machine.

"Silk—our fondest hopes have come true. They did talk about where they were going. I figured that with a new driver, orders might need to be reissued. They were and we know where these bandits are holed up. Now for the film. Get the quick drying apparatus ready. I want to run these right off."

It took more than an hour before the film was dry enough to use. Then Quinn and Silk watched the bank robbery unfold itself again. They saw the shooting, for the telescopic lens had picked up every detail. They saw the burly man dart out from the crowd to grapple with the crazy killer, saw him slugged and thrown into the getaway car. Quinn shut the projector off.

"You'll need two guns and a mask, Silk," he said quietly. "Be ready in ten minutes. We haven't much time to lose."

"They're going to be there for days, sir," Silk reminded him.

"But not that ugly looking gorilla who was willing to die if he could save other people's lives. I want to make an attempt at rescuing him—if it's not too late."

Quinn pulled down the shades in the library and stepped up to the fireplace. He touched one of the massive stones and a portion of the wall receded. He entered a compact, white tiled laboratory equipped with every chemical and piece of apparatus necessary to fight crime. He filled two thin vials with a yellowish fluid, rolled them in cotton and carefully tucked them away in his pocket. He donned a black suit and shirt, slipped his hood in place and hurried out the rear door. Silk had a sleek roadster purring sweetly.

THEY took it easy until they reached the highway. Then Silk opened her up. They were taking chances with motor cops, but such risks were necessary now, for Quinn had firmly made up his mind to save the gorilla-like man who had risked his life to prevent wholesale slaughter.

They passed the spot where the Black Bat had taken the getaway car from Sergeant McGrath, and Quinn grinned a little at the memory.

"Look out for a detective sergeant named McGrath," he warned Silk. "He's not exactly on our side and I rather aggravated him when I took the car away. Furthermore, McGrath is a human bloodhound. When his nose finds the scent, he'll never give up."

Silk grunted something, but kept his eyes and

The Bat saw four men, with pointing

attention glued to the road. They found the turns described by the driver of the bandit's car. Silk rolled to a stop, left the roadster well hidden by brush and with the Black Bat at his side, he carefully maneuvered his way through the darkness.

"Hold my arm," The Bat whispered. "I can see the farmhouse plainly—even see that it's painted red. There's a door at the rear, but no lights are showing anywhere, so unless some of the windows on the opposite side are boarded up, the bandits will be hiding in the cellar. Remember—there are six of them and they are well heeled."

Silk mumbled a reply, took The Bat's arm and let himself be led through darkness that defied his keenest stare. Yet The Bat moved quietly and avoided every pitfall.

"Maybe we'll find a trace of those vanished armored cars," Silk whispered. "Maybe McGrath wouldn't be sore if we exposed that racket. He's head of the squad working on the case."

"I doubt they'll be here," The Bat answered. "Armored cars would be spotted this far out of the city—and remembered. The moment we've cleaned up this mess and annoyed Snate a little more—then we'll find out what has happened to those cars. Careful now—no more talking. They've got heavy painted canvas drawn over the cellar windows, but I can see traces of light through some of the chinks in the framework around each section of glass."

They dropped flat and wriggled on their bellies across the newly mown grass. Both men were garbed in black. Had a guard been standing five feet away, watching intently, he would still have seen no trace of these two figures.

They reached one of the windows and The Bat pressed an ear against the glass. His sense of hearing, perfectly attuned during his months of blindness, functioned just as efficiently now.

The bandit with the gruff voice was talking.

"Take that big stiff and put him up against the wall. We're ten miles from no place so we don't have to worry about the noise our roscoes will make. Tie him up and we take pot shots at him. The guy who kills him loses. The stake is a grand apiece payable to the sharpshooter who can put the most dents in the mug's hide and still let him squeal."

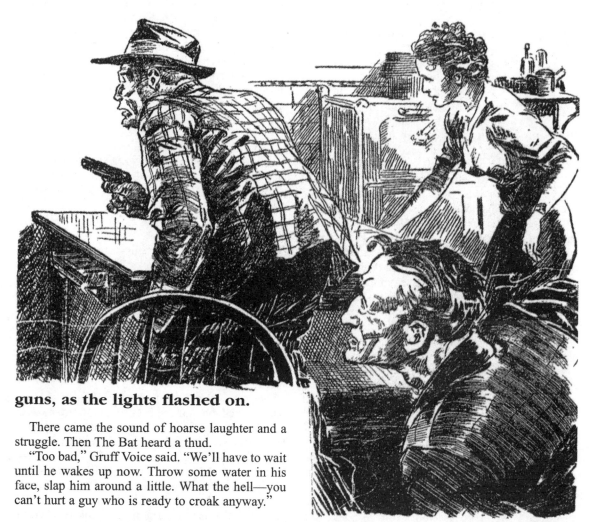

guns, as the lights flashed on.

There came the sound of hoarse laughter and a struggle. Then The Bat heard a thud.

"Too bad," Gruff Voice said. "We'll have to wait until he wakes up now. Throw some water in his face, slap him around a little. What the hell—you can't hurt a guy who is ready to croak anyway."

QUINN touched Silk's hand. Carefully both men drew their guns and wriggled toward the back porch.

"I'll go in," The Bat whispered, "because I can find my way through the darkness. You park outside that window. Break it down if you hear any shooting. And Silk—take these two glass vials. Throw them into the cellar if things get too hot. Then hurry down and drag me out if I can't make it under my own steam."

Silk tapped The Bat's hand twice in a signal that he understood. He took the glass vials and crept back to the window. The Bat approached the rear door, tried it and found it locked. His small kit of instruments opened the way for him and he walked across a kitchen. Two chairs in the middle of the floor were as plain to his eyes as beacons. Mentally he blessed the surgeon who had so miraculously cured him. And then The Bat thought of the girl. She had sworn to force him to accept her as a mem-

ber of his organization. Odd that he hadn't heard from her yet.

A board creaked and The Bat stiffened. He cocked his head to one side, but he heard nothing more. He took another step forward. A man's form flitted across his range of vision. The gun in The Bat's right hand exploded. The form stopped and slumped to the floor. The Bat moved forward a step. He heard a rush of many feet. He pumped four more bullets as fast as he could and then a mighty blow crashed against his temple. He reeled until he struck the wall. Lights flashed on. The Bat saw four men, all armed, with their guns pointed at him. His own weapons were on the floor, fallen from nerveless fingers.

And standing off to one side was a girl. Her hair was black instead of golden. She used too much makeup and she had a hard sort of look, but The Bat wasn't deceived. This was the girl who had done so much to restore his sight!

CHAPTER X
NEW RECRUITS

RUFF Voice was stocky, had cold, fishy eyes and a leering grin around his thick lips. His appearance matched his harsh tones.

"Well, if it ain't the big shot who tried to trip us up this morning? Are we glad to see you! Lucky, ain't it, that Slim came upstairs to get some water? He heard you pick the lock and we got here before you knew what happened."

"Extremely fortunate," The Bat said almost pleasantly, but his spirits were low. He was trapped, facing guns in the hands of four men. A fifth he had killed—the sixth was undoubtedly still in the cellar guarding the prisoner. Those facts, in themselves, were serious enough, but to The Bat's astounded senses the presence of this girl, working closely with the band of killers, was even more of a blow.

Gruff Voice twirled his gun carelessly. "We just lined up a nice finish for a sucker who tried to stop us this morning. You'll get the same medicine—after we pull that mask off your face and see who you really are."

He moved toward The Bat, but the girl's hand touched his shoulder and he stopped. She simply reached for the gun he held, examined it to be sure a cartridge was pumped into the firing chamber and then motioned the four men back.

"This man," she said very quietly, "killed Joey this morning. Joey and I were in love although you dopes probably didn't know it. I want the first crack at his murderer."

"But we gotta contact the boss," Gruff Voice protested. "We can't just knock him off. The boss will be sore."

"I'm not going to kill him," the girl said calmly. "All I'll do is plant a bullet in his hide where it will hurt the most. I want him to suffer—as he made Joey suffer—as he has made me suffer. Stand back—I need plenty of room."

The four thugs moved away, giving the girl every opportunity. She sighted the gun and smiled tightly.

"You're a very brave man," she told The Bat. "You're clever, too—the way you handled things and found this hideaway. Why don't you show how clever you are by catching the bullet I'm going to shoot? Why don't you just reach out, seize the slug and throw it back to me?"

The four thugs laughed uproariously. Then the girl stepped just a trifle closer and lifted the gun once more. Suddenly the weapon came hurtling toward The Bat. He caught it deftly and before the thugs could recover from their astonishment, the gun was spitting. Gruff Voice went down with a

hole in the middle of his forehead. The other three sprang toward The Bat. He sent one reeling backward. The other two fired rapidly, but The Bat was dancing lightly from right to left while his own weapon swung with comforting speed.

The reedy-voiced man, screaming in rage all the while, suddenly changed his tactics. He headed straight for the girl who had drawn off into a corner. She shoved a chair toward him and he tripped over it, went sprawling on the floor.

INSTANTLY she pounced upon him and wrenched his gun away. It spoke and one of the thugs who threatened The Bat suddenly let go of his gun and looked with amazement upon a bleeding, numbed hand.

"Good work," The Bat called out to the girl. "We've got them now."

He moved toward the reedy-faced man, but suddenly stopped in his tracks. From the doorway behind him came a harsh voice.

"You got who, wise guy? Elevate your mitts or I'll blow your backbone in half."

It was the one thug left to guard their prisoner in the cellar. During the excitement, The Bat had forgotten him. He raised his hands slowly.

"The same goes for you, Helen—I always figured you were a rat."

The girl was pale and a bit unsteady on her feet. She dropped the gun and backed up toward the wall.

"That's better," the thug approved. "Now Mister Hooded Guy—let go of that roscoe, walk over beside the dame and claw at the wallpaper. Remember— I've got ten shots in this gat and I'll pump all of 'em but one into your hide. The last one is for the dame—the dirty, double-crossing little rat."

The Bat dropped his gun and walked carefully toward the further wall where he stood, facing the girl.

"You were splendid," he said quietly. "But what did I tell you about horning in on dangerous business like this?"

"You'd have been unmasked and killed long ago if it hadn't been for me," she answered with a catch in her voice. "Now I—I don't know what will happen."

"Turn around, you," the thug ordered. "Turn around and rip that mask off your face. I want to see what you look like before I change that expression with lead."

The Bat turned very slowly, keeping his hands shoulder high. The thug was, perhaps, the smartest looking one of the lot. His gun was held as steady as a rock. Reedy Voice was trying to get up off the floor. The thug whom Helen had wounded sat in a chair, white as paper while he tried to stem the flow of blood from his wrist.

"Take off the hood," the gunman snapped. "Take it off or I'll blow it off."

The Bat's eyes narrowed behind the mask. There seemed but one thing to do—charge straight into the face of the spitting gun. He was doomed anyway and his only chance lay in forcing the killer to shoot too fast for accuracy. It looked like deliberate suicide, but The Bat's mind was made up. He'd rather die trying than merely standing there to face the inevitable stream of slugs. He tensed his muscles for the leaping charge.

Then a hand appeared behind the gunman. Something flew into the middle of the room, dropped with a slight crash and instantly the air was filled with a yellowish smoke. The gunman yanked the trigger wildly, but as he did so, The Bat moved fast. Bullets slammed into the wall behind the spot where he had been standing. That is, two of them did. The last one struck the ceiling and sent a shower of plaster down. For at that moment Silk had jumped with an inverted gun.

"RUN for it," The Bat shouted. "In the cellar— get the prisoner out, Silk. Helen—where are you?"

He tried to penetrate the yellow haze, but it was almost impossible. Here The Bat's abnormal eyes were no better than those of an average man. Already he could feel the effects of that stupefying gas. Two more minutes and he'd drop, too. Then he heard a moan. He whirled in the direction of it and took half a dozen long steps before he found the girl slumped against the wall.

He lifted her with great effort, for his muscles were beginning to react to the narcotic influence of the gas. Staggering, he reached the door, kicked it open and ran into the kitchen where the fumes were

less thick. He picked up a pan and hurled it at a window, smashing the glass and allowing cool air to enter. He sucked in lungs full, hurriedly unlocked the door and went out into the night.

Silk was kneeling beside a prone figure, chafing his wrists and trying to bring him back to consciousness.

"Are you all right, sir?" Silk asked anxiously. "And the girl?"

"We're both okay," The Bat answered. "What of the prisoner? Is that he?"

"Yes—one of them struck him quite hard, I think. I can't seem to bring him to."

"Run for the car," The Bat ordered. "Drive it here and lose no time. Take the adhesive out of the compartment in back and bring it to me. Hurry!"

The Bat eased the girl to the ground, ripped off his coat and made a pillow of it. Before Silk returned, she had opened her eyes and smiled wanly up at him.

"I hoped to show you I was worthy of joining your forces," she whispered. "I—I guess I bungled things."

"Bungled them?" The Bat held both her hands tightly. "You saved my life, Helen. Your name is Helen?"

"No—it's Carol—Carol Baldwin. Oh, Tony Quinn, I—"

"No names," The Bat whispered quickly. "Tony Quinn doesn't exist so far as you know. There may be ears."

"I'm sorry. If you'll let me go, now, I'll just drop out of sight."

"Let you go?" The Bat chuckled. "Oh, no! Once you warned me I'd beg you to join my forces. I'm doing just that. I need a girl like you and I owe you so much besides."

She sat up and blinked dizzily. But her lips were parted in a warm smile. Then Silk roared up in the roadster and The Bat went to work. He smashed other windows in the farmhouse, let the gas seep out and then entered, before any of the thugs awakened. He applied the adhesive scientifically until each man looked like a mummy. He rolled them as far apart as possible, stood up and surveyed his work with relish.

Silk came rushing out of a back room with two big valises in his hands."Here is the money," he enthused. "What a haul they made!"

"So Snate didn't get it," The Bat laughed. "Put it in the roadster. Pile the unconscious man in the front seat, help the girl in and you ride the rumble. I'll be out in a moment."

For The Bat had one more duty to perform. Methodically he applied his trademark to the foreheads of each thug—the tiny black bat that portrayed his handiwork.

Carol Baldwin

FIVE minutes later he sent the roadster heading for the highway. The girl spoke in a low voice.

"I joined Snate's forces weeks ago—just to lay my own plans to destroy him. Someday I'll tell you why."

Carol turned to the unconscious man at her side and gently wiped some of the blood from his face.

"You may not know it," The Bat said, "but that man saved the lives of a number of innocent people. One of Snate's gunmen decided to send a burst of machine gun bullets into the onlookers at the bank stickup. This man jumped the gun."

"I know," she replied. "They were talking about him and if you had been only a few minutes later, he'd be dead now. Snate gave the orders to murder him."

CHAPTER XI
THE COMMISSIONER'S VISITOR

NOT long after midnight, a figure, dressed completely in black, climbed silently up a porch pillar at the rear of Police Commissioner Warner's residence. He crawled to the top of the porch roof and then carefully pulled up several heavy objects at the end of thin, yet strong ropes. He carried these to the window of the room where the Commissioner was asleep.

A patrolman, on special detail, sauntered through the backyard and The Bat lay prone, watching the man in the darkness. After he had gone, The Bat crept to the partly opened window, raised it and slipped inside. He drew a gun, walked over to the bed and turned on the light.

The Commissioner sat erect, rubbing his eyes and trying to get his bearings. He saw the menacing gun first, raised his head and stared at the black hooded figure of the intruder.

"The Black Bat!" he said hoarsely.

"Right you are," The Bat replied. "Don't speak loudly and if anyone approaches, tell him you simply can't sleep and that's why the light is on. I'm not here to harm you, Commissioner. My work will enable you to put a much wanted man behind bars—where he belongs."

"Go ahead," Warner nodded. "You have my word that I won't try to get help or reach for the gun under my pillow."

The Bat chuckled. "The gun is no longer there. I removed it in case you acted before I had a chance to explain. Furthermore—your word of honor goes a long way with me."

The Bat stuffed his gun back into its holster. He walked to the window and picked up the bulky objects he had carried into the room. He set up a motion picture camera first.

"This was operating from a vacant office across the street from the Security National Bank," he explained. "It will show you just what happened and enable you to make a still of the man whose mask was ripped off."

"Great," Warner approved. "I'd give a lot to lay my hands on him."

"That," The Bat said, "will be very simple. Phone headquarters and have them send a detail of men to a red painted farmhouse along Spring Lane—just off Route 4. Every member of the holdup gang is there, either dead, wounded or securely tied up."

The Commissioner seized the phone and gave cryptic orders. Then leaned back against the pillows and watched the camera unreel the pictorial history of the holdup. After that The Bat played the recording.

"May I have those?" the Commissioner asked. "If you wish, I'll say they were delivered to me anonymously. There is evidence enough here to send every member of that gang to the chair."

"It's yours," The Bat nodded. "The recordings were taken from conversations of the gang as they fled. I purposely crippled their getaway car so they'd steal the handiest means of escape—another sedan I had planted in front of the bank. The recording device was hidden behind the rear seat. Your Sergeant McGrath will appreciate knowing that, Commissioner. I'm afraid he's just a little put out with me."

THE COMMISSIONER growled, "He even went so far as to demand that I give him a permanent assignment to run you down. I had to comply. You have broken laws, you know—and killed men. Necessary, of course, but still you are not an accredited officer. Just who are you?"

"A man—with a mission. I trust you, Commissioner, but if you don't know who I am, it will never be necessary for you to explain away something that might prove dangerous to your career. Now—in return for all this—I want full news of Oliver Snate. Have you any suspicion as to who is behind him?"

Warner showed his surprise. "You think that, too, eh? Well, so do I, although I've been laughed at for it. No, I haven't the slightest idea who is behind him, but I do know that Snate is probably the most powerful crook ever to rise out of the garbage heap he must have come from. He's a crawling maggot. He preys upon everyone, crook and honest man alike. He murders at will, laughs at the police and our puny efforts. Snate must be crushed and—I hate to admit it—but I think you are the one man to do that job."

The Bat retreated toward the window. "Thank you, Commissioner. Oh, yes, the money stolen from the bank. Don't bother to search for it. I—"

The Commissioner sat bolt upright. "Then

you're a crook, too?"

"Why not? You stated that I'm far outside the law. I might as well go the whole way. But you interrupted me. The money is just inside the door of your garage. And remember—I still have your word of honor not to try and stop me."

He stood for a moment, outlined starkly against the window. Then he was gone. The Commissioner lay back against his pillows, rubbed his chin thoughtfully and made a sudden decision. He jumped out of bed, hastily donned his clothes and phoned for his car.

Twenty minutes later he pushed the doorbell of Tony Quinn's house. Quinn, tapping his cane methodically, opened the door.

"Tony, it's Warner," the Commissioner said and tried not to put any of his chagrin into his voice. "I—I was just going by and—and I thought I'd drop in. I saw the lights on."

Quinn laughed. "Come in. Lights? Oh, yes, Silk leaves them on, unconsciously, I suppose. He thinks I need them. Something on your mind, Commissioner? You're out very late."

The Commissioner sat down and twirled his hat nervously. "I've got too much on my mind. The Black Bat for one thing. Frankly, I thought this mysterious, hooded figure might be you, but I—I know how wrong I am now. Forgive me, Tony."

"It's an honor even to be suspected," Quinn chuckled. "I've heard of The Bat and I appreciate the work he's doing. What made you think I might be he?"

"He is built like you, Tony, and he has a somewhat similar voice. But you—you're a—"

"BLIND man? Don't be afraid to say it. I'm used to that now. Commissioner, remember what you told me today? About cooperating with you? I've been thinking things over and I may be able to help. Snate is the man we must get first, but in getting him we must force him to reveal the identity of the man behind him. That man is far more important than Snate and in my mind there is no question of his existence. If he lives, or goes free, he will start a new gang, put another dummy like Snate at their head and carry on as before. That must be prevented. The angle to work from is that of the disappearing armored cars. How long since one dropped out of sight?"

"Three weeks to the day. It's almost time for another to vanish. I've assigned detectives to ride every car in the city. What good they can do I don't know. Sometimes I think it's like sending a man to his grave."

"Tomorrow morning," Quinn suggested, "why not call a conference of interested parties? Mr. Otto Fox, for instance. He owns the largest armored car concern in the country. Then there is Paul Stewart, the Commissioner of Correction. I understand he's not quite so popular of late. Many of Snate's gang seem to be paroled convicts whom Stewart was instrumental in releasing."

"That's right, but Stewart is honest," Warner insisted. "He's working with me, trying to pin enough on those paroled men to drag them back to a cell. So far the score is blank."

"Also," Quinn went on, "bring with you Peter Gage, who runs the *News-Record*. Snate has been hammering away at him and he has the courage to retaliate. I think he might help."

"We'll meet at your house," Warner approved the idea. "Ten o'clock, shall we say? I'll be going now, Tony. And watch out for Sergeant McGrath."

"McGrath?" Quinn frowned. "Why?"

The Commissioner smiled tolerantly. "Oh—just an idea of mine. You see, McGrath received a phone call tipping him off about the bank holdup, but before he could get into action, the thing was done. McGrath, however, was on the scene not long after and he is sure he saw your man Kirby acting suspiciously. Then he saw you crossing the street. McGrath has an idea you might be this new character who has come into life. The Black Bat."

For long minutes after the Commissioner departed, Quinn sat quietly staring into space with his apparently sightless eyes. A slow smile played around his lips. Silk entered with a tray.

"It's all right to send in Carol and our newfound friend," Quinn said. "Do you think he can be trusted, Silk?"

"Yes, sir. Very much so. His name is Jack O'Leary, sir, and he is commonly known as Butch. He once had pugilistic aspirations, but it seems he was framed into a faked bout and thrown out by the boxing commission. A little slow witted, perhaps, but he's as strong as a bull."

Butch marched into the room behind Carol. His head was neatly bandaged and in his eyes was the look that a St. Bernard might give its mistress after its life had been saved. Carol sat down while Butch clumsily arranged pillows at her back. Then he stepped before Quinn.

"Say—you look like you can't see. I figured you was this Black Bat guy."

"And if I am?" Quinn asked him.

BUTCH licked dry lips. "Well—maybe I ain't so bright, but if you need a door or somebody's face pushed in, I'm right there with my dukes. I was framed by a gang of hoods like these mugs that belong to Snate. I hate 'em and I'd work for nothin' if you'd give me a crack at mussin' 'em up." He gulped and moved one foot awkwardly. "That is—if you are the Black Bat."

"I am," Quinn answered quietly, "and I'm glad you asked to join forces with me. I would not have asked you because your life will be in constant danger from now on. I'll arrange a means of contact. Meanwhile you must never be seen with me—as Tony Quinn. Nor as The Bat if we can manage it. You'll be my left hand, Butch. Silk happens to be my right."

"You can count on me," Butch said very seriously. "Boy, are those hoods of Snate's scared of you. That's all they talked about. You want any good muscle work done, I'm your man."

"Thanks," Quinn nodded. "I knew you'd help."

"And I?" Carol asked with a smile.

"You," Quinn turned toward her, "are my eyes. You gave them back to me."

"But those pictures?" Silk put in quickly. "You gave the film to Warner. He'll spot Butch in a second."

"That portion of the film has been destroyed," Quinn said. "And—I think Warner has his suspicions anyway. Not definite ones," he added hastily, "but he more or less expressed himself tonight. We can trust him and he will never really know I am The Bat. Now, before we retire, there is work to be planned. Tomorrow we begin to really wear Snate down. Butch, I want you to wangle a job with the Star Express Service. That's Otto Fox's armored car company. We'll prepare false recommendations. Ride those trucks and keep your eyes open. It's a dangerous job. You may be aboard one of them when it vanishes." Butch nodded tersely.

"Silk," Quinn went on, "you will remain here. I may need you in a hurry."

Carol walked over to the davenport and sat down beside Quinn.

"I'm speaking for myself," she said. "First of all I'll wash this dye out of my hair and remove some of this awful makeup. I have a small apartment not far from here. You can reach me at any time, Tony Quinn."

"Good," Quinn smiled. "It's better that you are never seen with me—nor with the Black Bat, either. You'll work in disguise, as Silk will be forced to do. There must be no way by which either crooks or police can tie any of you to The Bat. Tony Quinn, being stone blind, wouldn't make new friends so you won't be able to come to my house except secretly. Quinn is supposed to be too disgusted with life to be interested in anyone. Perhaps you won't understand how that could be, Carol, but I do. I was really blind long enough to find out for myself."

She nodded and he thought her eyes were a little sad.

"Yes—I do understand," she murmured softly, "You see—my father was—blind."

CHAPTER XII
NIGHT BATTLE

 RSTWHILE District Attorney Quinn got no sleep that night. Butch departed for his rooming house with cleverly forged recommendations prepared by Silk. Carol, safely under Silk's watchful eye, returned to her apartment. And Tony Quinn went forth into the night as the Black Bat.

He had followed Silk and his captors to Snate's private hideout, so no time was wasted in finding the place again. Quinn parked his car well away from the address, walked toward the place through underbrush and soggy marsh. He donned his hood, made sure his guns were ready and then slipped up to the rear of the mansion-like dwelling.

It took him but a few moments to secure entrance through the cellar and, walking softly through the intense darkness of the house, he reached the door to Snate's study.

One of Snate's men was half asleep behind the big desk. The Bat saw him as plainly as though the lights were on. His presence signified that Snate needed a guard in this room at all times. Therefore something of either great value or an incriminating bit of evidence was kept there.

The Bat reversed one of his guns, smashed it down on the sleepy guard's skull and quickly bound him with adhesive. He carried the man to a supply closet, stowed him away inside and locked the door. Then he returned to Snate's desk and began searching the drawers. Nothing of interest showed up until The Bat tried to open the large lower drawer. It was locked. He fell to work on the lock and to his surprise discovered that it was a modern tumbler type. But his tools soon turned the latch. He pulled open the drawer and gazed thoughtfully at the telephone that lay inside.

He left the drawer partly open, arose and methodically unscrewed every electric light bulb in the study. Then he made a rapid investigation of the rest of the house. Two men, ostensibly servants, slept in an upper room. The Bat slugged one into unconsciousness and used his gun butt on the other.

Now he had the entire house at his command without undue danger of being surprised.

Returning to the study he sat down back of the desk, picked up the phone and held it to his ear. There was a click and a surly, hissing voice made him hold his breath.

"What the devil now, Snate?" the voice asked. "Didn't I tell you not to wake me up in the middle of the night unless something important turned up?"

The Bat took a bold chance. Speaking rapidly, as if badly agitated, he imitated Snate's tones as best he could, depending on the Unknown's sleepy brain to discount any slight difference in the tone.

"It's the boys, they're getting restless. We got to do something."

"Damn you, Snate," the man at the other end snapped, "you're getting more jittery by the day. Tell them we're going to pull another armored car job within the next forty-eight hours. I'm getting things set now—and if you waken me again with such a trivial excuse, I'll take steps to punish you. If the men won't obey, shoot one or two. The rest will toe the mark then."

The phone at the other end slammed down. The Bat carefully restored the instrument to its drawer, closed and locked it and then eyed a huge wall safe with considerable interest.

HE HAD a well founded hunch that Snate's accumulated wealth lay behind that great steel door. For now The Bat was positive that Snate was only a puppet and his master would hardly allow Snate to dispose of the huge profits of their joint reign of crime. Safe deposit boxes had grown unpopular with crooks of late because authorities had a habit of locating them and getting court orders to have them opened.

The Bat had tried to place the voice of Snate's master, but it was impossible. Obviously the voice was disguised until it became nothing more than a kind of hissing without tonal qualities. The Bat laughed to himself as he thought of the next time when Snate spoke over that phone and received a warning as to how the men should be handled.

The safe door intrigued The Bat, but he had no aspirations about opening it. Nothing less than a diamond pointed drill, plenty of soup and hours in which to work would break down that barrier.

Then a door slammed shut with a bang and The Bat jerked up. His two guns appeared with the ease and speed of a magician's feat. Backing quickly, he selected a dark spot and crouched there waiting. It was too dangerous to attempt a rushing escape for he had no idea as to how many men had entered the house.

"Hey!" That was Snate's voice raised in anger when no one came to receive him. "Something's happened," Snate went on, speaking to his men. "Two of you get at the doors. The others watch every room, especially the windows."

The door of the study opened and The Bat saw Snate and one wizen faced crook outlined against the light from the hallway. Snate snapped the switch on the wall and bit off a curse when no lights came on. He moved toward the desk. The Bat moved, too, sidling toward the door. He closed it very gently until Snate and his thug noticed that the light from the hall was being cut off.

Both spun around, reaching for their guns.

"You're about to commit suicide." The Bat's voice came brittle as thin ice. "Don't move and don't call out."

"The Black Bat!" Snate gulped.

That name seemed to do something to the warped brain of Snate's undersized thug. Either fear or drug-impelled bravado made him go for his gun. He was swift, too, and the gun was ejected from its holster by a spring. But the hammer never fell against the cartridge. The Bat's gun barked once and the thug spun completely around before he struck the floor.

That shot started things. Snate, half mad in fear of his own life, charged The Bat. His men were running toward the study. Snate dragged his gun out, tried to aim it in the darkness, but he had no target. The Bat, moving on rubber soled shoes, was no longer near the door. Snate turned around, swept out his free hand reaching for The Bat, and ran squarely into a teeth rattling punch on the mouth. At the same moment a hand that felt like steel twisted his wrist until the gun dropped. That same hand moved again with amazing rapidity until it clutched Snate by the throat.

"I COULD kill you now," The Bat hissed, "and the world would be the better for it, but the time is not yet ripe, Snate. So I'll compromise with the urgings of my heart and only knock you stiff."

Snate whimpered, tried to scream, but those fingers were too tight against his windpipe. He heard the rush of air made by The Bat's fist, felt a pile driver of a punch strike him squarely in the face and then Snate's interest in things animate ceased.

The Bat let him collapse to the floor. Someone shoved open the door of the study and for a second The Bat stood revealed. Two men at the door cried a warning and at the same time opened fire. A bullet whistled past The Bat's ear. His two guns pumped lead with a fury. One thug clutched at his stomach and fell. The other decided he might live longer if he beat a retreat and he did so—very hastily.

The Bat surveyed the study, saw that it had no windows and that ventilation was provided by a grilled ventilator. He had to leave through the door. Darting forward, he reached the hallway before any of the other gunmen responded to the shouts for help and the firing. The Bat's gun spoke and the light in the hallway went out. He sped to a small table lamp, hastily unscrewed the bulb and inserted a bit of metal into the socket. He felt a slight shock, saw the blue flash as the power was short-circuited —all over the house, the lights went out.

Now The Bat was in his element. Here, in the darkness, he could see plainly while his enemies blundered around, not knowing which way to turn. One was coming down the stairs. The Bat quietly seized a small chair and placed it on the stairs several steps from the landing. The descending thug tripped, fell headlong and when he tried to scramble to his feet, a gun butt put him out of the running.

The Bat headed toward the front door, opened it and then slammed it shut again as two bullets smashed into the heavy oak. There was a car in the driveway, its headlights on and flooding the porch. Those same lights would illuminate the rear of the house also. Another man was coming down the steps as quietly as possible. The Bat moved sideways, heard a board squeak and drew down the fire of the man on the stairs. The Bat shot once and missed. When the thug started back upstairs, he fired a second bullet that stopped the fight.

There were at least two men outside. The Bat could hear them talking. They'd expect him to emerge through the rear door and take his chances in reaching the thick brush that surrounded the house. Therefore The Bat did the exact opposite thing. He turned the knob of the front door, flung it wide and raced out into the night.

Guns cracked and he saw a burly man raise from the protection of a thick bush. The ground at The Bat's feet spurted dirt as another bullet hammered into it. In desperation, The Bat jumped and went into a nose dive that carried him across the ground and behind a hedge.

"I winged him," the thug yelled. "I put a slug in his carcass. Careful now—he may still be able to shoot."

THE Bat's nose dive to safety had been mistaken for the antics of a badly wounded man. He smiled tightly, rolled over and over until he was a dozen yards from the spot where he had vanished, and then lay prone, gun arm resting on elbow and weapon pointed straight out.

He saw one man move into his range of vision. The Bat's gun flashed. His aim was accurate, but the flame from the muzzle of the weapon drew down the fire of the last crook. There was nothing to do now but shoot it out. The Bat waited, tensely. He had one advantage. If the killer showed himself even slightly, he would see him. The headlights of the car streamed in a direction away from the two men and both were operating in total darkness.

Something dropped to the ground about twenty feet to The Bat's right, but he wasn't fooled by that trick. His gun swung left. He saw, as clearly as though a spotlight focussed on the subject, the stealthy movements of the last crook. The Bat fired twice, heard a scream of agony and waited until the flailing of limbs in the brush died away. He approached the wounded man, saw that his slug

had inflicted a deep scalp wound and he knew the battle was over.

He paused long enough to attach one of his tokens that emblazoned the image of a black bat on the man's forehead. Then he hurried to the parked car, got behind the wheel and backed to the road. He roared up the highway to the spot where he had parked his own car. There he disabled the sedan he had temporarily appropriated, climbed into his own sedan and drove away.

He left it parked ten blocks from his own home, slipped through neighbors' yards as quietly as a cat and reached his own back door. Silk was waiting anxiously. There was a smear of blood on The Bat's hand.

"You're hurt, sir," Silk gasped.

The Bat stripped off his hood, glanced at the hand and shook his head. "That's the blood of one of Snate's men. I must have got it when I pasted a black bat on his forehead. Tonight, Silk, my slippery one, I gave Snate a token of my respect. Unless I'm badly mistaken, I broke his nose—at least that's what I intended to do."

"I hope it was his neck," Silk grimaced. "Everything is quiet here. Butch left, as you know. Carol is safely in her apartment and you can contact her by phone whenever you wish. A lovely girl, sir, and clever as they come."

"Right you are." Tony Quinn picked up his cane, stared straight ahead and began tapping his way out of the kitchen. "Come along, Silk, I've something to discuss."

"One moment, sir," Silk said. "I'll phone Miss Carol you are back. Unless you need her, sir."

Tony Quinn shook his head. When Silk returned, he was sitting in the chair before the fireplace, eyes staring blankly at nothing and they seemed dead— like the eyes of a blind man. Tony Quinn took no chances that his secret might be discovered. Sergeant McGrath might have ideas and come snooping.

"SIT down, Silk," Quinn said. "We're in something of a jam right now. Butch can operate perfectly without anyone knowing he works for me. The crooks who might recognize him are either dead or behind bars. Carol can readily change her appearance. But you—Silk—I don't wonder you turned to house breaking. Any police officer could pick you out in a crowd of ten thousand. We've got to remedy that."

"But I have already arranged it," Silk broke in eagerly. "I haven't talked about myself much, sir, but when I operated during my prime, I took over quite a few rather intelligent people. I assumed a disguise that I worked on for years. I have small porcelain cups that fit to my molars and puff out my cheeks. A little color rubbed into the right spots on my face and a trick beard of the Van Dyke type, make me look quite distinguished, sir. Then a conservative suit, nose glasses suspended by a silken ribbon around my neck and I'm the very essence of a college professor. In fact, I was once known as The Professor."

"Great," Quinn cheered. "Have you any other accomplishments, Silk?"

Silk flushed a trifle embarrassedly.

"Well, sir, I have been known to put out some rather fancy kites—forged checks. I also possess the knack of imitating a person's voice. That used to be quite handy when I made phone calls in some other man's name."

"Silk," Quinn said, "you're going to be a priceless asset. Now to bed with you. I need rest also, because tomorrow Commissioner Warner is bringing three men here to confer with Tony Quinn, the blind man. Shortly after that, there is to be another armored car disappearance and then, my dear Silk, Snate is really going to get a headache. Tonight I talked to Snate's master and through Snate, I'll land him, too!"

CHAPTER XIII
THE DISAPPEARING TRUCK

 HEN Commissioner Warner swept the nose of the big departmental limousine into the driveway of Tony Quinn's home, he saw the blind man slowly making his way along the drive. Warner stepped on the brakes and the tires grated against the gravel. Instantly Quinn made a crazy jump for the bank. It was rounded upward and he fell on the slippery grass until he sprawled on his stomach. With a cry of fear he pulled himself along the turf until he was out of the drive.

Warner reached his side and helped him to his feet. "Tony, I'm terribly sorry that I frightened you."

Tony Quinn exhaled a long breath of relief. "I'm acting like a child, Commissioner. But the sound of brakes seems to get me. Every time I hear them squeal, I expect to feel the radiator of a car smash against me."

"Let me help you inside," Warner suggested, and swore at himself for being such a fool as to suspect Tony Quinn of being the Black Bat. "Fox, Stewart and Gage are already on the porch. Feel well enough to confer with us?"

"Oh yes, of course." Quinn flashed a quick smile. "Using my brain in trying to figure this thing out is all that seems to make living worthwhile. I have an idea, Commissioner, and it may work."

Quinn shook hands with the three men who waited on the porch. His eyes stared straight over their shoulders, but Tony Quinn's grip sized up each man as he held their hands in turn.

Gage had a plump, warm fist. His clothing seemed to smell of printer's ink, for Gage wasn't one to be content as an executive. He practically lived beside the great presses that pounded out his newspaper. Gage was big, rough, and ready.

Stewart was big, too, but in a different sort of way. There was no surplus strength in his muscles and the flesh on his face hung down in jowls. His handclasp was limp.

Otto Fox typified the go-getter type, slender, immaculately dressed and always nervous. His hand felt moist and cold, Quinn thought.

Silk served highballs and discreetly withdrew. Quinn took the floor.

"Gentlemen, the Commissioner has been good enough to ask my help. I've thought about this armored car disappearing act for many hours. I haven't solved the manner by which it is done, but— I think we might forestall any further attempts."

"Yes," Otto Fox leaned forward and clicked the ice cubes in his glass. "Tell me how you will do that."

"It looks to me like an inside job," Quinn offered. "Therefore the men who control it must be circumvented. There is a way. Each morning your crews, assigned to each truck, are given sealed orders. They don't know where they are going until the trucks start out. All armored car services operate that way. Therefore, instead of allowing regular employees to handle those sealed orders it is my suggestion that you, Mr. Fox, handle every detail yourself. You route the jobs, you issue the orders direct to the men."

"NOT me," Fox shook his head. "If anything happens, then I will be instantly blamed. You forget, these losses are not mine. Those shipments are insured and I do not care to draw down insurance company detectives on me."

"Let me handle it," Stewart spoke up. "I've an interest in this case. I'm being publicly censured for letting criminals out on parole, but I'm powerless to stop their release. All I can do is send them back. Doubtless many of them are helping this man Snate, and if I help to prevent these robberies I at least interfere with their plans a little."

"Why, of course," Commissioner Warner broke in. "Stewart is quite impartial and if anything happens, the blame cannot be thrown upon Otto Fox."

"I think it's damned foolish," Gage snapped. "If there are inside men, don't you think they'll get wise?"

"Let them," Quinn interrupted. "What can they

do? Stewart is to be given a list of the places where the trucks are to be sent. He will sort these clients under Otto Fox's direction and route the trucks secretly."

"Foolproof," Stewart exulted. "Quinn, Warner is right. You have got a brain in that skull of yours. Now tell us how we can pick up Snate and put him behind bars."

Quinn smiled wanly. "I can't do that, gentlemen. My thinking powers don't go quite that far. Someday I may have an idea, though, and I'll certainly expose it. I have no love for Snate."

When they were gone, Silk entered. "I thought you were going to trap those armored car thieves," he protested mildly. "But as I see it, sir, you've simply stopped them."

Quinn lit a cigarette. "I've laid the groundwork for the plan that will trap the master crook of this age, Silk. Do you think my puny little ideas will stop him? Oh, no. You see, the man who owns Snate was in this room just now. He is one of those four men."

"What?" Silk gaped. "Are you sure?"

"The master crook knows everything that goes on. Those three men stick with Warner as much as possible and one of them does so simply to gain knowledge and pass it on to Snate. In that angle lies his defeat, although he doesn't sense it. Prepare the car, Silk. Carol and I are going for a ride."

"It's quite ready, sir. And so is Miss Carol. She arrived a few moments ago."

Quinn took both her hands as she met him. He didn't speak, for words seemed unnecessary. Instead he picked up his cane, tucked her arm under his and permitted her to lead him out the door and into the roadster. It was hard to pretend blindness on a morning like this, and with a beautiful girl beside him.

She parked the car along a road that overlooked the bay. They sat staring at the water.

"You never know how blue the sky and the water can be, Carol," he said quietly, "until you've lived in darkness for months."

SHE turned to him "That's why I drove here, Tony Quinn. It's time I told you who I am. My father was a police officer—a detective sergeant. Eight years ago, Oliver Snate ruled a small midwestern town—not very far from Springville where Dr. Harrington brought back your sight. Dad fought Snate—and lost. Snate cornered him one night and put two bullets into his back. They paralyzed him for life. Another smashed through his temple, severing the optic nerves—blinding him. He was too weak for an operation.

"Dad heard of your fight against crime and followed you through every phase. Followed you with my eyes for I read him every scrap of information we could get from the newspapers. But Dad was doomed and he knew it. When the time came, he bound me by a promise to obey his instructions. I was to contact you, and through Dr. Harrington present you with new corneas for your eyes, if such an operation would be successful."

Quinn's face was strained, his eyes gaunt and starkly clear now. "Other doctors told me such an operation would be useless," he said, "How did Harrington do it?"

"Harrington could be as famous an eye surgeon as any of those you consulted. But he chooses to live quietly in a country town. No one but Dad could have persuaded him to operate on you—and Dr. Harrington used more than the corneas. He took entire sections of the eyes.

"Furthermore he performed a delicate experiment which had been successful on animal subjects. Dr. Harrington made the pupil larger and exposed more of the eye lens. He asked me to report the results and I did, immediately after the night when you saw me for the first time. You not only have new eyes, Tony Quinn, but exceptional eyes in the manner by which they function. The change which Dr. Harrington made cannot be seen by others, so there is no fear of their abnormality being discovered."

"You were there," Quinn said tensely. "You watched the operation and while I was under anesthesia I talked of what I hoped to do to Snate."

She nodded mutely. "It made Dad's death easier when I told him. He didn't live long after that. Now do you understand why I must be with you—must help you against men such as Snate? Oh, I know he won't be the last one, and those of his kind cannot be fought with fair means. Dad discovered that. So did I."

Quinn said nothing on the drive back. When the car stopped, he took her hand and held it tightly.

"Of course I could never do without you now, Carol, even if you hadn't told me any of this. You proved yourself when you had the courage and tact to enter Snate's mob and then save me from being unmasked and killed. And what you have told me makes me more resolved to fulfill my mission than ever before. No one is safe so long as men like Snate exist. They build themselves up until every boy with the slightest criminal tendency idolizes them, imitates them. Such a thing must stop and there is but one way: to crush those men and in crushing them make them humble.

"Show them up for what they are—stupid, vain, selfish killers."

"And you are going to do that?" she asked.

"Exactly. Snate's days of freedom, perhaps of life itself, are numbered. Tonight the Black Bat flies again and this time there is a trap to be baited and set. Snate may spring it and jump clear, but one day its jaws will close and that day is at hand."

QUINN waited until almost midnight before he ventured out of the house. He slipped through the back door, garbed entirely in black, with twin guns strapped in place and his black hood concealed in a specially constructed pocket.

Keeping the brim of his hat low, he stepped into a street two blocks from his home, hailed a taxi and had himself driven into the heart of the business section. There he became most cautious, for the scars around his eyes would be a dead giveaway if he were observed. He used dark sidestreets to reach the huge garage where Otto Fox maintained his armored car fleet and his general offices.

There were watchmen on duty, but they were old men, retired from the more arduous duties of guarding cash. Quinn fitted his hood in place, sidled through a small delivery door and found himself in a dark, oily smelling room. He walked across this, as sure footed as though every light were turned on. There were winding, steel stairs leading upward. He made his way softly around these until he reached the top and his goal—the entrance to the offices.

The iron barred door was locked and it took him ten minutes to open the twin locks. From this vaulted room the orders for each car were passed out and, sometimes, sacks of currency.

Once a guard walked by the door, tested it and passed on, satisfied. There was a small grill set high in the door. No light streamed from it and had there been light, it would have illuminated an entire section of the corridor. Therefore the guard was satisfied, for what manner of intruder could work in pitch darkness? Even the ray of a flashlight could be easily observed.

The Bat soon found what he was looking for. Neatly stacked under the locked cover of a rolltop desk, he discovered the orders for the following day. They were in large envelopes, all sealed with wax and impressed with the firm's seal. It was impossible to open the flaps without detection, but The Bat had other methods. From his pocket he took a small round silver bar with a slit running along it. He carefully inserted this through the flap, above the seal where the envelope came together loosely. Maneuvering the bar, he engaged the edge of the paper in the slit. Turning the bar slowly he rolled the paper tightly around the bar until he could pull it out.

One by one he treated each sealed envelope in the same manner, copying the contents until he had a complete list of every truck's destination. Next he consulted record books which he removed from a

steel, fireproof cabinet that gave way easily to his set of tools.

It was almost dawn when his work was completed. A difficult task that often threatened to be without result, yet it finally yielded the one item The Bat required.

The careful check he had made of the instructions and the record books revealed that there was one stop—to be made by one truck only—that wasn't recorded except on the sealed orders to the truck itself. The client was not listed on any billing or order accounts. It was the Triton Garage, a huge storage and repair place far uptown.

The Bat made his stealthy way out of the building, just as he had entered. The four guards who patrolled every portion of the grounds, except the record rooms, had no inkling that a hooded man had spent half the night in a room where even they were not permitted.

SILK raised the shades just before noon the next morning.

"You were late last night," he said diffidently. "I hope you were successful. And Butch phoned. He secured his job with the armored car concern and is assigned to Truck M. They letter, instead of number, their trucks, sir."

Tony Quinn whistled softly. Truck M was the one with the superfluous call. Things were shaping up nicely, yet if the Black Bat failed, Butch might lose his life. Not one of the armored car guards who had vanished with their rolling vaults had ever been heard from again.

"Work for you, Silk," Quinn said. "You might begin by stealing a set of marker plates—from a car whose owner won't miss them for a day or two. Then go to a used car exchange and buy the fastest job on the floor. Nothing flashy, but be certain there is plenty of power under the hood. After that, it will be best if you prepare yourself as The Professor and keep the disguise on until you hear from me. Should anyone call, let Carol answer the door and make our regrets."

"Yes, sir," Silk replied simply, but his eyes were shining brightly. Silk had been idle too long to suit his nature.

Quinn decided to go for a walk in the middle of the afternoon. With his cane tapping a path, he strolled out of the house, walked a dozen blocks slowly. He seemed to be worried about his health for he kept a muffler tied well up around his throat. As always he wore a wide brimmed hat pulled low, for Tony Quinn was known to be sensitive about those scars that marred his features.

Once he paused and turned deliberately around, as if hesitating whether or not to retrace his steps. But in reality he looked carefully up and down the

BUTCH

street. There was no one about and it was beginning to grow dark with the early dusk of winter.

Then he turned down a side street, sauntered up to a black coupé parked at the curb. When he was certain he was unobserved, he slipped behind the wheel and sent the coupé racing out into the highway. He parked in a deserted section, peeled off his grey topcoat and revealed his black outfit beneath. He changed to a black slouch hat that had been thrown on the seat of the car. From a concealed pocket he drew his hood and made it ready. He tested his two guns—and was off.

It took him only a few moments to reach the busy center of the city, but he went straight through, rolled uptown and finally selected a parking place which he could pull out of easily. He waited there for more than half an hour until he saw one of Fox's armored cars coming along. He trailed it, very carefully, for he knew that police might also have the car under observation. It made two quick stops.

Each time Quinn saw Butch emerge from the back with an exposed gun in his fist. Another man climbed out and the two of them entered the designated place of business while a third took up a station beside the truck. Butch usually heaved into sight first, holding heavy bags of money while his companion guarded every step they made. As they approached the truck, the rear door opened. Butch and his guard got in while the third man hurried to the front seat.

THEN The Bat raced ahead of the truck to avoid being spotted and parked just outside of the mouth of an alley that led to the big Triton Garage. When the armored car entered this alley, The Bat watched very carefully. He saw it roll into the garage and stop. Two minutes later it came out again.

The Bat saw the two uniformed drivers at the wheel and there seemed to be nothing wrong. He noticed also that there was a V–shaped crack in the window beside the driver. But instead of turning south and heading toward the banking sections where the deposits were to be made, the truck turned north, speeding up.

The Bat followed, at a safe distance. He saw the truck swerve sharply and turn onto a narrow little street. Three minutes later, The Bat reached the corner and suddenly reached for the hand brake. Another car, with weak headlights, was approaching and taking up more than its share of the road. It pulled over finally and The Bat watched it pass by. It was a florist truck of the light delivery type. He snapped off the emergency, started down the street again and found that it was blind!

And there was absolutely no sign of the armored truck!

Leaping from his car, The Bat made a swift inspection of the few garages on the residential street. There was none in which the armored truck might have been hidden. He returned to his own car and sat behind the wheel trying to puzzle it out. His eyes were extraordinarily good and there were no kinks in his brain. He had seen that armored car turn down this street. It was impossible for it to have driven out again without his seeing it. Yet— the Earth might just as well have swallowed the truck for all The Bat could figure out.

He backed his car out of the street and headed back to the Triton Garage. Somehow he knew the secret to all this lay at that point.

CHAPTER XIV
BUTCH FINDS TROUBLE

JACK "BUTCH" O'LEARY found that working for The Bat was a simple process. Everything seemed arranged for him. The forged papers he carried were accepted as genuine and he was instantly given a job as an armored car guard, just as Quinn planned.

Not long afterward, Butch knew why. The guards working for Fox's service were quitting rapidly. Their sole conversation was of the permanent disappearance of more than thirty men and eleven trucks. Most of the guards were new, attracted by the double wages being paid.

Butch got himself rigged up in one of the green uniforms used by the service, buckled on the forty-five automatic and began to feel important.

"Lemme see the guy who tries to hijack the

truck I'm on," he told the three men who were to ride with him. "Trouble with this whole setup is that the mugs who went out and never came back, couldn't take it. Hell, why didn't they put up a fight? All they had to do was fire their guns a few times and draw down a raft of cops. But did they do it? No, because they were too damned scared to shoot."

Loomis, a white-haired employee of the company for more than twelve years, was doubtful.

"You didn't know those others—who have disappeared. They were competent guys. We have target practice twice a week and all those men could knock the head off a match at thirty paces. They weren't scared easy, either. No, sir, whatever happened to 'em happened so fast they just didn't know what to do. And I been lucky too long. One of these days it'll get me, too."

"Stick around," Butch snorted. "Me—I'll take care of you. Only keep your eyes open, see? Maybe if we do that, we'll get the jump on the guys who been taking the cars."

At nine, the armored truck rolled out. There was a weary detective riding with the two guards in back. Two more were up front. At a tiny desk inside the rolling vault, Butch broke the seal of the first route order.

"Alston Trust to pick up payroll for Esquire Shoe Company. Twenty grand for delivery at six bells tonight. That's a funny time to deliver a payroll."

"They make it up first thing in the morning," the detective explained disgustedly. "Don't ask me how I know. I been checking these things for weeks. They got a safe over there that nobody could crack."

They made the pickup and Butch turned to the second sealed order. All day long they followed that procedure. It grew hot inside the truck; the detective peeled off his coat. Then Butch picked up the last order of the day.

"Triton Garage to pick up day's receipts and then home, boys, without the boogy man laying his mitts on us. That's on account of I was along. He musta saw me and got scared."

The driver took the order, drove uptown and turned down a narrow alley leading to the garage. The great doors opened as the truck hove into sight. It stopped inside the garage and Butch climbed out, drawn gun in his hand.

There was an office directly across the wide floor and he hurried there. He heard something of a swish, heard a motor start at the same moment and began to turn around. Something whizzed down and collided with his skull. He dropped to his knees and a grinning thug brought down the short iron bar again, almost cracking Butch's thick skull.

BUT Butch was tough. At least Butch wasn't completely out as he fell. He had his eyes slitted and was conscious of what went on. He saw that the armored car he had worked in all day was now covered with a huge canvas. There was a pungent, choking odor in the air. He saw also an armored car, the counterpart of his own truck, even to the letter M painted on the door, rolling out.

Even Butch's slow witted brain caught the idea. The real armored car stopped when it entered the garage. The huge piece of tarpaulin, held in position and out of sight, dropped down and as it struck the truck, deadly gas bombs broke. The crew had no time to shoot. Then a duplicate truck rolled out to provide an alibi for the Triton Garage. Plenty of witnesses could swear that the armored car left the garage all right.

"Will I slit this big ape's throat?" a voice asked, and Butch promptly closed his eyes and fought to recover his strength.

"He's out stiff—damned near dead from those socks you handed him," another voice rejected the idea. "Drag him into the empty stock room. We'll take care of him when we cart the others away. There'll be blood stains if you bump him here and we can't take chances."

Someone grabbed Butch's feet and pulled him across the floor. Butch remained as limp and passive as he could. His life depended upon the way he played possum. He was in a serious predicament, but Butch felt no fear. He remembered a cold-eyed man with a scarred face, and if Butch needed assurance, it lay with that calm person. The Black Bat wouldn't rest long now. Butch had a well confirmed hunch that The Bat wasn't very far away.

He was thrown into a corner. Someone slapped him across the face. Butch didn't move a muscle.

"He ain't dead yet, but I think the big lug is breathin' his last. How about the guys in the truck?"

"All dead," another man reported and Butch had to restrain a shiver from running up and down his spine. "That gas don't fool around, Limpy. Remember that last guard we socked? When he didn't die, the boss tested the stuff on him and he was dead in less than three minutes."

"Sure—why not? Ain't it the same stuff they feed the poor death house chumps out west? That's where Snate got the idea. Boy, was there a haul in that truck! A hundred and fifty grand if there was a cent."

"Yeah," the other thug mumbled, "and what do we get out of it? A measly hundred bucks a week with a promise of a big cut later on. If you should ask me, it's too damn much later on. We get about two or three hundred grand apiece coming to us and all Snate hands out is promises."

"Shh, Limpy. You wanna have that gas tried on you? Snate don't take no back talk from nobody—'specially lately. Somethin's got in his hair. You know what? He's scared. Scared stiff!"

"Who wouldn't be?" the first thug asked. "That Black Bat is got himself nine or ten lives. Ain't no bullet made with his number on it. If he gets just a little closer to this racket, I'm pullin' out—cut or no cut."

THERE was silence after that. Then Butch took a chance and opened his eyes a crack. He shuddered. The bodies of the truck guards were being carried into this small room. Their faces were suffused with a peculiar greenish tinge. Loomis was there, and the weary detective who rode the truck. Snate's batting average was running a hundred percent—except for Butch.

Perhaps thirty minutes crawled by. Butch wasn't sure, for it seemed like a year to him. He was alone in the little room, alone with four dead men. Carefully he crawled over toward the bodies and groaned a little when he saw that they had been stripped of their guns. He heard someone approach and tried desperately to get back to the side of the room where they had flung him. He was too late.

"Hey, look at that big guy," someone hissed. "He's alive. Get busy with that knife."

That was enough for Butch. He suddenly arose, looking as big as a mountainside to the two men in the room. He reached out one mighty paw and the fingers closed around the knife man's throat. They squeezed—once—and bone cracked. Butch flung a lifeless body from him and looked around for the second thug. He was gone, but as Butch headed toward the door, a menacing gun stopped him. Three men backed him into the little room. Only one had a gun. The others looked on with obvious interest.

"So," it was the man called Limpy who spoke, "you're a tough guy, huh? You rubbed out Slim, did you? Well, you were gonna die anyway—only nice and easy—with some swell gas—but now you're gonna take it in the belly—every damn slug in my gun."

Butch's eyes protruded and his vast body shook with rage. Yet even his slow-witted brain told him there was no hope. He couldn't jump the gun. There wasn't room enough. Slowly he backed away until he felt the cold wall at his back. The trio advanced, step by step, glorying in their new found control over life and death.

Then Butch saw the door behind the men silently open. A black-gloved hand emerged and it held a gun. There was a single shot. Limpy gave a scream, whirled around and fell headlong. The other two men reached for their weapons, but their hands

froze. Standing in the doorway was a figure that had grown to be the nemesis of the underworld. The Black Bat faced them, two guns at a ready angle.

"Back up," he ordered. "You," he indicated Butch, "get out of here."

"Sure, sure," Butch grinned happily. Then he used his head. "I dunno who you are and you look like a crook to me, but thanks anyway. Just lemme take care of these two mugs in my own way. Then, if you wants, you can plug me. I'll die happy."

He received a curt nod of that hooded head. Butch spat into the palms of his hands, hunched his shoulders and then spread his arms wide. The two thugs cowered, bleating in terror. Butch grasped each one by the scruff of the neck, lifted them completely off the floor and brought their heads together twice. Then he dropped them, wiped his hands on his thighs and faced The Bat inquiringly.

"Run for it," The Bat whispered. "This place is full of Snate's men and they'll be down here like flies."

BUTCH made a line for the door, racing across the huge empty space of the garage. He heard someone shout. A gun barked. Butch felt a mighty blow against his forehead. He reeled, clutched at the air in a vain effort to find something by which he might support himself, and then his huge body collapsed like an empty sack.

The Bat leaped out of the small room, fired half a dozen quick shots toward the ramp that led to the upper floors of the garage and drew a squeal of pain from one of the thugs who hid there. The others ducked. Then a siren cut loose.

The Bat glanced out of the nearest window. Two cruisers, crammed with detectives, were pulling into the areaway before the garage. Other things happened so fast they seemed amazing. A heavy car came rumbling down the ramp. It braked to a stop beside Butch. Two men jumped out, picked up Butch's limp form and threw him inside. The Bat snapped a pair of hasty shots, missed and raced toward the rear of the garage seeking an exit. There was none!

He saw the bandits' car speed by the detective cruisers with an exchange of shots. One of the cruisers turned to take up the chase while five detectives raced toward the doors of the garage. At their head was Detective Sergeant McGrath.

The Bat surveyed the garage quickly. There was no sign of the real armored truck and The Bat possessed no idea that it had remained inside the garage while a ringer rolled out. Powerful elevators had raised the truck to a dismantling room where it was already beyond recognition.

There was one thing The Bat wanted to do

before he beat his retreat. The armored car guards lay in that empty stock room, mysteriously dead and showing no signs of violence. While Sergeant McGrath and his men cautiously approached the building, The Bat hurried to the stock room. Using one of his sharply pointed tools, he deftly made a small incision on the arm of a dead guard. The blood, still warm, flowed under pressure of his fingers and he mopped up a quantity on a clean handkerchief.

As he turned away his eyes passed over the two unconscious thugs. They wore regulation overalls and mechanic's smocks on the back of which were emblazoned. "TRITON GARAGE" in bold sewed-on letters. Just above these were faint marks in the cloth where other letters had been previously sewed. The Bat spelled out AJAX AUTO REPAIR. He made a mental note of this.

Then he set to work formulating a plan to escape McGrath. Watching carefully, he waited until McGrath and his men entered the building. They were bunched together, and started an extensive search of the place. McGrath motioned toward the ramp and they headed that way. The Bat selected that auspicious moment and stepped into the open with both guns drawn.

"Don't move," he called out. "This is The Bat! Remain exactly where you are and drop your guns to the floor. Drop them!"

The Bat's guns barked in unison and the bullets slammed into the wall above the heads of the detectives. That was warning enough. Their guns clattered to the cement floor.

"Turn to the right," The Bat commanded, "and walk straight ahead until I tell you to stop."

MCGRATH obeyed, but he shouted a warning. "You may think you're some kind of a tin god, but one of these days I'll run into you first, Bat. That's the day you'll roost in a cell."

"I'll be looking forward to it," The Bat answered gaily. "Now—all of you stand just where you are. McGrath—I'll give you the honor of removing yourself and your men from my presence. All of you are now standing on the platform of an elevator. Pull that rope at your left and take a ride."

McGrath ground out an oath, but he glanced over his shoulder at the eerie figure in black, took firm cognizance of the two menacing guns and shivered. McGrath was too wise to resist. He possessed a good trait of biding his time. He manipulated the rope and the lift began moving slowly upward.

The Bat sped toward the door. He raced around the garage, cut through an alley, removing his hood as he ran. He vaulted a fence with ease, reached the street and headed directly to the spot where he had parked his car. Two minutes later he drove north.

CHAPTER XV
THE BAT'S DILEMMA

BUT The Bat was intensely worried over Butch. The fact that the fleeing bandits had stopped long enough to pick him up meant but one thing to The Bat's agile mind. Butch had learned something of extreme importance. Yet The Bat knew that he was powerless for the moment. McGrath might test out a theory that Tony Quinn was The Bat by hurrying to Quinn's home and demanding an explanation if Quinn didn't happen to be there to receive him.

The Bat stopped at a busy corner, drew his collar up and his hat brim down. He stepped into a drugstore, reached a phone booth and dialed Police Headquarters.

"Commissioner," he said when Warner was on the wire, "this is Tony Quinn. I've been sitting in front of my fireplace thinking, since dinner, and I need your help on one detail. Will you check your records and call me back? I want to know the last port of call that each of those vanished armored cars made the day of their disappearance."

"Of course, Tony," the Commissioner assented. "I've bad news for you, though. There has been another one of those jobs pulled. McGrath is working on the case now. Stewart prepared the sealed orders and swears no one knew what was in them but himself. It is impossible for any other person to have known the route of any truck and prepared the trap by which this latest one vanished."

"You suspect Stewart then?" Quinn asked.

"What else can I do?" Warner answered. "Yet I simply cannot persuade myself that he is our man. But I'll call you back in a few moments, Tony."

He hung up and The Bat sped back to his car. He reached his home and was inside his study just as the phone rang. He was breathing hard, but he governed his voice well as he answered.

"It didn't take me long to find them," Warner said. "And I have still more news for you. First, the armored cars used to make different stops at the end of their day's run. Usually it was at some bank where deposits were made. We checked carefully and there is nothing significant there. Now, this last truck to vanish: it must have either driven into, or been near the Triton Garage, because Sergeant McGrath was investigating some shooting there and found the murdered armored car guards. They died of some violent poison."

"Are you sure the truck visited the Triton?" Quinn asked. "Did it have orders to go there?"

"We don't know yet," Warner answered. "Have to check with Otto Fox first. Two mechanics disclaim any knowledge of the truck and simply said a car drove in, dumped out the dead guards and got away after a lot of shooting. The mechanics were badly injured and couldn't tell us much. They weren't with the Triton very long. Came from one of that garage's branch plants known as the Ajax Auto Repair up on Lenox Street."

"Someone," Quinn offered, "was close to the crooks and they were forced to get rid of their death cargo fast. There is no other solution."

THE Commissioner chuckled dryly. "Someone was close all right. Those mechanics didn't know it, but The Bat was there. That's what all the shooting was about. McGrath is running down some idea of his now. One of the men with him reported all this to me just a minute ago."

"Thanks," Quinn answered. "That may help me."

He hung up and slowly turned away from the phone. Then he jerked erect and one hand darted for a gun. It leveled at the man who stood not a dozen feet away.

"Who are you?" Quinn snapped. "And keep your hands right where they are."

The man was about fifty with hair grey at the temples, a fat, round face and nose glasses fastened securely in place with a flowing black ribbon hanging loosely around his neck. He wore a wide, black, loose flowing bow tie, a morning coat and grey striped trousers. To Quinn's momentary amazement the man smiled broadly.

"I'll be certain not to move, sir, until you've put the gun away. Fooled you, didn't I?"

"Silk," Quinn gaped. "You're perfect! No wonder the suckers fell for your line. You reek importance and money."

"Thank you, sir," Silk answered and he was highly pleased. "I'm quite ready to begin work."

"Great. Drive at once to the Ajax Garage and Repair Plant on Lenox Street. Investigate the place carefully and if you value your life, don't give your identity away. That garage may prove to be a mare's nest of spies and cutthroats. Butch has been snatched from the Triton Garage and the Ajax may be another hideout for the mob."

"I'll be careful, sir," Silk said. "And might I suggest that I stop and pick up Miss Carol? She's rather champing at the bit, sir. Wants something to do. Perhaps we can satisfy her desire for action by letting her drive me. The mission is comparatively tame, sir."

Quinn had no time to discourage the idea. A car had stopped outside with a squeal of hastily applied brakes.

"Run for it," Quinn cried and donned a grey tweed smoking jacket as he spoke. "The back way, Silk. The car is parked at the usual place."

"But you, sir?" Silk protested.

"I'm going to have company. Sergeant McGrath is coming to call. Now will you hurry?"

Silk was out the back door as the front doorbell buzzed. Quinn quieted his nerves, picked up his cane and slowly tapped his way to the door. He opened it and his attitude was one of expectancy.

"Yes? You'll have to announce yourself. I'm blind."

McGrath narrowed his eyes. "I'm a detective lieutenant—sent here by the Commissioner. May I come in?"

Quinn moved aside and indicated the direction of the study with his cane. "Certainly, Sergeant. I suppose your visit is about the armored car guards who were found dead at the Triton Garage. I talked to Commissioner Warner about five or ten minutes ago concerning them."

MCGRATH stopped in his tracks and Quinn, fumbling his way along, bumped into him head on. "Oh—I'm terribly sorry," he apologized.

"Wait a minute." McGrath gripped Quinn's arm. "Did you say you talked to Warner ten minutes ago?"

Quinn nodded assent. "Is there anything so peculiar in that? I phoned him fully fifteen minutes ago and he called right back with the information I wanted."

McGrath walked over to the phone and got the Commissioner on the wire. Full confirmation of Quinn's statement was followed by an irate order from Warner.

"McGrath, you fool, if you pester Quinn, I'll have you broken. You're going a little mad with this idea of the Black Bat. Listen to me now—never mind talking. You talk too much anyway. I thought Quinn was The Bat myself, but I changed my mind. You change yours, do you hear?"

"Yes, sir," McGrath gulped. "But you can't blame a guy for thinking. This Bat is clever and so is—the other person we referred to. The Bat acts just the way I'd expect this other man to act and they are precisely the same build. I'm wrong though, and I admit it. He simply couldn't have been at the Triton and reached this house fifteen minutes ago. Sorry, Commissioner."

Quinn was staring somewhat to McGrath's left. "I really don't get the gist of all this," he complained in the annoyed tone of a blind man, helpless to determine things for himself.

"It doesn't concern you, Mr. Quinn," McGrath said in an abashed voice. "All I wanted was to phone the Commissioner from some place where I knew my words wouldn't be overheard by anyone we couldn't trust. Thanks for the use of the phone."

"Not at all," Quinn followed him to the door. "I have few callers and I'm even delighted to see you, Sergeant."

McGrath didn't grasp the significance of the remark until he was in his car. Then he snapped off the tip of a cigar so violently that he tore the wrapper. He hurled the cigar away and swore vigorously.

Quinn made his slow way back to the study and sat down. For fully twenty minutes he remained immovable. Then he arose and stood, apparently looking at nothing, but in reality he studied each window. If anyone lurked in the darkness outside, he could have seen them. Certain he was unobserved, Quinn moved toward the fireplace and entered the small laboratory he had constructed behind it with his own hands.

He went to work swiftly now. First he took the blood-stained handkerchief from his pocket, put the stain into a solution and divided the fluid into five equal parts. Methodically he tested each portion with reagents. In the third test tube he obtained a precipitate and he set it down, satisfied.

"The armored car guards were killed with cyanogen gas," he told himself. "Somehow it was administered to them very effectively and in a well enclosed area where it could work so fast they had no time either to draw guns or call out."

HE TOOK the time to reload his guns before he removed his jacket and revealed the somber garb of The Bat. This time he was forced to use one of his own cars, but he took the precaution of removing the marker plates and substituting ones stolen by Silk. All this took time that he hated to lose. For one thing, he knew that Silk had accepted his silence as consent and stopped to pick up Carol. Silk might run into almost any kind of high danger at the Ajax Garage if it was infested with Snate's rats. Mentally Quinn damned McGrath and his suspicions.

He drove slowly out of the garage, turned up the street in front of his house and made certain McGrath had placed no shadowers on his trail. Then he opened the car wide and roared north toward the Ajax Garage.

It was early morning now and it was easier for him to prowl unrecognized, yet he took no chances. He parked the car and walked briskly along until he reached the entrance to the garage. He looked vainly for signs of Silk's car. Something gleamed brilliantly in the gutter. He picked it up and for the first time since he had gone blind, Quinn felt the full pangs of fear.

What he had picked up was a vanity and on its cover were emblazoned Carol's initials!

Butch was gone—kidnapped by Snate's men! Carol and Silk had disappeared as mysteriously and thoroughly as those vanished armored cars. The Bat was stymied completely. There seemed to be no way in which to turn. Snate would be clever enough now to shift his headquarters and there was no doubt that he had several other hideouts.

CHAPTER XVI
THREE PRISONERS

 AROL and Silk parked half a block from the entrance to the Ajax Garage.

"The orders were explicit," Silk lied honorably. "This is a job for one person, Miss Carol. Two of us would make too much noise. You will have to remain in the car. Keep the motor going in case I make a hasty exit. I don't know what I'm going to find in this garage, but since The Bat has sent me, I'm sure there must be something of consequence."

"But I'm only being a chauffeur," Carol protested. "I want an active part in this work. It is as much my fight as it is The Bat's. I even dyed my hair again."

Silk was agreeable to the idea, but Silk was also smooth. "Supposing you went into the garage and were accosted? What would a girl be doing in a garage at almost midnight? No, Miss Carol, it's my job alone."

He smiled at her, straightened his cutaway and drew himself up pompously. He marched straight into the garage, spotted an attendant who looked more like a ruthless killer than a mechanic and walked up to him.

"I," Silk announced, "am Professor Calkins of the University. My car has broken down several blocks away. I want a wrecker and prompt service for which I will readily pay—"

"Go away," the pseudo-mechanic growled. "We're full up and we don't work nights."

"But I'm in trouble," Silk went on.

"Will you beat it?" the thug barked. "Or do I heave you out on your ear?"

"That," Silk said angrily, "is quite enough. I'll see about this matter later on. Good night!"

He walked toward the door, glanced over his shoulder and saw the thug sauntering toward the ramp. Silk stepped quietly into a small office and crouched there, waiting. After five minutes he emerged again, scurried across the wide garage until he reached the base of the ramp. He crept up this very cautiously and halfway to the top paused long enough to remove a gun from a hip holster.

He heard someone descending and he ducked into the second floor where he knelt behind a car in dead storage. The thug who had received him was hurrying down the ramp with two men in tow. Silk smiled grimly. The gang was holed up somewhere on either of the two floors above. It took him fifteen minutes to investigate the third floor and be certain there were no concealed rooms. On the fourth he stood gazing thoughtfully at the east wall. There was one corner which ended too abruptly and left a considerable space unaccounted for. Unless one looked for a hidden portion of the garage, it would hardly have been noticed, but Silk's eyes and wits were sharp.

He tiptoed to the farther wall and gradually approached this cubicle in the corner. He knew that Carol would be growing both impatient and worried, but Silk dared not hurry his movements. There was too much at stake now.

WITH his back flat against the wall he put an ear to the cubicle and listened intently. No sound reached him. He studied the blank wall again and smiled tightly as he saw minute cracks in the shape of a narrow door. Gun ready, he moved toward it. Somehow Silk had a hunch this was too easy. A mob like Snate's would naturally have alarms set, yet he saw no trace of them.

There was a box-like arrangement about waist high on the wall. Silk had passed it already. He stopped abruptly and squinted in the faint light to make out a similar box-like arrangement on a pillar directly opposite. He knew what it meant. He had passed through an invisible ray of light and set off an alarm.

He was in for it now and wisdom told him a quick retreat was in order. He started for the ramp.

"Hold it!" a harsh voice snapped. "One more step and I'll bury lead in your back."

Silk sighed, dropped his gun and raised his hands. He turned around and saw two thugs approach him. One held a submachine gun at a ready angle. He was done this time. There was no bucking one of those fast shooting babies.

The second thug drew a heavy pistol, clubbed it and moved in rapidly. The gun butt swung twice and Silk hit the floor with a thump. The lights spun in a galaxy of motion until unconsciousness swept him into temporary oblivion.

Two more men came running up the ramp. The pseudo-mechanic indicated Silk.

"That's him—he called his-self a Professor. I thought he was a phony. Joe says there ain't no crippled car within ten blocks. But there is a buggy down the street with a girl in it."

"Okay. Bring 'er in."

The thug moved Silk's limp body with his foot and then grinned.

"We got something this time. I'm betting my share in the last armored car job that this guy is The Bat. Put him in the bus. We'll grab the girl—she must be in on this or she wouldn't be hanging

Silk listened intently.

around—and scram before somebody else shows."

Carol saw nothing suspicious in the two men who sauntered up the street. They separated just before they reached her car, one crossing the street. The other walked directly toward her and as he drew opposite the car, he sprang for the door. Carol quickly snapped the lock on the door, but while her attentions were centered on this man, the second had approached quietly. He yanked open the door, clapped a huge paw over her mouth and threw her into the rear seat. He climbed over himself and held her so that she could neither move nor scream.

The car pulled away from the curb, slowed as it approached the garage and allowed another sedan to precede it. Then both cars were off. In the first, Silk lay stunned into insensibility. In the second,

Carol fought vainly against a strength five times her own.

Her eyes were covered by a handkerchief after a few moments and the thug at her side gave a growled warning.

"I can't hang onto a wildcat like you forever, so unless you are good, I'll knock you stiff."

CAROL knew he meant it and estimated that her chances of escape were far better if she remained conscious. She gave her assent with a nod of her head. The thug let go of her, but he kept his right fist curled and ready to swing if she attempted to reach the door of the speeding car.

"You're making a mistake," she said. "I'm not worth kidnapping. Nobody cares enough about me to pay any ransom—even if my friends could raise the money."

"Now listen, baby," the thug smiled crookedly, "don't stall with me. You're workin' for The Bat and we know it. So just be nice and quiet because I'm tellin' you I wouldn't care if I slugged you so hard you'd never wake up."

Carol made no reply. She didn't attempt to move the handkerchief around her eyes for she sensed such an action would bring a prompt reprisal. She tried, instead, to visualize the path of the car, but she had started this angle too late. Carol hadn't the slightest idea of where she was.

An hour later, the car rolled over gravel and came to a crunching stop. Carol was helped out, firmly gripped by the forearm and propelled into a house. Then the bandage was yanked from her eyes. She saw two things simultaneously. Silk, who was sprawled, half dazed, in a big chair—and Snate, who regarded her with a contemptuous sneer.

She paid no attention to Snate, but hurried to Silk's side. "Are you hurt?" she asked.

"Who," Silk asked with a quick wink, "could hurt The Bat?"

Carol grasped the situation at once. Snate thought Silk was The Bat. So long as he assumed that, Quinn would have a good chance to prowl.

"I—I never thought they'd get you," she said slowly.

"That's enough gab," Snate barked. "Take the man into the next room and leave him there. I'm going to have a little talk with this dame. Maybe she can tell me a few things I'm curious to know."

Silk put up no fight as he was led into a room that was plunged in pitch darkness. He was thrown into a chair about five feet from a small table. Silk barely made out the lines of the furniture in the room. He settled back to think.

He had awakened from his coma halfway to this place and overheard the men talking of their great capture of The Bat. At once Silk decided to act out the part. Snate would be less on guard if he believed The Bat was dispensed with. The thought that Snate might work fast and murder the man he believed responsible for his troubles occurred to Silk, but he dismissed it with a shrug. Tony Quinn was in this game wagering his life against the outcome. Then why shouldn't The Bat's righthand man take the same attitude?

Minutes passed and Silk worried about Carol, worried about Butch and The Bat also. Suddenly the lights were turned on. Snate entered with a swagger and a malicious grin. For the first time Silk noticed that an automatic had been lying on the small table, almost within reach of his right hand. Snate picked it up.

"YOU," he announced triumphantly, "are a cock-eyed liar. You're not the Black Bat because if you were, you'd have grabbed that gun long ago. I know The Bat can see in the dark—you can't. Now—either you talk or I'll have the boys pistol whip you until your face is ribbons. Who are you? Where is The Bat and who is he?"

Silk's lips compressed themselves into a thin line. Defeat made him more bitter than hopeless. He should have suspected something of this kind when he was left apparently alone in a pitch dark room.

"Now listen," Snate went on. "You think you're a tough guy. Well, so am I. You'll tell us how to contact The Bat or—I'll have the boys work on you and I'll personally put a slug in that dame's skull. Which is it?"

Silk's eyes flashed around the room. There was no doubt in his mind but that Snate was telling the truth and he was fully capable of carrying out his vicious threats.

There was nothing to do but stall—and hope.

"You win," Silk said. "But I can't tell you how to contact The Bat because I don't know how myself. He contacts me. The girl also. He's no fool, Snate. He knows we were always in danger of being captured and he knows your methods of making people talk, too. If we don't know anything, we can't talk, can we?"

"There's a way for you to reach him," Snate thundered. "How?"

Silk heaved a mock sigh of resignation. "Okay—I'm licked. His instructions were to write a letter to the *News-Record* and he'd come to whatever place I designated."

Snate showed smug satisfaction.

"He'll come, all right, because he won't get a letter from you, wise guy. It'll be from me—and if he don't show, you and the dame get knocked off. I'll prove both of you are here by sending him a little token. This time The Bat is done. He's a sap—like cops and all guys who call themselves 'right.'

He'll give up his life to save yours and the girl's. That's what he'll think. And when he finds out what he's got himself into—well, now, won't that be just too bad!" Snate sneered.

Silk glared at him wordlessly.

CHAPTER XVII
THE TRUCK DOUBLE

HE BAT didn't wait to puzzle out his next move. He swung into action at once. Stowing the broken vanity case into his pocket, he stepped into an alley, slipped his hood into place and made his way to the back of the big garage. There was a small door at the rear and it gave way to his tools. Inside he heard no sound and no one lurked in the darkness waiting to pounce on him.

His sensitive eyes saw a folded piece of paper lying in the middle of the floor. He estimated the chances of it being a trap, rejected the idea when his abnormally keen sense of hearing detected no sounds of the breathing of men who might lie in wait. The garage was empty and The Bat knew it.

He picked up the object, found that it was a newspaper and spread the sheet wide open. He looked at the dateline, the paper's masthead and the edition. It was a copy of Gage's *News-Record* and this particular edition wasn't due to be released to the newsstands for almost half an hour yet. The print itself was still moist!

The Bat's eyes narrowed beneath his hood. He selected the first likely looking car in the garage, started the motor and shot out to the street. It didn't take long to reach Gage's newspaper building, but the main difficulty now lay in securing admittance without being seen.

He found, after a full half hour's prowling, a small elevator that ran directly up to where he knew Gage's offices to be. The Bat stepped into the lift and sent it moving upwards. It stopped automatically and without making a sound. The doors parted in the middle and they were very well oiled. He opened them a crack and looked into Gage's private office.

Gage was sitting behind his desk, feet propped up on the edge. Otto Fox was pacing the floor, hands clasped behind his back, chin resting against his chest.

"I tell you Stewart is the man," Fox stated with finality. "He must be. No one else could have known where that armored truck was being dispatched. He sealed those orders."

"But Stewart insists he told no one. He left the orders in your office," Gage argued. "And he'd be a complete fool if he was responsible for the truck's

disappearance. The blame was certain to be shoved right down his throat."

"That's just it," Fox put in irritably. "He's smart enough to realize that a vast amount of suspicion also creates doubts as to its authenticity. He hopes that no one would believe he could possibly be foolish enough to go ahead with his plans after he was made solely responsible for the safety of the truck. Did you know, Gage, that the truck carried an extra heavy load this afternoon? One bank shipped two hundred and fifty thousand dollars in notes of hundred dollar denomination. The rest of it brought the total up to almost half a million."

Gage whistled in astonishment. "I didn't know that, but it still makes little difference to my way of thinking. Oh, I realize that even Commissioner Warner suspects Stewart. It is true that plenty of mugs slipped through his fingers from the various prisons of this state. It's true that he may not have tried to prevent this, but he has his side, also. He insists he did try to stop it and was powerless."

FOX rumpled his thinning hair. "Then in heaven's name, who is it? You, Gage? Or me? That's silly, of course. I stand to lose more than anyone from these damned thefts. In fact my business is completely ruined. And you—what interest could you have in piling up money when you've more than enough now?"

Gage nodded. "I see your point. Say—that suit of yours is soiled—did you know it?"

Fox dabbed at some black spots near the right coat pocket.

"Damn the suit," he raged. "What's a suit compared to the losses the banks and insurance companies are suffering? And mark me, Gage, this isn't the finish. I can sense greater and more atrocious crimes ready to burst wide open. Something must be done and I'm going to suggest that Stewart be arrested."

He banged the door on his way out. Gage sat immobile for a moment or two. Then he furtively looked around the office, reached for the lower drawer in his desk and pulled out a heavy manila envelope. He dumped the contents on the desktop and The Bat, who watched every move, gave an almost audible gasp.

That manila envelope had contained a necklace of emeralds and jade. Nothing extremely expensive or particularly significant to one who did not know, but The Bat had last seen the necklace around Carol Baldwin's lovely throat!

He drew a gun, parted the elevator doors and stepped into the office. "Keep your hands on the desk," he ordered brusquely. Then he moved to the doors and locked them from the inside. "Gage— where did you get that necklace?"

"The Black Bat!" Gage drew a sharp breath. "I—I'm glad you came. I—I was trying to formulate a plan to reach you without actually advertising for you."

"Why?" The Bat asked.

Gage shoved the necklace and the envelope across the desk. "You don't have to keep that gun pointed at me. I'm your friend—I hope. Anyway, I've tried to work with the police on this case and I've fought Snate to a standstill. That proves I'm on your side."

"It proves nothing," The Bat snapped. He scooped up the necklace, jammed it into his pocket and then extracted a letter from the envelope. He read this, but his eyes also watched Gage. The note was very brief.

> The Black Bat: Either you show up before morning at the last house down Strawberry Lane or two people will croak—slow. Stay away or bring the cops and you'll see how we do it.

There was no signature and the note had been typewritten. The Bat felt the texture of the notepaper by gently rubbing it between his fingers and then picked up similar looking sheets from Gage's desk. His sensitive touch told him the paper was of the same quality. He held both sheets to the light. They were similarly watermarked.

"Get up!" he ordered Gage. "Walk over against that wall where I can watch you while I experiment a bit."

GAGE obeyed and The Bat sat down at a typewriter—the only one in the office. With one hand he copied the note from Snate's mob. It took him but a moment to compare some of the printed letters. There was no question in his mind now. This note had been typed on Gage's own paper and on Gage's own machine.

"How did you get this letter?" he demanded.

Gage shrugged. "I can tell by the way you're acting that you believe I wrote the letter. I didn't! I was called out about an hour ago. Someone wanted to see me about an exclusive story he wouldn't trust a regular reporter with. Of course I went—and was tricked. Nobody met me. When I returned, the letter was lying on my desk."

"Not a very convincing story, Gage. In fact it smells to high heaven. You've read this—written it too—unless I miss my guess. Two of my people are being held prisoners. They must have been forced to state how their captors could get in touch with me. I have no arrangements made for such an emergency and certainly if I had, it wouldn't be through the medium of a newspaper. Do you think I want my business blasted over every front page in the country? Those people of mine never talked because they had nothing to say. You wrote this letter to me, placed it on your own desk and pretended you found it there."

"I told the truth," Gage said. "So help me."

The Bat's hand moved to his pocket and threw the newspaper he had found in the Ajax Garage upon Gage's desk.

"That edition of your paper—when did it come off the presses?"

Gage glanced at the edition banner. "About three quarters of an hour ago. You must have got that somewhere in the plant. That edition hasn't been distributed yet."

"That's what I thought." The Bat picked up the paper again. "Stay just where you are, Gage. I may change my mind about you—I hope so—because I've admired the way you've fought Snate, but if you send out any alarm for me, I'll shoot. That's a warning."

He stepped back into the lift and sent it down. At the bottom he listened a moment. Gage certainly wasn't creating a rumpus. The Bat smiled a little and ran to the spot where he had parked his car. He stripped off his hood before he reached the street and made his way back to his home without detection.

There he sat down, glanced at a clock and saw that he had but a few hours to the deadline. At dawn Snate would murder Silk and Carol. Butch hadn't been mentioned in the letter, therefore Snate didn't know that Butch also was a member of The Bat's ring.

He took out the necklace, laid it on the table and his nostrils twitched for it smelled faintly of the perfume that Carol used. Then he looked startled. The necklace was composed of large and small beads. As he recalled it, they were systematically strung, first a large bead and then a small bead. Now their positions were changed. Several small beads and then a larger one, followed time after time by similar arrangements and between each set a firm knot.

He gasped as he realized their true significance. The small beads represented dots, the large ones dashes and the knots the end of a word. Carol had restrung her necklace so that it spelled a message in code.

QUINN charged into his library, found a book on codes and hurried to decipher her message. Gradually his pencil marked out letters until a sentence was created.

AJAX TONIGHT
LOOT HIDDEN THERE

Quinn was up and out of the house within a minute. It was clear that Carol had heard Snate's men talking and knew that they intended to remove the hidden loot from the Ajax Garage before morning. It was likewise certain they would bring their treasure to the same hideout where Carol, Silk and Butch were held prisoners. Carol was telling him in the only way she knew how that the trail was still wide open.

He drove his car into an alley, donned his hood and proceeded to make his way to the big garage. Lurking in the darkness outside, he saw a car pull up before the closed doors and stop. A man got out and entered the garage through a small door set in the huge roller type one. He emerged after a few moments and walked down the street. The Bat maneuvered his way to the parked car, crawled into the tonneau and crouched there, hard against the back of the front seat.

As he had expected and hoped, a mechanic emerged after a few moments and drove the car into the garage, up the ramp to the third floor and left it there. The Bat got out, listened intently for a few moments and then began his prowl.

A cold horror possessed him, for if he was too late and the loot had already been removed, his chances of reaching Carol and Silk were practically ruined. To obey the orders of that note meant instant death, for Snate's men would be lying in wait, ready to blast the life out of him at the first opportunity. The Bat could do them no good alive and they had suffered enough humiliating experiences at his hands already not to withhold their fire when the chance to exterminate him arose.

There was nothing on the third floor and The Bat was torn between the problem of searching the second or fourth floor first. He decided to go higher and climbed the ramp to the top. A weak light cast a yellowish shadow of light over the parked cars. The third floor had not been lighted. To The Bat's mind this was significant. If men of Snate's mob were in the habit of coming here, they would need light enough to see their way between the cars.

As Silk had done, The Bat carefully studied the architecture of the place. He spotted the cubicle setting off one corner of the floor, remembered that the building itself presented a square appearance from the outside and knew that a secret room was located behind those jutting walls. But unlike Silk, The Bat moved warily. He saw the apparatus used to create an invisible beam of light and avoided it. His eyes, efficient as they were, quickly made out the lines of the hidden door. He approached it softly, guns ready. Then he heard the whine of a motor in first gear. A car was coming up the ramp.

HE DUCKED hastily and watched a light delivery truck bearing the name "Campbell The Florist" on its panels stop at the top of the ramp. Two men alighted, leaving the cab doors open. The Bat watched them rap smartly against the hidden door, saw it open and they vanished inside. Before he could get into action, the two men emerged again, this time carrying heavy valises which they threw into the back of the truck. When they disappeared, The Bat made his catlike way to the truck. As he passed the front of it, he paused. There was a V-like crack in the window beside the wheel.

Instantly his mind clicked. He had seen that odd shaped crack before—on the window of the armored car that rolled out of the Triton Garage.

"A confounded jackass," he berated himself. "That's what I've been. An armored car window wouldn't be cracked. They're bulletproofed and they'd cobweb instead of cracking."

He hurried to the rear of the truck, opened the door and got inside. There he squatted, pursing his lips in a noiseless whistle of amazement. He had solved the mystery of the disappearing armored car. It was vividly clear to him now.

The real armored car had never left the Triton. Instead, this truck had rolled out, looking exactly like the armored car. It had turned into that dead end street and there it had undergone an astonishingly quick and efficient change. The truck was so constructed that the sides of the body could be literally turned inside out. What had looked like the formidable steel sides of an armored car became only the exterior of a florist's truck. No wonder the disappearance of Fox's armored cars had been so mysterious and complete.

For the inside, this florist delivery wagon was the counterpart of the outside of the vanished truck. It occurred to The Bat, then, that the small cab was also the same color as the armored car. Undoubtedly provisions had been made to remove all identifying marks so that not the slightest trace remained to give any suspicion that this florist delivery wagon could possibly resemble anything like an armored car.

CHAPTER XVIII
THE BAT TAKES A RIDE

EARING the two men come out of the hidden room, The Bat lay prone on the bottom of the truck. Wisely, he had moved the valises of money to the far end of the vehicle so that when one of the thugs glanced in to see that it was safe, his eyes didn't wander far. The Bat was pressed against the panel separating the truck from the small cab. His black clothes merged with the darkness and he was unseen.

He remained in that position while the truck moved down the ramp, through the big garage doors and finally turned into the street, heading north. It traveled sedately along, obeying every traffic regulation even at this hour of the morning. The thugs were taking no chances on being stopped.

The driver turned sharply after half an hour of that and headed for the river. They were far uptown, where the estates of wealthy people formed the landscape of the river's bank. The truck turned into a driveway, rolled straight through the doors of a five car private garage and stopped. The Bat tensed now, for what happened from this moment on depended solely upon his prowess.

He softly opened the rear door, stepped out and made a nosedive from the garage to behind a hedge that bordered a path leading to the big house.

"Hey!" one of the thugs whispered softly. "The rear door of the truck is open. You damned nitwit, we might have spilled all that dough out in the road."

"I closed it," the second man snapped. "And what's more, I think I heard a funny noise just now, like somebody runnin'. What if it's the—Black Bat? I wouldn't want to meet that guy now. Not after the boss snatched his pals. Between you and me, that guy's scared me outta this racket. I'm ready to pull my freight the second I'm handed my cut."

"Me, too," the other man agreed. "Remember what he did at the boss' other hideout? He killed three men and wounded three others. That bird can shoot like he's got telescope lenses in his eyes. I ain't afraid of the cops—not any part of 'em—but this Black Bat—I don't like him at all."

Each man picked up a valise and walked quickly toward the back door of the mansion, as though they feared the darkness. The Bat followed along, slightly behind them and well protected by the hedge.

"But what we got to be afraid of?" one of them assured himself. "The Bat ain't gonna let the boss polish off his pals. He'll give himself up—wait and see. He's that kind of a guy."

"Yeah—he'll give himself up," the other snorted, "with a couple of spitting roscoes in his mitts. If that guy shows, I blow, cut or no cut. And I got a funny feelin' about him—like he ain't licked yet."

They looked up as the rear porch light was snapped on. The Bat, crouched in the darkness, saw Snate himself step out to greet the men. But the greeting wasn't pleasant.

"Where you tramps been? We got work to do and you mugs hold up the parade. Get that stuff inside and count it. And no chiseling. I know just how much is in that haul. Leave them hundred dollar bills alone, hear me? Take just one and I'll know it. Now scram!"

THE door closed and darkness surrounded The Bat again. He lost no time now. The house was pro-

vided with a cellar hatchway through which entrance was gained by opening a set of slanting doors. There was a huge padlock closed by some competent looking brass staples. The Bat drew out his kit of tools, selected a pair of small but very sharp cutting pliers, and in half a minute the hasps were cut. He opened the hatchway doors very gently lest they squeak.

Closing them over his head, he knelt beside another door barring the entrance to the cellar itself. This door was also well sealed, but he forced his way through it quickly.

There were no lights on in the cellar, but that hindered The Bat not at all. He avoided empty ash cans that were strategically placed around the cellar floor in what seemed to be an arrangement indicative of a crude alarm system.

Then The Bat hesitated. To his exceptionally keen ears came the sound of steady scraping, like the claws of a giant rat digging its way through cement and stone. He traced the origin of the sound and was confronted by a solid steel door with only a small closed trap set high in the center of it. Someone was behind that door, someone who was evidently a prisoner. The scraping was very clear now.

The Bat's hopes mounted high. Could this be Carol and Silk trying to dig their way out? Was his mission to be accomplished so easily? The Bat tapped on the steel panels.

"Who is it?" The voice came from within and to ordinary ears would never have been distinguishable.

"Butch," The Bat whispered. He knew the imprisoned man couldn't hear him and the word came involuntarily. He heard Butch yelling inside, but The Bat was at work. He examined the lock and groaned. It was practically pick-proof and no key that he possessed would fit it. He stood erect and tried the little trap door set in the steel. It opened by pressing a spring latch.

"The Bat!" Butch was peering out. "I can see the outlines of your hood. Boy, you didn't come too soon. Those babies are getting ready to knock me off."

"I can't open this door," The Bat whispered. "There isn't time enough for that. Take this gun and use it if I'm not around when they come for you. Silk and Carol are prisoners in this house, too."

"So that's who it is," Butch gasped. "I heard the mugs talkin' about two more saps they're gonna experiment on. I'm first and I know what they mean. It's a poison gas they use on the armored cars—to kill the men inside. Thanks for the gat. Will I polish off them babies when they show!"

Someone walked across the floor upstairs and The Bat quickly closed the small door, scurried through the cellar and merged with the inky darkness behind the staircase leading to the first floor. A weak electric light bulb was turned on.

A door opened and three men came down, talking audibly. One said, "You handle the stopwatch, Rocky. I'll heave the bomb through the little door and Ted watches the guy croak. You sure that gas mask is okay, Ted? If it ain't, you'll hear the angels singin'."

"IT'S okay," a muffled voice came from behind a gas mask. The three men strode toward the steel behind which Butch waited eagerly. He didn't know that there wasn't a chance for him. He'd have no opportunity to shoot before that tiny bomb of deadly gas would smash against the floor at his feet.

The thug with the stopwatch carefully set the hands, nodded and a second man opened a small wooden box, removed the tiny glass bomb packed in cotton and carefully held it between two fingers. He took a step toward the door and stopped—very quickly.

"The first one of you who makes a sound will die!" The Bat stood directly behind them, a gun covering the trio. "You have the keys to that door. Open it!"

The thug with the gas bomb turned slowly and his jaw sagged. He gasped, "The Black Bat!" Then he realized the import of that small bomb he held. "No, you don't, Bat. This little thing I got in my hand will kill you in one minute flat. Put down that rod or I'll throw it."

"And kill yourself?" The Bat asked contemptuously. "If you have that much nerve, go ahead and throw it. You'll die during that same minute, too."

"D-don't throw it," the crook with the stopwatch quavered. "He's right. That gas will polish off all of us."

"Open the door," The Bat warned. "And do it quietly. Not another sound out of any of you."

One of them drew out the key, inserted it in the lock and swung the door wide. Butch, looking up like some monstrous shadow, emerged, blinking his eyes against the weak yellow light from a single overhead bulb. He held The Bat's gun in his fist and started for the trio of crooks aggressively.

"No," The Bat hissed. "There is no time for that. You three men get into the cell. See how you like being cooped up in darkness for awhile."

They obeyed, but as they marched through the door, The Bat's extraordinary ears picked up a few words of a mumbled conversation. The thugs seemed almost willing to obey him, but as the last one stepped well into the cell, he swung around suddenly and drew back his right hand.

"See if you can scare this," he howled and the glass bomb started its fatal flight through the air.

But The Bat was prepared for this. With his foot he gave the iron door a quick shove and it slammed shut. The glass bomb struck it, burst and the thugs inside screamed in terror. They fought for possession of the one gas mask. Those screams died away within a single minute.

"They asked for it," The Bat told Butch in a whisper. "Now to get Carol and Silk out of this place. Walk softly, Butch. We don't know how many are upstairs."

"But I got lots to tell you," Butch gripped The Bat's arm. "I know how them armored cars disappeared. I was gonna tell you back in that garage, but things happened too fast."

"I know how they vanished. Follow me, Butch, and you'd better remove your shoes. They squeak."

BUTCH obeyed quickly and they stole up the stairs, paused at the door while The Bat listened and then he gave the signal to proceed. He opened the door a crack and looked into a spacious kitchen. No one was in sight, but some kind of a stew bubbled aromatically on an electric range.

"Remain at the back door!" The Bat ordered. "Open it quietly and be ready for a quick getaway! Don't use your gun unless absolutely necessary."

"Right," Butch replied. "I'll just bust their necks with my bare hands."

The Bat swung open the door leading into a serving pantry and peered through a small serving window. He looked out into a handsomely furnished dining room. Now voices came quite clearly and one of them was Snate's hoarse bellow.

"We're all set," he gloated. "Before dawn The Bat walks down that road to Strawberry Lane. He won't think anything will happen until he reaches the house I told him to enter, but he'll get his belly full of lead before he even gets within a quarter of a mile of that place. There are four guys waiting—with sawed-off shotguns. They can't miss him."

"Gosh, boss," another man breathed in admiration, "you're a smart guy."

"Sure I am," Snate patted himself on the back with words. "Don't the papers play me up big? Listen, the other day I saw a bunch of kids playing cops and robbers. The cops were getting the worst of it and gave up to the crooks. What do you think the leader of them kid crooks called himself? Oliver Snate! Ain't that somethin'?"

The Bat's eyes grew hard and his lips compressed firmly. It was something! The glory that the press had placed over Snate's head was bearing fruit. Snate was becoming something of an idol to the boys who lived in the slums.

Snate spoke again. "Joey—you better go up and see how them two birds are getting along. I ain't heard a squawk out of the man in an hour and before that he yelled his head off until I slugged him."

"Gonna give them two the works, boss?" someone asked eagerly. "The dame, too?"

Snate emitted a sigh. "Sure. She's tied up with the Black Bat, that dame, so she's poison, even if she is a looker. Both of 'em get the gas—just as soon as the boys report in that The Bat has been blown in half."

One man emerged from a room opposite the dining hall. He scampered up a flight of stairs. The Bat set his finger firmly against the trigger of his gun and edged his way along the wall until he reached the hallway. If Snate or one of his men happened to come out while he went up the steps, it would be all over.

But luck was on The Bat's side now. He reached the staircase without detection, went up the steps three at a time as noiselessly as though he were a ghost. There was a long corridor at the head of the stairs and The Bat was just in time to see a man backing out of a room. The man closed the door, locked it and started for the stairs.

SUDDENLY his face drained of color and his hands shot high above his head.

"Go back in there," The Bat hissed, "and don't make a sound."

The thug's knees quaked, his lips moved in terror and his eyes bulged. This hooded figure in somber black was the very essence of defeat and death to him. He made no attempt at tricks.

Carol, tied to a chair in the middle of the room, strained against her bonds and at the gag that was inserted between her lips. Silk lay in a corner savagely trying to extricate himself from the folds of several strong leather straps that pinned him with cruel tightness. He rolled over, saw The Bat and actually shivered in delight.

"Untie them," The Bat whispered to his prisoner. "Work fast if you want to live."

The thug freed Carol first and she hurried to the protection of The Bat's free arm. He held her closely and whispered, "Don't talk. Don't move unless necessary."

Silk stood erect in a moment. His disguise was still intact, but he looked badly worn. There was an ugly gash on his temple near the hairline and a bruise discolored one eye. But Silk remained riveted to the spot. He knew that undue walking could be heard downstairs. The Bat nodded in approval. He stepped up to the thug, indicated that he was to turn around, and then smashed down with his gun butt. Silk caught the man before he hit the floor. He eased him down so that no noise was created.

"The window," The Bat whispered. "Out that way."

Carol shook her head. "Barred," her lips formed the word.

"Then follow me," The Bat hissed. "The slightest sound will give away the party. If anything happens, run for the kitchen. Butch is there—waiting."

They both nodded mutely and The Bat led the way to the head of the staircase. There he stopped and signaled the others to stand back. A man was coming up.

He reached the top, turned right and a hand suddenly clapped across his mouth. At the same moment a fist slugged him under the chin, snapping his head back. He went limp. Silk laid him down gently and The Bat nursed bruised knuckles. Silk hastily searched the man and stood up with a gun proudly flashing in his fist.

"You first," The Bat whispered to Carol. "Go straight to the kitchen. We'll cover you."

She hesitated, as though she didn't want to obey the order. The Bat jerked his head toward the steps and she went down slowly and softly. She reached the bottom, turned toward the dining room—and then all hell broke loose!

One of Snate's men glanced out of the library and saw her. He shouted a warning and jumped for the girl. The Bat's automatic slammed once and the bullet found a vulnerable mark. The thug dropped in his tracks.

"You next," The Bat told Silk, "I'll cover you."

"Sorry, sir," Silk said quietly. "You're more important than I."

"Get on with you," The Bat snapped. "Hurry!"

SILK could do nothing but obey. He poised at the top of the steps and then launched himself down them at a terrific speed. A crook loomed up in the doorway of the library. The Bat fired and he drew back with a curse. Silk was getting ready to run for it, exposing himself to the gunfire from inside the library. It was a risky business, but he never hesitated a moment. As he went into the lurch that carried him past the range of gunfire, The Bat's automatic blasted seven fast shots. Silk made it safely.

The Bat whirled, streaked for the nearest room and scooped up a chair as he crossed it. He could hear the thugs running up the steps. He swung the chair against the window, smashed it and shattered the remaining glass with the flat of his gun. He turned toward the doorway and pulled the trigger to send a warning shot out. The gun clicked. There were no more bullets in the magazine and no time to insert a fresh clip.

He was on the second floor and the drop was dangerously high. If he miscalculated, there would be at least a broken leg and now the slightest delay meant instant death whether it was within the house or just outside it.

Suddenly a blast of firing sounded. Men screamed and the shooting increased as new guns added to the din. Downstairs, Butch and Silk were firing rapidly. The Bat wormed his way through the window, hung by his fingertips a moment and then let go. He landed in a clump of bushes that scratched him, ripped his clothes and knocked the wind out of him for a moment. Then someone helped him to his feet. It was Carol.

"I have a car ready," she whispered tensely. "Oh—if only Silk and Butch make it!"

They did. Both of them appeared a moment later. Carol signaled by blinking the lights of the car she had rolled out of the garage. They jumped in and The Bat, who was at the wheel, sent the sedan rolling at top speed in second gear, toward the road in front of the house.

As he turned into the street, he saw a man running madly from the front porch. There was a coupé parked at the curb and he ran directly across the range of the headlights.

"Stewart!" Silk gasped. "He must have been in there!"

"Never mind him now," The Bat said hoarsely. He stripped off his hood with one hand. "Silk, load your gun and hand it to me. I'm going to stop this car soon. You take over and go straight back to the house. Straight back—understand?"

"We ain't gonna be in on no more fun?" Butch asked disappointedly.

"There's going to be plenty of it—later on. Right now I have a job that is a solo. Wait for me."

The Bat slowed, pulled into the curb and stopped. He climbed out, grinned a farewell and vanished into the darkness.

The Bat watched Silk, Butch and Carol disappear down the road. Then he made his way to an all night drugstore and stepped into the phone booth. He dialed Commissioner Warner's home.

"I'm sorry to awaken you at this hour, Commissioner," he said cheerfully. "This is The Bat!"

HE HEARD Warner's quick gasp of astonishment and then went on talking. "If you want to help me solve the mystery of the vanished armored cars and trap Snate and his real master, there is one thing you must do immediately."

"Yes," Warner said softly. "Anything you say. But I warn you—no matter how much help you are in this case, if you're caught it's a cell and, perhaps, the electric chair for you."

The Bat chuckled. "Let me worry about that, Commissioner. Now phone headquarters and have cars sent for Otto Fox, Paul Stewart and Peter Gage. Have them taken to your office and hold them there for an hour and a half. Don't, under any

circumstances, allow any one of them to use a phone, communicate with any person other than yourself, or leave your office. It's vitally important that they be held and yet not realize the fact."

"I'll do it," Warner agreed, "because I am so certain you are trying to help the side of the law—even if you smash every doggone law that's ever been enacted in so doing. They'll be with me until"—he glanced at a clock beside his bed—"three–forty."

"Just long enough," The Bat answered. "Lie like the devil to them and don't even mention my name. Before dawn you'll have Snate and his real master as well."

The Bat hung up, paused to check three addresses and made notes of them. Then he spent almost all the allotted time in making a very discreet search of three homes—those of the suspects whom Warner now had closeted in his office at headquarters. At the last one, The Bat found what he wanted, yet so quietly done were all his operations that no servants were awakened, nor the slightest alarm raised.

CHAPTER XIX
MASTER OF CRIME

 N THE mansion once more, Snate wiped the blood off a light wound along his left forearm. His face was a mask of intense hatred.

"Listen, all you guys," he snapped.

"Get out of here—fast. The cops will come like flies in a minute. We'll meet again—at the river hideaway. It's time for a split pretty soon, but I got to contact a guy I know to see if the land lies clear. Scram—all of you."

Snate himself beat a hasty retreat for the garage and piled into a coupé. He heard sirens in the distance and took the first road to the left. His anger was subsiding for he knew he was safe for the moment. Then Snate began to think seriously about all this. The Bat hadn't fallen for his trap, had in fact secured the release of his friends. To Snate it smacked of the near supernatural. How had The Bat ever discovered this hideout, so securely nestled among the estates of wealthy people? Besides seeing in utter darkness, did The Bat also possess some abnormal powers of magic? More and more Snate thought of dumping the whole business, taking his share of the loot and running for it.

In twelve years of law breaking he had never met a policeman he feared a fraction as much as he feared The Bat. It was time to clear out—with a whole skin and a fortune that would keep him for life.

Snate doubled back over several highways, crossed town twice and finally headed straight for the only remaining spot where he considered himself safe. It was a small, dilapidated dwelling in a poor section of the city. To this place Snate had transferred all his business, even to the contents of the vault. A smaller safe guarded the accumulation of loot now.

He drove his car into a ramshackle old shed at the rear of the place, entered cautiously, with a gun in his fist until he was satisfied that The Bat hadn't preceded him. Snate sped directly upstairs and opened another locked door. Inside the room was his big desk. He unlocked the lower drawer, removed the telephone secreted therein and picked up the receiver.

There was a click from the other end. "Chief," Snate breathed the word. "I got a lot of bad news. The Bat didn't fall for my little plan. He got away, damn him, and he took that dame and her pal along."

"You utter fool," the hissing voice of his master made Snate shiver. "I told you to be careful. The Bat won't stop now. We must get clear before he reaches us. We're ready for that anyway—after one more job is pulled. Your organization is breaking up fast, Snate. Three of your men have written affidavits exposing your whole setup."

"What?" Snate half screeched. "Tell me who the dirty rats are. Tell me where I can find them. I'll—"

"Silence," the voice rasped sternly. "I'm talking now. Here is what you must do—and without the slightest delay. Once, Snate, you were a safe cracker—a rotten one perhaps, but you can still open a box. You've got nitro, so take along a bottle of the stuff. Go to the offices numbered 501 in the Carlton Building. There you will find a small safe that should be simple to open. Inside it is the letter which the three traitors signed. Take that—and whatever else there is of value to give the job an appearance of being just routine burglary. Then get together every cent of cash we have. Have it as compact as possible and come to me. Do you hear that?"

"COME—to—you?" Snate asked doubtfully. "Ain't that dangerous?"

"Of course it is. Our whole business is dangerous. Are you becoming frightened, Snate? Are you turning rat, too? Remember this—if you cross me, you'll die a slow, miserable death. We'll share that money between us. You've got to come here."

"Okay," Snate licked his lips. "I was going to suggest we let the boys cool their heels anyway. It took our brains to think up this racket and we ought to get all the profits."

"It took my brains, Snate," the voice hissed. "Now get busy. I'll be waiting here so don't delay."

Snate checked a heavy automatic to be certain it was loaded. Then he went to the vault, but hesitated before opening it. Somehow Snate didn't feel quite right about this business. Cheating his own men formed no part of his problem. It was The Bat who worried him. That hooded figure in black seemed to be everywhere at once.

Snate was going to be glad when there were many miles between him and this city.

He secreted a small electric diamond-pointed drill under his coat. That would be essential for the work at hand.

He spun the combination, opened the vault and quickly stowed the sacks of currency and the small boxes of gems into two huge suitcases. He locked these, slipped downstairs and out the back door. There were no neighbors and he was quite unobserved. He got into his car and headed back to town.

He parked it directly outside the Carlton Building and locked it with some misgivings, for he might need a quick getaway. The cash inside the car convinced him the doors should be secured however. He sauntered toward the entrance to the building and found the big doors open. The lobby was dimly lighted.

He went up the stairs, disdaining the elevator lest its motor attract the watchman. Snate found 501 quickly and opened the door with a set of master keys. There was something written on the glass panel, but he paid no attention to it, since the hallway was in darkness and he dared not use a flashlight.

Closing the door softly, he moved across the small reception room. He drew his flashlight now, placed his hand over the lens and parted his fingers a trifle to emit only a slender beam of light. The only door he saw was marked. "Private." He grinned sardonically, stepped into the main office and saw the safe.

"Cheese box," he muttered triumphantly and went to work. He drilled the holes with practiced skill, poured in his soup and covered the safe with rugs that he took from the floor. He set the fuse, lit it and then ran for cover. The explosion was well muffled—Snate knew his business. He crouched in the darkness waiting to see if the rumble attracted any attention. When no one came, he approached the safe, removed the carpets and threw the ray of his flash into the yawning box. There was no sign of an envelope, but he did see a neatly stacked wad of currency—all brand new. He flipped part of it through his fingers.

"Two hundred grand in five hundred dollar notes," he exulted. "To hell with the letter. I don't see it and I'll be miles away from here if it's ever found."

HE STUFFED the money under his shirt and tiptoed to the outer door. He stepped into the corridor, saw no one and reached the lobby without detection. He was gloating inwardly. Why tell the Chief about the haul? He'd simply say that the safe was empty. It never occurred to Snate that he might get away with all the loot. Memory of that hissing voice gave him no doubts as to the nature of the man who possessed it.

He inserted his key in the door of the car, had it partly open when a man moved into his range of vision. Snate's stomach took a bad turn. It was Detective Sergeant McGrath and he looked as though he meant business.

"Snate—I want you," McGrath yelled.

But Snate plied into the car, tramped on the starter and was off. He raced madly along the deserted street and groaned when he spotted headlights in the mirror. He turned corners wildly, pushed the gas pedal to the floor along the avenues and finally there were no longer any signs of a pursuing car. He breathed in relief and pointed the hood of the car toward his real destination.

He stopped a block down the street, looked up and down carefully, and when he saw no one, dragged out the heavy valises and began running toward a brownstone front house.

He pressed the door bell and cursed his mentor for not being there to receive him. At any minute a patrolman might come along and grow suspicious at the sight of a man carrying two valises at this hour of the morning. Also there was a better than even chance that McGrath had sent out an alarm.

He heard burglar chains rattle, locks pulled back, and finally the door opened. Snate stepped in, set the bags down and mopped his forehead. His host stood in the darkness of the hallway, a gun in his hand.

"I almost didn't make it," Snate gasped. "We ain't got no time to lose, Chief. Sergeant McGrath nearly nabbed me and he'll have the whole damned police force looking for me now. You all ready to blow?"

"Snate!"

The man who was his master no longer bothered with a disguised voice. The time for that was over. He had played safe only in case one of Snate's men might stumble on the phone and hear his voice. Now he surveyed Snate angrily.

"Have you gone crazy?"

"Me—crazy? Say—I just did what you told me. I opened that box easy, but there wasn't anything inside. I got all the dough from the last few jobs in these bags. You got the rest of it, ain't you?"

"Snate—what's this about? Who told you to come here?"

Snate's jaw fell. "You did."

"You fool. I've been home only a few moments. The Police Commissioner sent for me—with some trumped up excuse that held me in his office. I thought this might happen. It's the work of the Black Bat! Didn't you kill him?"

SNATE wrinkled his face into questioning lines. "I told you he got away, didn't I? Listen—I'm not crazy. You asked me to come here with your own lips. I phoned—on the special wire—to get instructions. I—"

"I never talked to you, Snate! It's all up now! That was The Bat you talked to! There's but one thing to do. Run for it! Come upstairs—to my study. I'll get the rest of the swag, we'll divide it and travel."

Snate raced up the steps behind the man. In an elaborately furnished study, the real leader of Snate's men opened the valises, examined the contents quickly and then faced Snate angrily.

"You're holding out," he snapped. "There's something under your vest. It bulges. Come clean, Snate. You know better than to trick me."

Snate licked his lips. "I—I wasn't holding out, chief. It was like this, see? I opened the safe you told me about and found two hundred grand in there. So I copped it. Ain't that okay?"

"I didn't tell you about any safe, but if you have two hundred thousand dollars, it's quite all right. Let me see it."

Snate dumped the loot on top of the desk. He stepped away, waiting for further orders. Snate was ill at ease in the presence of this man. Somehow he reminded him of a snake—a crawling thing ready to strike a man in the back. Snate surreptitiously patted the gun under his armpit.

"Get my hat and coat from the rack in the corner," Snate's master ordered brusquely. "We're leaving at once."

Snate then made the greatest mistake of his life. He turned his back on a man he didn't trust. Snate was halfway toward the clothes rack when he sensed the danger. He swung around, but much too late. The man from whom he had taken orders held a gun. It exploded and the bullet plowed through Snate's fat back, rasped against his spine and he spun around like a top gone wild. He plunged to the floor unconscious.

The man who had betrayed him smiled thinly, opened one of the valises and began hurling Snate's latest haul into it. He paused, gasped and held one of the packets of money under the light. It was banded and upon each band was the insignia of The Bat.

"Damn him," the Unknown almost shrieked. "I should have emptied my gun into his stomach so he'd die slowly. He even planted counterfeit money for Snate to steal."

He hurled the worthless money to the floor, closed the bag and picked up both of them. He raced down the steps, opened the front door and stopped.

METHODICALLY, as though his life depended upon it, he counted twelve husky detectives and twelve submachine guns all pointed squarely at him. The valises thudded to the porch and he raised both hands. Commissioner Warner and Sergeant McGrath seized his arms. Handcuffs clicked. Warner stepped back with a dubious shake of his head.

"Otto Fox—you very nearly got away with it."

As the cavalcade of police cars pulled away from Otto Fox's house and two ambulance orderlies carried out Snate, a shadowy form watching from a thick shrub across the street smiled contentedly.

CHAPTER XX
THE BAT EXPLAINS

 UINN, Silk, Butch and Carol sat around the fireplace. There was a peaceful, satisfied grin on Quinn's face.

"Thanks to Carol we finished up the case quickly," he said. "Sending your necklace in the form of a coded message saved the day."

Carol laughed. "It wasn't hard to convince Snate that you'd recognize my necklace. I overheard them talking about the Ajax Garage. And after all my part was so very small."

"Your part," Quinn reminded her, "began long ago—with the restoration of my sight. Now to get on with the story. You know how the armored cars vanished. The drivers are entombed in thick slabs of cement and dropped somewhere at sea. I'm reasonably certain of that because Snate maintained a launch that used to put out to sea quite frequently."

"But I don't see how you got wise to Otto Fox," Butch broke in. "I don't see nothing that shows he was the real big shot."

"There wasn't much," Quinn admitted. "I knew the brains behind Snate lay within the skull of one of three men: Stewart, Gage or Fox. Fox seemed to stand the greatest loss because his business was vanishing almost as fast as his armored cars, but— the loot he obtained more than repaid him. Fox tried to pin the guilt on Stewart with voiced suspicions and upon Gage by planted evidence.

"When his men captured you and Carol, Silk, he suspected you were friends of The Bat. Therefore he also believed that I'd begin looking for you by starting at the garage. Under ordinary circumstances he might have planted his men there to shoot me down, but it was more advantageous to plant evidence that might convict another person—Peter Gage.

"So when Fox slipped into Gage's private office after luring him away by a trick, he stole one of Gage's newspapers, not yet released. He dropped this in the garage. The ink was still wet, but Fox became careless there. He thrust that wet newspaper into his coat pocket. Later on I saw how the ink had stained the cloth. Gage noticed it also!"

He stopped and lit a cigarette before he went on. "I had Commissioner Warner get Fox, Gage and Stewart out of their respective homes. After they had gone, I slipped inside by committing a little fancy burglary. I looked for one thing—a private telephone on a private line that connected with Snate. I found this—in Fox's bedroom. Then, fortunately, Snate phoned. I acted out the part of Fox and gave Snate some instructions which he followed to a tee.

"Snate broke into the offices of the United States Attorney and robbed the safe of a number of counterfeit bills that were to be used as evidence against a crooked engraver. By so doing Snate violated federal laws. You see—it might have been hard to pin much on him because he remained in the background. But a federal offense—with Snate's reputation and record—meant Alcatraz. Fox, too, would have been difficult to convict, so I let him reveal himself. Warner and Sergeant McGrath were warned to be on the lookout. McGrath even tried to accost Snate as he left the offices of the Federal Attorney. That was to scare Snate so he'd run immediately to Fox's house. Fox also tried to pin suspicion on Gage by writing me a note on Gage's paper and with his typewriter."

SOMEONE rang the front doorbell and Silk jumped up. Quinn's eyes, sparkling brightly as he reviewed the case, assumed the dead expression of a blind man. Butch and Carol quickly vanished into another room.

Commissioner Warner, Stewart, Gage and Sergeant McGrath came in, faces aglow in victory.

"We got them," Warner sat down with a sigh of relief. "Fox was our man. He shot Snate and tried to make away with all the loot. Snate won't die and he is charged with robbing the Federal Attorney's office and what do you think he got? Counterfeit money! You should see the way the newspapers played it up. Made a stupid fool of him."

"I wrote an editorial about it," Gage broke in eagerly. "I made it quite plain that all crooks of Snate's type are arrogant fools without the brains of a two hour old mouse. If Snate ever built up an aura of glory, it's dashed to pieces now. The whole country is laughing at him."

"Very good work," Quinn said quietly. "Did you handle it, Sergeant McGrath?"

McGrath looked slightly confused. "Well, I got the credit, but it isn't really mine. The Black Bat prepared the traps and he sprung them, too, I suppose. But how are you going to give credit to a man you can't identify—a man who commits every crime on the books to gain his own ends? You know, I don't understand that guy. I don't get his point—unless he's looking for revenge. Just like you might, Mr. Quinn. Why, if you weren't blind, I'd swear you were The Bat."

Stewart contained himself no longer. "I almost

laid my hands on Snate not many hours ago. I actually tracked him to his hideout, but The Bat was there ahead of me and making a target range of the place. I ran for it, knowing I'd be of no help."

"What of my idea—about the armored cars' sealed orders?" Quinn asked.

"Didn't that help at all?"

"Help?" Stewart cried. "No—I'm sorry, Quinn, it didn't. In fact that idea placed me in a very embarrassing position. I made up and sealed the orders as you suggested, but Fox threw them away and had a clever forger make up new ones—in my handwriting. If Fox hadn't confessed to that, I really think Commissioner Warner would have arrested me. Incidentally the racket of paroling unworthy convicts is broken up. Fox was behind it."

Quinn folded his arms. "Then I guess the case is closed. I'm only sorry I didn't have an active part in it. Still, Snate is behind bars and that gives me a lot of satisfaction."

Sergeant McGrath eyed Quinn askance as the four men arose and went to the front door.

"Just the same," McGrath said, "The Black Bat reminds me of you, Quinn. If he ever looks you up, tell him for me that what he's done means nothing—nothing at all. If I can throw him into a cell, I'll do it—so fast he won't know how he got there."

Quinn smiled. "But really, Sergeant, I don't know The Bat. He wouldn't contact me. I'm help-lessly blind and I could be of no value to his work."

"Yes," McGrath grated, "if you are blind. But no offense, Quinn. I'm just suspicious of everyone."

SIMULTANEOUSLY, Warner and McGrath extended their hands.

Quinn took Warner's and shook it warmly.

"Everything is forgiven, Sergeant McGrath. Being suspected of acting as the Black Bat is an honor, I assure you."

"Aw, what's the use," McGrath said disgustedly. "That's Warner's hand you're shaking, Quinn. I'm over here."

They trooped away. From another room Carol's merry laughter broke the stillness and Butch joined in. Silk seemed a little despondent.

"I'm sorry it's over," he said. "Now what are we going to do?"

"Do?" Quinn chuckled. "Silk, before another hour has passed, someone will rise up to take Snate's place—Otto Fox's too. Crime doesn't stop, but we won't stop either. The Black Bat isn't dead, Silk. He's just asleep, roosting on the rafters until someone gets the idea he is greater than all law and order."

Carol put her hand on Quinn's arm. He looked down at her, covered her hand with his own, and they walked back into the library to sit before the cheerful fire.

THE END

THE BELFRY by Will Murray

The Black Bat came into the world at a synchronistic time.

The year was 1939. Superman was taking the comic book world by storm. The Great Depression seemed to be easing, and in the world of pulp magazines a raft of new characters were being launched, among them Street & Smith's *The Avenger* and Thrilling's *Captain Future*. Soon, a flood of fresh pulp heroes and comic book superheroes would be competing for the nation's entertainment dimes—the price of most such magazines. Not all would survive for long.

Thrilling had acquired a title called *Black Book Detective* from an obscure publishing house and soon decided that its original hero, investigator Jonathan Drake, was not working. Editor-in-chief Leo Margulies decided to make it a showcase for a new recurring pulp hero in the vein of their long-running *Phantom Detective* magazine.

On radio, The Shadow was proving to be a gigantic hit, and the Street & Smith pulp magazine built around the mysterious character continued to outsell all rivals. So it was decided to create a character more in the mold of The Shadow than The Phantom had been.

Prolific pulpster Norman A. Daniels was selected for the task. Years before, Daniels had written a slew of Phantom Detective novels for Thrilling.

"Leo asked me to think of something to compete with The Shadow," Daniels recalled. "I came up with this character I called the Tiger because in the initial episode, the hero had been doused with acid. His face was lined like a Tiger's. He wanted to change the Tiger to the Black Bat because he wanted it to go into *Black Book Detective* magazine."

Thus did blind District Attorney Anthony Quinn become the night-seeing Black Bat. The rewrite failed to capture all the corrections possible, thus the frequent references to the Black Bat's "catlike" eyes and reflexes.

Daniels was paid for the story early in December 1939, indicating that he had written the bulk of it in November. No doubt Margulies—who had a member of his editorial staff make the changes—wanted the new character to resemble The Shadow even more closely than Daniels depicted him. For inspiration, he need have looked no deeper than the back files of the Thrilling line.

Back in 1934, Margulies launched a new title under the general editorship of Jack Schiff featuring a masked crime fighter named The Bat. "C.K.M. Scanlon" was the byline—in reality a house name. The author's true identity has never been verified, but the gas gun-wielding Bat was modeled after several similar pulp protagonists penned by Zorro's famous creator, Johnston McCulley. Since McCulley also wrote for Thrilling—his Green Ghost series in *Thrilling Detective* had just concluded—it seems probable that McCulley was the mystery writer.

That is speculation. More likely, Margulies borrowed a leaf from the issue of *The Phantom Detective* that went on sale in mid-November. It featured *The Yacht Club Murders*, in which the Phantom battled a masked murderer calling himself the Bat.

Author Charles Greenberg described him this way:

> A figure which might have been spewed from the bowels of hell crouched four feet away. A wide-brimmed, black slouch hat, pulled low, almost concealed the black velvet mask beneath it. It was a mask which covered every bit of the face, straps from it going back to be fastened to the base of the skull. There was a cross gash opening for breathing, and diamond-shaped slits for the eyes. A black cape, close-gathered at the neck, dropped in a tentlike flare about the crouching figure. Whalebone ribs in it enforced the flare from the body. Black-gloved hands were thrust through long slits in front of the cape. The right hand balanced a long, slender, evil-looking rapier. Swaying slightly, that figure personified evil, stealth and crime. It looked like some monstrous bat!

From the slouch hat to the batwing cloak, the description perfectly fits the Black Bat! Greenberg, in turn, might well have taken his inspiration from Mary Roberts Reinhart's famed play-turned-film, *The Bat Whispers*. That cloaked Bat was also a criminal.

While the premier Black Bat novel was moving along the Thrilling production chain, a weird thing happened. At DC comics, editor Vincent Sullivan, seeing the phenomenal sales of *Superman*, asked artist Bob Kane if he could come up with a super-hero of his own. Kane remembered this as taking place around the holiday season of 1938-39.

Enticed by the money to be made, Kane began sketching a character he initially called Bird-Man, a red-suited hero with a black domino mask and hawklike wings. This evolved into the Bat-Man, thanks in part to writer Bill Finger, who had been working with Kane.

> He was a shoe salesman then and deeply into pulps like *Doc Savage* and *The Shadow*. But he had aspirations of becoming a writer. I called Bill and

said, "I have a new character called the Bat-Man and I've made some crude, elementary sketches I'd like you to look at." So he came over and I showed him the drawings. At that time, I only had a small Halloween mask, like the one Robin later wore, on Batman's face. So Bill said, "Why not make him look more like a bat and put a hood on him, and take the eyeballs out and just put slits for eyes to make him look more mysterious?" At this point, the Bat-Man wore a red union suit; the wings and trunks were black, the mask was black. I thought that red and black would be a good combination. Bill said that the costume was too bright—"Color it dark gray to make it look more ominous." So I followed his suggestions. The cape looked like two stiff bat wings attached to his arms. As Bill and I talked, we realized that these wings would get cumbersome when Bat-Man was in action, and changed them to a cape, scalloped to look like bat wings when he was fighting or swinging down on a rope.

Finger recalled his role identically:

> I got Webster's Dictionary down off the shelf and was hoping they would have a drawing of a bat, and sure enough they did. I said, "Notice the ears, why don't we duplicate the ears?" I suggested he draw what looked like a cowl. He experimented with various cowls. I suggested he bring the cowl nosepiece down and make him mysterious and not show any eyes at all.... I didn't like the wings, so I suggested he make a cape and scalloped edges so it would flow out behind him when he ran and would look like bat wings.

Unknowingly, they were fashioning a crime-fighter whose costume eerily paralleled the Black Bat, who had yet to see print! The Black Bat lacked any insignia or bat ears on his hood, but met with in a dark alley, the Caped Crusader and his cloaked counterpart would be mistaken for twins! Early on, the Black Bat wore a Shadow-style slouch hat, but that was soon discarded.

"I was very much influenced by The Shadow and Doc Savage, The Phantom, things of that sort," Finger once admitted. In this instance, he probably meant the hero of *The Phantom Detective* magazine, not Lee Falk's seminal costumed hero of newspaper syndicate fame. But it might have been either hero.

"He was a pulp reader," Kane recalled. "As a matter of fact, I read all the pulps that Bill Finger read. He'd give me his magazines, and I did read them. I was influenced by *Doc Savage* and the pulps, to some extent."

Batman debuted in *Detective Comics* #27, May 1939, which went on sale March 30th. *Brand of the Black Bat* finally saw print in the July 1939 *Black Book Detective*, which went on sale April 28th—less than 30 days later!

When that happened, the bat guano hit the fan.

"There was a lawsuit almost pending," Finger recalled. "It was a weird coincidence. Apparently the character had already been written and on the drawing board. Whit Ellsworth used to be a pulp writer for Better Publications. So, through Ellsworth's intervention, a lawsuit was averted. They were ready to sue us, and we were ready to sue them. It was just one of those wild coincidences."

Fortuitously, F. Whitney Ellsworth had recently written several *Phantom Detective* and *G-Men* lead novels for Better, which was a Thrilling imprint. Before that, he toiled as a DC editor in the mid-1930s. Soon, he was back at DC, possibly as a result of his face-saving intervention.

An agreement was reached. Batman would remain a comic book character exclusively, and the Black Bat would never migrate to the four-color field.

"I knew nothing about that," Daniels revealed. "That was all done in the office. They never told me anything about it. They never asked my advice."

When *Brand of the Black Bat* was adapted for *Exciting Comics* #1 in 1940, they renamed their bat-hero the Owl, but were forced to change it to the Mask when a rival publisher released another masked hero by that name. Remnants of the earlier Owl script remain in the comic book story reprinted in this volume, including the original birdlike beaked mask and the panel on page 124 where the Mask is described as looking "like a big black bird."

But the coincidences didn't stop there. Thrilling editor Mort Weisinger soon joined DC Comics to edit *Batman*, after helping launch the Black Bat. He soon enticed his former boss Jack Schiff to write *Batman* scripts, and before long Schiff, too, was a *Batman* editor. One of their writers was, briefly, Charles Greenberg who wrote *The Yacht Club Murders*. The only one who didn't join the Bat team was Norman Daniels. He remained busy with the Black Bat and the Phantom all through the 1940s.

The parallels did not stop there. Batman's origin was finally told in *Batman* #1 in 1940. The grisly account of the murder of young Bruce Wayne's parents and his subsequent decision to fight crime is now part of the popular culture. Pondering his future, Bruce Wayne muses, "Criminals are a superstitious, cowardly lot. So my disguise must be able to strike terror into their hearts. I must be a creature of the night, black, terrible... A... A... A bat! That's it! It's an omen. I shall become a bat!"

As almost everyone knows, a flying bat was Wayne's inspiration. This sounds suspiciously like the scene in C. K. M. Scanlon's "The Bat Strikes," where a bat flaps into private detective Dawson Clade's cabin, and he exclaims: "That's it! I'll call myself 'The Bat.'"

Thrilling editor Jack Schiff, who broke into DC Comics as a Batman scripter in 1941, subsequently editing the Batman titles from 1942 through to early 1964, in later years marveled at all the Bat-coincidences, remarking, "It's funny. Not until it was brought out so sharply—that Batman was a combination of The Bat and the Phantom Detective— did it really hit me. There's no question in my mind that (those characters) must have influenced Bill and Bob. And then the whole business of the Bat and the origin is so similar. Bill [Finger] was honest and if I had cornered Bill with that—I don't know why I didn't—he would have admitted it."

What Schiff didn't know at that time was that the borrowings went deeper. The first Batman story was based on a 1936 Shadow novel written by Theodore Tinsley, and some of its art Bob Kane purloined from Tom Lovell's interior artwork! The Batman was built from the scraps of many pulp heroes!

As for Norman Daniels, he never paid attention to the wave of *Batman* comic books which roosted on America's newsstands side-by-side with *Black Book Detective*.

"I've never seen one," he once remarked. "I never had anything to do with them, and I never bothered with them." Furthermore, Daniels commented, "I can't see very much of a connection between the two."

The printed record begs to differ.

For this exciting debut volume of the Black Bat, we have paired the long-running cloaked crime-buster's first two cases. We have already told you about *Brand of the Black Bat*, for which Thrilling art director Alexander Samalson had commissioned a rather generic cover situation augmented by a flying bat. For *Murder Calls the Black Bat*, which Norman Daniels wrote in March of 1939 under the working title of "Murder Calls the Bat," he splurged and had the great Rudolph Belarski execute a stunning full-figure depiction of the Black Bat in all his sable glory. Rarely did the Bat appear in full costume on his covers. In the trademark Thrilling style pioneered on the covers of *The Phantom Detective*, Tony Quinn's hooded face looked down upon an exciting and suspenseful scene on most subsequent covers. Naturally, we have reproduced the classic Belarski image for our own front cover.

By the way, "G. Wayman Jones" was a Thrilling house name that went back to the first years of the outfit, and masked a host of writers on the early Phantom Detective novels, until that byline was changed to "Robert Wallace." It had been retired back in 1933, but Margulies revived it for this series. Although Norman Daniels wrote nearly every Black Bat novel, writers like Norvell Page and Lawrence Donovan would occasionally pitch in. We'll explore some of those other scribes in future volumes.

Now, go with Tony Quinn, alias the Black Bat, as he embarks upon his second suspenseful case... as *Murder Calls the Black Bat*! •

An arm encircled McGrath's throat (Chapter VIII)

Murder Calls the Black Bat

By G. WAYMAN JONES

Author of "Brand of the Black Bat," "Alias Mr. Death," etc.

CHAPTER I
DEATH BY THE GUN

THE GRAHAM COMPANY wore the expensively modest front that might be expected of one of the world's most famous jewelry shops. Within its doors were consultation rooms and never a sign of such plebeian objects as showcases. Gems were brought directly from the huge vault to the customers who were served in those private rooms. Buying a diamond from the Graham Company was like purchasing currency at the United States Mint. Graham's diamonds were just as negotiable.

Perhaps that was why the clerks looked up in utter amazement as Mrs. Van den Killan swept into the shop with fire in her eye and acid on her tongue.

Clarence Graham, head of the firm and fifth in a long line of antecedents who had carried art, heard her voice even above that of his secretary as she switched on the inter-office phone.

"What's all the excitement?" Graham inquired mildly. "By all means send Mrs. Van den Killan in."

She came, slamming the door behind her. She deposited a wrapped package on Graham's desk.

"And this," she shrilled, "is what the name of Graham means! I bought a tiara here seven weeks ago. I paid one hundred and thirty thousand dollars for it. It's incredible! Most incredible!"

"My dear madam"—Graham arose and helped her into a chair—"please calm yourself. If there is anything wrong with the tiara, we shall certainly remedy the condition."

"Wrong with it?" she half screamed. "Wrong with it? You have the complacency to sit there and ask me what's wrong with it? The whole thing is a fake. It's paste! Paste, I tell you! Worth about one thousand dollars."

Graham smiled. "There is, of course, some error. Perhaps if we—"

"My husband is ready to go to the police!" the woman snapped. "I purchased the tiara believing it was the original worn by the Czarina. I took it abroad with me, to an important function in Amsterdam."

She leaned forward and banged the flat of her hand against the desk. "You can imagine my utter embarrassment when the Belgian Ambassador's wife swept through the ballroom wearing an identical tiara."

"What?" Graham arose. "But that is impossible. There is only one tiara like that which I sold you. The other must have been false."

Mrs. Van den Killan screwed up her face in distaste.

"Of course I thought that, too. I removed mine and later on I learned that the Belgian woman had purchased her tiara just three days before, especially for the occasion. Therefore I took steps to find out whether or not the one you sold me was false. I am quite certain that I was the one who was cheated, Mr. Graham."

WITH fingers that shook, Graham unwrapped the package, exposed a large plush case and touched the spring controlling the lid. It flew back and the tiara gleamed warmly under the light of a desk lamp. Graham lifted the flashing collection of gems from the box, placed it on the desk and put a jeweler's loupe to his eye. The magnifying glass brought each finely cut gem into bold prominence. Graham heaved a sigh of relief.

Then he touched a button on his desk. Two minutes later a short, round-shouldered man with a closely trimmed beard entered the office with a hobble that appeared to be characteristic.

"*Ja, Herr* Graham," he said and looked over his thick glasses. "You sent for me, *nein?*"

"Dr. Wohl," Graham said, "I want you to look at this tiara and tell me its worth. Mrs. Van den Killan wishes a new appraisal of the piece."

Wohl picked up the tiara, glanced at it critically, and brought it close to his eye.

"Dr. Wohl," Graham told Mrs. Van den Killan, "is one of the most famous jewel experts in the world. He will reassure you as to the genuineness of this tiara, for I am sure you are mistaken, madam. Graham sells nothing but perfect stones."

A moment of tense silence passed. Then Graham looked at the gem expert

"Well?" he asked impatiently.

Wohl set the tiara back in its plush case and drew himself fairly erect, "This tiara," he said in a matter-of-fact voice, "is worth about one thousand dollars. It is of the finest paste, created by an expert—but it is worth no more than a thousand dollars, *mein Herr.*"

"But that's the tiara we sold Mrs. Van den Killan seven weeks ago?" Graham cried. "It was perfect then—had been appraised at a hundred and fifty thousand dollars! How can it have changed to paste?"

Wohl shrugged indifferently. "That I do not know. There are many ways—perhaps a substitution was made by someone in the family. Perhaps by clever thieves. Who knows? I am not a policeman—*nein.* Only a gem *expert,* and I say this piece is a lie, a fake."

Graham dismissed the expert with a wave of his hand.

"Mrs. Van den Killan," he said slowly, "I don't know what happened. Frankly, I cannot imagine. We sold you this tiara as a genuine bill of goods. You must have been tricked somehow and this paste replica substituted. I cannot say as to that. But in view of the prestige of Graham's and the value of your account, I shall make good your loss at once. I hope that will be satisfactory."

"Thank you," the woman said. "I don't know what happened, but that tiara is exactly as it came from your shop, Mr. Graham. I took it to Europe the day after it was delivered. It was in the custody of the ship's purser on the way over and then was placed in a Paris bank vault. Upon my return yesterday, I brought the tiara to Harriman's Jewelry Store for appraisal—after what had happened abroad. He insisted it was a fake."

"I shall try to determine what happened," Graham said suavely. "At the earliest opportunity you will be called back and told what we are able to discover. Thank you for your patience, Mrs. Van den Killan, and I assure you that this has all been most unfortunate."

WHEN he closed the door behind her, Graham almost staggered back to his desk and slumped in the chair. He looked keenly at the tiara. Even to his trained eyes it looked like the real thing.

Or did it? Weren't some of the stones lacking in warmth? Didn't their glow reflect a certain coldness? Of course, Wohl was right. No one could dispute his word.

DR. WOHL

Graham arose suddenly, walked over to a wall safe and opened it. He drew out three steel trays of cut diamonds, opened them and gazed intently at the stones. He fastened the loupe to his eye and examined some of them. His face grew as pale as the whiteness of a pearl. His breath came in rasping gasps. With a trembling finger he pushed the buzzer for Wohl.

The expert shuffled into the office, his bald pate glistening, his watery eyes regarding Graham suspiciously.

"Wohl," Graham said, "look at these. We've had them in the store for the past six months. They were brought here and passed by you as perfect gems. They don't look right to me. In heaven's name, man, don't tell me are they phonies, too?"

Methodically Wohl went to work. While Graham paced the floor, he examined each stone and made two separate piles of them. One was twice as large as the other and it was to this pile that Wohl pointed.

"Mein herr," he said, "those are fakes. Pure fakes, worth a fair sum as excellent replicas—but not diamonds, *nein*. Not diamonds."

"But they haven't been out of my safe since you passed them as genuine!" Graham roared. "Wohl, are you slipping? Did somebody pass these fakes over on us as the real goods?"

Dr. Wohl drew himself up. "I," he stated pompously, "have worked with diamonds for thirty years, *ja!* Not once have I been accused of carelessness.

When those diamonds came to me for appraisal, they were genuine. What happened to them after they left any hands, I do not know or care."

"Yes—yes, of course," Graham groaned. "You're one of the world's greatest experts. You worked in Amsterdam for many years, in a position of great trust. But it's incredible! Approximately two-thirds of these gems are paste. Wohl—the rest of the stock! Maybe it's been tampered with, too! Listen—go back to your office. I'll send in the stock, tray by tray. Examine it all. Work as you've never worked before. We carry millions of dollars' worth of gems here. If two-thirds of them are fakes, I'm bankrupt! Insurance companies won't pay. They'll claim these gems were fakes when they were insured. They'll be in the right, too, for how could such substitution be made?"

For two hours Graham sweated profusely, locked in his private office. Every ten minutes Wohl shuffled into the room and made two piles of stones. Opals, emeralds, rubies and sapphires. Out of each tray, two-thirds were phonies—masterly reproductions of the real thing, but fakes just the same.

"Not a word of this," Graham told Wohl, "We have a few hours to see if we can find out what has happened. Keep on sorting the stock. Don't talk to anyone."

Graham's phone buzzed, He answered it in a curt voice and his shoulders drooped as he listened.

"All right. Send him in."

A MAN of about thirty entered the office, carrying a three-carat diamond in the palm of his hand. His face was almost as pale as Graham's.

"Yes, Mr. McFayden," Graham snapped at his chief clerk. "What is it?"

McPayden swallowed hard. "I—I really can't account for it, sir. Mr. Philip Mitchell purchased this stone yesterday, as an engagement ring for his fiancée. He paid us three thousand dollars. And—and now he maintains this stone is a fake."

Graham seized the gem and held it under the light. Then he motioned McFayden away angrily.

"Tell Mr. Mitchell there was an error. Tell him we'll replace this stone at once—within two or three hours. Tell him anything, man, but get out of here. Get out, I say!"

McFayden backed hastily out of the office. Graham took a drink of water, passed a hand across his tired face and groaned aloud.

"Tricked! Fooled completely. A million dollars' worth of stock stolen right under my eyes and replaced with fakes. I must be dreaming! Such a thing couldn't possibly happen!"

He sank weakly back into his chair.

Perhaps half an hour more had passed, when in

the outer office McFayden looked up from his desk with an air of irritation as an underclerk approached.

"Mr. Graham wants you—at once," the clerk told him. "His secretary just called to say you are to go to his office."

"More of this mysterious business," McFayden grumbled to himself. "Next he'll be accusing me of planting that phony chunk of paste in our stock?"

Passing from his desk into the anteroom of Graham's private office, he nodded to Graham's secretary and walked over to the door of his employer's private sanctum. He tapped on the panels and waited for Graham's voice to bid him enter. Nothing happened so he rapped harder.

"Are you positive he's in there?" McFayden asked the secretary.

"Positive," she answered, "Wait—I'll get him on the inter-office phone,"

She flicked down the button and called Graham's name. There was no reply. She jumped to her feet.

"Something has happened! I know it! McFayden—open the door?"

McFayden turned the knob slowly and eased the door open. The secretary looked over his shoulder— and a terrible sight met their eyes. Graham was seated behind his desk. His head hung limply against his chest and in the solid, high backed chair, he looked like a gnome. They saw his right hand slowly dip into the drawer of the desk and remove a gun. Slowly he raised it until the muzzle almost touched his temple.

"No!" McFayden yelled. "No! Don't shoot, Mr. Graham! Don't shoot!"

BUT Graham paid no attention. He acted as if he were already living in another world. His finger squeezed the trigger. His head jerked to one side and blood spurted, staining the chair and seeping to the rug. The hand holding the gun dropped from sight. The gun hit the floor with a thump.

Graham's secretary gave a long drawn-out sob that welled into a scream of horror. She and McFayden backed out of the office and McFayden closed the door.

"Stay here," he told the secretary grimly. "Don't let anyone in."

McFayden dashed out of the office. The secretary glanced at the closed door of the death room.

"Me stay here with—that?" she screamed, and rushed after McFayden.

He had stopped dramatically in the center of the store.

"Mr. Graham just shot himself!" he yelled. "Committed suicide! I saw him shoot! Get the police! Get a doctor! Hurry!"

CHAPTER II
MURDER CALLS

 THE expensive sedan stopped in front of a neat, smartly appointed home in one of the better sections of the great city. Oaks and elms, scores of years old, shrouded the house. Shrubs, well trimmed, and flowers of myriad colors made a showplace of the estate. A plain oak plank fastened to the gate bore the owner's name:

TONY QUINN

A man got out of the sedan and hurried up the path to the house. Philip Harriman had reason to be in a hurry. His usually polished, suave exterior, known well to his best customers, was missing. It was difficult to realize that he was a prosperous, much-envied man who owned one of the three greatest jewelry firms in the country, for he looked more like a worried, distraught man who had been caught short in a market crash.

He pressed the bell and the door opened almost immediately, as if the servant who answered had been watching. Harriman knew "Silk" Kirby, Tony Quinn's butler. Silk nodded in recognition, also.

In appearance, Silk was little like the preconceived idea of a butler in a wealthy man's home. He was too slippery-looking and his eyes were cold as ice. His forehead was high, above a pointed, narrow nose, and a mouth too small.

"I'll announce you, Mr. Harriman," he said.

"Let me go right in," Harriman begged. "It's terribly important."

Silk's hand checked the jeweler.

"Sorry, sir, but Mr. Quinn doesn't receive many guests since—since he became blind. He's rather sensitive, you know."

"But this is vitally important—means millions!" Harriman exploded. "Tony is still my attorney. What difference does it make if he's blind? I still need his advice."

Silk's expression didn't change, but he seemed to take cognizance of Harriman's anxiety. He gestured and led the jeweler into a huge living room. Before the fireplace there, in a big leather chair, sat a slender, well-built man. He sat erect, his head cocked to one side as if he had heard the voices in the reception hall. But his eyes stared straight ahead—the lifeless, glassy eyes of the blind.

His face was not pleasant to look upon. Deep, ugly scars had been burned in the flesh, especially about the eyes. It gave him a sinister appearance.

Harriman stepped forward. "Tony," he cried eagerly, "Tony Quinn! It's me—Phil Harriman. I've got to talk to you."

Tony Quinn's voice was flat, a low mockery of the ringing tones that once had stirred juries and made criminals writhe in fear. Something seemed to have gone out of Tony Quinn when he became blind. There was defeat and desolation in his voice.

"Come in, Phil. Sit over there. The green chair. I can hear you best there."

Harriman sat down and Silk quietly withdrew. Harriman lit a cigarette and tried to compose himself.

"You're a wonder, Tony," he said. "Every time I come to see you, I'm told exactly where to sit and what my chair looks like."

TONY QUINN smiled ruefully.

"I keep track of the furniture," he said slowly. "When a blind man moves about, he must know where every article that may trip him is located. Now, Phil—what's worrying you? I recognize the note of excitement in your voice."

"I need advice," Phil Harriman said quickly. "You were in private practice before you became the best D.A. we ever had. I was one of your clients and I still consider you my attorney. Oh, don't hold up your hand to stop me. You're blind, but that hasn't affected that keen legal mind of yours.

"Listen, Tony! There's something downright hellish going on. This morning Mrs. Van den Killan— yes, *the* Mrs. Van den Killan—came into my office with a tiara she'd purchased from the Graham Company about two months ago. She wanted me to look it over. Well, I looked it ever and I even had Anghis Khan—my gem expert and one of the best in the world—do the same. The tiara was paste! The most perfect reproduction I've ever seen in my career—but paste nevertheless. I—I had to tell her."

"So?" Tony Quinn tapped his fingertips together and looked mildly interested.

"That," Harriman went on with a groan, "is only half of it. Anghis Khan and I couldn't believe our own eyes. The tiara is composed mostly of diamonds with a few rubies and emeralds sprinkled through it for color. To assure ourselves that our eyes were still good, we got some our own gems out of stock for purposes of comparison. That, Tony, is when I received the greatest shock of my life. My own gems were paste reproductions of the originals. Like Mrs. Van den Killan's tiara, they were superlative work and could pass any casual inspection. Khan and I examined every stone in my stock—and three-quarters of them are phonies!"

Tony Quinn leaned forward. He gripped the cane he held and the knuckles of his hands gleamed whitely. That was his only outward show of interest.

"An inside job, Phil," he said flatly. "Must be!"

Harriman groaned again. "Yes, yes, of course. I thought the same thing. But every one of my employees has been with me for years—more than

half were employed by my father as well. They can't be dishonest. And—well, because of that paste tiara I've been wondering if Graham has suffered a similar loss. I'm going to see him as soon as I leave you. Tony, I'm virtually bankrupt. I need an attorney. I need you. There will be all kinds of legal angles to this. Will you help? Will you tell me what to do?"

"One thing right now," Tony Quinn said quietly. "Go to the police; then, if you take your insurance papers to any reliable attorney, he'll tell you if you are covered. It's an odd case, Phil. I'd enjoy handling it if—well, if I was worth anything to anybody, including myself. But go to the police at once before the man or men responsible get clear."

Harriman stood up and jammed his hat down hard.

"Exactly. I just wanted to be certain I was right. And consider yourself still my attorney, Tony. I won't take no for an answer. Now I'm going to see Graham and then to the police. Thanks, old man."

SILK let Harriman out and closed the door quietly. He heard Harriman's car start away from the curb, then he walked briskly into the living room. Tony Quinn still faced the fireplace, unseeing eyes as blank as ever.

"Silk," he said slowly, "you heard Harriman's story?"

"I heard it," Silk answered. "Sounds like the screwiest setup ever."

"There's more than appears on the surface, Silk. Graham wouldn't sell a fake tiara, or even a fake quarter-carat diamond. He's like Harriman—completely honest and operating his business on that principle. They carry tremendous stocks of gems, the finest in existence. If someone has been clever enough to appropriate three-fourths of Harriman's stock, he has probably also taken as many from Graham. It may be the police will find themselves stumped. It may also be, Silk, that the Black Bat will take a hand in this. The case sounds interesting."

"Yeah," Silk said eagerly, "it does at that. And we've been laying low, boss. Much too low for me."

The phone buzzed and Silk sped away to answer it.

Harriman's voice came over the wire, trembling and high-pitched.

"Let me talk to Tony Quinn, Silk. Hurry!"

"Sorry, sir," Silk said. "Mr. Quinn doesn't answer the phone anymore. I'll take any message."

"Oh, damn it, why does he have to be so sensitive about his blindness!" Harriman rapped out nervously. "I tell you—"

"I'm sorry," Silk broke in. "Mr. Quinn doesn't like to move about too much, sir. It's rather difficult for him. If there is a message—"

"Yes—yes, there is. Tell him that Graham just committed suicide! They won't let me into his place of business—it's full of police. McFayden, Graham's clerk, saw Graham shoot himself through the head. There was some kind of a suicide note, I hear. I'm going to Police Headquarters at once. Quinn will understand what I mean."

"Thank you, sir," Silk said and hung up. As the connection was cut off, his face lighted up. He hurried back to the living room.

"It was Harriman," he reported. "Says Graham just bumped himself off. Harriman's going to the cops right now."

Tony Quinn's lips pursed and he whistled softly. For a moment the blankness in his eyes faded and they became alive and real.

"Something is brewing, Silk," he said softly. "But it's Harriman's battle right now. We'd better get to bed."

CHAPTER III
THE BLACK BAT

BUT at one a.m., Tony Quinn was not asleep although all the lights in his room were out. Silk, in his own quarters on the first floor, also had too much on his mind for slumber. Too many things had happened to let sleep come easily. More and more Tony Quinn sensed that this was no more an ordinary case than he was an ordinary man.

As had been the case when he had heard of Graham's suicide, Tony Quinn's eyes were again eager and alive; not blank and staring. In his face, also, was none of the persistent inquiring look of a blind man. The room was black as midnight, but Tony Quinn could distinguish each object as clearly as if a beam of sunlight were fastened upon it. Not only could Tony Quinn see, but his eyes were exceptionally acute!

His pose of a blind man was one so perfect that only a period of actual blindness could have schooled him. And that was true! Once a promising young district attorney, Quinn had fought bitterly against all crime. He fought physically, too, one day in open court. Certain phonograph records, containing evidence enough to convict an important crook, were destroyed by acid flung by the hands of this crook's band of criminals.

Tony Quinn had stepped directly in front of the records as he sought to save them. The acid had struck his face and burned deep, ugly scars. It ate away his sight and made horrible mockery of those eyes.

Totally blind, with no hope of a cure, Tony Quinn had resigned and settled down for a life of darkness with no hope of release save in death. But when his sight failed, his other senses grew so

acute that he acquired the hearing of a jungle beast on the prowl. His fingertips, resting against an object, could form in his mind every feature of its shape. Only actual colors escaped his senses. But his instincts were quickened until he could acutely feel the presence of anyone in a room.

Then, on a night of darkest despair, had come a girl—a girl whom he could not see. She called herself Carol Baldwin and through her he had met an unknown country doctor many miles from the city. Under his hands, Tony Quinn had undergone an operation which not only restored his sight but even added to it. By some miracle of that surgery, he was enabled to see as plainly in darkness as in daylight.

He had returned home from that obscure country place presumably from a vacation trip, apparently as blind as ever. But with such a firm purpose fixed in his mind that only three people shared his secret besides the surgeon, who had since died.

Carol Baldwin knew. She lived quietly just a few blocks away and was prepared to take an active part in Quinn's work at any time. Then there was Silk Kirby, who had come to rob Quinn and remained to become his most trusted assistant. And Silk had become invaluable to Quinn, since not only was he a reformed burglar whose loyalty to Tony Quinn now approached fanaticism, but he was an ex-confidence man, glib as the best in that racket.

And finally there was "Butch" O'Leary, a tremendous hulk of a man who had attracted Tony Quinn's notice during a bank robbery when Butch had leaped at a machine gun armed thug who was in the act of mowing down a score of bystanders. Quinn had known at once that Butch was a man he could trust.

ALL three were faithful, willing and anxious to help. For Tony Quinn had created for himself an utterly new life. Because the underworld in general secretly gloated over the blindness of the ex-D.A. and called him "blind as a bat," Tony Quinn had become a "bat." The "Black Bat" who prowled by night and matched his wits against the keenest in the world of crime.

He had become a Nemesis, a dark blot of shadow soon feared by every man who lived by violence or by his wits, and now was a scourge of the underworld of crime. For each time the Black Bat acted, he left a vivid token of his work. His victims bore the brand of the Bat—a miniature black bat, with wings outstretched—stamped on their foreheads.

Financially independent, Tony Quinn had resolved to devote his whole life to an endless fight against crime in all its rotten, lecherous phases. Yet on the surface he remained the old Tony Quinn, scarred and blind for life. His secret was carefully guarded.

Now Tony Quinn propped a pillow against the head of his bed and reached for a cigarette. He could clearly see the pack in the darkness, even its coloring. Suddenly his hand paused and stiffened. His head turned slightly, like that of a listening dog. From downstairs he heard a soft thump and a muffled groan.

Silk heard things, too. Someone had raised a window in the dining room. Raised it very softly and with all the skill of a trained burglar. Silk took a gun from his bureau, walked in bare feet to the hall and then moved silently toward the dining room. A gust of cool night air swept in on him and he shivered. The window was open.

Silk passed by the portieres draped artistically at the side of the door. Something swished. A gun butt cracked against his skull and at the same time an arm encircled him, keeping his limp body from crashing to the floor. His lips were sealed by a hand clapped across his mouth.

The intruder laid the stunned Silk carefully on the floor and then, with a grin, started up the steps. Killing a blind man was the easiest stunt he'd ever had to do. He'd wake the poor sucker first, give the fool a chance to act, so it would seem as though the burglar had shot to create an avenue of escape for himself.

The killer reached the landing at the head of the stairs and stood listening. He could hear the rhythmic breathing of a man in a sound sleep. His lips curled sardonically. He'd make that sleep permanent. Wasn't this blind guy an ex-D.A. and was anything sweeter than polishing off one of his breed?

The killer stepped into the bedroom, saw the recumbent form under the covers and crept forward, gun carelessly held in his hand. He smiled confidently and prepared to awaken the sleeping man. His mouth opened and stayed that way. For a hand had dropped on his shoulder. A hand with fingers of steel. He was spun around as easily as though he were a top in the hands of a child.

He tried to raise his gun, but it was wrenched from him.

With a savage oath he ducked and twisted, finally tearing himself free of the restraining grasp. All thoughts of murder left him.

Only one idea was in his mind now—escape!

HE jolted a quick blow to the face of the towering man who held him, missed and squirmed until a whole side of his suit tore loose. Like a deer, he bolted out of the room. Behind him rushed Tony Quinn.

He reached out and touched the fleeing man's shoulder.

The killer gave a howl of dismay and took a flying dive down the staircase. He tripped a quarter

THE BLACK BAT

of the way down, and tumbled over and over. But when he hit the bottom, he bounded up again like a rubber ball, racing along the hallway toward the front door.

Quinn, hurrying down the stairs, hesitated to shoot. But with the quick realization that his midnight visitor might have some mysterious knowledge that Tony Quinn was the Bat, Quinn raised his gun to put a slug through the intruder's leg. But the killer carried a spare weapon. As he reached the door, he jerked this out of a shoulder clip and flung it up toward the man on the stairs.

From the dining room came a single shot. The killer's sadistic leer changed to a look of mingled agony and surprise.

He turned about methodically, as if undecided what to do, took one step toward the door and then pitched forward on his face.

"Good shooting, Silk," Quinn called softly. "Turn on the lights and watch yourself. He went down like a dead man but you never can tell."

The lights flashed on. Silk, nursing a bump on his head, came cautiously into the hallway, his still smoking gun gripped in a steady hand. He approached the still form of the killer and nudged him with his foot. Then he calmly stowed the gun and knelt.

"Got him through the heart," he told Quinn. "A damn easy way for a mug like this to die. They got electric chairs for his kind."

"Odd," Quinn said. "What made him come

here? Not mere chance, because he made no attempt to rifle drawers. He came straight upstairs and when I grabbed him he was ready to fire at the blankets I'd rolled up beneath the bedspread. He came to kill, Silk."

Quinn turned the dead man over and calmly searched his clothing. From an inner pocket he drew out ten one-hundred dollar bills.

"Blood money. This man is probably a hired killer. And what's this?"

He turned a sealed envelope over and over in his hands. It was labelled, "TO THE POLICE" in bold, flowing handwriting that was somehow familiar. Quinn walked over to the desk in the study and sat down.

"Maybe we oughta call in the cops," Silk suggested, doubtfully. "Or should I dump the guy some place and forget all about this?"

"Silk"—Tony Quinn laid down the letter he had extracted from the envelope—"we will notify the police that a burglar entered the house and when he pulled a gun, you shot him. The whole affair was staged to look as if a burglar had broken in, and it will remain so. Your gun did the killing. You take the responsibility. There won't be many questions. The whole thing is much too clear cut. Then, after the police have gone, we notify Carol and Butch to come here at once."

"Y'mean—" Silk asked eagerly.

"I mean the Black Bat is taking a hand in something that's pretty vicious, Silk. Harriman was a friend of mine. I liked him and he trusted me. Harriman—is dead!"

"But how'd you know?"

"Read the letter, Silk."

SILK picked up the letter carefully, holding it by the edges. His face grew grim and somber as he read the brief contents.

TO THE POLICE:
    This is the only way out. For four years I have steadily appropriated stock from my own store and substituted for it certain paste replicas of the original gems. I never intended these to be sold and used them only to keep up my inventory. Now I am revealed. Though these people I have served for many years will never forgive me and my friends be unable to grant me forgiveness in their minds, I pray that my God will forgive. I take the only way out.
                                        Philip Harriman

"Poor guy!" Silk shook his head sadly.

"Your sympathies are cockeyed." Quinn said. "If Harriman wrote that note, what is it doing in this mug's pocket? Why did he come here to kill me anyway? We don't even know If Harriman is dead."

"He seemed okay when he phoned about Graham bumping himself," Silk offered. "A little excited maybe, but he didn't sound like a guy who was goin' to knock himself off. Say—" Silk was suddenly assailed by a horrible idea. "You don't think maybe this killer was sent here by someone who knows you are the Bat?"

"No. There was an entirely different reason. I was to be killed because the man who directs these crimes believed Harriman may have told me something—as an attorney, of course. Something he didn't want revealed. To work, Silk. First we must dispose of this shooting affair. Remember—this crook is just a burglar who pulled a gun and you were forced to kill him. Call Sergeant McGrath."

"McGrath?" Silk gaped. "But that heel will suspect you did it. He'll suspect all kinds of things. He already thinks you are the Bat, boss. Sure, I know he ain't got a thing to go on, but just the same McGrath is a square cop and he's sworn to get the Bat. No use letting him stick his mug in on this business,"

Quinn smiled a little. He well knew what Silk Kirby meant. He was referring to a case not long past when Tony Quinn had come closer to being unmasked than at any time since he had undertaken his self-appointed mission to do his share to clear the world of crime. And by that same Sergeant McGrath. Quinn had at last managed to slide out, and in his rightful character innocently plead ignorance, stressing his blindness.

But it had been a close call, and because McGrath had a one-track mind he had stubbornly refused to give up his idea that Tony Quinn was the Bat—and that he was not blind. His trouble was that he could prove neither assertion. Still he refused to admit he was wrong, and had become rather annoying to the former district attorney. Quinn was remembering all that as Silk made his remonstrance.

"We don't call him"—Quinn's smile, grew a little wry—"and his suspicions will grow still greater because he will believe I am afraid of him: afraid be might learn something to prove his accusations. No, call him, and get it over with. And, Silk, you *never* saw this suicide note."

CHAPTER IV
WAYS AND MEANS

 ERGEANT McGRATH came on the wings of a screaming siren. He was a chunky, beef-faced man with a determined slant to his chin. A policeman for twenty-odd years, Sergeant McGrath was as tenacious as a bulldog and as stubborn. Thoroughly honest and capable, there was not an iota of mercy

in his makeup. He had sworn to uphold the law and if it meant his own skin, he would carry on. And Sergeant McGrath had sworn to get the Bat.

Tony Quinn, cane between his knees, sat in his accustomed chair in front of the fireplace. Sergeant McGrath made a swift examination of the dead man on the floor, listened to Silk's story and had fingerprint men dust the open window. They found marks made by the dead crook's gloved hands, characteristic marks predominated by a scar on the surface of the glove's index finger.

McGrath strode into the living room, pulled up a chair and sat down facing Quinn.

"Hello, Sergeant." Quinn smiled welcome. "Sorry to make more work for you."

"Work?" McGrath snorted. "This job is a pipe. It's okay—on the level, Quinn. Silk blasted that mug out all right and a good job, too. He was a guy named Mercy Grogan—one of them mugs who'll pull anything for a thin dime. Silk is lucky at that, because Grogan was a killer."

"I recall the name." Quinn stared straight into the fireplace with his blank eyes. "Silk *was* fortunate. I was, too. I couldn't have defended myself, not being able to see."

Quinn's apparently sightless eyes watched the big officer. McGrath was getting set to pull a fast one. Quinn could sense it and he steeled himself.

"Uh-huh," McGrath said doubtfully and lit a cigarette.

McGrath took half a dozen deep drags on it and suddenly flipped the flaming cigarette straight at Quinn's nose, it missed Quinn's face by a fraction of an inch and landed in the fireplace. But Tony Quinn never moved a muscle. His staring blank eyes never flickered. And that had taken tremendous will power.

McGrath sighed deeply and relaxed. No man possessed of his sight could have avoided jerking his head back, or at least blinking as the cigarette came flying toward him. Quinn seemed to be blind all right.

"It's been a hell of a night," McGrath went on. "You're lucky you're not the D.A. anymore, Quinn. Because the guy who is in your shoes now is going to have his hands full. First of all a jeweler named Graham cleaned out a few million bucks worth of his stock and put phonies in their place. Then he bumped himself off, right in front of his secretary and a clerk. He left a note explaining things.

"Next about twenty big shots come flocking to the station carrying jewels. They all had been tricked. They'd paid fancy prices for a lot of junk. Then another jeweler named Harriman disappeared and we get complaints about him, too, so we investigate and sure enough he's done the same thing. Maybe he bumped himself off, too. We'll know pretty soon. To top it all off this guy Grogan gets blasted clean to hell."

Quinn's face was drawn and sad. "Did you say I'm lucky not to be the D.A., Sergeant? I'd sell my very soul to step back in that office and direct this jewel case you're talking about."

McGrath turned a beefy red. "Yeah—yeah, and you'd do a good job, too. Say, I didn't mean it that way. I—I know how you feel, Quinn. I'm sorry."

Quinn laughed grimly. "Forget it, Sergeant."

McGRATH put a friendly hand on Quinn's shoulder and began to say something. Then his old doubts assailed him again. He kept quiet, but he walked over to the desk and used the phone. He spoke in monosyllables and once grunted in surprise.

He hung up and returned to Quinn's side.

"More trouble. They just located Harriman. He drove his car off a cliff at the Palisades Road. Burned up pretty bad. Oh well, when they save the state a lot of dough, you can't get sore at 'em. Just the same it's going to be one sweet mess to clean up."

"You're right," Quinn said slowly. "Perfectly right, Sergeant. A sweet mess."

When the house was finally cleared and the body of the thug taken away, Silk sat down weakly and mopped his forehead. Quinn still remained seated before the fireplace. Not until more than an hour had passed did he move.

Then, at his gesture, Silk pulled down the curtains. Quinn arose, walked briskly and with no pretense of blindness now, to the book-lined wall of the room. He manipulated a section of the bookshelves and it opened to let him into a white-tiled laboratory equipped with almost every modern device for use in searching out the tricks and mistakes of criminals.

Quinn took the suicide note supposedly written by Harriman from his pocket. Carefully he smoothed the paper and deftly applied a spot of colorless chemical to several written words. The ink smeared and faded slightly. Quinn then placed a section of the letter beneath a microscope.

"Find anything?" Silk asked hopefully.

"This note," Tony Quinn replied thoughtfully, "was written more than seventy-two hours ago. It's a good stab at reproducing Harriman's handwriting, but Harriman never wrote this note. Why? Because Harriman only discovered today that his gems were phonies. There was no reason why he should have been planning suicide so far in advance."

"But how did that mug I killed get the note?" Silk asked.

"We'll never know, definitely," Quinn answered. "However, it's safe to assume that Harriman must have been murdered. This note was supposed to have been placed on his person, but somehow it wasn't. Perhaps the crook you killed forgot to take care of that detail in the excitement of murdering Harriman. It does indicate that we have a place to start in this investigation, Silk. We begin at once!"

"Me, too?" Silk perked up.

"You mostly. Silk, you know how to disguise yourself in two different makeups. Put one of them on at once. Then use the secret exit at the end of the estate. Go out and learn all you can about *Mynheer* Van den Killan. Everything, no matter how small, may be important. Find out about his habits, his friends, his finances. See if there is a possibility that he may have substituted that paste tiara for the real thing without his wife knowing it."

"I'm on my way." Silk grinned from ear to ear. "I wasn't a confidence man for nothing, Boss. I'll case this Van den Killan guy until I know which side he sleeps on."

Silk walked briskly to the door, hesitated a moment and turned around.

"What about you, Boss? Say, you don't think those mugs may come back and try to knock you off?"

Tony Quinn smiled tightly.

"If they do, I'll be quite ready for them. It may be reasonable to assume they'll come, because evidently they believe Harriman told me something. My silence must be important to their state of well-being. Don't worry about me, Silk."

TONY QUINN spent another twenty minutes examining the suicide note. He was firmly convinced now that it was a forgery and a good one. If that note had been found it would plainly have indicated that Harriman had died a suicide. With his gems missing and paste replicas in their place, the police were bound to assume that he had appropriated them and when he was on the verge of exposure, had taken the easiest way out.

But what of Graham? The other jeweler had suffered a similar loss. According to the meager information that Quinn possessed, two persons had been eyewitnesses to Graham's suicide. Still, he couldn't help wondering about it.

Quinn slipped out of the hidden laboratory. His eyes seemed to film over and he used his cane in making his way across the room. He sat down before the fireplace again, assimilating every phase of the case in his agile mind. He was lining up probabilities and theories. An investigation was in order and soon the Black Bat would prowl again while the underworld shuddered and crawled back into its filthy hole.

The phone rang. Tony Quinn got to his feet slowly and made his careful, methodical way to the instrument. Every movement was that of a blind man. Silk was on the wire, agitated and plainly worried.

"Boss, there's three or four guys casing the house. I slipped out the back like you said, but on a hunch I took a gander around the place. They're watching the place all right and they don't look like cops to me."

"Thank you, Silk," Quinn answered. "Don't return. Carry out the orders you already have and don't worry about me."

Quinn hung up and frowned. It was somewhat difficult to formulate a plan of action when he had to retain his pose of a blind man. If those thugs ever guessed that he could see, they might quickly associate him with the mysterious Black Bat, because of his known hatred of criminals and the criminal world when he had been district attorney. And should that news ever reach Sergeant McGrath, it would be all up.

Quinn turned around and for one of the few times in his pretended career of a blind man, he almost gave himself away. Standing in the doorway was a tall, wide-shouldered, sleek-looking man. He had a narrow waxed mustache and thick lips. His clothing was expensive-looking and showed reasonably good taste. His voice, too, was well modulated when he finally announced his presence.

But the most significant thing about him was his right hand buried in the pocket of his coat. Quinn knew the fingers of that hand were curled about a gun.

With a supreme effort, Tony Quinn forced himself to disregard this intruder. He was supposed to be blind and therefore he could not show that he realized someone was in the house.

SILK

CHAPTER V
PUSHOVER MURDER

QUINN used his cane, tapping his way across the floor toward his favorite chair beside the fireplace. The man in the doorway spoke and Quinn swung around, almost tripping himself on a chair.

"Is there someone here?" he asked querulously. "I thought a heard a voice."

"You Quinn?" the intruder asked. "Sorry if I scared you. The front door was open so I just walked in."

"Yes—yes, I'm Tony Quinn. You'll have to excuse me. I—I'm blind. Your voice—it isn't familiar—"

"We never met before," the caller said. "My name is Topping. I'm a pal of Philip Harriman. You know him, don't you?"

"Harriman? Oh, yes. Yes, of course. He was here to see me only this afternoon. About some trouble at his store. I expected he might contact me again."

"He asked me to bring you to him," Topping said and grinned. It was a knowing grin that he believed Tony Quinn could not see. "Harriman's in a lot of trouble and he wants you right away."

Quinn hesitated. To walk out with this man might mean quick death—a bullet, or a knife in the back. Yet if he refused, the same treatment might be administered immediately. Quinn recognized his danger before him, but danger made his blood ran quicker, his heart pound faster. And there was a chance, too, that he might learn something that would aid him in this puzzle that had unexpectedly confronted him.

"I'll come at once," he said. "My hat and coat are on that hat rack in a corner. Would you mind getting them? I'm a bit clumsy when I look for things."

"Sure, pal," the man who called himself Topping said blandly. "Glad to help you. Tough being blind. You can't see at all, can you?"

"Not a bit. Thank you for helping me with my coat. Now, if you'll take my arm and guide me down the porch steps. I know the rest of the way. Is Harriman far from here?"

"I've got a car," Topping informed. "A couple of my pals are with me, but you don't have to mind them. They're friends of Harriman's, too. Say, did he give you—all the details of his trouble?"

Tony Quinn's right foot moved off the path and hit a small shrub. He stumbled and only Topping's quick movement saved him from a bad fall.

"I'm sorry," Quinn apologized. "No, Harriman didn't tell me anything to speak of. Some trouble about his jewels being missing. He wanted advice as to his insurance."

"Yeah—yeah, but he's worse off, now. He's got to see you. Okay, pal, up with your leg. You're getting into a car. That's it. Now just sit down. Fine! I'll get in beside you."

Tony Quinn's eyes stared straight ahead, but they saw Topping nudge one of the two men on the sidewalk. His lips moved in soundless words.

"Blind as a bat. This job is a pushover."

The car rolled away and Tony Quinn braced himself for trouble. They would hardly attempt murder on a lighted street or in traffic. Until they actually hit the outskirts, he was comparatively safe. He took a firm grip of his cane and waited for the inevitable moment when he would be forced into action.

The car headed north, turned more than a dozen corners and passed directly by Graham's jewelry store. At the next corner the driver turned again, applied the brakes and finally stopped at the curb.

TOPPING took Quinn's arm.

"We're here, pal. Now all you got to do is follow me. I'll keep your arm. So will my friend. He'll take the other arm, see? That's so you won't trip and hurt yourself."

"Thank you," Quinn said. "Thank you very much. Where are we? Seems as though I smell the river."

"We're about three blocks from it," Topping answered. "Harriman's holed up—I mean he's waiting down the street."

They walked for a third of a block. Topping held Quinn's right arm and a pudgy, dark featured thug had his left. Another man trotted well ahead while the fourth, who had driven the car, brought up the rear.

Quinn saw Topping gesture and the man in front nodded. He veered off the sidewalk, looked up and down the deserted street and then hastily pulled up a sewer cover. He rolled it two or three feet away and then moved aside. Quinn felt the little hairs at the tape of his neck rise up. They were going to let him walk right into that sewer. That suited him perfectly. He'd vanish as a blind man, but once, in the darkness of the sewer, he could easily swim to safety.

"We cross the street here," Topping said. "Just hang onto my arm. Now this way."

Quinn's head was high, his blank eyes staring straight ahead. He moved toward the gaping sewer and felt like cracking the smirking thug who stood just out of his reach.

Suddenly Topping gave Quinn a shove. The apparently blind man stumbled forward. His foot went out, then down. His body followed and he plummeted through about eight feet of space before he thudded against the muck at the bottom of the sewer. To Quinn's amazement there was no water and an instant later Topping jumped down followed by two of the other men. The driver apparently had returned to the car.

Quinn was roughly seized. All pretense was gone now. Topping's voice was harsh.

"Okay, you wise D.A. Maybe Harriman didn't tell you much, but we don't take chances at this stage of the game. It's lights out for you, but you oughtn't to kick. Hell, it's a favor! I'd rather warm a morgue slab than be blind anyway."

"You—you're going to—to kill me?" Quinn asked incredulously and with just the right amount of fear in his voice. "But I don't understand. You're making a mistake."

"Maybe," Topping said, "but orders are orders. When Grogan didn't knock you off, it was put right up to me. I'll make it easy. Now don't try to fight or I'll bust your jaw. Get moving!"

A flashlight illuminated the sewer as they trudged along through the muck. Quinn stumbled and clutched at the rounded sides of the tube every few steps. Then Topping nodded to one of the other men and at the same time brought Quinn to a stop.

The thug seized a rusty handle set in one side of the pipe. He tugged and a section slid out. Quinn was forced through and he found himself in a narrow passageway carved out of rock and earth. Newly dug, too, if the smell of the dirt meant anything. There wasn't room enough to walk erect. He had to crawl.

Gradually he sensed that he was climbing upward. Then he came upon a room, dug like a small cave. Inside were cots, food and tables with cards flung upon them. In one corner empty tin cans had been hurled with the carelessness of a bachelor camp.

"Sit down," Topping commanded and gave Quinn a hard shove.

QUINN reeled forward, tripped and fell heavily. He lay there, moaning gently. Topping sat down on a rude bench.

"Now this job has got to be done with class," he told his two aides. "We can't muff it or the cops will get wise. Also watch that blind guy. He can't see, but he used to be a pretty smooth article. Here's the dope and it's right from upstairs, see?"

"Hey, Blackie," one of the thugs asked, "you never told us much about the guy who pays off. What's he look like? Where does he get all this mazuma he tosses around?"

"Blackie," alias Topping, ground out an oath.

"You were told to ask no questions. I'll tell you this, though, so it'll settle the thing once and for all. Nobody knows what the chief looks like—not even me. When I meet him, it's in a dark room where I can't see no more'n this blind guy. He gives his orders in a whisper and he always leaves fifteen minutes before I do. But he pays off and this is the biggest deal anybody ever cooked up. So we don't ask questions."

"Okay, Blackie," the thug muttered. "Only I don't like workin' fo' a mug I don't know."

"Well, stop being nosey," Blackie snapped. "I don't like it and neither does the chief. Now listen—this blind guy is important, see? He's a pal of the cops. They're bound to make a careful investigation. So here's what you do. Get one of them big buckets which we used to haul dirt in when we were digging. Fill it full of water—and get the water from the river, understand? Shove his head in the drink and hold him there until he's dead. Then take him to the real sewer, toss him in and he'll float to the river."

"I get it," one of the thugs grinned. "They'll find him floatin' around and think maybe he fell offa the pier. A blind guy might do that."

"Smart, ain't you?" Blackie snarled. "Well, that's the way it's got to be. I'll take his hat and cane, beat it to the pier where the sewer comes out and plant them there. I'll make a mark with my shoe like he slipped. Nothing to it. But you guys watch him. Give me about fifteen minutes to get things set and then hand him the works. Stay right here in the cave after you finish the job. I'll be back."

Tony Quinn pulled himself up against a wall of the cave. It was illuminated by two lights that derived their juice from dry cell batteries. He spoke in the whining, pleading tones of a blind man at his wits' end.

"I—I haven't done anything. There's no reason to kill me. I—I'm blind. Let me go. I won't tell the police what happened. I couldn't anyway because I can't see you."

"Which makes it swell," Blackie leered. "Like I said before, this job is a pushover. Okay, boys. Fifteen minutes and then dunk him in some water."

Blackie took Quinn's cane and hat, stepped through the door into the dry sewer and vanished. Quinn lurched to his feet, reeled forward a few steps and one of the thugs hastily drew a gun. Then he grinned sheepishly and put the weapon back in his pocket. Quinn's hands were stretched out before him. He struck the wall, reeled back and his hands dropped on a chair. He fumbled around and sat down. There was a small table just in front of him. He found this, apparently by sense of touch.

ONE of the thugs picked up a huge bucket, signaled his companion and went for the river water. The other killer pushed a chair up to the table and sat across from Quinn. Being alone with a man he intended soon to murder got on his nerves. Somehow he didn't like this. It was too easy. He drew his gun again, placed it on the table and kept one hand curled around the butt.

Quinn was feeling over the table, as if trying to ascertain his position. Finally he sighed, as if in resignation of what was to come. The killer, gripping his gun, presented a problem. Quinn had intended to act swiftly, but now that did not look possible.

One hand dropped into his pocket and the thug's gun came up to cover him. Quinn kept right on fumbling, as though the gun didn't exist. He pulled a pack of cigarettes from his pocket, extracted one and put it in his mouth. The killer relaxed, but he kept the gun ready.

Quinn seemed to have some trouble with the cigarette. His hand shook badly. Some of the tobacco dropped out of the paper tube and then the whole cigarette came apart. Quinn fingered the slip of paper, rammed some of the tobacco back into it and rolled the cigarette again. He moistened it with his lips.

The chair crashed against Quinn's shoulder.

"Would you mind giving me a light?' he asked. "I don't know where you are, but I'm quite harmless. A cigarette builds you up a little. I—I wish I had a drink."

The thug lit a match and held it toward the end of the cigarette. Suddenly Quinn's lips pursed and he blew violently. The loosely packed tobacco, in the split paper, flew out and into the thug's eyes. He howled and clawed at his face. Quinn leaned across the table and belted him on the chin.

The man went catapulting backward, stumbled over a chair and fell heavily. But he was up again in a flash, and the fallen chair came with him. He hurled it and Tony Quinn had to raise one arm to shield himself. The chair crashed against his protecting arm and shoulder. The thug reached under his coat and a spring holster threw a gun into his fist. He fired one shot and the bullet whined by Tony Quinn's ear.

Quinn made a dive toward the table and swept the battery-powered lamp it supported to the floor. The cavern was plunged into semi-darkness illuminated only by a weak light in a far corner. The killer fired two more shots, but he was nervous and jittery. This man who had been so blind could now see. Those dead eyes contained life and they glistened like the eyes of a cat in the gloom.

Quinn danced agilely to the left. The crook followed him and tried to center his gun. His finger grew white against the trigger but Quinn saw this and was ready when the fourth shot rang out. Before the crook could get his bearings again, Quinn was upon him. He seized the thug's gun hand, jerked the weapon free and hurled it into a corner. The gunman gave a bleat of fear and hastily retreated.

But he was by no means finished. His side coat pocket contained a single shot derringer and he swept this into view. He held his fire now, though, depending on that one small pellet of lead to finish off this strange being who moved so fast. The Bat whirled suddenly and did a nosedive along the floor. Not toward the crook but toward the corner where he had flung the gun. His fingers closed around it.

The thug fired and the sharp crack of his small weapon was echoed by the roar of the Bat's larger one. The thug dropped both arms suddenly.

His eyes bulged, his chin dropped an inch. Then he plummeted to the ground. There was a hole squarely between his eyes.

IN ten minutes the second thug returned. He backed into the cave, carrying the bucket half filled with water. As he turned, he saw Quinn in the dim light, saw his very much alive eyes and also the gun. He glanced toward his pal and saw him dead.

With an oath he whipped out a gun with amazing speed. It blasted once. Then there was another shot and the thug dropped to his knees. The vicious look on his face changed to one of bewilderment as death reached out with unerring aim. Between his eyes was a bluish hole. For this second time the Bat's aim had been true.

Quinn searched the man he had killed first. In a vest pocket, folded over several times, he found a crude map. There was no time to examine it so he stowed the paper away. Then he went through the clothing of the other crook, but found nothing of interest.

Quinn hurried to the door leading into the sewer. He slammed it behind him and had the feeling that he was sealing up a tomb. He hastened down the sewer, and the extreme darkness meant little to him for his super-sensitive eyes penetrated the gloom as readily as though it had been illuminated. He had to go through the sewer to the river, just as Blackie had planned, for a blind man certainly would never find his way out of the sewer in any other fashion.

He made out another rusty handle, tugged at it and water rushed over his ankles. The real sewer had been built next to the abandoned one. He stepped into the waist deep water, waded his way along until he could see river lights. Then he let himself drop and the current caught him. He was swept out and hurled into the river. His body turned over and over.

He began to shout for help. His voice rang loudly and to his relief someone called back words of encouragement. He heard someone dive into the river and a moment later strong arms kept him afloat. If Blackie were watching now, he could only assume that Tony Quinn had been extremely lucky and that his own men had failed so badly they would flee for their lives.

CHAPTER VI
WAYS AND MEANS

T was a patrolman who had rescued him. Quinn was wrapped in a blanket borrowed from a watchman's hut on the pier.

"I really don't know what happened," he mumbled while his teeth chattered. "Two men took me for an auto ride. Then something happened. I fell through a hole. Then someone put my head underwater and held it there. I fought, got away and drifted through some kind of a tube. The next thing I was in the river."

The patrolman nodded sympathetically and touched his head for the benefit of the pier watchman.

"Sure, sure, friend. Of course you couldn't see nothing, huh?"

Tony Quinn's eyes were absolutely blank. "No. You're quite right. I'm blind. My name is Quinn. Tony Quinn."

The patrolman gasped and hustled Quinn into a radio car. Twenty minutes later he was safely home. Silk had returned and was there to minister to him. After the police left, Silk gave vent to his feelings.

"Plague them guys! Boss, you just got to start things rolling so we get a crack at 'em. Taking you out, thinking you were blind, and trying to bump you that way."

"It's a complication I couldn't foresee," Quinn admitted ruefully, "and I very nearly lost my bout with Fate. But the only two men who knew I wasn't blind are dead. This man called Blackie will believe some miraculous piece of luck saved me. What did you find out about Van den Killan?"

Silk sat down. "Not so much, Boss. He's a Dutchman—you know that, of course. Lived the first thirty-five years of his life in Amsterdam. Then he went to South Africa where he got interested in a diamond mine. Say—is that guy crazy about jewelry! He buys up every important piece he can afford and he's got plenty of rocks in his safe. Credit is okay, bank account on the level. He's married, but has no children. He's supposed to be retired, I guess. Wife pals around with a bunch of society people, especially one guy named Clifford Carlyle who has plenty of dough, too."

Outside a siren wailed and died. Silk sprang to the window.

"Boss, it's Police Commissioner Warner and Sergeant McGrath! What can you tell 'em? That cop who rescued you musta turned in a fast report."

"I'll tell them the truth," Quinn said, and smiled. "You were out on an errand when those thugs took me. Remember that!"

Silk let Commissioner Warner and Sergeant McGrath in. Warner rushed up to Quinn and shook his hand fervently.

"Just heard what happened, Tony. Great heavens, that must have been an awful experience!"

"It was," Quinn replied with a wan smile and pulled the blanket closer about him. "I really don't know yet how I survived. Three or four men came for me. They took me somewhere—don't ask me where, because I don't know. They ducked my head in water and held me there until they thought I was drowned. I held my breath as long as possible although I did swallow and breathe in some water. Then they threw me into some kind of a tube. Unless my sense of smell has gone as completely as my sight, it was a sewer. I felt cold air as I dropped off a regular falls. Then I began to yell for help."

"Yeah?" Sergeant McGrath stepped in front of Quinn. "What would them mugs want to bump you for? Unless"—he added this slyly—"you had pulled a fancy trick on them sometime or other, or they thought maybe you were going to—some little trick like the Black Bat would pull, for instance."

COMMISSIONER WARNER whirled around. "Sergeant, you've said enough. Why in thunder you keep intimating that Tony Quinn is the Black Bat is beyond me, He's blind... do you hear? Totally blind! Every doctor he's been to says the same thing. The Black Bat happens to be your pet hate. Well, perhaps he does deserve a good stiff prison sentence. He has broken about every law man ever created. Yet that doesn't make him Tony Quinn, you fool. Lord only knows how you ever got that wacky idea in the first place, McGrath, but it's about time you forgot it."

McGrath grumbled something under his breath and backed away. Warner apologized profusely.

"The Black Bat put one or two things over on McGrath and he can't get it out of his system," he said to Quinn. "Of course McGrath is perfectly right in trying to unmask the Bat. The fellow should be brought to justice, heaven knows. Someday he may turn into a real criminal himself and stop running down crooks and he'd be a tough one to catch. Tony, what's your theory as to the reason for this attempt on your life?"

"Attempts," Quinn corrected with a wan smile. "I'm beginning to think that the man that Silk killed was also trying to murder me. The reason? There can be only one. Philip Harriman came to see me this afternoon. He told me that some kind of a stupendous robbery had occurred at his store. He asked my advice, as an attorney. Perhaps these crooks believe he told me more than he did. Still, I don't understand it. I can't imagine what they would think Harriman told me that could interest them. Anyhow—didn't you tell me Harriman had committed suicide?"

Warner pulled up a chair and sat down. He leaned close to Quinn.

"I'm beginning to wonder, Tony. It was Harriman's car all right, but—well, it caught fire after it plunged off the cliff and there wasn't much left to identify. The body we found was charred from the flames, and all that was left to identify it as Harriman's was his signet ring."

"The fact remains, though, that Harriman's stock of gems has been thoroughly plundered and some damned good paste replicas put in their place. Graham's stock is similarly depleted, but Graham very definitely committed suicide. We have two witnesses who saw him put a bullet through his brain. I wonder—was it really Harriman who was destroyed in that car?"

"Then you think that Harriman may not be dead and that he not only robbed his own store, but Graham's as well?"

Sergeant McGrath strode forward.

"That's what I think," he growled flatly. "Look—those two jewelry stores were like banks. There were time locks on the vaults and no cracks-man in the world could have busted in. Weren't any signs the vaults had been touched in any way. My idea is that Harriman looted his own stock and maybe Graham played along with him. Only Graham couldn't take it and bumped himself."

Quinn nodded slowly. "Perhaps you are right, Sergeant. Still, if Harriman is the man behind the robberies—and he isn't dead—then why should those thugs come here to kill me? Harriman couldn't have sent them. He knows very well that he told me nothing of importance."

Sergeant McGrath's face grew grim. "I think maybe he did. What's more, he also found out that you are the Black Bat. He told you too much and he wants to kill you before the Bat goes into action. He didn't try it that first time because he didn't find out the truth about you until later."

QUINN shrugged and his blank eyes looked straight into the fireplace.

"It's a reasonable theory, Sergeant, if you really believe I am this rather spectacular creature who calls himself the Black Bat, I'm genuinely sorry you think that way because it makes a lot of trouble for you. You keep chasing clues frantically and your mind makes them point to me. But I assure you, I am quite blind. In fact I'd sell my very soul to be this Black Bat."

Commissioner Warner arose and gestured to McGrath.

"You're more of a fool than I thought, McGrath. Suspicions, suspicions. Why don't you get some that will clear up this damned case? Why don't you locate those stolen jewels? They can't just vanish. Go out and find the Black Bat, too, if you wish. Find him—throw him in a cell and I'll see that he's given the justice he deserves. Now get out of here. Wait for me in the car."

McGrath, his face flaming red, skulked to the door. Silk gave him a crooked grin and a low chuckle. Commissioner Warner put a friendly hand on Tony Quinn's shoulder.

"He's obsessed with the idea you're the Bat. But between you and me, Tony, this Black Bat has done the department a lot of favors. If I could help him in any way, at any time—well, you know how it is. My duty is to put him behind bars. But my heart tells me to shake his hand."

Solemnly, Warner picked up Tony Quinn's hand—and wrung it. Then he nodded to Silk and vanished into the night.

Silk, his features aghast, hurried to Quinn's side.

"Say, did you hear what the commissioner said? Why, that guy, too, practically accused you of being the Bat!"

"But in a nice way." Quinn grinned broadly. "In a very nice way, Silk."

Silk shook his head. "They're up a tree, anyhow. That's plain enough. They're doing a lot of guessing and getting nowhere." He paused, and his forehead wrinkled thoughtfully. "And another thing," he cried. "What's happened to all the stuff already stolen? If Graham bumped himself off because he figured things were getting too hot, he must have hidden the rocks somewhere. The same goes for Harriman, unless… Boss, do you think Harriman is really dead? Maybe he and Graham were in cahoots. Graham got scared, finished himself off and Harriman planted some stooge in his car and burned him up."

Tony Quinn rubbed his chin calculatingly.

"Those theories of yours, Silk, jibe with those of Commissioner Warner and Sergeant McGrath. The police are quite satisfied that Graham did commit suicide, so I suppose we shouldn't question that fact. *However,* Silk, I make it a habit of questioning all facts, especially those which are most obvious. The stolen gems must be hidden somewhere, true. Yet, to find them we must first locate our master crook.

"There are a few suspicions in my mind already. Harriman is, of course, one suspect. I hate to think that of him for he was—or is—my friend. Still he may have duped all of us cleverly. We'll try to find out. First of all, I'm going to examine Graham's jewelry store—from the inside."

"How?" Silk asked incredulously. "McGrath said it's just like a bank."

"I don't know how, just yet," Quinn admitted. "But there are always ways and means."

CHAPTER VII
THE TRAP

 OISELESSLY, Quinn slipped through the secret door and into his laboratory. There he divested himself of his lounging robe and other outer clothing. He donned a black suit, a black shirt. His shoes were black, with spongy rubber soles and heels. An automatic went into a spring shoulder holster and a black hood was thrust into a side pocket. He drew on black gloves and donned a wide-brimmed hat pulled low over his face.

With a few swift changes that would be complete, once the black hood was slid over his head and scarred face, Tony Quinn had become the Black Bat. In darkness, which his own eyes could so readily penetrate, he would be nothing more than a deeper shadow in shadows.

Quinn nodded to Silk, opened a door and stepped down a ladder into a tunnel. But unlike the one inside the old sewer, only Quinn knew this tunnel, for he had painstakingly helped to dig it. He hurried along and came out through a secret door set in the floor of a garden house.

Slipping across the lawn he emerged on a side street along which there were no houses and little traffic. He turned a corner, looked carefully around and then bolted toward an old coupé that stood at the curb in front of a boarding house.

Butch, the Bat's giant assistant, lived in that boarding house and left this car at the curb for the Bat's use. Quinn climbed into it and drove away.

The Bat took a mighty risk in these expeditions, for should anything happen, he would be recognized upon close inspection. Those telltale scars were known to practically every policeman in town and there were eighteen thousand on the force.

So every movement the Bat made was cautious and planned ahead of time. That was why he was now somewhat worried. He had to invade a virgin territory of which he knew nothing and a dangerous territory at that. A crook with his plans all laid out would have a difficult time breaking into the Graham Jewelry Company—yet the Bat intended to do just that. He was far from satisfied with the story he had been told of Graham's suicide, even though two persons had witnessed the act and there had been a note in the dead man's handwriting. The Bat knew only too well how weak the human eye can be—and how unseeing under certain circumstances.

He left the car and merged with the shadows of the great buildings until he reached the store. Windows were covered by steel curtains and burglar alarms would guard every foot of the interior.

The Bat stepped into a doorway and eyed the building doubtfully. Despite the darkness, every detail was clear to his supersensitive eyes. Someone was moving around, just inside the door. A watchman, of course. Probably there would be one or two others and most certainly every window and door would be provided with an alarm system.

Then the Bat smiled a bit. He returned to his car, drove to a quiet section of the city and phoned his own home. Silk answered and the Bat gave precise instructions.

"I'll wait exactly five minutes after you reach the place," he said. "Be sure to impress Butch with the idea of caution. We can't slip now, Silk. It would be disastrous."

The Bat glanced at his watch, walked to the street and picked up a loose section of curbing that had fallen away. He put this into his car and drove back to the neighborhood of the Graham Company.

AN hour slipped by before he went into action. He made sure the street was deserted and that no patrolman was in sight. Then he drove slowly down the street, cut close to the curb and as he passed in front of the jewelry building, he hurled the piece of curbing.

It struck the large plate glass window in the center and smashed it. As the Bat stepped on the gas pedal, he heard the automatic alarm system banging away. He drove for blocks, parked and got out. He made his way back toward the building and saw the radio patrol cars, the protective agency's police and the firm's watchmen gathered in front of the building surveying the damage. No one had seen the Bat hurl that piece of curb; nothing was missing from the window. The radio car began pulling away, but the protective agency's police guarded the shattered window,

Then a truck, once painted a dull gray and now covered with the white from plaster and with several other hues from paint, pulled to the curb. Two men climbed down. The larger one, a veritable giant, wore a painter's cap low over his face. He began fussing with ladders and lengths of board. The smaller man nodded affably to the police.

"Got here in quick time, huh, boys? Say, that's some hole in the window. Got to board her up tight until tomorrow. She'll need a whole new pane of glass then."

The two men measured the window, dragged lumber into the jewelry store and then the smaller man returned to the truck for a box of tools. As he crossed the sidewalk, he loosened his collar with a violent stretching of his neck.

In the darkness, the Black Bat's scarred features were transformed into a grin. It was working very well indeed. Butch, who was the huge, ungainly carpenter, and Silk, who was now in disguise, had secured admittance to the jewelry store. There were usually ways and means accomplishing any purpose.

The radio police gradually left. The agency police stuck around until the window was boarded up effectively. Then, as the two carpenters went back into the jewelry store for their equipment, the watchmen took over.

Exactly five minutes later, the Bat drew his hood over his features, transferred a heavy automatic to a side coat pocket and edged his way through the shadows toward the building. He slipped down an alley, vaulted a fence and came out in the rear of the jewelry house. A light winked twice and the delivery entrance door swung wide. Silk grinned broadly.

"If you were working against the law, Boss, every cop in town would have a big headache."

Butch stalked up, towering above the Bat and Silk. He nursed a fist tenderly.

"Them three watchmen are out, Boss. They won't do no squawkin'."

The Bat never doubted that, for when Butch hit a man, he stayed down. He moved into the store, closing the door behind him. Silk flipped a switch. All the burglar alarms were in working order again. The phone rang. The Bat answered and told the inquiring protective agency that everything was in order once more.

"Now," the Bat told Silk and Butch, "watch the doors. Silk, take the front, and you take the rear, Butch. If you see anybody—even the patrolman on the beat—give me a warning. I'm going upstairs to the office where Graham met his death. Don't walk near the safes or the consultation rooms. There will be infra-red warning rays around them."

THE Bat hurried up the elaborate, modernistic staircase, found the office labeled with Graham's name and stepped inside. He passed by the secretary's desk, stopping only long enough to glance in the desk drawers and at the appointment book.

He closed the private office door behind him and went directly to Graham's desk. Using a flashlight with a taped lens, he made a rigid examination of the premises, especially the area directly around the solid, high-backed chair in which Graham had been seated when he died.

The rug was a light green and a spot of blood showed vividly plain. From its location the Bat estimated that it had come from Graham's temple through which the slug had smashed its way. He turned the light on the chair itself and suddenly his eyes contracted behind the slits of the mask. On the back of the chair, halfway from the bottom, was a jagged smear of dried blood. It clung to the deep red leather of the back and might have escaped less critical and observing eyes than the Bat's.

The Bat walked behind the chair and squatted. He noticed that he was completely hidden from the view of anyone standing in front of the desk or from the doorway to the outer office.

"Graham was murdered," the Bat told himself. "The killer knocked him unconscious, hid behind this chair and when McFayden and the secretary entered, it was the killer's hand they saw rising from beneath the desk. Graham's hands were hanging limply down. But the killer got some blood on the sleeve of his coat and unknowingly brushed it against the back of this chair. "It's murder—not suicide."

He began examining the papers on top of the desk. There was nothing of interest but the Bat's keen eyes saw a pad. On the blank surface of the top piece of paper were slight indentations, as if someone had written on the pad and that writing had been torn off.

The Bat hurried into the secretary's office and opened the pencil sharpener so that he was able to spill some of the dust from the pencil lead onto a bit of paper. He carried this back into Graham's office and gently blew some of the finer particles of graphite dust onto the scrap pad.

The dust settled into the indentations to bring into relief what had been traced there.

Vaguely, the Bat made out a drawing of what seemed to be an immense diamond. It was crudely done but plain enough. Below it was one significant word. "Kill—"

It looked as though there had been other words written as well but not firmly enough to make an impression on the under sheet of paper. The Bat opened a drawer, found Graham's check book and compared the writing in it with the writing that formed the one word—"Kill." It matched!

"Graham wrote this," the Bat told himself grimly. "He was in the presence of his murderer, knew he was doomed to die and wanted to leave some clue that the killer wouldn't recognize. That clue is in the drawing of the diamond. It must be! But Graham didn't fool the killer for he must have recognized the danger of the drawing and the few words written below it. He removed that paper from the pad but in his excitement forgot that there might be an indentation from the point of Graham's pencil."

The Bat carefully stowed the slip of paper into a pocket. Then he searched the desk drawers thoroughly. There was nothing of interest, but in the bottom of the wastebasket he found ashes of what seemed to have been a letter. Working swiftly, the Bat extracted a glass cutter from a small kit of instruments that he carried.

He sped down into the store proper and cut two six-inch sections of glass out of a counter.

RETURNING to the office, he slid one piece of glass beneath the ashes until the charred bits of paper were upon it. The second piece of glass he used as a cover, pressing the ash firmly down with it. He held the two pieces of glass together with rubber bands that he took from Graham's desk. Then he replaced the waste paper in the basket and covered up all other signs of his work.

One thing the Bat knew now. Graham had been murdered cleverly but he had tried to leave a clue to the identity of the killer. He had failed—but only

partially. That drawing of a diamond might mean something.

As he crossed the floor toward the door he heard a soft whistle from downstairs. Instantly he sped to the stairway landing and peered down. Shadowy figures were before the drawn curtain of the front door and a peremptory knocking indicated that the visitors sought to summon the watchman.

"Silk," the Bat whispered hoarsely, "you and Butch go out the rear exit! Get on to that all-night drugstore and wait. I'll call you soon as I can. Hurry!"

Silk didn't protest. When the Bat issued orders, they were to be followed explicitly, no matter what the consequences. Silk hated to leave the Bat in a trap, as this looked to be, but he went anyway. It wouldn't help any if all three of them were trapped.

The front door opened and two men came. One held a gun in his fist.

"Odd," he grunted, "where those watchmen are. *Herr* Wohl, do you think—"

"*Ach*, I do not know," a gruff voice responded. "Perhaps we should the police call."

The two men stepped deeper into the store and reached the weak rays of light from the bulbs above the vaults. One was a thick-set stoop-shouldered man who wore nose glasses and had a pompous mien. The other man was slender and nervous. He held the gun.

CHAPTER VIII
ESCAPE IN THE DARK

MOVING cautiously, the two invaders reached the stairway and peered up into the darkness. Neither one took note of the slightly darker section of shadow that was the Bat.

"Something is wrong," the slender man said sharply. "I think we ought to phone the police. Maybe the man who broke the window came back."

"*Ja,*" the heavier man retorted. "It iss, perhaps, better."

They turned to hurry toward the phone on a desk in one corner. Then a voice came down to them from the upper regions of the store. It was a soft, yet commanding voice.

"Both of you—don't move unless it is your wish to die! You—with the gun—place it on the floor and then kick it into a corner. If you doubt I'm in a position to enforce my orders, look up here."

They looked, faces pale, mouths agape. The Bat had turned the tiny ray of his flash upon the gun he held. The slender man bent down, put the gun on the floor and kicked it out of sight. Then the two men walked slowly up the staircase, hands shoulder high.

"You are showing remarkable judgment," the

Bat told them. "Now—into Graham's office where we can have a little talk."

"Just a minute," the slender man said hoarsely. "If you're a crook and want us to open the vaults, we simply can't do it. They are equipped with time locks."

"I'm not interested in the safe," the Bat said pleasantly. "I want information."

"Where are the watchmen?" Wohl demanded.

"Sleeping," he was told. "Peacefully sleeping, gentlemen. Right this way. And please stop for a moment while I make certain you are not further armed."

They were not. A moment later all three were in the quiet security of a dead man's office. The Bat perched himself on a corner of the desk and waved the two men into chairs.

"Mr. Wohl," he said gently, "please take that scowl off your face. You're a dignified, capable-looking man when you don't scowl."

"Mein Gott!" Wohl exploded. "Who are you? How can you see that I scowl? All is darkness here. I cannot see any part of you."

"They call me—the Bat. Like my namesake, I am able to see in darkness, Mr. Wohl. Now if you'll introduce yourselves, we'll get down to business. I mean no harm."

"I'm McFayden," the slender man burst out, "And I trust you. I've heard of you often. You're no crook. You fight crooks. I'll tell you anything you want to know. This man with me is Wohl, the gem expert who works here. I'm chief clerk. We got word from the protective agency that the window had been smashed so we came down to see what had happened."

The Bat nodded. "Now just relax. McFayden, you were one of the witnesses to Graham's suicide. Give me all the details."

McFayden shuddered and the Bat saw his lanky frame tremble.

"There aren't many. I—I knew something had gone wrong. He was so nervous and worried. Then when I came back to talk to him—he'd sent for me—I saw him sitting right there, behind the desk. Then, while I watched him, he raised his right hand, took a gun out of the drawer and before I could even move, he—he shot himself through the head! Miss Curtis, his secretary, saw him do it, too. We ran for help. He—he was dead when I returned."

"I believe you," the Bat answered simply. Then he turned to Wohl who sat bolt upright in his chair. "And you, *mein Herr,* I have known of for a long time. You are one of the best jewel experts in the world. For years you worked in Amsterdam as a diamond cutting supervisor. Am I right?"

WOHL nodded sadly. *"Ja.* And I wish I had never left Holland. *Ach,* this suicide, this robbery!

It iss beyond me. Now I have also lost my chob, *ja.* Who would hire a man who permitted millions of dollars' worth of false chems to be placed in here as real ones? Harriman's expert, he also is much worried. I talked to him but a few hours ago."

"Where?" the Bat queried.

Wohl looked a bit startled to the Bat's sensitive eyes.

"We had dinner in the hoffbrau—*Unter-den-Linden* it iss called. For two hours we talked—until we heard the news of *Herr* Harriman's death."

"And Harriman's expert is whom?"

"A great man, *ja!* Greater than I, for he spent many years in India where truly great chems are sold. Rajas and princes trusted him. He iss himself an Egyptian. His name—Anghis Khan."

McFayden arose abruptly and the Bat's gun covered him. "Don't shoot," the jewel clerk quavered. "I—I just want to get a cigarette from the desk. Haven't any of my own."

McFayden walked around the desk and it seemed to the Bat as though he took plenty of room. The chief clerk's right hand came up, brushed back his hair and then he walked toward the desk. He took a cigarette from the container, lit it and returned to his chair.

Somehow, the Bat didn't like that bit of action. McFayden's face seemed to have suddenly become crafty, too.

"I'll be going now," the Bat said. "You men have been of great help to me. Please remain exactly where you are. After five minutes you may do anything you please."

Gun leveled, he backed toward the door. More and more the Bat sensed danger although nothing had happened outside the private office and the same eerie silence held sway over the store. He opened the door, clumped through the secretary's office, stepped into the hallway and closed the door with a thud. But a split second later the door was open a crack and the Bat stood outside listening. The inner door was still open.

McFayden's voice was low, hardly more than a whisper, but the Bat had the hearing of a blind man. Every word carried plainly.

"The Bat, is he? Well, I'll show him, with his damned mask. Graham used to keep a lot of valuable stuff in his wall safe When I passed by it, I put my hand through the warning ray. By this time the protective police and the regular cops will be covering the place."

"You fool," Wohl grated. "That was the Bat. I am sure of it, and he iss not one to fight. Also he iss honest—the friend of the police, though they will not openly admit it. He did not harm us and you—you have called the police to shoot him down. *Ach,* that was wrong; he was not a burglar."

"That's what you say," McFayden whispered triumphantly. "But I happen to know he's killed a lot of people. Crooks maybe, but just the same he's wanted for murder. And he broke in here, didn't he? That man isn't safe to be loose. Next thing he'll turn crooked as they're all saying he will, and then what'll happen?"

THE Bat waited to hear no more. He rushed down the steps, two at a time. But he stopped quickly. Cars were pulling to the curb and uniformed men were rushing toward the door. By now the whole building was surrounded!

But the Bat remained calm, as he thought swiftly. All exits on the lower floor were definitely out of the question. The windows on the second floor were heavily barred and also eliminated. There remained only the roof.

Then a harsh voice demanded entrance as the banging on the front door grew peremptory. Sergeant McGrath! The Bat's heart began pounding. Of all men, McGrath would be the most persistent, once he learned it was the Bat who had invaded the premises.

McFayden passed within five feet of the Bat as he rushed down the steps. Wohl stood in the doorway at the office. The Bat sidled away, merging with the darkness. At any moment the lights would be turned on.

He studied the layout of the second floor, seeing as clearly through the darkness as a normal man would if the whole place was brilliantly illuminated. There was an iron ladder leading to a trap door set in the ceiling. That meant a roof exit. It would be protected to keep intruders from coming down, but hardly fastened so that it couldn't be opened from within.

He also saw a door, half ajar, leading into a stockroom. The Bat ran lightly toward the ladder. As he reached for the rungs, the lights were turned on and a score of police burst into the store. The Bat couldn't risk climbing the ladder now. Instead he bolted into the supply room and gently closed the door.

Sergeant McGrath was giving crisp orders.

"Keep your eyes peeled and your guns ready. It's the Bat! Take him alive, do you hear? Shoot if you have to, but aim low. McFayden, you and Wohl stay downstairs! This Bat can shoot faster than chained lightning. I'm going up. The rest of you search the first floor and watch me, too. Come flying if you hear a shot. And I'll show myself every minute or two. If he knocks me cold, I won't show. That'll be a signal for you boys to start in."

The Bat, listening from the other side of the storeroom door, gulped and broke out in a cold sweat. McGrath was clever—clever and capable. He was coming up alone so that none of his men might suffer needless risk. He depended on the fact that if the Bat struck, the police downstairs would close in. Whatever else he might be, McGrath was no fool.

McGrath inspected Graham's offices first and then darted into the room where the jewels were weighed and examined, a miniature laboratory. Finally he stepped cautiously down the corridor, gun hand extended slightly and the weapon nosed up so it could instantly be snapped down in firing position. He saw the storeroom door and the ladder to the roof as well.

On the other side of the storeroom door the Bat waited with held breath. McGrath kicked the door wide and eyed the darkened room suspiciously. He saw the light switch about three feet from the door and stepped toward it.

Something came flashing out of the air. An arm encircled his throat and prevented any cry for help. At the same time he felt his gun hand gripped so hard that nerves and muscles felt paralyzed. He gave a wrench, trying to free himself, but only succeeded in getting more firmly in the grip of his unseen adversary.

THEN a voice breathed softly in his ear:

"Sorry, Sergeant. I don't like to do this." And a fist slugged McGrath across the back of the neck.

Stunned, the officer reeled away a step as the grip on his throat relaxed. He was straightening up to hurl himself forward when the Bat's fist exploded against his jaw. McGrath started for the floor, but the Bat seized him and laid him down gently. Hastily he stripped off the officer's coat and donned it. He placed the unconscious sergeant's gray fedora on his head and backed out of the storeroom.

Below, a dozen patrolmen were positive they saw Sergeant McGrath emerge from the room.

The Bat had his hood stowed away in a pocket, but the fedora hid his features well. He hurried to the ladder and swarmed up it. Pushing open the trap door at the top, he stepped out on the flat roof.

The next office building was across an alley about four feet wide. The Bat raced across the roof, jumped and landed lightly. He was up again in a flash and three minutes later he was opening an office door and racing to pick up a telephone.

Butch's rough voice greeted him with a bellow of relief.

"Gosh, boss, I figured the cops had you that time. We shouldn't oughta have left, but Silk says we gotta, so we did. You okay?"

"So far," the Bat said grimly. "All that worries me is Sergeant McGrath. He thinks Tony Quinn is the Black Bat and in about two minutes he'll wake up and be trying to find out again. I'll be coming by where I told you to meet me, Butch. Stand ready! There is no time to lose."

The Bat hurried down to the lower floor. Peering through the glass door in the lobby he saw more police hurry into the jeweler's building. McGrath had apparently awakened and put up a howl. The Bat opened the doors, slipped out and reached an alley on the far side of the building. He raced down it, cleared two low fences and finally came out near the spot where Butch had left his coupé parked. He got in, started away and turned on a radio concealed under the dash.

A general alarm was being sent out and the report made the Bat sweat profusely.

"All cars… All cars… Converge on Twenty-two thirty-eight Teneyke Boulevard. Close all streets and surround the house. Keep guard and allow no one to enter. Wait for Sergeant McGrath's orders."

The Bat wheeled around a corner and tramped on the brake. Before he could pull to the curb, a man came running toward the car. The Bat slid over in the seat and opened the door beside the wheel. Butch jumped aboard and took over.

"Faster, Butch," the Bat groaned. "They're closing in now. Hear the sirens?"

CHAPTER IX
MURDER AGAIN

 RIMLY Butch bent over the wheel and the powerful motor under that dilapidated hood did things for him. He reached the extreme end of Tony Quinn's estate and slowed a trifle. The Bat leaped, landed as confidently as a cat and vanished through a section of high stone wall. Hastily he doffed his hood, stripped off McGrath's gray coat and hat, hid these under his own black coat and moved across a path toward the garden house. Through the darkness he could see a score of police taking up positions all about the mansion. McGrath was certainly determined to satisfy himself this time. If Tony Quinn should not be at home—

The Bat sidled into the garden house and vanished through a whole section of wall. Two minutes later he was in his own laboratory. The rumble of voices from outside was harsh. The Bat stripped off his clothes in a flash, rolled them into a ball and tossed them, with McGrath's coat and hat, down the secret passageway.

Now he was Tony Quinn—blind Tony Quinn— who listened intently at the secret door leading into the living room. The police hadn't reached that room yet. Trust Silk to see they were delayed as long as possible.

"Nevermind what I mean!" Quinn heard Sergeant McGrath bark at Silk. "I'm an officer of the law and I'm going to search this house! Where's Quinn?"

"He's about somewhere," Silk answered nervously. "I—I don't know exactly where, because I've been busy in the kitchen. Probably he's sleeping. He should be at this hour."

McGrath pushed Silk out of the way and strode into the living room. He stopped dead and stared, with his mouth hanging wide open. In the deep leather chair before the fireplace sat Tony Quinn. His cane was between his legs and his sightless eyes were staring in the general direction of the hallway.

"What's the matter, Silk?" he asked querulously. "What's wrong? Silk! Silk—where are you?"

"Coming, sir," Silk called back and the relief in his voice was plain to Tony Quinn, at least. "It's Sergeant McGrath and about a hundred cops, sir. They're all around the place. I think he's gone nuts, if you'll pardon me, sir."

"Tell him to come in."

Tony Quinn was looking straight at Sergeant McGrath. Once Quinn's lower lip quivered as though he might enjoy a lusty laugh. McGrath's hair was tousled. His jaw was swollen and somewhat out of kilter. He was in his shirt sleeves and the shoulder of his shirt was ripped. But more than anything else, Quinn enjoyed the stupefaction on the detective's face.

"Where is the sergeant?" Quinn went on impatiently. "Ask him in, Silk. All policemen are friends of mine. I've told you that often enough."

McGrath walked up to Quinn and stood looking down at him. Certainly this man was blind.

"I—I guess I made a mistake," McGrath mumbled. "I figured this time I had you. But listen, Quinn—maybe I'm wrong, and maybe I'm just a sucker. If I'm wrong, I apologize. If I'm a sucker, get this! I'll run you in if it's the last thing I do."

Tony Quinn's forehead wrinkled into deep lines. "I'm afraid I don't understand, Sergeant. Have I done something to aggravate you? I'm terribly sorry. I'm afraid I was asleep when you arrived. Dozed off in my chair here. Bear with a blind man. Sometimes sleep comes with great difficulty and when I manage to drop off, I usually finish my nap wherever I happen to be."

"It ain't that!" McGrath howled. "It's this! Look at the damned thing if you can see!"

HE pointed dramatically to his forehead. Emblazoned in the center of it was the image of a bat, wings outspread. But Tony Quinn looked slightly to McGrath's left.

"I apologize again," he told the officer. "Sorry I can't look, Sergeant. You'll have to describe what it is you wish me to know about."

"Aw, forget it!" McGrath swung around. "I guess I'm nothing but a fool. A fool, and the laughing stock of the whole doggone police force."

He gave orders and the house was cleared of policemen. The quiet that fell with the slamming of the front door almost hurt. Silk was mopping his face and drinking a rye highball concocted of nine-tenths whiskey.

"Silk," Tony Quinn still looked directly into the fireplace and his lips didn't seem to move. "Silk, make certain McGrath left no guard."

Silk returned after a few minutes.

"They're all gone, Boss. I'm sure of it. Butch is on the lookout, too, and he just passed me the high sign. Are we going out? You haven't had any sleep."

"Sleep can wait."

Tony Quinn arose and, tapping his cane before him, walked slowly toward the secret door. Then, like a ghost, he vanished from sight. Silk slipped through the door, also. He found Quinn switching on a powerful lamp on the laboratory bench. Beneath it, Quinn put the charred paper he had taken from Graham's wastebasket.

"This," he said to Silk, "I found in Graham's office! If Graham wanted to destroy this letter permanently, he'd have burned it elsewhere. I think someone other than Graham set fire to the paper because he wanted no one to see it and he, himself, didn't want to take a chance on having this letter found on his person."

Quinn carefully raised one of the glass slides. With a delicate brush dipped in a colorless shellac, he set the remnants of ashes so he might work with them freely. Next Quinn slid a strong magnifying unit over the ashes and peered through.

"This letter," he said in an excited whisper, "was written on Philip Harriman's stationery and it was signed by Harriman. The few words that are left show some kind of a deal was in order. Unfortunately not enough is left to give me a clear picture."

Quinn set this clue aside, took from his pocket the folded paper which he had removed from one of the thugs who had tried to murder him. This gave him much more satisfaction.

"It's a floor plan of some kind of a store," he told Silk. "Look—even the counters are blocked in and so is a safe. A big one if the map is drawn to scale."

"But what good is it," Silk queried, "if it doesn't say where this place is located?"

Quinn smiled grimly. "It does, Silk. A draftsman evidently drew this up. His first sketch was erased, but take a look at those block letters which didn't erase perfectly. They indicate the two streets that form a corner where this store is located. Get me a directory, Silk. Hurry!"

Silk procured one. Quinn riffled the pages, found the street section and then slowly leaned back in his chair.

THIS," he said, "is a map of the interior and exterior of a jewelry store owned and operated by a man named Robert Gill. I know the place. Its amount and quality of business is on a par with that of Harriman's and Graham's. Silk, we've got to get busy. Gill's is the next place slated to be robbed. Put on one of your disguises, and hurry. Then get Butch's coupé and wait for me near the gate." Within fifteen minutes, the Bat was driving the coupé toward Gill's store. Silk looked puzzled.

"What good is a floor plan," he asked, "that doesn't show those crooks how to bust in a vault? And another thing—there must be somebody you suspect."

"I don't know exactly what those floor plans mean," the Bat admitted, "but I'm going to find out. About suspects—there are several in my mind. Harriman, of course, may not be dead and may be working undercover. I have to think that. Then there is a man named Wohl, who was Graham's gem expert. He and McFayden, Graham's chief clerk, were the men who came into the store when I was there. McFayden acted suspiciously and I don't trust him. He tricked me, sent in an alarm after he'd practically promised not to interfere. Perhaps I was questioning him too closely. When I pretended to leave, he made definite statements that indicate he doesn't particularly like the Bat."

With the hood over his shoulders, the Bat sent his coupé across town, down an avenue and finally they saw the store owned by Gill, the jeweler. It was an imposing place. Steel curtains were drawn down inside the windows and undoubtedly every modern alarm device was in use.

As the Bat slowed and rolled to the curb half a block away, lights suddenly flashed on in the store. At the same instant the burglar gong on the wall outside began to clang. Sirens whined. Radio cars were coming in all directions.

"There was another alarm flashed through," the Bat whispered. "Someone must have tripped a ray and put in an automatic call to the police."

"Look!" Silk pointed to the main entrance of the store. "There's a guy coming out."

"Gill!" the Bat said explosively. "I've seen his picture in the papers often. Silk, we're trapped! The radio cars have sealed up all side streets and the main thoroughfare. If we try to get clear now, they'll stop us for investigation. They'll strip this hood from my head. Even if I take it off right now myself, somebody is bound to recognize these scars—and won't that make Sergeant McGrath happy."

"What'll we do?" Silk cried anxiously.

"Duck! Make it seem this car is empty. They'll pay all their attention to Gill for a few minutes and—Gosh, Silk, we're sunk! Here comes McGrath in his squad car. Must have picked him up by radio."

Sergeant McGrath was coming hell-bent. Brakes and tires squealed in unified protest as he stopped the heavy squad car. He was out of it in a flash. Silk placed a hand lightly on Bat's arm.

"Listen, Boss, it's the only way. I'll swipe McGrath's car and make a run for it. They'll chase me, but that bus of his looks like it could run rings around them radio cars. The side streets will open up and you can make a break for it."

"Good man, Silk." The Bat nodded. His hand dipped into his pocket and he handed Silk a sticker, fashioned after the likeness of a bat. "You'll make it all right. Plant that sticker on the windshield when you abandon the car. That will prevent McGrath from blowing anyone else for the theft. Keep your head down. They'll probably open fire."

SILK slipped out of the coupé, made a wild dive toward the building shadows and then sidled half a block down the street. True to the Bat's theory, all police were clustered around the excited jeweler. Silk darted across the road and leaped into the detective's cruiser. The motor was still humming. He released the brake, slid low behind the wheel and tramped hard on the gas pedal.

McGrath was the first to notice the theft of his car. He shouted a warning. Radio cars started after the cruiser. McGrath clung to one and began emptying his gun at the fleeing squad car. But Silk knew how to handle a car. He raced around corners, doubled back down avenues and finally pointed the nose of the cruiser for the outskirts.

No one noticed the dilapidated coupé that slowly pulled away from the curb and vanished into the night.

CHAPTER X
TORTURE FOR SILK

OOLLY Silk glanced up in the rearview mirror and grinned. All signs of pursuit had gone. He was alone and streaking down a highway miles from the city.

But was he?

As Silk swept around a hairpin turn, lights suddenly flashed for a second in the mirror. Silk tensed. He was being followed—and by a car being driven without lights. They had been turned on momentarily, as the driver rounded the curve.

Police wouldn't do that. They would have opened fire if they were as close to the stolen police car as this mystery car was.

Silk felt a hollow sensation in the pit of his stomach. Was it possible that the burglars who had been in Gill's store had watched Silk steal McGrath's car and were following it? Had they also noticed that the Bat had made good his escape—and thought now they were on his trail?

Silk estimated his chances for escape from the pursuers and realized they were few. The car behind him was as fast as Sergeant McGrath's cruiser and once the men in it opened fire the chase would end abruptly. If that did happen, Silk had to let the Bat know what had occurred. He fumbled in his pocket and found a piece of paper and a pencil.

Placing the paper on one knee he scrawled a brief message while he piloted the speeding car with the other hand. Then he jerked open the glove compartment in the dashboard. There were several envelopes inside, used by McGrath to file his reports. Silk addressed one—not to Tony Quinn, for that would have been too dangerous—but to Carol Baldwin.

This done he suddenly eased up on the gas pedal and the pursuing car gained on him so rapidly that Silk could almost make out the marker plates. Silk determined on a bold move. He stepped on the gas again and pulled away, for the pursuing car had slowed considerably to avoid crashing.

Suddenly Silk yanked the wheel and sent his car careening off the highway. The pursuers flashed by and brakes began to squeal. But Silk had seen the marker plate. He hastily made note of it on the letter.

Then he backed around and headed toward the city.

All hope of escape was gone now for those men who were following him would start shooting at any minute. Silk sealed the envelope, fastened a one dollar bill to a small portion of the flap and kept his eyes on the highway until he saw a rural free delivery box ahead of him. Abruptly he slowed, stopped beside the box and thrust the envelope and dollar bill inside. He had already hastily written instructions to forward it special delivery. All he could hope for now was that the letter would be picked up in time to give Carol an opportunity to warn Tony Quinn of his danger.

As he pulled away from the mailbox, the pursuing car was sweeping down on him. But he was certain they had not seen him mail that letter.

He eased up on the gas pedal, pulled well over and waited for the pursuing car to pass. It drew abreast and Silk saw the snout of a tommy gun covering him.

"Stop!" a hoarse voice yelled. "Stop or you'll fill yourself full of steel jackets!"

Silk groaned and clamped his foot on the brake. The windows of the cruiser were shatter proof, but steel-jacketed machine gun slugs would smack straight through. Trying to run for it would be suicidal and they would catch him sooner or later anyway. Silk stopped the car, got out and raised his hands shoulder high.

HE was thankful that he was in disguise. Two men covered him and one gestured with the muzzle of his gun for Silk to step into their sedan. He obeyed. The police cruiser was left where he had parked it and the sedan headed back toward the city.

"You've made a mistake, gentlemen," Silk said uneasily. "If—if you're kidnapping me, I won't be a profitable undertaking."

"Maybe," one of the men grunted. "But you will be profitable for an undertaker if you don't talk. We saw you swipe that cop's car. What was the big idea? But don't bother to talk now. Just lift your mitts nice and high while I give you a frisk."

Silk was searched thoroughly, but not until his captor encountered the small Bat sticker did Silk really lose hope. As the thug brought this out his eyes flashed and for a moment a wave of fear came over him. Then, remembering the gun he held and that two other armed men were with him, his confidence came back.

"The Black Bat!" he snarled, and the gun jabbed Silk harder.

"The Bat?"

The man at Silk's left gaped. The driver swerved the car crazily for a second as he squirmed around in the seat for a quick look.

"It's him all right," the leader of the trio grunted. "Man, won't the boys be glad to see him!"

Silk remained silent. He knew that adopting Tony Quinn's identity was tantamount to swift death, but the Bat needed time to get organized. Silk was narrowly watched now, but he was alert also, taking in every detail of the route to his destination,

The sedan entered the outskirts of the city, rolled down a quiet avenue and as the first streaks of dawn broke over the towering buildings, the car nosed into an alley and stopped beside a loading platform. A gray hearse was parked beside the sedan. Silk shivered. This was getting just a little too close to the ultimate finish.

"Get out!" he was harshly ordered. "Keep your hands way up. The first phony move means a belly full of slugs."

They pushed him up the four steps of the loading platform. A sliding door opened and he was shoved inside. The hearse belonged here, all right. Silk was a prisoner in an undertaker's place of business.

A tall, wide-shouldered man with a narrow, sleek mustache listened to the report of his underlings and jerked his head toward Silk as the Bat's name was mentioned, He took the seal of the Bat and waved it under Silk's nose.

"So *you're* The Bat. I expected a powerful man, an intelligent-looking man—not a rummy heel like you."

"That's good," Silk breathed in relief, "Because I don't know who this Bat guy is. Sure I swiped the bus, but I didn't know it was a cop's car. I was casing the Gill Jewelry place—getting set to make a play for the stuff in the window when the alarm system goes off. I figured if I was caught, they might say I was the one that had busted in, so I grabbed that police bus and beat it. I found that funny looking sticker on the seat and shoved it in my pocket. I'm a right guy and if you boys made a mistake, I ain't the kind to hold it in for you."

THE tall man grinned crookedly. He had black eyes that looked sinister to Silk and his lips were thick. Otherwise his features were regular, almost handsome. Silk had seen him somewhere. He was certain of it, but recognition refused to come.

"Now listen," this man told Silk, "you're going to talk. If you want to save yourself time and a lot of unpleastness, you can either admit you are the Bat now—or tell me just who he is."

"I'm dumber than a clam," Silk said. "Because I don't know what the devil you're talking about."

The tall man scowled. He lashed out and the back of his hand struck Silk across the mouth. Then the man walked over to a telephone and dialed a number. At a signal, one of Silk's captors stepped behind him and pressed his palms against Silk's ears. The man at the phone asked for someone and apparently didn't reach his party, for he hung up at once.

Five minutes crept by and the phone rang. This time Silk was permitted to listen.

"Chief," the tall man said, "this is Blackie. We got a guy down here who we think is either the Bat or somebody who helps him. He's a thin guy, about five feet six or seven. His hands are skinny, too, and he don't look like so much."

Blackie listened for a few moments and then said: "Okay. We'll find out what he knows. Can we make him talk? Listen—I know ways that would make the mummy of Tut-ankh-Amen squeal. I'll let you know when he sings."

Blackie rose from the chair behind the desk and approached Silk. He put his hands on his hips and surveyed the prisoner contemptuously.

"I've an idea," he said slowly, "that you might be a stubborn fool, so just to save time I'll give you a sample of what's in store for you unless we hear all you know. Boys, put him on that slab and strap him down."

Silk managed to get in one husky punch against the eye of the thug nearest him before they pounced down, lifted him up and deposited him on a long table used in embalming work. Straps pinned him firmly to the table. Blackie picked up a scalpel and fingered it.

He pulled up Silk's trouser leg and made a deft incision. Silk bit his lower lip. Not that it hurt—so far. There was hardly any pain from that sharp blade. Then Blackie took a blunt object that looked like a piece of dark crayon. He suddenly rubbed the point of it against the open wound on Silk's leg.

Instantly a flash that felt like a bolt of lightning shot through Silk's body. Blackie kept on rubbing the object and Silk's senses spun crazily. He never believed anything could involve such excruciating agony. Sweat poured down his face, turned his face gray under the disguise, and made his mouth go dry from sudden fever induced by the pain.

"And that," Blackie grunted in high satisfaction, "is a sample of what's to come. That dark stuff is silver nitrate and if it hurts a little just chalk that up to modern medicine, because the stuff also sterilizes the wounds. You won't die of poisoning—but you might die of shock induced by pain. Maybe it would be wise if you told me who the Bat is?"

"Maybe," Silk said through clenched teeth. "But I can't tell you something I don't know."

AGAIN the knife cut deeply into Silk's leg and once more the silver nitrate seared through the wound until Silk's senses reeled. His tense body relaxed, his head fell back and he surrendered to blissful unconsciousness.

"Wake up!" Blackie slapped him hard. "Wake up!"

Silk opened his eyes. "The beauty of this treatment," Blackie went on maliciously, "is that when one leg goes numb we still have the other. Then, the arms. It will take many hours before you finally die. Let's have it, you dope. You're not the Bat because he's a bigger man than you. But you know who the Bat is—and I'm going to find out. Do you tell me? Or shall I cauterize another little incision?"

"Go—to—hell!" Silk mumbled through parched lips.

He braced himself for another gouging with the silver nitrate pencil. But as Blackie bent over Silk, the light struck him and something clicked in Silk's mind. He knew who this man was. What good that knowledge would do him had become problematical, but Silk had not given up hope yet.

Two minutes later he lapsed into unconsciousness once more and all Blackie's slapping could not bring him back to his senses. Blackie shrugged and turned away.

"We'll wait until he wakes up. Anyway I've got to get busy. You boys watch him. If he gets away, I'll give you a taste of that silver nitrate stuff."

CHAPTER XI
THE TIPOFF

 ASILY the Bat made his escape from the police lines, for Silk had drawn practically every car away. He drove to the street where Butch lived, parked the car and gave Butch a covert signal. Ten minutes later, the Bat was in his laboratory, peeling off his hood and clothing to become blind Tony Quinn once more.

An hour passed and no word from Silk. Quinn grew nervous, although none of it showed in his placid features as he sat before the fireplace. Quinn took no chances, even when he was home, and supposedly alone. There might be others besides Sergeant McGrath who were suspicious. So if anyone peered through the windows of Tony Quinn's home, they saw only a blind man, idling time away by living in his thoughts.

At five-thirty there was still no sign of Silk, and Tony Quinn had to act. He arose, tapped his cane slowly and made his way into the reception hall. Here no one could see him from the windows. He picked up the phone and dialed a number. The voice that answered was wide awake and crisp.

Carol Baldwin even put some of her personal beauty into her words. She was Tony Quinn's dream of feminine perfection come true. She, alone, had given him back his sight and restored his peace of mind. Her own father had been shot by a criminal. The bullet had lodged in his brain, blinding him by severing nerves. It was the healthy corneas from his eyes that had been transplanted in Tony Quinn's. And her father's dying wish had been that she in some way ally herself with forces that opposed crime. For this reason she had become Tony Quinn's capable and trusted assistant.

"Can you come over?" Quinn asked. "It's important. Drop by and pick up Butch. I'll wait for you—in the lab. Use the entrance and be careful you aren't seen."

"Has something happened, Tony?" she asked anxiously.

"Yes—it's Silk. I'll explain when you come. Hurry!"

During the thirty minutes that elapsed before the arrival of Carol and Butch, Tony Quinn grew more and more worried. If Silk had been caught by the police, Sergeant McGrath would have been on the job long before now. And Silk had got away to too good a start on the police cars to be caught. There was something else and it could mean but one thing. Some clever crooks—in all likelihood the same who had been attempting to rob the Gill jewelry store, had observed Silk steal McGrath's car and had followed him. They must have had good reason for that, also—had probably in some way identified him with the Bat. Just how, he could not guess, unless the crooks had caught a glimpse of the Bat's black costume, and then seeing Silk escaping had leaped to the conclusion that he was the Bat, and had discarded his black hood in order to escape. Even if they did not believe Silk was the Bat, once they had caught him, Silk had that Black Bat sticker and if it should be discovered, he would be subjected to all manner of ways and means to make him talk. Criminals, the entire underworld, would give a good deal to lay their hands on their enemy, the Bat.

CAROL entered through the secret door. Butch closed it as he stepped into the room. Quinn took both Carol's extended hands.

"Silk has disappeared," he said swiftly. "I don't know what happened, but if he was making some kind of an investigation, he'd have called back by now. Somebody's got him—that's the only answer—and we must rescue him."

He turned his head and spoke to the hulking man.

"Butch, the only work for you at the moment is to prowl around the underworld. Visit the bars and other hangouts. Try to learn something about a crook named Blackie—a rather tall man whose most outstanding feature is his waxed mustache. Also listen and see if you hear any undue talk about the Black Bat."

"I'm on my way."

Butch nodded and vanished through the hidden door. Carol sat down while Tony Quinn paced the floor nervously.

"I'm worried, Carol," he said presently. "Silk is invaluable to our organization, besides being one of my best friends. If I only knew where to begin. But I haven't the least idea how to start. His disappearance is of course mixed up with these jewel robberies, but just who has been getting away with those millions of dollars' worth of gems—"

"There are no suspects?" Carol asked.

"Suspects! Oh, yes—but nothing definite. Graham's store, as you know, was robbed of gems worth millions. Harriman's place was also looted, and something happened at Gill's place only a short time ago. Graham is dead. So is Harriman—as far as anybody knows. Yet there hasn't been any clue as to who actually got away with those gems—if those two men did or not—or where the gems are right now."

"Tony," Carol said tensly, "suppose I make the rounds of those three jewelry stores? I'll be a hard customer to please and stay one as long as possible. Perhaps I'll learn something. The chance is small but unless you have something definite to work on, I think we should risk it."

Tony Quinn nodded, "The stores will open for business very soon now. If you learn anything, no matter how meager, let me know. And be very careful, Carol. The brains behind this business belong to an exceptional man. He'll be suspicious and wary. The slightest slip will mean death."

She pressed his hand, smiled at him and left.

The silence of early dawn settled on the house after Carol left. But sleep was out of the question for Tony Quinn, weary as he was after the strenuous night just past. Silk was in jeopardy and there seemed to be no way of helping him. He might even be dead!

Tony Quinn's expression never changed, but deep within his breast a spark of hatred fanned itself into active flames—hatred for the men who might have harmed Silk Kirby.

Butch phoned in twice, with nothing to report. At ten-thirty Carol called.

"IT'S worked out wonderfully," she said. "I visited Graham's store first. I'm not sure what happened there, but someone else is taking over the business. I overheard clerks talking about Graham's secretary, the one who saw him commit suicide. They said that she had quit—refused to return because of the terrible thing she witnessed.

"I rushed home and changed my clothing and my appearance slightly. From a porter in the building, I learned the name of the ex-secretary. I went back to the store, told some smirking man named McFayden that I was a close friend of this girl and that I wanted the job she was throwing up. I had some references with me—you know the ones you fixed up for me to use whenever I needed them. And I got the job, too! Almost instantly, because they needed someone immediately. This McFayden seems to be in temporary charge and it wasn't difficult to convince him. Tony—I think he rather likes me."

"Which is one more reason why I'll punch him in the nose sooner or later," Quinn laughed tightly. "Good work, Carol, but watch yourself. That may be a nest of murder you're sticking your fair head into."

She laughed gaily and hung up. Quinn returned to his chair in front of the fireplace and sat down, cursing his helplessness. As a blind man he couldn't stalk the underworld—could not even show his face outside the door of his own home except to stumble along in his pretense of being blind. He couldn't visit such people as McGrath, or the police commissioner, or anyone actively connected with the jewelry firms. Tony Quinn was not supposed to be interested in such things. He was supposed to be a disillusioned, bitter young man whose affliction had made him practically a hermit.

"Police Commissioner Warner," Tony Quinn

muttered. "1 could bring him here. He might know something, Damn it, I can't just sit here like a fool doing nothing."

He got up and walked to the telephone. The commissioner was instantly available to Tony Quinn. Half an hour later he arrived. Quinn let him in, apologizing for Silk's absence.

"I wanted to see you about last night's episode," he told Warner. "You understand, I hope, that I am not a coward, but being blind and unable to help myself much, I feel that perhaps those men might try to kill me again. Also I think I know why those two attempts were made."

Warner sat down, lit a cigar and applied his lighter to Quinn's unlighted cigarette.

"I'll post a twenty-four hour guard if you wish. But I suppose you wouldn't want that. I can see it in your face. Just tell me why you think they tried to murder you. Perhaps I will get some clue to start the ball rolling."

"Suppose the thieves trailed Harriman here— you remember he came to see me to discuss a legal question shortly before his auto accident—and believed he had told me much more than he really did," Quinn said. "They insured his silence with death and want to take the same means to keep my lips sealed."

WARNER sighed. "It sounds logical enough, but I'm not sure that Harriman really is dead, Quinn. It may be that he himself is the one who reasons you know too much; that he inadvertently told you more than he meant to, although perhaps you haven't realized that fact yet. Oh, damn it, Tony, I'd give my last dollar if you were back as D.A. Your brains turned the trick in cases as difficult as this one.

"And I've further news for you. I'm telling you all this, Tony, because it is my opinion that a fine legal mind is going to seed in your skull. You think that because you are blind you are unable to help at all. That's not true. Not so many weeks ago you helped tremendously in running down a mob of killers just by reasoning things out. I want that same kind of help in this case."

"I'll do what I can." Tony Quinn's tone did not show much enthusiasm. "Have there been any more developments?"

"Several very significant ones. First of all a jeweler named Gill—you probably recognize the name and know he is as prominent as the other two—is involved. When the news broke about Graham and Harriman, Gill got excited and examined all the stock in his store. He had his expert, some Italian named Professor DiNonno, go over the stuff, too, They were convinced every bit of jewelry in the store was the real thing.

"Then, just before dawn this morning, Gill went to the store. He was still worried, and couldn't sleep. He opened the vault—and found that three-quarters of his stock had changed into paste overnight. It was the McCoy when he put it in the vault at six o'clock and at four the next morning it was phony paste. This whole business smacks of the supernatural."

"And the other complication?" Quinn asked quietly.

"Did you ever hear of a wealthy man named Van den Killan? He's Dutch and rich as Croesus. Anyway, Van den Killan has always been deeply interested in gems. Now he comes into the open, and buys up the three largest businesses in the country. Yesterday he purchased Graham's business, and Harriman's, and this morning he bought out Gill."

"But how on Earth—" Quinn began.

Warner laid a firm hand on Quinn's knee.

"I know just what you're thinking. How could one man possibly have enough cash to buy three concerns like that? Frankly, it required little cash because the stocks were so badly depleted that the value of each firm lay mainly in its name. Gill had to sell out because he was on the verge of bankruptcy. The heirs of Graham and Harriman wanted to have the businesses liquidated—immediately—and pulled strings to get the probate court to agree, because if they didn't there just wouldn't bc any estates."

Quinn mulled that over for a moment. "Then Van den Killan, from all appearances, had the best motive of anyone for looting those stores. He has entered the jewelry business and at the same time has eliminated his stiff competitors."

Warner sighed. "Just what I figured. But listen here, Tony, we can't be saying anything like that. Van den Killan is an important man. He's been decorated by several governments. His wealth is so great that it looks as if his going after more money is downright foolishness. What's more, now he'll be in the millionaire income group and have more taken away from him in taxes than this added burden warrants. I agree that some people can't seem to get enough money, but Van den Killan is different. He's given large sums to charity, he doesn't live like an emperor and his reputation for honesty is something to contend with."

TONY QUINN shook his head thoughtfully. "Those gems are somewhere. You're certain they haven't been marketed?"

"I'm not certain of anything except that Graham is dead. And certain of that only because I've seen his dead body. But those stones haven't been sold openly. The F.B.I. is helping us and they have covered the whole country. No, Tony, those gems are being held somewhere for the opportune moment when they can be turned into cash. That's a fairly simple deduction. What actually gets me is how on Earth they vanish."

"Have you examined the vaults?" Quinn asked.

"Examined them? Humph! We practically tore Harriman's vault apart. Graham's was bigger, but we went over it carefully enough. Gill's vault hasn't been examined yet. What mystifies me most of all is that the substitute phony gems meet the specifications of the originals as to weight, cutting and color. Only an expert could tell the difference.

"What's more, everybody who has heard or read of these crazy cases is having his own gems examined, which brings us to another new complication. So far well over a million dollars' worth of stones, in the hands of people who bought them from either Graham, Harriman or Gill, have turned into paste. It's incredible."

"It is," Tony Quinn admitted. "The most amazing thing I've ever heard of. Sounds almost as though there might be some new scientific device for turning real gems into paste. There you would have your perfect solution. And Van den Killan would possess the only strong motive."

"I've even thought of that," Warner groaned. "But I can't feature any man destroying almost ten million dollars' worth of jewels just so he can take over three important jewelry stores. Unless"— Warner drew a sharp breath. "Do you suppose such a thing could exist and, perhaps, another device to turn the paste gems into the real ones?"

"That's much too wild a conclusion to grasp at, Commissioner. Give me a few hours to concentrate on the subject. I might think of something."

Warner arose. "Thanks, Tony. I need your help. In fact, if I knew who this Black Bat was or how to reach him I'd beg him to give us a hand. Outlaw he may be, but that man is clever."

Tony Quinn's lips parted in a wan smile as he shook hands with the commissioner. "Now you're talking like Sergeant McGrath, Commissioner."

"I know," Warner replied. "It's foolish of me, but I can't help expressing a hope, can I? If you weren't blind... Oh, let's forget it! You aren't the Bat and he wouldn't be apt to help anyway. Phone me if you think of anything, Tony, and if you desire a guard, I'll post one when you say the word."

CHAPTER XII
THE BAT MOVES IN

FOR ten minutes after Warner left, Tony Quinn sat before the fireplace. His fingers were curled into fists and he methodically beat the arms of his chair. Silk was still unheard from! No clues had developed as to his whereabouts, and now the matter of the disappear-

ing jewels had become more complex than ever.

"I've got to get out!" Tony Quinn told himself over and over again, "I've got to do something before I go mad. There must be some way that I can operate without being recognized. Silk can do it."

Suddenly he leaped to his feet. Silk was in disguise. Silk Kirby could always take on a new personality without undue trouble. Then why couldn't Tony Quinn?

He headed for Silk's room, but halfway across the hall he hesitated and sighed. Silk wasn't scarred from deep-burning acid. All he had to do was cover his face with makeup and saunter out.

"Just the same," Tony Quinn said savagely, "I'm going to give it a try."

He rushed to Silk's room, found the flat makeup kit and hurried back to his laboratory. There, under powerful light, Tony Quinn began work. He knew a great deal about the art of disguise, for that subject came under his studies of crime and criminology.

He regarded his deeply scarred features in front of a mirror. Deftly he experimented with the creams and flesh tints. He filled in the scars on his face, burned deep by powerful acid, brushed over the waxy preparation that now concealed them and surveyed the result with considerable satisfaction. Next he used two aluminum cylinders that fitted snugly inside his nostrils. They broadened the shape of his nose, made him look entirely different.

EVEN his chestnut hair became jet black under the influence of a chemical. Within twenty minutes, Tony Quinn had vanished and an utter stranger looked back at him from the depths of the mirror. Now he could venture forth and work without fear of someone detecting the scarred face of blind Tony Quinn! His spirits soared, for now the Bat could work without a telltale hood.

The phone rang. Carol's voice was clipped and worried.

"Tony, I returned to my apartment during lunch hour and found a letter from Silk there. I'll read it to you."

Hurriedly she did. It read:

Car following. Looks like snatch or bump. Marker plates on car MA4975. Will stall as long as possible.

Quinn made a note of the numbers. "Good, Carol," he said tightly. "If that car isn't stolen we'll have a clue. Return to work and watch yourself. If I find Silk and rescue him, someone at the store may think you tipped me off. You're new and they're bound to figure you as a plant if anything happens that they can't account for."

"Tony, do you really believe someone at the store is responsible for these crimes?" Carol asked breathlessly.

"I do," Quinn said, "so watch out."

"Tony—" Carol's voice grew soft and warm. "Tony, be careful. Don't take too many chances—please."

"Don't worry about me," he told her. He hung up and hesitated a moment. He wanted to find out in whose name that car was registered, but dared not use the phones in his house.

Working swiftly, he changed his clothes and donned a light gray suit. He examined his disguise once more, made certain there was no danger of any part slipping or fading away. Then he stuffed his black silk hood into a pocket, stowed a gun in a shoulder clip and supplied himself with several Black Bat stickers.

He used the secret means of leaving his house, after first locking up securely. He drove for downtown, entered a crowded drugstore and took no pains to conceal his features. It was a rather novel thing, this openly flaunting those who looked for the Bat. Tony Quinn liked it.

"This," he told the Motor Vehicle Department clerk he got on the wire, "is Sergeant McGrath of Police. Headquarters. I want the name and location of a marker numbered "M-A-four-nine-seven-five."

"The owner, Sergeant," the man told him after a moment's wait, is listed as Oliver Beam, an undertaker, at one–nine-O-nine Boulevard Drive."

Quinn hung up, returned to his car and drove it to within five blocks of the address just given him. There he got out, patted the comforting weight of his gun and was grateful that darkness had again set in. He walked directly past the undertaking parlors.

SILK KIRBY no longer possessed much feeling in his legs. Half a dozen incisions cauterized by the silver nitrate pencil had paralyzed the nerves. But now Blackie was ready to start work on Silk's arms.

"Don't be such a martyr," he told Silk. "Why not tell us who this Black Bat is? Why not save your own skin? We could use a guy like you in this outfit. You've got guts."

Silk managed a grin, but there was no mirth in it.

"Sure. You'd use me to fill up one of them caskets. Go ahead, Blackie, I'm a better man than you are. I'll never talk."

Silk had abandoned the idea of convincing these men that he knew nothing. They were positive that he did. Blackie shrugged and reached for the scalpel. Silk shut his eyes tightly and held his breath. He wouldn't be able to stand many more of these sessions, but hope was still high in his heart—and so was faith in the Bat. Sometimes the Bat could work wonders. If it was humanly possible, the Bat would be at work now, closing in gradually.

He felt the scalpel rest lightly against his forearm. Then one of the gang called out.

"Blackie—guy on the phone for you."

Blackie hurried into the next room, but Silk could hear his voice.

"No. I've given him the works but he's tongue-tied. Sure I can make him squawk, but it'll take time. Listen: this Black Bat is smarter than you think. If he's working on this case, we've got to find out who he is before he gets to us. I'm warning you, I'd rather have every cop and G-Man in the country on my heels than this Black Bat. He's not human."

There was a significant pause for a moment and then Blackie gave a sigh of resignation.

"Sure, I know you're in charge. Okay. I won't fool around any longer. We'll kill him and bury him somewhere. I still think it's a mistake, but what you say goes."

Blackie hung up, returned to stand beside Silk and picked up the scalpel once more.

"It's the finish, sucker. Orders are orders and you're slated for a nice quick burial. The only way to save yourself is by talking. What's the word?"

"You know I won't talk," Silk said calmly. "Get it over with."

Blackie fingered the scalpel and drew down the corners of his mouth. He poised the surgical instrument above Silk's throat and got himself set for the death thrust.

He heard a commotion behind him and turned. One of his men stood in the doorway—with a knife in his throat! He seemed to be supported by some invisible strings, for plainly he was dead. Strangled cries came from the throats of the two thugs watching Blackie. He turned deathly pale and dropped the scalpel.

For the dead member of his outfit wore a brand. The brand of the Bat! The silhouetted image of a bat was pasted squarely in the center of his forehead!

"The Bat!" Blackie yelled.

"Look out!" Silk screamed a warning, "There are three of 'em in here."

BLACKIE scurried to the table and smashed a hard blow against Silk's jaw. Then he did one of the most foolish things in his life, though he had no idea of that. He swept the single lamp in the room off the table, smashing it. The room was plunged in a darkness that neither Blackie nor his two aides could penetrate.

But there was one present who could. The Bat saw the three men, poised with guns, ready to open fire. He smiled a little and picked up a folding chair, one of the kind commonly used by undertakers. Raising it above his head he hurled it straight at the trio.

One man went down. Another fired wildly at

the door. Only Blackie retained any measure of calmness. He decided this was no place for him.

Quietly he edged back until he reached the rear door. Once he aimed his gun at the shadow that was Silk on the long table, but changed his mind about squeezing the trigger. The Bat might open fire too, shooting at the streak of flame Blackie's gun was bound to make.

Instead, Blackie turned the key in the door, quietly pulled it out and opened the door far enough to insert it in the outer side of the lock. Then he stepped out, closed and locked the door and ran for it. His two men inside would keep the Bat busy. If they were killed, that was their tough luck.

The two men trapped in the room realized that they had been tricked. One was on the floor, half conscious. The other backed into a corner. He saw something like a dark blob of shadow move into the room and he snapped a single shot. Before he could shoot again, the dark blob took rapid shape and came hurtling toward him. A hard fist exploded against his jaw and he went down.

The other thug reeled to his feet and the Bat felled him again with a single blow. He knelt beside the two men, pasted his insignia upon their foreheads and then took time to scribble a brief note with gloved hands. He thrust it under one thug's vest, leaving half of the note exposed. Then he hurried to the table, unstrapped Silk and carefully drew him over one shoulder.

The shooting was certain to bring police and he had to get away quickly. Moving like a ghost, the Bat approached the front door. Escape through the rear was impossible, for Blackie had locked that door.

Distantly the Bat heard a siren. He hurried into the deserted street and by using alleys and courtyards reached his parked car unobserved.

But the sirens were moaning nearer and in numbers now and he knew all cars would be stopped. The Bat opened the baggage compartment of the coupé, gently tucked Silk inside and then removed his hood. He stowed this in Silk's pocket, unstrapped his shoulder clip, and hid gun and clip

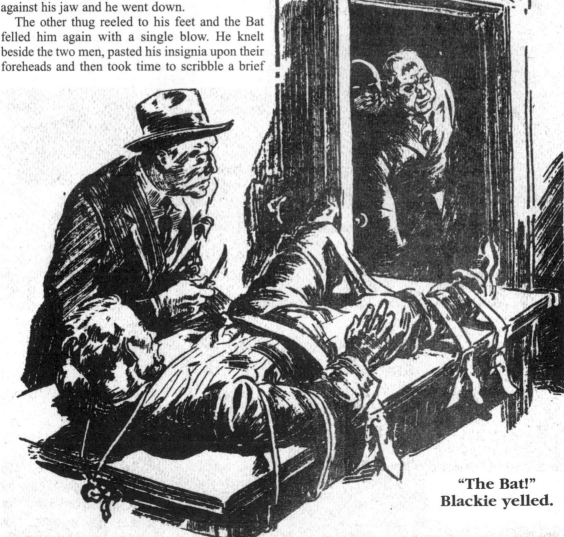

"The Bat!"
Blackie yelled.

behind the front seat of the coupé. He drew on a neat gray felt hat, got behind the wheel and drove sedately down the street past the house from which he had just escaped.

A patrolman held up his hand. Tony Quinn stopped and stuck his head out of the window. A detective cruiser howled up. Sergeant McGrath came striding toward the car.

"How long you been here?" he demanded.

Tony Quinn took a long shot. His usually well modulated voice took on a high-pitched, excited tone.

"Just driving through, Officer. I dunno what all this racket is about."

SERGEANT McGRATH turned a flashlight full on Tony Quinn's disguised features. He wasn't particularly impressed by the wide-faced stranger in the car, nor did he pay much attention to him.

"Beat it!" He waved Quinn on. "And fast. There's liable to be some shooting." He jerked around to one of the patrolmen. "You sure those mugs you found in that place had the Bat's

weakly. "But man, you didn't come too soon. They were set to slit my throat. Hey, what the devil? Who are you?"

Silk had taken it for granted that this man beside him was Tony Quinn, but as his vision cleared, he saw an utter stranger at the wheel.

Tony Quinn laughed. "Like it, Silk? I used your disguise kit. For a first attempt it isn't bad."

Silk relaxed. "Oh, boy, did you scare me! Good? It's perfect? You don't need any lessons, Boss?"

"As you said," Quinn remarked, "1 did come just in time. Things have developed, Silk. Developed to a point where there are a couple of very good suspects in our gem robbing with which your recent little playmates are tied up somehow. Up to now our murderous, thieving friends have had their own way, but from now on I'm taking the aggressive. They'll know just how much I mean business when they see that thug I had to kill. He saw me slip into the undertaking parlors and came at me with his knife. I was forced to get to him first."

"Boss!" Silk raised his head quickly. "I found something, too. Listen—did you get a dark-haired

signature pasted on their heads? Let's go!"

Tony Quinn drove rapidly out of the danger zone, pulled up on a quiet street and fished Silk out of the baggage compartment. Silk was still dazed and extremely weak from the siege of pain inspired from Blackie's sadistic impulses.

"I knew you'd show up, Boss." Silk grinned

guy with a big mouth and thick lips? Dressed like a dude?"

"He got away," Quinn answered. "A rat, if there ever was one. Left his pals to shift for themselves. Do you know him, Silk?"

"Do I know him?" Silk sighed. "That was Blackie Burns—the slickest jewel thief in the world! He works on only big stuff, Boss. That guy has swiped more rocks than any man alive. I can't figure him now, though. Usually he works solo and takes all the profits for himself, but now he takes orders from some other guy. I heard him talking to the big boy over the phone."

"I know Blackie, too. He is the man who took me for a ride that ended in a cavern. Perhaps"—Quinn's eyes narrowed—"Blackie is in on the deal only long enough to gain the confidence of the real leader. Then Blackie means to perform his little solo act. We can't be sure of that, but it's possible—and must be taken into consideration. I'll drop you near the east gate, Silk. After I park the car near Butch's, I'll come back and help you inside."

Quinn looked at Silk's swollen, discolored legs and muttered an imprecation.

"I hope Blackie and I will meet again—*soon*. Don't try to walk, Silk. Just lay low until I come back."

CHAPTER XIII
THEFT

 HEN Carol Baldwin returned from lunch that afternoon she found a black-haired, wide-faced stranger seated in her office, McFayden was holding a spirited conversation with the man.

"I tell you, Mr. Gordon," McFayden was saying earnestly, "if you would permit me to examine your necklace, I'm certain I could tell you whether or not it is one of these astoundingly good copies."

"No," Gordon answered and smiled brazenly at Carol. "I insist on seeing Van den Killan. If his experts tell me it's genuine, I'll be satisfied. You are only a clerk. You have admitted as much to me."

McFayden spread his hands in a gesture of despair. "Very well." He glanced at Carol. "Miss Baldwin, will you ask Mr. Killan if he will see Mr. Gordon about a necklace? Priceless, he says. Personally, I wonder."

But Gordon ignored that stab. He only kept on grinning and hardly removed his eyes from Carol. She could almost feel his stare and she was worried. Comparatively unknown in this city and her association with the Bat never suspected, Carol had resorted to only a very slight disguise in obtaining her position. But she was suspicious about this stranger. He looked too fatuously guileless to be true.

She called Van den Killan and sent Gordon into the inner office. The big Hollander greeted him with outstretched hand.

"I am told you have valuable chems, *Mynheer*," he said affably.

"Sure." Gordon removed a plush box from an inner pocket, opened it and carelessly flung a necklace on the desk. "Tell me if I was stuck. I paid two hundred and ten thousand dollars for that baby and she don't look worth it, but the little woman has got to be pleased."

Killan held the glistening string of diamonds to the light and drew a sharp breath.

"To me it looks real. And a lovely piece of work. But my experts, I have three of the best in the whole world. I let them look at it. Wait!"

Wohl came into the office first. He glanced at Gordon and then his eyes fastened on the necklace that Killan held.

"Himmel!" he cried. "Where did that come from?"

The expert who was introduced as Anghis Khan entered next. He wore a fez and sideburns that ran down half the length of his oval face. He was dark-featured and almost slant-eyed, showing traces of Oriental blood. Professor DiNonno proved to be a squat, swarthy Italian. They clustered around the necklace, fighting among themselves over its estimated value. Finally Gordon arose.

"If you men don't mind, I'd like to get this over with. The way you're acting, I think it's one of them phonies floating around town. Go ahead—tell me. I can take it."

ANGHIS KHAN turned and spoke in an Oxford accent.

"But of course it is real, my dear chap. It's worth every cent you paid for it. In fact, it might bring a great deal more. Because of the enormous thefts committed—those of which you have undoubtedly read—this necklace has increased in value about twenty to thirty thousand dollars. Articles like this are now extremely rare!"

"I will pay," Van den Killan stated pompously, "two hundred and fifty thousand dollars—cash. You will sell, *Mynheer?*"

"I will not," Gordon retorted. "I bought that baby for my wife and it's hers. How much do I owe you for giving me the good news?" He drew out a massive handkerchief and wiped his forehead. "Gosh, it would have been a blow at that—paying two hundred and ten thousand for a lot of glass junk."

"Perhaps"—Van den Killan moved toward Gordon and seized his arm—"I should tell my partner about this. Perhaps we can go yet higher. That necklace I must have."

"Partner?" Gordon frowned. "How many of you guys are in this business?"

Van den Killan disappeared for a moment and returned with a middle-aged man in tow. He was introduced to Gordon as Clifford Carlyle and looked much like the popular version of a college professor. He wore glasses suspended from a silken cord around his neck. His vest was white edged and every article of his clothing matched.

Gordon picked up the necklace, put it back in its box and backed up a little as if he were afraid of this congregation of gem experts.

"It is agreed," Van den Killan said, rubbing his hands. "Perhaps we can talk it over tonight, *ja*? At my house—or your hotel? I am prepared to go higher, *Mynheer*. That necklace I must have."

Gordon shrugged carelessly. "You can come see me at nine. I live at the Alexrandria Hotel, but I think you're wasting time, gentlemen. I like this doodad myself."

Gordon closed the office door, walked by Carol Baldwin and then hesitated. He returned to her desk and took a card from his pocket.

"Did anybody ever tell you how beautiful you are?" he asked her and laughed when she turned pink. "No offense meant. Maybe one of those men in there would like my card. And, say, you might look it over yourself, sister. It's got my name and address on it."

He turned away, whistled blithely and vanished out the door. Carol looked at the card contemptuously. Then her fingers felt something on the reverse side. She turned it over and her face really turned red.

Pasted in the center of the opposite side was—a black bat!

AT eight o'clock Tony Quinn, in his disguise of Rex Gordon, had dinner in the grill room at the hotel. He noticed that two waitresses served him. At nine, Hans Van den Killan was announced and sent up to the suite.

Killan sat down and rubbed his face.

"Business always goes better with a drink," he observed. "Permit me to order something, *Mynheer*."

"Gordon" crossed his legs, dug himself deeper into the wide-armed chair he occupied and grinned like a contented kitten. A bottle of rye was sent up and Van den Killan prepared highballs. The man he knew as Gordon drank his slowly.

Then Van den Killan began to talk about what had brought him there. He spoke of the necklace at once, raising the ante, but got only slow shakes of Gordon's head as a reply.

"I don't think you can do any business," the man he called Gordon said finally. "The necklace is over there in my bag. I check out in the morning. Maybe if the little wife don't like it, I'll ship it back and take your offer of twenty thousand more'n I paid for her."

Van den Killan looked sad, but recognized the finality in his host's voice. He arose, shook hands and departed. Tony Quinn, alias Gordon, stepped over to the window and watched the Hollander enter his car and drive away. He smiled thoughtfully and turned back.

The bait had been seized. News of the existence of this rare necklace had probably spread rapidly and without doubt had reached the ears of the man behind this series of bizarre thefts. Perhaps that man *was* Van den Killan, after all. Anyhow, whoever he was, a man as avaricious as the master thief would surely make an attempt to steal the necklace. But he would find a tornado when he tackled Rex Gordon.

Suddenly the lights flickered in an unaccountable manner. All at once Tony Quinn felt a wave of weariness creep over him. He hadn't taken time out for much sleep since Harriman had visited him many hours before, but he shouldn't feel this sleepy.

Abruptly he stiffened with a sharp realization. He had been drugged.

Quinn half staggered toward the table on which Van den Killan's bottle of whiskey still rested. He picked it up, spilled some of it into a glass and tasted the stuff cautiously. There was no taste beyond that of good rye.

Reeling now, Quinn headed to the telephone. He had been tricked beautifully, all right. If he could reach Silk or Butch... or Carol... But Quinn's hand had only touched the telephone when the drug's influence took over his entire system. He dropped to his knees, then quietly fell to the floor where he lay breathing stertorously.

To his befuddled senses, it might have been hours later before Tony Quinn stirred. He was aware of a buzzing sound that was even louder than the ringing in his ears. The phone! Memory came back with a bitter rush. He lurched to the desk and hauled himself to his feet. An anvil chorus beat out its measures in his head.

Silk was on the wire, anxious and distraught. Quinn ordered him to remain at the house. Then he sat down on the bed and gently massaged his temples. A drink of water made him feel a little better. Finally he lifted his suitcase and put it on a chair. Its contents seemed intact when he opened it, and to his amazement the plush jewel case rested in exactly the same position in which he had placed it.

HE opened it and the necklace glistened under the light. Then Quinn applied a magnifying glass to his eye but he did not study the gems. Quinn was no expert in diamonds. But he did carefully examine the clip of the necklace. There should have been a faint scratch on the underside of the snap. It was not there. Not that he expected that it would be, for the necklace had been a lure for this master thief, and apparently he had taken the bait.

"The cleverest act of substitution I've ever heard of," he told himself grimly. "Worked quick, too. They must have made up this replica and stolen into this suite with it while I was under the influence of that sleeping drug. If I was just a man named Gordon who had bought his wife a necklace, I'd be completely fooled and leave the city thinking I still had the original."

Was the brain behind this jewel plot Hans Van den Killan's then? Had he slipped a drug into the whiskey, returned later and made the substitution? Quinn had told the Hollander where the necklace was so that he might properly bait the trap. No one else had heard unless—

Quinn made a quick study of the suite, looking for wires and a microphone, though there seemed little possibility that anyone would have time or opportunity to install one. As he had rather expected he found no trace of one, but realized that if by any long chance there had been one the thief could have removed it easily.

He picked up the bottle of whiskey, corked it and slid it into his pocket. He transferred the contents of the glass, containing a few drops of rye, to a small vial and put this in his bag also. Then he checked out, took a cab to the railroad terminal and vanished in the crowd there. If he was trailed, Quinn knew that those who watched him would be satisfied that he had gone, wholly unaware that he had also been neatly tricked.

Once he felt sure he had outwitted anyone who might possibly be watching his movements, Quinn climbed into a taxi and had himself driven to a busy spot where his old coupé was waiting. He stopped long enough to buy the latest edition on the newsstand, stopped several blocks from his home and read the brief newspaper items that concerned this strange jewel robbery case. Most of the facts he already knew but there was one item indicating that a meeting of police and jewelers was being held at the home of Hans Van den Killan. Quinn's lips compressed in a thin line. There was more work for him.

CHAPTER XIV
THE SMELL OF BLOOD

HANS VAN DEN KILLAN greeted his guests warmly; he seated them in a spacious living room and his servants passed around drinks. Clifford Carlyle, the Hollander's new partner in the former Graham jewelry business was there, offering suggestions for the benefit of Police Commissioner Warner. McFayden lurked in a corner, apart from the others. Wohl, Anghis Khan and Professor DiNonno were arguing heatedly, paying no attention to the other guests. The last to arrive was a man named Fawcett, a jeweler who had requested the privilege of attending.

Commissidner Warner finally arose and spoke quietly.

"Gentlemen, we are here to study this problem that confronts us. During the past few days astounding thefts have been committed and the direct results of them have been suicide, bankruptcy and the loss of

The drug took hold of him.

faith in all jewelry dealers. Men and women who invested large parts of their savings in gems have discovered that they have been tricked.

"Two such people attempted suicide not three hours ago. They were elderly men who dared not risk their superfluous cash in bonds. They bought diamonds and got—cut glass! Customers who have traded with the firms owned by Graham, Harriman and Gill have discovered that their purchases were frauds.

"On the surface it appears that the jewelers deliberately substituted the fakes and took the real gems for their own use. My opinion is that this theory is wrong. I believe that a super-criminal is responsible."

"And so do I." McFayden stepped into the center of the room. "Furthermore I know his identity—as much as anyone does, at least. It's the Black Bat. He was in our store. I saw him with my own eyes. So did Wohl."

Wohl waved his hands excitedly.

"*Ach,* gentlemen, this man called the Bat—he came one night and he talked good sense. For myself I do not believe he is a crook."

Warner sat down slowly.

"Yes," he said. "I know both of you met the Bat. Sergeant McGrath came close to landing him that night. I regret that he did not succeed, for the Bat is a dangerous man and you may be right, Mr. McFayden. But to the business of the evening. We have with us Mr. Fawcett, who is also a jeweler. He insisted that he be allowed to attend. Now we shall hear from him."

Fawcett nodded curtly and walked to the center of the room.

"I own a jewelry shop two blocks from Maiden Lane, as most of you probably know," he said crisply. "I came here mainly to talk about protection and ask your advice as to how I can properly safeguard my goods. This afternoon, I purchased the Bourbon tiara, the crown jewels of Spain's royal family. If they are lost, I am utterly ruined, for every cent I could scrape together is invested in them."

"You put them in a bank, of course?" Warner asked.

Fawcett shook his head. "I didn't have time. They arrived much too late. They are in my office safe and I shall personally guard it until morning."

Warner's gaze centered on Van den Killan's fat face. The Hollander seemed hypnotized by Fawcett's statement. He kept muttering "Bourbon tiara" over and over again.

SUDDENLY Van den Killan's expression changed. His jaw hung slackly down, his eyes were wide and he was licking his thick lips. Clifford Carlyle jumped up and turned pale. McFayden gave a strangled cry. Off in one corner the three gem experts, Wohl, DiNonno and Anghis Khan stared in awe. Warner turned quickly, and drew a startled breath.

Standing before the heavy curtains shrouding the French windows was a broad-shouldered man dressed entirely in deep black. There was a hood over his shoulders and cold eyes flashed through the slits in the mask. He held a gun in each hand.

"Gentlemen"—the Bat bowed ironically—"I am here only to listen and observe. If you will carry on, just as though I were not present—"

"That man's a thief and killer!" McFayden yelped.

He took a step in the direction of the Bat. One of the guns centered on his chest and he stopped, licking his lips and swallowing with difficulty.

"Sit down, McFayden," the Bat said pleasantly. "We're interested in facts tonight, not your stupid suspicions. Commissioner Warner—carry on."

Warner cleared his throat "I suppose there is nothing else I can do. But I warn you, Bat—one of these days you'll be brought to justice."

"For heaven's sake, get it over with," Carlyle shouted irritably. "Do you think I enjoy standing here, facing a masked man with two guns, while you make ineffectual threats, Commissioner?"

Warner shrugged. "Very well. Here are the facts as I know them. Millions of dollars' worth of gems have disappeared and the cleverest replicas ever created have been put in their places. When or how these gems were stolen we don't know. Possibly two dead men might enlighten us, but unfortunately we do not have communication with the spirit world. The fact remains that because of these thefts the value of gems like diamonds, emeralds and rubies has skyrocketed. It means that the thief will profit more than ever if he can sell his stolen goods."

"True!" Hans Van den Killan broke in excitedly. His fat face was flushed. "But we can do nothing. Of course the diamond mines are not operating full blast these days, but they will start again, if we do not recover the stolen chems. It would be fatal to the jewelry business should the diamonds be discovered after the diamond syndicate releases more stones. With rubies and emeralds the danger is not yet so great."

"What about insurance coverage?" the Bat asked calmly.

Warner waved his hand in exasperation. "We can't do anything with it. The companies naturally contest every attempt to collect, maintaining that the gems must have been fakes when they were insured. Can anyone prove they were genuine? How the world could such substitutions be made? I don't blame the companies for holding up payment."

The Bat's eyes flashed around the room.

"I notice a man who is a stranger to me—"

FAWCETT, the jeweler, arose slowly. He was by no means confident that this eerie masked figure wouldn't open fire at any moment.

"My name is Fawcett. I—I'll pay you a thousand dollars to help me. I'll—"

"I don't require fees for my work," the Bat answered. "I heard you tell about the Bourbon tiara. It was foolish of you to advertise your possession of it."

"He'll have protection—plenty of it," Warner snapped. "These depredations are at an end. From now on every jewelry store will be guarded, every suspicious person stopped and questioned. My mission is twofold—to round up the men or man responsible for this gigantic theft, and return to their owners the jewels that have been stolen from them."

Van den Killan caught the Bat's eye. The fat-faced gem fancier still seemed fascinated by Fawcett's tale.

"You—have the Bourbon Tiara," he asked awedly. "The royal chewols? I would half my fortune give to own them."

"We can talk that over later," Fawcett snapped irritably. "Right now I'm afraid. Graham is dead. So is Harriman. Maybe they didn't commit suicide. Maybe they were both murdered! I don't want to be the third man to die. I—I—Oh, why did I ever buy that damned thing anyway?"

All eyes were upon Fawcett. He was pale and shaken. Van den Killan hastened to pour him a glass of brandy. In the commotion, Commissioner Warner was the first to glance at the further end of the room. He caught a sharp breath. The Black Bat was gone.

During the excitement, the Bat had quietly slipped through the French window and vanished into the night. Thirty minutes later Tony Quinn, dressed in baggy tweeds and a smoking jacket, tapped his way across the living room of his own home. Silk, walking with some difficulty, entered with a tray of food.

"Nothing happened while you were away," he reported. "No sign of McGrath. Did you learn anything?"

"That the whole gem industry may be shaken by this series of thefts," Tony Quinn replied. "It's worse than I realized, Silk. And your legs, How are they?"

"Just stiff," Silk replied. "Blackie cut pretty deep, but that silver nitrate he rubbed into the wounds cauterized and sealed them. They're healing fast. I'm ready for action, Boss. Any time you say."

"It may come quickly, Silk. Tonight a jeweler named Fawcett made a blunder. It may prove fatal to him. He admitted buying some particularly valuable gems. When he mentioned the fact before the select audience that heard him, I could almost smell blood."

"You mean—one of them guys that was at that meetin' is the killer?"

"There isn't much doubt about it," Quinn answered wryly. "They all have their reasons. Hans Van den Killan would sell his soul to own the jewels he craves. McFayden is a little rat without morals or conscience. Clifford Carlyle, Van den Killan's partner, is something of a blank space. I can't figure him out. Even Fawcett acted suspiciously in revealing that he owns those gems. Then there is Wohl and Khan and DiNonno. Those men know jewels. They came into contact with most of those stolen. The only thing to be said in their favor is that they have long records for honesty and efficiency here and abroad. I have personally checked that myself."

"IT'S that little squirt McFayden," Silk reasoned. "But there's Blackie, too—somewhere on the outside lookin' in. I don't like the setup. Blackie ain't the kind to work for somebody else. He's a lone wolf and he goes in for big stakes. Never heard of him working with a gang before."

"True," Tony Quinn reasoned, "but Blackie's real identity may not be known to the backers of this crime. They may believe he is nothing but an ordinary gangster looking for easy money. Blackie, you see, might be planning far ahead, laying the groundwork for a coup that will result in his getting all the loot. Or Blackie may have changed his stripes and all this telephoning he does to some superior is faked to deceive his own men.

"We're no nearer the truth now, Silk, than we were at the moment when Harriman came to see me. I laid a trap myself tonight, baited it and had it sprung right in my face. Two years ago I purchased a necklace because I was able to obtain it at a bargain. It was stolen from me tonight and I don't know who took it. Van den Killan is the most logical suspect, but others also knew I had it. All that was left for my trouble is this little souvenir."

Tony Quinn tossed the replica of his diamond necklace on the table. He picked up the phone and called Butch.

"Work for you," he said. "Leave at once and cover the Fawcett Jewelry Store near Maiden Lane. Conceal yourself and watch everyone who even looks in the windows. Take down a description of each person who acts suspiciously. And be ready for action when the store opens in the morning. I may appear in a disguise as a black haired, boy-faced man without these scars. I'll wear a gray suit and hat. Got that?"

"Got it," Butch replied. "Is it okay for me to tell Carol you're safe? She's been calling every few minutes, Boss."

"I'll tell her myself," Tony Quinn said. "Get busy, Butch, and no slip ups."

Tony Quinn deflected the receiver a moment and then called Carol. It would be soothing to hear her calm voice, almost unusual to talk rationally with someone unexcited. Quinn's heart beat just a little faster when she answered the phone.

CHAPTER XV
MURDER

NTIL the early morning hours after dawn, Tony Quinn stayed in the privacy of his laboratory. There he first analyzed the contents of the whiskey bottle from which Van den Killan had poured a drink for the man he believed to be Rex Gordon. The liquor contained an appreciable quantity of chloral hydrate.

"Doped," Quinn muttered. "Just as I thought—and only Van den Killan had access to that bottle. It was delivered sealed."

He examined the contents he had taken from the glass from which he had imbibed the sleep-inducing potion. To Quinn's amazement it was pure rye and nothing else. It contained no trace of a narcotic. His case against the Hollander broke down rapidly.

Suddenly Quinn recalled the fact that two waiters had served him in the grill room of the hotel. Had he been drugged then? Possibly the action of the drug had been carefully studied by the person who ordered it administered and it had not taken effect until after Van den Killan left.

"The man who stole the necklace might have slipped some of the same drug in the whiskey bottle," Quinn reasoned aloud. "That would throw the blame on Van den Killan all right. Only he forgot to put more of the drug in the glass that I drank from."

"I got an idea," Silk put in. "Suppose Van den Killan knew danmed well you'd suspect him. Maybe you were drugged in the grill room and this Dutchman shoved that Mickey Finn in the bottle because he figured you'd have it tested anyway. But he didn't put any of the stuff in the glass, so you'd figure he couldn't have done it and the guy who did was trying to put the blame on Van den Killan."

"We're getting nowhere," Quinn said irritably. "The fact remains that Van den Killan knew where the necklace was and he had every opportunity to grab it. Breakfast, Silk, and in a hurry. While you're getting it ready, I'll put on my handsome face."

At ten minutes of nine, Tony Quinn, in his disguise of Rex Gordon, walked into the ornately furnished jewelry store owned by Fawcett.

"My business is with Mr. Fawcett personally," he told a clerk. "Most uimportant. You might whisper it concerns the Bourbon gems."

The clerk nodded knowingly. "Yes, sir. Mr. Fawcett is waiting in his office. He's been there since before the store opened. Up those stairs, sir. The last door at the end of the corridor."

Quinn found the office and tapped on the panels. There was no reply and he grew tense. He tried the knob and found the door unlocked. As he opened the door his hand drifted toward a shoulder holster and froze there. Fawcett was in his office all right. But Fawcett lay sprawled across his desk in a pool of thickened blood. He had been dead for some time.

Quinn closed the door quickly. He stepped over to the body and made only a brief examination. Fawcett's throat had been slit from ear to ear. There was no sign of any struggle and Quinn reasoned that the murderer must have been in the office with Fawcett's knowledge and consent. Probably someone the murdered man trusted.

He saw a huge, modern vault in a corner and with gloved hands he tried the great door. It was securely locked. Quinn frowned. Would the killer have taken time to close and lock the safe if he had robbed it? Or hadn't the Bourbon jewels been placed in it at all?

SUDDENLY Quinn tensed. His abnormal hearing detected the sound of hoarse breathing outside the door. From below came the sound of a stifled groan. Quinn hastily backed into a washroom, then he drew his mask over head and shoulders, removed his guns and snapped off the safety attachments.

"Mr. Fawcett," It was the voice of the clerk to whom Quinn had talked. "Mr. Fawcett!"

The Bat took a long chance. He opened the washroom door slightly and called back a summons to enter.

The clerk came in first and behind him stalked Blackie Burns, with a gun in his fist. Two of Blackie's men trooped in also. They all stopped in amazement at the gory sight before them. Blackie gave a strangled scream of rage. He lifted his gun and crashed it against the clerk's skull. Then he gave crisp orders to his men.

"We been buncoed, but this ain't the finish, boys. Not by a long shot. I just got to make certain I'm right. Joe, beat it downstairs and make sure nobody gets in here. Snap it up."

"Shall we swipe some of the rocks downstairs?" Joe asked avidly. "There was a lot of 'em, Blackie."

"All trash probably," Blackie snapped. "Beat it—and never mind the stuff downstairs. It's five-and-ten junk compared to what I'm after."

Blackie walked directly over to the safe. He took a slip of paper from his pocket and began twirling the dial. He had the combination, for the door swung wide within a minute.

The Bat watched Blackie scoop out the contents of a drawer until he found a crimson plush-covered box about ten inches high and two feet long. He opened the cover and sighed—a single, long drawn out breath of relief.

"It's okay," he said quickly. "Now we run for it. I don't get the meaning of that stiff, but let the cops worry. They'll figure the guy who bumped him swiped the jewels, too. It's a cinch for us."

The Bat's guns came up and he raised his foot to kick open the door. Suddenly a siren whined and a dozen quick shots came from downstairs, in the store proper. Then Sergeant McGrath's voice yelled orders and there was more shooting.

"Stung!" Blackie gasped. "Stung proper! This was a plant! Stay by the door and hold 'em off while I see if there's an out. Pump them cops full of lead if they show."

"Yeah, but I don't wanta be caught in this room with a stiff, Blackie," the thug still with him whined. "They're liable to think I did it."

But Blackie was paying no attention to his aide. He ran to a window and peered out. A bullet smashed through the glass. Blackie pumped two quick shots into the courtyard and drew back. He spotted the washroom door and rushed toward it, barged into the small room, gun extended.

Something whizzed behind him. The gun flew from his grasp and a brawny arm wrapped itself around his throat. He struggled with all the strength of desperation, but that locking arm never relaxed until Blackie slumped, his face blue and his breathing difficult. Then the Bat slugged him under the chin, raised the limp form and draped it over one shoulder.

THE thug in the office spun around as he heard footsteps. His gun blasted once and the bullet ripped past the Bat's head. The Bat's guns roared and the man went down with a bullet in each leg.

Footsteps and hoarse shouts announced the arrival of the police. The Bat looked about for an avenue of escape. There was none! Deftly he slipped Blackie off his shoulder and dumped him in a corner. Then he flattened himself behind the office door.

Sergeant McGrath burst into the room, gun drawn. Another detective was right behind him. They saw Fawcett's corpse, saw the unconscious wounded thug, and sped toward them.

Neither heard the door close gently. Then McGrath sensed the presence of danger. He straightened up from his examination of the dead Fawcett—to look into the decidedly dangerous end of a heavy automatic. His fellow detective already had his hands raised high.

"Reach, Sergeant!" the Bat said with a chuckle. "I'm sorry to do this, but necessity knows no such thing as friendship."

"Don't call me your friend," McGrath bellowed. "This time I've got you cold! You're a killer! A rotten, cowardly killer!"

"You have me cold, as you say," the Bat said, and laughed, "except for the fact that you are at the end of my guns. Fawcett was dead when I arrived. The wounded man is unfortunately my work. I had to shoot that thug or be killed myself. He is, of course, your prisoner, and you are welcome to get anything out of him you can, if he knows anything much—which I doubt."

"You can't get away with it," McGrath snarled. "This store is full of police. There isn't a chance for you! Not even if you shoot us down."

"But I wouldn't do that—unless it was positively necessary, Sergeant. Please don't make it so. Now put your gun in one of the desk drawers. Your pal will do the same. Turn your backs to me while I search you. Not that I think you carry two guns, Sergeant. A man of your prowess wouldn't find use for a second one—but—we can never be sure."

The Bat searched the two men deftly. Forcing them to face the wall and place their hands high up against it, palms level with the wallpaper, the Bat stepped toward Blackie. The gem thief was groaning and trying to sit up. The Bat moved to cover him also.

"Blackie," he said. "Blackie—wake up! Get to your feet!"

Blackie obeyed that voice, for it possessed an almost hypnotic influence. His eyes opened wide when he saw the masked figure.

"Blackie," the Bat said, "we're going out of here, you and I. Escorted by none other than Sergeant McGrath and his worthy assistant. It's up to you now. I'm going to hand you a gun. Put it in your side coat pocket, understand? You'll keep McGrath's friend covered while he escorts you to a police car. Can I depend on you, Blackie?"

"If it'll get me out of here, I'll do anything," Blackie retorted.

His wits had snapped back to normal and he recognized the fact that the Bat was trying to effect an escape for both of them.

"How do you expect to get away with it?" McGrath growled at the wall. "With that hood on your head the boys will know you."

THE Bat chuckled happily. "Ah! I shall remove the mask, Sergeant. Your long-felt desire to see my ugly face is to be gratified. Now follow these instructions or by thunder you'll never go home to your wife and family again. Blackie has a gun, too. You will pretend we are your prisoners. You will take my arm. Your friend will take Blackie's. To all appearances you will be escorting us to your service car. But you will be our prisoners; we'll shoot if you disobey. Blackie, you carry that jewel box."

"Take off the mask," McGrath raged. "Take it off and I'll do anything you say. I know the face under that hood. And you're right about it being ugly. Acid burns don't make a man look beautiful. Tony Quinn, you're at the end of your rope now."

"Turn around, Sergeant," the Bat said quietly. "I'll show you what I look like."

Both detectives turned. Blackie, wholeheartedly aligned with the Bat now, kept them covered. McGrath held his breath as the eerie figure in black began removing the hood. His jaw dropped as far as it would go when he saw the features of the man under the mask. Automatically he checked every detail of the face. The wide nose, the thin lips, the pleasant eyes and the straight black hair. Certainly this was not Tony Quinn. There wasn't the slightest resemblance.

"Like me?" the Bat asked with a wide grin. "I'm not exactly good-looking, but certainly not ugly. Ah, we go into action! Your men are coming up. Take my arm, Sergeant, and if you feel something prod your ribs occasionally, don't try to brush it away because the trigger of my gun is unusually sensitive. Ready, Blackie?"

"And how!" Blackie grimaced. "You're okay, Bat. I figured you were on the side of these heels, but I was wrong. You won't be sorry you helped."

"March!" the Bat ordered.

It was a strange procession that wended its way down the steps and through the store. Plainly it seemed that Sergeant McGrath had captured a prisoner and was hurrying him to one of the police cars. Detective Halloran also had his man firmly held by the arm. The only thing lacking was the smile of triumph that was usually on McGrath's features when he had effected an important capture. McGrath's face was strained and pale.

"You're doing splendidly," the Bat whispered out of the corner of his mouth. "Keep it up—and live, Sergeant."

THE four of them piled into a detective's cruiser. McGrath started the motor and drove away.

"I suppose it's the end for me now," he said tensely. "You won't dare let us live after I've seen your face."

"I promised," the Bat said, "that you would not suffer any bodily harm and I meant it. We'll drop you somewhere on the outskirts. The walk back will cool you off, Sergeant. You're steaming like a locomotive."

"Hey, wait a minute," Blackie growled from the rear seat. "You got me out of an awful mess, Bat, but these two cops don't live, get me? They take the works. Why damn it, my mug is on file. They'll identify me and then every cop in the world will be on my trail."

"They will not be harmed, Blackie," the Bat reiterated. "Sergeant McGrath is a friend of mine and even though I've just met this other detective for the first time, he's a friend also. By all means they do not die."

"Yeah?" Blackie grated. "We'll see."

Halloran gave a shout of strangled horror as Blackie shoved his gun against his head. Blackie squeezed the trigger, but only empty clicks resulted.

"Pull off the road and stop," the Bat ordered McGrath. He had swung around in the seat and his gun covered Blackie now. "Blackie, your heart is as dark as your name. You're a born killer and hardly fit to live, but I'll give you a break you don't deserve. Get out of this car and run for it! At the next corner is a dairy truck. Steal it—unless your conscience bothers you. Get going! Can't you see I won't be able to hold McGrath in check much longer?"

CHAPTER XVI
USELESS BAGGAGE

JUST for an instant Blackie gaped, but he obeyed. Once he glanced over his shoulder, as though he expected the Bat's gun to cut him down. He jumped into the dairy truck and sent it rolling away.

The Bat saw something else, too. It escaped the eyes of the two detectives, for they could see nothing but the muzzle of the Bat's gun. A rickety old coupé whined by, but it slowed as it began to near on the dairy truck ahead.

"And now," the Bat told McGrath, "we'll part. I'm sorry to have inconvenienced you."

"Rats!" McGrath rasped. "Of all the lowdown, mangy cusses I've ever run up against, you're at the bottom of the heap. Sometimes I used to call myself a fool for trying to run you down, but now—I'll get you if it takes my last breath."

The Bat smiled contentedly, reached into his pocket and drew out two pair of handcuffs.

"These are yours, gentlemen. You will clasp one section around your wrist. Sergeant, hook yourself to the wheel. Your friend will use the blanket rack in front of him. Hurry now—or would you prefer to be slugged?"

The detectives obeyed. McGrath sullenly, Halloran with something of a wry smile.

"Okay, Bat," Halloran said. "I don't know what your game is or why you let that killer get away, but I'll say this—you kept your promise. Me, I'm glad to be alive after watching that lug try to blast my head open. So you unloaded the gun you gave him? All time I been covered with an unloaded gat. I take my hat off to you, whoever you are."

"And you, Sergeant?" The Bat stepped out of the car and bowed slightly toward McGrath. "Aren't you the least bit appreciative?"

"The night they pull the switch on you, I'll laugh out loud!" McGrath thundered. "That's how much I appreciate you."

The Bat grinned. He saw a car coming down the road. Quickly he ran toward it, raised his head and flashed Sergeant McGrath's badge.

"Car broke down," he told the gawking boy who stopped for him. "Step on it. I left my buddy in the car with a killer. Got to get help."

In the car Sergeant McGrath tugged vainly at the handcuffs.

"He took our keys and the key to this car also," McGrath snapped. "But I admit I was wrong. Tony Quinn certainly wasn't under that mask. I've been a fool."

McGrath's free hand scooped up a piece of black silk. The Bat's hood. He flung it back on the seat angrily. A nice souvenir to be left with. Well, he'd get the man who wore it yet—even if he wasn't Tony Quinn.

As soon as he was well out of sight, the Bat got from his commandered car and dashed for the nearest phone booth. He had to get all necessary work done before McGrath was released and put a description of the Bat over the radio. A few minutes after that happened, every patrolman in town would be on the watch.

The line was busy when the Bat called his home. He fretted impatiently and tried again. This time Silk answered.

"The address," Silk said smoothly, "is Two Thirty-five White Street. Butch just called."

"Stand by," the Bat ordered. "I may need you. How are the legs?"

"Aching—to get busy. Don't forget me if you need help, Boss, especially should you meet up with a certain party. I'd like to be there."

NUMBER 235 White Street proved to be another funeral parlor. When the Bat reached the place he surveyed the neighborhood and spotted his coupé parked two blocks away. Butch was impatiently waiting back of the wheel.

"I saw them cops lead you outta that jewelry store downtown," he said excitedly. "Holy gee, Boss, I thought it was all up. And in that disguise I wasn't even sure it was you. But I followed, like you said, if things went wrong. I parked way up the road and when this guy beats it I tailed him, figuring that if you needed help, you'd give me the high sign as I went by."

"Good work, Butch. Now I'm going to need your muscle. I allowed the man you followed to go free just so that he could lead me to such a hideout as this. We're going in after him."

"Lead me to it!" Butch clenched his fists. "That must be the guy who started to make hamburger outta Silk. I'll make a stew outta him. Just lead the way."

The Bat smiled, but there was no mirth in that contortion of his lips. He surveyed the funeral parlors for a moment or two and then signaled Butch.

"It's up to you," he said, low-voiced. "If Blackie spots me—and he knows what I look like in this disguise—I wouldn't get any further than the front door. You walk in—and look sad, if a St. Bernard like you can do such a thing. Get as many of those men close to you as possible and then go to town. Got it?"

"Yeah—oh yeah." Butch's face lit up in enthusiasm. "Will I take 'em."

Butch straightened his coat, slicked down his thinning hair and put a mournful expression on his huge face. He opened the door of the undertaking parlors and removed his hat subserviently. A squat, apelike man came from a rear room to greet him.

"I wanta get prices on a nice job." Butch looked at the rug. "It's—it's for a pal o' mine, see? Nuthin' too good for him, y'understand."

"I'm sorry," the squat man said. "But we're full up, mister. Why don't you try somebody else?"

"Because I like this joint." Butch looked up slowly. "My pal liked this joint. You gonna let me see the boss, or do I pull the joint apart, huh?"

The squat man backed away hurriedly and disappeared. But he returned in a moment and there were three burly men at his side. They ranged themselves like a formidable army phalanx, on either side of Butch.

"Now what was it you were sayin', wise guy?" the little man demanded.

Butch's saddened features suddenly lighted up once more. His right hand moved at an astounding speed for a man his size. Giant fingers closed about the little man's throat, lifted him high into the air, a kicking, squealing creature. Two of the larger men reached for Butch and their smaller companion descended like a tomahawk. They went down under the impact. The fourth thug howled in rage and charged. He ran straight into a punch that seemed to explode something within his skull. He dropped heavily and didn't even quiver.

The other three were trying to get up, but Butch stood close by and rapped them hard on the top of their heads as they came up. He was enjoying himself immensely and secretly hoped the Bat would arrive by way of Bermuda. At least he did until a harsh voice snapped a command. Then Butch poked around to stare at a gun, and behind it a dark-featured man with murder glittering in his eyes.

"Reach, you big palooka!" he commanded. "Quick, or I'll chill you."

BUTCH backed up a few steps and elevated his arms. Every muscle and nerve was tensed. Butch couldn't think too fast, but he had the power of a piledriver and the speed of a flashing piston. Blackie recognized that and took care not to get too close.

"What's the big idea?" he demanded of Butch. "This is a funeral home. Haven't you any respect for the dead?"

"Yeah," Butch growled. "Boy, I'd have a lot of respect for you—dead. But see'n you're alive, I'll hang a couple of lanterns on your eyes."

"Walk into the rear room," Blackie snapped. "Come on—no stalling. Somebody sent you here and I want to find out just who it was. Maybe a mutual friend, eh, gorilla?"

Butch marched into the rear room. The first thing he saw was a large, red plush box on a table. Pasted on the cover, now open, was a paper representation of a black bat!

Blackie saw it too and gave an alarmed shout.

"So that's the game? While you kept me busy, your pal busted in here, huh? Okay, you big lug. You work for the Bat. For a minute or two I figured him for a right guy, but all he did was get me free from the cops so he could trail me here. Well, he's gone—and he's got the swag I risked my hide for. But I've get you, Big Boy! When the Bat returns that bunch of rocks, he can have you back."

Blackie's four aides were clustered just inside the door, eyeing Butch malevolently. Blackie hurled the empty jewel box on the floor and swore.

"Sap, that's me! I fell for the Bat's line, but this ain't over yet. Not by a long shot."

"Quite right, Blackie," a voice said calmly.

Everyone in the room spun around, while a chorus of rasped breaths exploded. The Bat, hood over his head and shoulders, stood just inside the door. The guns in his hands menaced the quintet of crooks.

"Butch, come over here beside me. Draw your gun and watch these men. If one of them so much as sneezes, shoot him! They'd do the same if our positions were reversed."

"Next time," Blackie raged, "you'll get it, you wise guy! First you played me for a sucker and then you swiped that bunch of rocks. Well, try and sell 'em. It can't be done except through the right channels and I know 'em. You don't!"

The Bat moved into the room and flung a glistening diadem of jewels on the table.

"Those," he said calmly, "could be peddled at Woolworth's. Others played you for a sucker, too, Blackie. You swiped a nice mess of paste."

Blackie's face contorted into a mask of passionate rage. He seized the shimmering stones set in a golden crown. He forgot that guns menaced him, forgot everything but the fact that he had been buncoed. He ran over to a window and tried to scratch the glass with one of the diamonds. Failing, he gave a shout of rage and hurled the thing to the floor.

"Easy, Blackie," the Bat warned. "Now listen to me. You work for someone. That man has tricked you as neatly as he has tricked everyone else. Do you think the police descended on Fawcett's jewelry store by sheer accident? Do you believe Fawcett's murder wouldn't be pinned on you if the police managed to arrest you? It was a plant—meant to strap *you* in the chair. Who staged it, Blackie? Who is the man you work for—the man who has robbed people in this city of millions in gems?"

BLACKIE'S face turned crafty. "I don't know what you're talking about. I work for myself, see?"

"But you practically admitted, by your own words and actions, that you *were* given a bad steer," the Bat went calmly on. "Someone baited that trap for you. Baited it with worthless paste. He'll do that again, Blackie. He'll do it because he's afraid of you. He's got what he wants from you, and now you've become useless baggage. Next time you may not be so lucky. What if I hadn't been there?"

"Hey, Boss," Butch stepped forward. "How about me taking him apart, huh? What he needs is a little of that persuasion stuff."

"No," The Bat rejected the idea. *"We* don't handle things that way—not at this stage of the game. Blackie will think over what I've told him. I'll contact you again—when I'm ready to hear you talk. Until then, Blackie, watch your step."

Butch caught a significant glance from the cold eyes behind the mask. He stuffed his gun into his pocket and fell to work with vigor. In three minutes Blackie lay sprawled on top of his own men, all piled in a heap. Butch wiped his hands and grunted his satisfaction as they went out of the door together.

He was silent for a long time as he drove the Bat in the general direction of his home. But Butch didn't like the way things progressed, and finally said:

"Maybe you made a mistake lettin' that bird go," he offered.

The Bat had stripped his mask off and was folding it into a compact wad as he answered.

"No, Butch. Blackie is a peculiar type of crook, He's clever and he usually gets what he goes after. Silk knew him, years ago. Blackie is in this game to get everything for himself. He won't welch now—when his goal seems near at hand. Nothing would have made him talk. And, of course, I couldn't very well notify the police to come and get him because I want Blackie loose. Sooner or later he'll lead me to the man we want. Your job is to try and pick up

Blackie's trail. It may be impossible because he'll lay low, but do your best."

CHAPTER XVII
CAROL'S DESTINY

A S the shadows lengthened, Carol Baldwin glanced at the clock and made ready to call it a day. She was locking her desk when McFayden barged into her office in the jewelry store.

"You're to take this package to the Harriman branch store on your way home," he said with a wide smile intended to open the way for an extended conversation. "It's important, so don't fail to deliver it at once."

"Leave it on the desk," Carol replied. "I'll stop off with it. Don't worry."

McFayden walked toward the door, hesitated and turned back for another look at this blond vision of loveliness. Carol met his stare coolly and he flushed. She picked up the small package, slipped it into her purse and with a final adjustment of her hat, walked down the stairs, through the store and into the street.

"Cab, lady?"

A taxi pulled up at the curb. The driver was grinning at her. Carol felt a sudden premonition of danger. She turned to rush back into the store, but a man stood directly behind her.

"You better take a ride, lady," he said. "It would be healthier than yelling for the cops."

She glanced down and saw that his hand was deep in his side pocket. There was no question as to what that hand gripped. Carol retained her composure with an effort.

"Is this a threat?" she asked. "What are you after?"

"Get in the cab and find out," the man smiled thinly.

Carol didn't know him, for she had never seen Blackie Burns before. Yet she did recognize the menace he offered. Her eyes flashed to one side. A patrolman was casually making his way down the street. Carol took three steps toward the taxi and suddenly veered to the left. Instantly, Blackie seized her by the arm and literally hurled her into the cab.

"Hey!" The patrolman broke into a run. "What's the idea?"

Blackie's concealed hand moved a trifle.

"This!" he snarled.

A gun exploded. The patrolman stumbled and fell heavily, skidding across the sidewalk. He raised his head, tugged at his holstered gun and then the agony from a wound in his shoulder overcame him. He fell back limply.

The taxi cut into the traffic, raced by two red lights and swerved around a corner. It stopped beside a sedan.

"Get into that other bus and make it snappy!" Blackie rasped.

Carol obeyed. There wasn't anything else she could do. The cab pulled away and before it reached the next corner, two radio cars flashed by in swift pursuit. Blackie scowled, snapped an order to the driver and the sedan headed north along an avenue.

"Well, Beautiful"—Blackie regarded his prisoner appreciatively—"you didn't get so far in trying to take a powder on me, did you?"

"You," Carol returned crisply, "are an insufferable, stupid moron. The type of a coward who doesn't give the other fellow a chance. Did you have to shoot that patrolman?"

"Sure," Blackie declared complacently. "He'd have bumped me if I hadn't stopped him. Now listen, Baby, you keep that tongue of yours in check, see? If it didn't wag so much, *you* wouldn't be in this jam."

CAROL leaned back against the cushions.

"I don't know what you mean," she said shortly.

"Aw, stop trying to kid me, will you?" Blackie grinned. "Not so very long ago a certain party phoned me. You tuned in on that call somehow. What's more you ain't no friend of Graham's old secretary. We checked up. You notified a guy who goes around masked like it was Halloween about that phone call. So he came to see me and he made a lot of trouble. You tipped him off, so you must know who he is. Think that over."

"Are you certain," Carol asked blandly, "that you weren't recently behind the bars of an asylum? There's no necessity for lying. You know I carry a package meant for the Harriman Jewelry Company. That sly Mr. McFayden handed it to me. Just another idea on how to rob the store, I suppose. Everything else you mention is a complete puzzle to me. The package is what you want."

"Hand over that purse," Blackie ordered. "Oh, you'll get it back. I just want to see whether or not you travel heeled."

He dumped the contents of the purse on the seat, rifled through the myriad articles a woman carries, then tossed the wrapped package McFayden had given her into Carol's lap.

"Open it," he ordered, "and see if it's jewelry I'm after."

Carol broke the cord, peeled off the paper and revealed a small jewelry box. She pressed the spring and the lid flew open, There was nothing inside.

"McFayden," she breathed softly. "This is his work! He sent me on a fool's errand, thinking I'd take that cab planted in front of the store. You're one of his men. He's the thief who has robbed the store, and you're in it just as bad as he is. I don't know why either of you should want to kidnap me, but—"

"Now ain't that nice," Blackie sighed. "You sure pick things up fast, Beautiful. Only you're a little wrong. I'm the boss of this outfit; not that sneaky guy McFayden. It depends on me just how you're treated. Now, if you'd whisper the real name of the Black Bat, I might get soft-hearted and let you out."

Carol sniffed. "I don't know what you're talking about. The Black Bat?"

Blackie crossed his legs. "Okay, lady. All I know is that you work for the Bat and soon as you're missed, he'll come flying. He'll find you, too, because that guy is smart. Twice he surprised me, but this time I'll do all the surprising. You can relax. Nobody's going to hurt you—yet."

Carol glanced out of the car window and saw that they had left the city and were heading toward Connecticut. Once or twice she had a glimpse of the Sound. They were silent as the car whizzed along, then at last it passed through a small town, tuned to the right and headed straight toward the Sound waterfront.

Carol had a mental vision of being held prisoner aboard some boat. So far as she could reason, it would be impossible for the Bat to find her now. She had left no clue, wasn't expected to report for hours yet, and inwardly she was glad. For if Tony Quinn ever realized she was a prisoner, and guessed where she was, he would come quickly and run straight into a death trap.

SUDDENLY Carol made a lunge for the car door. She had it half open when Blackie's big paw descended on her shoulder. He hauled her back and shoved her against the seat.

"Spunky, ain't you?" he said, and grinned at her. "You'll lose some of that. Okay—we're here. Like the scenery?"

Carol could hardly keep her tears in check. She peered out of the window and saw that the car had stopped inside a high concrete gate. The door was swinging shut now. A small gray stucco building occupied the center of the enclosed area and piled in several places were huge, concrete boxes.

"Nice, huh?" Blackie smiled. "Them things are burial vaults, lady. They put people in 'em and plant 'em in graveyards. You'll know just how it's done if your mouth freezes up. Now get out of this car, and no funny tricks. You can't get away from this place—not unless you got wings."

Carol stepped out of the car. Two men in overalls smirked at her. Blackie took her arm and she was forcibly led into the stucco building. There she saw various molds for casting these huge vaults. A furnace was roaring at one end of the building.

"Pleasant little place," Blackie said blandly. "We make metal vaults, too, for ritzy people. The business is on the level and nobody suspects the place, so it won't do you much good to start hollering. Nobody ever comes here. Now let's go into the office and have a little talk, huh?"

Carol walked between the half-finished vaults and shuddered. Anything could happen here. Why, she might be murdered and buried in one of those concrete boxes! Blackie, as she had heard him called by his men, was wholly capable of such a deed. Carol could tell that by the chilly glint in his black eyes and the malicious grin across his lips.

She sat down in a swivel chair. Blackie draped himself on a corner of an old desk.

"Now listen to reason, lady," he said. "You know we got the goods on you, Nobody else could have tipped the Bat as to where we had one of his pals. Know what happened to him? The Bat's pal, I mean?"

"How could I," Carol queried with just the right degree of innocence, "when all of this is just a mystery to me? I don't know what you're talking about. I didn't tip anyone off and I did not listen in on a single phone call. Where could I have listened from? You mean from the jewelry store?"

Blackie grimaced and walked toward a door at the further end of the office. He gestured for Carol to follow him. She was led into a dark, damp room, shoved into a chair and Blackie deftly tied her. Then he stepped back.

"Rubbing out dames ain't my style, lady, but you got only a few hours to make up your mind. Just start praying that the Bat will get here before the big shot does. You see, the boss in this racket ain't as soft-hearted as me."

"Thank you," Carol said stiffly, "for such consideration. I'll remember it when you are brought to trial for kidnapping. Just who is this man you call your boss? I thought you were the head man around here?"

"You'd like to know, wouldn't you? Maybe you will, but keep on hoping you never know because once that happens, you'll die. I'll bring some food and water later on. If you feel like yelling, go to it. Nobody can hear you. The Bat will start looking for you at the store and he'll get the dope that will lead him right here."

BLACKIE went out, closed and locked the door and eerie darkness descended on Carol. With a supreme effort she retained control of her nerves. Once she laughed mirthlessly. Wasn't this what she had wanted? An active part in the Bat's campaign against crime? Hadn't her father's wish led her into these dark, dismal passages where danger lurked every inch of the way?

Thoughts of her father gave Carol back a large

measure of composure and courage. He had suffered and died so that crime's vicious tentacles might not sweep out and encompass all that was decent and right. Could she do any less?

Grimly, Carol tested the bonds that strapped her to the chair. Ten minutes of frantic pulling and tugging only tired her. Yet there was one thing she could do. Blackie expected the Bat to find this hideaway and put in an appearance. There would be a trap set—a death trap! She might be able to warn the Bat. To do this she had to retain full control of her wits and never relax her vigilance for a single second. She banished all thoughts of fear and kept listening intently for the first sign of the Bat's coming.

Outside of the building, Blackie surrounded himself with the seven men who presumably worked in this vault manufacturing plant. He gave the men precise instructions.

"Leave the gate open so he'll walk right in. That guy is bound to find this place. I have a man planted at Graham's store who will slip him the location of this place. Let him inside and then go to work. No matter what happens, the Bat is not to leave this place alive. Don't kill him unless necessary, but if it looks like he's getting away, blast him down. That's all—except I might mention a reward of two grand for the guy who grabs the Bat."

Blackie stalked back to the office and sat down. He picked up the phone, dialed and called the city.

"Blackie," he reported. "Things are shaping up swell. Our customer arrived okay and we're trying to make a sale right now. If the other party arrives we close the deal. Got it, Boss?"

"Good, Blackie," the voice at the other end said. "I was beginning to lose faith in you. And let me assure you once more that the affair at Fawcett's was not of my doing. It happened to be a trick of someone else. We're almost ready to close up and nothing must interfere."

Blackie replaced the receiver and leaned back, highly gratified at the way things were going. He grinned at the telephone and thumbed his nose at it once.

"Yeah," he soliloquized, "we're about ready to close up. Only when that happens, Mister Wise Guy, you'll be on the outside of the door."

CHAPTER XVIII
DEATH VAULT

 PEERING toward the sidewalk, Butch's coupé stopped along the curb of a street not far from the river. The man who emerged looked carefully around before he ventured far from the car. Tony Quinn was in his disguise of Rex Gordon. In it he could move about more or less freely so long as he kept a watchful eye out for the police.

He had attempted to change this disguise, but it had not worked out too well. Certain peculiarities of Tony Quinn's face made radical changes of appearance difficult and then, too, he had little time to experiment. Still it was better this way than appearing in the hood of the Bat!

He kept well to the shadows of the building line as he hurried up the street. Certain he was unobserved, Quinn ran lightly into the middle of the street, quickly propped up the sewer lid and dropped into the abandoned drain, letting the lid fall back into place.

He jerked his gun out and stood quietly listening. No sound reached him. He drew his hood from an inner pocket, donned it and hurried down the tube until he found the rusty iron grip of the secret door.

The first thing he saw when he stepped through the door was that the two dead men lay just as he had left them when he had escaped from the cave. The Bat shivered a little as he crossed the room carved out of the earth. At the far end he pulled away a packing case and discovered what he sought—a narrow, round tunnel. He wriggled through the opening and crawled steadily upward along the slanting shaft.

Finally he reached a spot where a smaller cavern had been cut. The ceiling of this was propped up with heavy two by fours. And that ceiling was smooth and looked like concrete. He pulled away the timber, stood erect and was able to place the palms of both hands against the cement square. He pushed with all his strength and the section of ceiling moved up.

By using the timber props as supports, the Bat finally got this trapdoor half open. He seized the edge of the floor above, hoisted himself up and lay, panting from his exertion, on a cold cement floor.

His super-sensitive eyes made out his surroundings, despite the intense darkness. He was in the massive vault at Graham's jewelry store. This fact did not startle the Bat, for by careful reasoning he had already guessed that the tunnel would lead him here.

When, as blind Tony Quinn, he had been led to the sewer, he had observed that the underground tube lay only a block from where Graham's store was located. The cavern, dug just outside the sewer, had showed plenty of evidence of fresh soil being carried through it. All that meant another tunnel, dug in the direction of Graham's store.

In this feat of engineering lay the answer to the mysterious burglary of Graham's gems. Harriman's store and Gill's also might be similarly tapped by underground passages.

The Bat drew out a map which Silk had obtained for him. It showed the routes of every sewer line in the city, both old and new. Gill's store, the Bat noted, was almost as close to the sewer as Graham's, but Harriman's place of business could never be reached by any subterranean passages originating in a sewer. The Bat pursed his lips in a soundless whistle.

If there was no tunnel beneath Harriman's vault then suspicion fastened on Phil Harriman tenaciously, or on somebody in his store. Graham's and Gill's stores could be robbed from inside but Harriman's, without a tunnel, had to be burglarized by opening the vault door, an impossible act except by one who knew the combination and had free access to the premises.

THE Bat thought also of the tiara which had been shipped abroad. It showed that at least part of the loot had already been disposed of through foreign channels. The tiara, according to Mrs. Van den Killan, who had been in possession of the duplicate of faked gems, had been worn by a woman at an affair in Amsterdam. Van den Killan was a Hollander and bound to have good connections in the Netherlands. If he was engaged in criminal work his wife probably knew nothing about it, and the presence of the tiara at the ball might very well have been a sheer accident which Van den Killan could not have foreseen.

The Bat made a swift examination of the interior of the vault. Then he closed the trapdoor, placed the uprights to support it and slipped back down the tunnel into the sewer. By consulting the map again he proceeded to a point from which Gill's store might be reached by the least amount of digging. He saw another of those rusty iron handles, pulled it and stepped from the abandoned sewer into another cavern. He found the tunnel and five minutes later pulled himself up into Gill's massive vault.

"It looks," the Bat surmised, "as though Harriman or somebody close to him is elected. Unless his store is also equipped with one of these tunnels I can only assume that he or one of his aides robbed his stock. And a tunnel under his safe—at least one made from a sewer—is practically an impossibility."

Returning to the cavern dug alongside the old sewer, the Bat found evidences that it had also been used as a hideout. The tunneling operations must have taken a long time to accomplish and the crooks who performed the work had probably lived in the cavern. The Bat examined a heap of rubbish in one corner. He found several empty books of matches. One advertised a filling station in Eastown, a small Connecticut village. Another bore the ad of a grocery store in the same town, There were others, mostly all identified with that small village.

"The crooks must have lived there for an extended period," the Bat reasoned. "How else would they have obtained these match books from so many different sources in the same town?"

On the rickety table he discovered a worn pack of playing cards and a small pocket calendar. This made him draw in a quick breath. It was issued with the compliments of the Sherbrooke Burial Vault Company of Eastown, Connecticut.

In the Bat's mind facts clicked. Funeral parlors had been used by the crooks and there was a definite connection between such places of business and a burial vault concern. Where could the master thief find a better spot to work unmolested? A burial vault manufacturing plant would hardly fall under suspicion of any investigators and the necessary equipment used in preparing the copies of the stolen gems might well be housed there.

The Bat decided to examine this Connecticut burial vault concern without further delay. Another angle struck him The real gems were shipped abroad—or part of them, at least. No better method could be employed than by enclosing them either in a burial vault, a casket, or even the body of someone whose remains were to be shipped abroad.

He made his way out of the sewer and hurried to a phone booth. Hurriedly calling Silk, he learned that there was still no word from Carol. The Bat's worries increased. Above all things he did not want to risk her safety. But without a clue he could only work as rapidly as possible in running down the mob and hope that he might find some trace of her whereabouts during this work.

IT was long after dark when the Bat reached the small Connecticut town and drove to the vault manufacturing plant, or near it, rather. He left his coupé and reconnoitered. He saw the high concrete wall that surrounded the plant and also saw that the door, set in that wall, had been left slightly ajar. There were no lights in the yard, but that wasn't unusual. It was long after working hours. The open door attracted him, but Quinn knew better than to expose himself so boldly.

Moving into the dark shadows cast by the high wall he stood there, listening intently. He was rather far from the town itself, and there were no houses nor other places of business within half a mile.

Then he stiffened. His extremely sensitive hearing detected the sound of someone moving about on the other side of the wall. The Bat glanced up. If the plant employed a watchman, which was unlikely, he would be using a flashlight or lantern. Some of the light would illuminate at least a small portion of the yard and reach to the top of the wall. But there was not the faintest trace of light.

He heard the man on the other side of the wall curse once as he stubbed his foot against something. The Bat smiled grimly.

He noticed that electric light poles were ranged

about twenty feet from the wall. In the darkness they were almost invisible, but the Bat's eyes saw them as clearly as though they were flooded with a spotlight. He moved toward them. His clothes were black and when he pulled up his coat collar, the whiteness of his shirt was covered.

He drew on his black hood, wrapped his arms around a telephone pole and shinnied up it slowly and cautiously. From a point twenty feet away he knew he was invisible to ordinary eyes.

Halfway up, he surveyed the vault manufacturing plant. He penetrated the darkness easily and picked out two forms standing just inside the gate. Both men carried clubs and wore guns strapped to their thighs. Two others were slowly pacing a beat around the plant itself.

The Bat slid down silently, made his way to the rear of the plant and finally clambered up a tree. He crawled out along one branch until he could drop directly on top of the cement wall. Landing like a cat, he clung to the rough surface for a moment, then went over the side. For a second more he hung by his hands, then let go and hit the ground with a soft thud. He was up instantly and running toward a far corner of the premises, where the darkness was intense.

A guard strolled by, glancing up at the wall every few steps as if to make sure no intruder scaled it. He heard a slight scuffling sound behind him, reached for his gun and then tried to yell a warning. An arm curled around his throat, muffling the cry. A fist struck hard at the back of his neck. It was a scientific blow that brought immediate results. The guard went limp.

Carefully the Bat carried the guard he had captured into the darkest corner, set him down gently and made a brief examination. He nodded, satisfied. The guard would be unconscious for many minutes.

As softly as the nocturnal creature for which he was named, the Bat crossed the yard and edged his way toward the factory building. One of the other two men on guard shivered and patted his holstered gun to reassure himself. He knew that the Bat was expected to pay this place a visit, and the reputation of the Bat had penetrated every inch of the underworld. This man was afraid. The Bat could strike swiftly and with terrible effect. Only the promise of rich reward kept the fellow who was watching for him going.

HE started his patrol that stretched around the corner of the building. A shadow moved out and he started back in terror. Too late he tried to sing out a warning. The Bat's right fist cracked against the guard's jaw. His left followed with a second paralyzing blow. As the guard slumped toward the

ground, the Bat caught him and eased the fall.

He straightened up and those exceptional eyes spotted danger. The other guard, assigned to the factory door, had heard the scuffling. He barged around the corner, gun ready. The Bat's right hand moved like the strike of a cobra. There were two shots, almost blended into one. The guard spun around, dropped heavily and lay moaning.

In a flash the Bat raced toward the factory door. From the wall gate two more men came sprinting toward him, shooting as they came. Slugs slammed into the stucco wall of the building, but the thugs were shooting in darkness and at a shadowy form that flitted like a ghost. The Bat fired from the hip and one man tumbled into a heap. The other turned tail and raced toward the gate. The Bat let him go.

He reached the factory door and pushed it open. Nothing happened. He stepped inside and someone moved. The Bat turned his head and through the darkness saw two advancing forms, clubs held high. He ducked under one swinging blow, drove a fist deep into the stomach of one man and sent him reeling back. The other killer brought his club down in a vicious arc.

It was impossible to duck it, but the Bat rolled back with it and avoided the full fury of the blow. Before the killer could raise his club again, or reach for his gun, a fist exploded against his jaw. He sat down, half dazed. The Bat stopped long enough to smash him again, wheeled and rushed the other man who was getting to his feet.

The impact of the two bodies sounded like a head-on collision of two heavyweights in the ring. The Bat took a blow over his heart, leaped back to avoid another lashing punch and then came in, fists swinging. He struck a mighty blow full against the killer's nose, rapped a second to the chin and finished up the fight with a one-two that connected squarely with the man's jaw.

Gun in hand now, the Bat turned slowly. His eyes penetrated the darkness and he saw a small door to his left. Alert, he moved toward it, wary of a trap. Suddenly a beam of light came from beneath the door. He raised his gun and his finger tightened on the trigger. The door swung open slowly and the Bat gave a low cry of horror.

Inside the room, tied to a heavy chair in the center of the floor, was Carol. She was gagged, but her eyes implored him to run. The Bat refused to obey that plea. He knew only that the girl he loved, the girl who willingly risked all manner of peril for him, was in danger.

"Carol!" he shouted and rushed through the door.

Too late he realized that he had been tricked, after all. With all his thoughts centered on Carol, he had relaxed his vigilance for a bare fraction of a necessary second.

Something crashed down on the back of his neck. He hurtled forward under the force of the blow, fell to his knees and tried to lift the gun. Another blow caught him on top of the head. The room began spinning. Carol's face, a mask of horror, rocked and gyrated like some figment of a wild dream. Vaguely the Bat felt strong hands seize him. His mask was ripped off and he heard a grunt.

"YEAH, that's him!" Blackie gloated. "What he runs around with a mask for, I don't understand. It's the Bat and we've got him now. Grab his legs and help me toss him into that vault. The big one!"

The Bat was lifted, carried across the room and hurled into a spacious burial vault. Blackie stepped back, manipulated a block and tackle device until the heavy lid of the vault swung directly over the concrete box. He kept pulling the chain and the lid dropped slowly. Blackie stepped back with a sigh of satisfaction.

"Let's see him get outta there. He walked right into it—just as I figured he would, once he spotted the dame. Now we know she's connected with the Bat, so it's curtains for her."

"What about him?" One of the men pointed toward the burial vault.

"He'll keep," Blackie said. "Nobody could raise that lid and he'll be there when the boss shows. This is the best night's work we've ever done."

"But he'll smother in there," Blackie's aide cried.

Blackie assumed an expression of mock sadness.

"Now won't that be just too bad. Listen, I'm going into town. You and Joe take this dame down to the Sound and find a small boat, tie a lot of weights to her legs and when you get far enough out, toss her over. Better take this bottle of chloroform along. It'll make things a lot easier and she won't rock the boat. The Bat can stay here and rot?"

CHAPTER XIX
SILK TAKES A HAND

NLY shortly before dark, not long after Carol had started her long car ride, though as yet nothing was guessed of that, Silk had received a phone call from the Bat.

"I'm heading out to the Sherbrooke Burial Vault Company out near Eastown, Connecticut," he told Silk. "That firm may have a tie-up with the Grady Funeral Parlors and with Blackie. It looks to me like some setup to work in with this series of jewel robberies and worse crimes. If I don't come back, you'll know where to start looking, Silk."

"Can't I go along?" Silk implored. "My legs are okay now."

"Stay where you are!" the Bat ordered. "It anyone comes to see me, stall them. When you hear from Carol, tell her to lay low. She'd better not report for work again at the jewelry store. I'm afraid they may get to thinking it was she who tipped me off as to where you were being held, Silk."

Silk hung up glumly. Then, instead of waiting for Carol to phone, he called her apartment. There was no answer. Silk hung up thoughtfully, then made a sudden decision. Working fast, he disguised himself, locked the house and departed via the secret exit. He hurried to Carol's apartment and rang the bell.

When there was no response, Silk called the superintendent of the building. He hadn't seen Carol, although she was usually home by this time. Silk determined on a bold move. He taxied to the Graham Jewelry Company and rang the night bell. A watchman opened the door a crack.

"You mean Van den Killan's secretary? No, buddy, she ain't here. Say, maybe… But no, that can't be! Who'd want to snatch her?"

Silk's eyes grew wide with horror.

"What do you mean?" he asked. "She's my sister. What's this about a snatch?"

The watchman shoved his cap to the back of his head and frowned.

"She was leaving when I reported for work. A minute afterward a cop was plugged right outside. He said, later on, that a dame had been forced into a taxi and taken away. But it couldn't be your sister, buddy. She'll turn up. Maybe had a date with a boyfriend."

The watchman turned away, then seemed to have another thought.

"Say, buddy, I did hear somebody tell the hack driver to head for some town in Connecticut… Eastown, I think it was."

Silk moved away, thanking the man. Cold perspiration formed little beads on his forehead. Carol had been kidnapped! The Bat's hunch was right. They figured Carol had tipped off the Bat.

What to do? The Bat couldn't be contacted for advice. If anything must be done, Silk was now on his own. He didn't know which way to turn. He needed the Bat. Perhaps in some manner the Bat had also discovered that Carol was gone. It might be that he was following her already. Silk hoped so, sincerely. Carol's brave act had saved his life and Silk was grateful.

"The Sherbrooke Company was what the Bat said—where he was going," Silk muttered. "To Connecticut. I could drive there in less than an hour."

HE bribed a taxi driver to skip traffic lights, dismissed the cab far uptown and hurried into a garage that specialized in renting cars. Silk showed credentials, made a substantial payment and drove a fast roadster in the direction the Bat had taken. By guarded inquiry, Silk located the Sherbrooke Company and as he drove down the dark lane leading to the place, he doused his lights.

Suddenly Silk tramped on the brake, turned the wheel sharply and left the road. He made a complete turn, in a field, headed back in the direction from which he had come and made sure the car couldn't be seen from the road. He climbed out and made his way across a marshy field until he crouched behind the thick trunk of a tree about a hundred yards from the plant.

Two quick shots startled him. Silk drew his own gun and made ready to move into the battle. As he neared the gate set in the high wall, he saw headlights of a car turned on. Silk dropped flat, parted thick grass and watched. To his amazement, he saw someone carried out of the plant and hustled over to a big car. The headlights reflected against the wall and Silk made out the identity of the prisoner. It was Carol!

Her arms were tied and two men threw her bodily into the rear seat. One climbed in after her, while the other manned the wheel. Someone ran up to the car. It was Blackie, and Silk's eyes narrowed in hatred. But he bided his time and finally Blackie and one other man began carrying limp burdens across the yard. Silk grinned at that. The Bat had been here all right. And he had left copious evidence of his work.

Blackie drove out of the yard first. Silk let him go. He wondered about the Bat, where he was, but reasoned that if Blackie had captured him, the Bat would have been spirited away, also. Silk was positive none of those limp forms had been that of his employer.

The car, with Carol in the tonneau, rolled out of the yard, stopped, and the driver returned to close the gate. Then the sedan rolled over the narrow road.

Silk began running toward his own roadster. He piled into it, smashed his way through underbrush and without turning on his lights set out in pursuit.

As Blackie's car reached the main highway, it turned left. The second car took the right turn and Silk followed that one. Carol's safety was the paramount thing right now. Silk was torn between a desire to rescue her and to return to the plant in search of the Bat. It was a decision that worried him, but he depended upon the Bat's prowess. Carol was just a helpless girl, probably on her way to certain doom.

Silk trailed the car expertly. When it left the highway five miles south, Silk turned also and in time to see the sedan roll through the gates of someone's estate. He could smell the Sound and as he reached the gates, he saw the water.

Jamming on the brakes, Silk leaped out of the car, drew his gun and raced through the gates.

There was a marker with a name printed on it suspended from the rustic fence. Silk skidded to a stop, long enough to read the name,

"Clifford Carlyle," he grunted. "That's the guy who is partners with Van den Killan. So these mugs are using his estate. huh? Maybe Carlyle can explain that."

SILK noticed the sedan parked alongside the big house. He made a circle of the place and came out on the opposite side, along a smooth, sandy beach. Silk wished now that he had the Bat's eyes. The eerie darkness presented a problem. Silk couldn't see more than four or five feet.

Then a muffled scream made his blood run cold. He snapped off the safety of his automatic and ran straight toward the sound. A dark figure loomed up. The man whirled as he heard Silk. A gun appeared in his hand and a jagged streak of flame cut the darkness. The bullet fanned Silk's ear. He squeezed the trigger of his own gun. The man spun around and dropped.

"Got him, Bat!" Silk yelled. "There's another mug! If he hurts the girl, we'll drown him. Let's go!"

"No!" the second thug shrieked, "No, I—I won't hurt the girl. D-don t shoot. I don't want to fight the Bat. Blackie made me do this!"

There was genuine terror in his voice. Only a matter of minutes before the Bat had been dumped into a burial vault with a heavy lid placed over it. The thug had witnessed that piece of drama with his own eyes. Yet, the Bat was here! He had escaped, performed a superhuman feat which no ordinary man could possibly have accomplished. The Bat's reputation assumed a near supernatural phase in the frightened crook's mind.

Silk's trick of pretending that the Bat was here had worked splendidly. The thug began running madly toward the house. Behind him he left a rowboat that gradually slipped out to sea.

The thug racing away tripped on his own feet once and fell headlong. He arose and darted crazily along the beach. Then a bullet zipped by him and he stopped abruptly. Hands reaching for the stars, he stood trembling like a leaf in an autumnal wind. A gun prodded his spine.

"Where is the girl?"

"In—in the rowboat. She ain't hurt, honest. You can't blame me for this. Blackie made me do it. I—"

A gun butt crashed against his skull and silenced him. Silk was racing toward the water before the thug had completed his fall. He peered through the darkness and exclaimed in horror. The rowboat was drifting out on the Sound. Silk stripped off his coat, forced his shoes off without untying the laces and gave a running dive into the surf. He swam with the short, chopping strokes of an inexperienced swimmer, but managed to reach the boat.

A rope dangled off its prow. He seized this, pulled himself up a little and saw Carol lying in the bottom of the boat. Silk had to exert all his strength to swim and tow the craft behind him. Finally, however, he beached it. In a flash he raised Carol's head, saw the chloroform-soaked sponge and hurled it into the water.

With Carol in his arms, Silk waded ashore. He set her down gently, untied the ropes and chafed her wrists. At last she opened her eyes and gave a violent shudder.

"It's me," Silk told her soothingly. "It's Silk. You're okay, Carol."

SHE sat up.

"Silk—you! Silk! They got him! Tony is in a burial vault. He'll smother! I heard Blackie say no man could live more than half an hour in that vault. W-what time is it?"

Silk gulped. Far more than half an hour had passed since he had started trailing Carol. By now the Bat must be suffocated.

"Put your arms around my neck," Silk told Carol. "We're going back!"

Silk helped her into the roadster. He rolled out of the estate, stepped hard on the gas pedal and tore up the highway. Too late! The thought hammered at his brain. Carol was sobbing quietly, her head against Silk's shoulder. It looked like the end of the Bat. He had probably died trying to save her, and she had been the bait in the trap that had spelled his doom.

"He'll be all right," Silk soothed her, but he couldn't get much assurance in his tone. "No bunch of punks like Blackie and his gang can get the Bat. And maybe we're in time at that. Look—there's the road leading to the plant. Hang on—it's going to be rough sailing."

CHAPTER XX
THE FINGER OF SUSPICION

DAZEDLY, consciousness returned to the Bat soon after the lid of the burial vault sealed him into the crypt. He opened his eyes and for a moment was gripped by a horror more grim than anything he had endured since the days of his blindness. Ordinary darkness meant little to the Bat, for his eyes could penetrate it. But now, not knowing where he was, he could see nothing but blackness just as intense as the utter stark inkiness of the blind.

He rubbed his eyes and sat up. His head bumped against something extremely substantial. Eagerly he felt around until he realized that he was confined in some kind of box. The Bat gave a sigh of relief.

Anything was better than a return to blindness. His mind, attuned to accept such dire possibilities, had instantly grasped the idea that the blow on the head had returned him to the Stygian pits of his former affliction.

He was bathed in perspiration and his head ached like a sore tooth. He sat up, as far as he could, and the sensitive tips of his fingers grimly related the whole story to him. The Bat knew where he was now—in one of the huge burial vaults of six- or eight-inch-thick concrete.

He wondered if Blackie had sealed him inside. Regardless of whether that was so or not, precious little air was coming into his tomb, and if anything was to be done, action was necessary.

The Bat turned over clumsily, raised his back and set it firmly against the lid of the tomb. The muscles in his shoulders stood out like whipcords, his arms became massive pedestals that supported him and gradually raised the concrete lid.

A little fresh air entered and the Bat eagerly sucked his lungs full. Things cleared a bit after that, but when he released, he knew only too well that three men wouldn't have the combined strength to raise this lid far enough for him to squirm through.

He remembered Carol, tied in that chair. The Bat wasted no more time. His agile mind sought a way out of this death trap—and found one. A slight, hazardous chance, but a chance nevertheless.

In his pocket he had a clip of steel-jacketed .45 bullets. Blackie had not taken time to search him. After all, a man entombed in a concrete burial vault that weighed more than a ton wouldn't be able to put any kind of a weapon to use.

The Bat slipped several of the cartridges into the palm of his hand. Then he set his back against the lid once more and exerted all his strength to raise the lid about half an inch. He held his breath, supported the massive load on one arm and deftly inserted a cartridge into the crack between the casket and the lid. Now, at least, he would get fresh air.

Again he performed the same backbreaking stint until the second cartridge was inserted on the other side. There was some danger of the pressure exploding the bullets, but the Bat had made certain that the steel-jacket tips were pointed outside. Now he had two small but sturdy rollers beneath the lid. Gradually he eased the lid forward, rolling it by fractions of an inch on the bullets. He inserted two more and now he could move the lid faster and easier.

AT last he had cleared almost two feet of space. Wriggling his body, he managed to raise his head out of the tomb. For a moment he rested, waiting for his strength to return and the ache in his bones and muscles to subside.

Further and further he shoved the lid out, then, until its own weight raised the end near the Bat. It teetered like a seesaw for a moment, then raised up and slid off the vault. One corner broke and the whole heavy affair smashed to the floor.

The Bat leaped out of the vault. In the darkness that no other eyes than his could have probed, he saw his own gun, kicked into a corner. He leaped for it, picked it up. The weight of it felt good in his hand. He made sure it was loaded and ready for action.

Rushing to the door, the Bat flung it wide, then ducked back. A car, driving without lights, had pulled into the yard. Two people were getting out and the Bat's gun came up. He stepped outside the door.

"Reach!" he snapped.

There was a grunt of dismay from one of the intruders and a short little cry from the other. They turned to face this menace and the Bat gave a shout of delight. In the darkness he recognized them. Silk, dripping wet, had driven the car; Carol was standing beside him.

"Boss!" Silk shouted.

Carol rushed toward the Bat and for a long minute was enfolded in his arms. Silk danced about, asking a dozen questions and getting no reply whatsoever.

"Boss, we figured you'd be dead! I was set to track down Blackie and strangle the rat. What happened? How'd you get loose?"

The Bat led them into the plant and pointed to the broken vault lid.

"There's the answer," he said cheerfully. "I raised the lid, shoved bullets under it and pushed the lid off."

"Let's get out of here," Carol suggested with a shudder.

"In a few moments," the Bat said. "The inventive mind behind this series of crimes isn't operating this plant because it's a good place to dispose of his enemies. He must have a laboratory somewhere in which he makes up his paste copies of the stolen gems. This is the likeliest spot for such work. I'm going to look around. Silk, watch the gate and if anyone comes, warn me."

The Bat opened various doors and found only supply rooms or small workshops. Then, leading off the west wall of the small office, he found a door that refused to open. He rapped the panels smartly and his knuckles stung. He kicked up a piece of metal and tapped against the door. It rang metallically. The door was made of steel and probably as secure as a vault.

Prowling around in one section of the plant the Bat found an oxyacetylene torch used to weld together the sides of the metal burial vaults. He rolled the heavy apparatus to the steel door, started the intensely hot flame and cut through the steel as if it were soft cheese.

He cut away the entire lock and the door swung open. The Bat switched on lights and Carol gasped in amazement. The interior of that room was lined with work benches on which was the equipment necessary to the manufacture of paste jewelry. There was a massive safe set in the concrete wall. The room itself was a veritable vault.

THE Bat used the torch again and this time he spent precious minutes before he had the vault door open. But his work gratified him a moment later, for within the vault he found more than half of the stolen loot.

"This," the Bat said softly, "is the headquarters of the criminal chief of all this business. Here is where he studies the gems so he can make perfect duplicates of them. Still we don't know who he is and he will, of course, have no outward connection with this joint. But we've put an awful crimp in his plans now. Silk, get on the phone and call the State Police Barracks nearest this spot. Tell them to rush a detail up here, that over two million dollars' worth of stolen gems are in this vault. Later on

The oxyacetylene torch cut though the steel.

Commissioner Warner will contact them. Hurry!"

"Wait!" Carol gripped the Bat's arm tightly. "There is something more I haven't told you. I was so glad to find you uninjured, Tony, that it slipped my mind. McFayden is the man to blame for all this danger you and I have barely escaped. It was McFayden who sent me on a trumped-up errand so that I might be kidnapped. This man you call Blackie is just his agent."

"McFayden!" the Bat frowned. "That complicates matters, but he'll have some explaining to do. All the more reason why we must hurry. Should Blackie or any of his men return before the troopers arrive, it will be up to us to hold them off."

Silk rushed into the office and got on the phone. The troopers would be sent immediately, he was assured.

"Outside," the Bat ordered when Silk returned. "We'll wait in the darkness until the police arrive and then run for it."

"Boss," Silk said, "the mugs who snatched Carol were on that fellow Carlyle's estate. You know, he bought into the Graham jewelry store with that Dutchman Van den Killan. Maybe Carlyle and McFayden are in cahoots."

"We'll soon know," the Bat replied. Twenty minutes later three State Police cruisers rolled into the yard. A captain was the first to enter the burial vault plant. He saw the yawning safe door, saw the gems gleaming brilliantly and also he saw—the insignia of the Bat pasted upon the vault.

"It must have been the Bat who phoned," he shouted. "And me thinking he was just a myth. Spread out, boys! Maybe some of those mugs will come back and I'd like to surprise 'em. Keep your guns ready."

"Say, Captain," a trooper asked, "what if this Black Bat should show up? Do we take him? Do we open fire on him?"

"You do not," the State Police captain ground out. "If he shows, I'll personally shake his hand. Maybe I'll even kiss him, I dunno. He put us on the trail of the biggest haul in stolen stuff that's happened in a century. Look at them rocks sparkle!"

"What's next on the progtam?" Silk asked as a few moments later he was driving the Bat and Carol toward the city.

They were all squeezed into the seat. The Bat's arms rested around Carol's shoulder.

"Back to the house," he told Silk. "We all need a rest. But not a long one. Blackie happens to require some attention and he'll get it—soon. Then the brains behind him will pay the piper. Those murderers have pulled their final trick."

"Promise you'll be careful," Carol begged. "I never realized before just how much you meant to me."

SILK sighed and glanced the other way. The Bat looked into Carol's shining eyes.

"And I've never fully realized just all that you have done for me. In that vault I thought for a moment that blindness had come once more. The veil which you tore away from my eyes, Carol. I thought you were gone forever. It's odd how clearly you can think under such circumstances. I'll never place you in peril again."

"Oh, yes, you will," Carol countered. "This case isn't finished yet, and if I can help in any way I'll do all you ask and more, if possible. Don't forget, this fight against crime is as much my battle as yours."

They were silent after that, and shortly had reached the rear of Tony Quinn's estate. By using the secret entrance, the Bat and Carol reached the house while Silk parked the coupé near Butch's rooming house.

The Bat stood before a mirror and slowly removed all traces of his disguise. The scars returned, making a mockery of his face. He grimaced at them. Carol touched his arm.

"Don't, Tony. Those scars are the brand of the Black Bat. Unless you had suffered so, the Bat would never have been born. They don't matter to me, for I know the man behind them."

Tony Quinn's eyes gradually became fixed and glassy. The old expression of lassitude returned. He donned his tweeds and a smoking jacket, picked up his cane, and slowly tapped his way toward the door leading into the library.

"Just practice," he assured Carol, "It's been hours since I was blind Tony Quinn."

He tapped his way across the room and sat down in his accustomed chair before the fireplace. Silk returned and prepared a light meal. They ate it, in that same room, for Carol had to be ready to see if anyone came. Her connection with Tony Quinn was unknown to any but Silk and Butch.

"When do we get McFayden?" Silk asked impatiently. "He's been breathing free air too long to suit me."

"Silk—Carol," the Bat said slowly, "I don't like to contradict you, but I'm afraid you are wrong. Perhaps McFayden did send you on a fool's errand, Carol, one by which you were exposed to danger. Yet McFayden is not the man I want. I believe he was duped himself into sending you into Blackie's hands."

"Do you mean he isn't the brains?" Carol asked, surprised. "But he must be, Tony. McFayden could have called that number and ordered Silk's death. He was able to gain access to Graham's vaults and rob them. He tricked you—almost threw you into Sergeant McGrath's arms."

"I reiterate"—Tony Quinn looked blankly into the fireplace—"McFayden is not our man. You see, I know the identity of the brains behind Blackie and all this murder and robbery. I've been sure of it for hours."

Silk started to object, but Quinn suddenly raised his hand in a gesture for silence.

"Someone is using the secret entrance," he said in a low voice.

Silk whipped out a gun and covered the hidden door. It opened and Butch came in, panting and excited.

"Boss?" he cried. "Boss, it's McFayden that's back of all the hellishness! I spotted that dirty little rat trying to get rid of a chunk of rock. A big diamond he couldn't afford to buy. The mug he tried to hock it with turned him down and McFayden beat it so fast I lost his trail. But it's him, all right."

CHAPTER XXI
NOCTURNAL VISITOR

POLICE COMMISSIONER WARNER tossed nervously in his sleep. Perhaps the shadow of a man who entered his bedroom by way of the window was responsible for that. The lamp beside Warner's bed was turned on. He sat up quickly and one hand darted beneath his pillow for the gun he invariably secreted there.

"It isn't necessary to go for a gun, Commissioner," a voice said calmly. "Or if you believe a weapon so necessary, please accept mine."

A .45 automatic hurtled through the air and dropped on Warner's bed. His eyes, now accustomed to the light, made out a weird form standing three feet away. It was a man, dressed entirely in black. A broad-shouldered, yet agile type of person. There was a black hood drawn over his head and throat.

"The Bat!" Warner exclaimed. Involuntarily his hand darted for the gun, then paused. "Excuse me, sir," he said a little sheepishly. "I did that purely from instinct. Take your gun, Bat."

The Bat sat down on the edge of the bed. The cold eyes that gleamed through the slits in the mask made Warner chill. Yet he knew those eyes were those of an honest man, of an individual who fought on the side of the law. Without the law's red tape, possibly, and without much mercy for desperadoes who shot and killed their way to riches.

"Thank you," the Bat said calmly. "I haven't misjudged you, Commissioner, and right now I particularly need your confidence. I'm on the verge of unveiling the mind behind this weird business of the jewel robbers and subsequent murders. I know his lieutenant; I know how the whole sordid business was done, but as yet I have no proof that will hold up in a court of law. That proof I must allow

you to furnish, for I doubt any judge or jury would be swayed very far by the words of a masked man sitting in the witness stand."

WARNER grinned. "And I doubt very much that Sergeant McGrath would estimate your true value to our side, sir. But you say you know who is behind this. Great heavens, tell me! Give me one clue and I'll do the rest."

"That clue will come later," the Bat answered. "For the moment it is necessary for you to call a conference or every man interested in this case. That means McFayden, Clifford Carlyle, Van den Killan, Wohl, Anghis Khan and Professor DiNonno. Request that all of them come to your home at three o'clock—this morning, of course. Have your men awaken them with that message. Do not allow any detectives to be planted outside the house. Sergeant McGrath may be with you, though, and two or three other trusted men. It's possible you may need them."

Warner glanced at the clock on his night table.

"That gives me three hours. I'll do it, Bat."

"And I can give you some cheerful news," the Bat went on. "At least a part of the loot is recovered. It ís now in the hands of the State Police in Connecticut. You might send several men to the Sherbrooke Burial Vault Company near Eastown, Connecticut. The killer, you see, owns that burial vault concern. He also owns four funeral parlors in this city. The object of that is to provide a safe hiding place for the jewels. He has encased them in the cement of burial vaults. Possibly some are even already interred."

Warner reached for the telephone and gave orders to the inspector in charge of Headquarters. He hung up slowly.

"I've tried to figure out the man behind it all, but damn it, Bat, I can't," he said mournfully. "The whole trouble is that almost everyone connected with the case has such a sound, honest reputation. Take Van den Killan—he has the most logical motive, because he has acquired ownership of three important business houses for a song. But Van den Killan is immensely rich and honest enough. Carlyle, his partner, is more or less unexplained and my suspicions have fastened on him strongly. He bought into the business with Van den Killan. He is wealthy, but there has been considerable talk of certain deals—strictly business and within the law, of course—that he has pulled in his day.

"Gill is bankrupt, and anyhow a man wouldn't put himself out of business in order to rob others, McFayden, in my opinion, is a sneaking little rat, but he doesn't seem to have the brains necessary for a job of this sort.

"Anghis Khan and Professor DiNonno I've

investigated thoroughly. They have handled millions of dollars' worth of gems here and abroad. If they had crooked tendencies, they would probably have shown them long before now.

"The same goes for Dr. Wohl. He worked in Amsterdam supervising the cutting of extremely valuable gems. Why, he even cut the great Mogul Diamond with his own hands!"

"And Harriman?" the Bat asked softly,

COMMISSIONER WARNER jerked erect.

"There you have touched upon the most logical suspect. The condition of the corpse we found in his car indicates that it was purposely disfigured and burned so it could not be positively identified. What I believe is that Harriman substituted the body of another man so we'd think he is dead. Graham is, of course, out of the question as a suspect."

"Graham," the Bat said quietly, "was murdered. And I might suggest that you investigate the floors of Graham's and Gill's vaults. I've already located the tunnel that leads directly into their safes, but I don't think you'll find one beneath Harriman's."

"So that was how it was done!" Warner ejaculated, his jaws closing with a snap. "But I can't agree with you, Bat, that Graham was murdered. Two witnesses saw him shoot himself."

"Nevertheless he was murdered," the Bat said. "And then, too, there is another murder you haven't mentioned. The murder of Fawcett."

The commissioner smiled a little. "That one is on the records as being either your work or that of Blackie Burns. We discovered Blackie's identity when McGrath had to go through about ten thousand rogue's gallery pictures to place Burns, but he did it all right. McGrath also sent in the two men you left in that funeral parlor. We questioned them for hours, because of that note you so kindly left on one of them. Those men were just paid mobsters who haven't the vaguest idea as to what it's all about. They don't even know Blackie's real identity."

The Bat laughed. "Nor does the man who hired Blackie. That precious scoundrel, Blackie Burns, is working both ends against the middle. He intends to make away with the loot—and soon, too. I had hoped either he or the man who employs him would fall into the hands of the troopers in control

of the burial vault plant. But if they did come back there, they probably saw the police cars and lights and fled. Perhaps it is best because men would have died in that encounter, and there has been enough of murder in this case."

The Bat touched the switch on the night lamp and plunged the room into darkness. For a moment he hovered above Warner. "And I thank you for another clue you just gave me. A clue I found impossible to locate myself. It merely clinches the case, but it is essential."

There was a rustling sound at the window and then complete silence. Commissioner Warner leaned weakly back against the head of the bed.

"*I gave him a clue?*" he mumbled. "*I just gave him a clue? I don't remember saying anything to give him a lead.*"

THINGS were getting a little too hot for Blackie Burns. First of all, he was pretty certain now that the police had identified him as one of the topnotch jewel thieves in the racket. Then there was the episode at the burial vault plant. Blackie had narrowly missed capture there. Only the fact that he had spotted the State Police cars parked along the road saved him. As it was, more than half of the looted gems were now in possession of the police. It was time for a showdown and Blackie's avaricious nature asserted itself.

Ten minutes before, Blackie had entered a room that was plunged in complete darkness. There, by prearrangement, he had found the unknown for whom he worked. He had listened to suave promises, boasts that the finding of more than half of the gems meant little, for there would be other jobs soon.

But Blackie was not satisfied. The Bat was closing in too fast. Blackie wanted to get out with a whole skin—and as much of the loot as possible.

Therefore, instead of obeying the orders of the man whose orders he had been docilely taking, Blackie had slipped out of the darkened room instead of waiting ten minutes as he had been requested to do. He was out of the secret meeting place as fast as the mysterious man who guided his criminal activities, and when he saw a man hurrying down the street, Blackie went in swift pursuit.

The man he trailed shortly entered a house. Blackie's eyes narrowed. It was time for the showdown. He hefted the weight of a gun in his side coat pocket and went on.

He paused abruptly and looked up and down the street. Somehow Blackie was afraid. He cursed the Bat, but chilled at thought of him, too. Then he climbed the steps of the brownstone front house he had seen his quarry enter, rang the bell and when the door was opened, Blackie grinned and shoved his gun against the man's stomach.

"Sorry," Blackie grated. "Keep your hands up, Boss. I don't like to do this, but I got a hunch you're going to pull out."

"You fool!" the man in the shadows snapped. "When the time is ripe, you'll get your share of the stuff. Didn't I order you not to attempt to prove my identity? Coming here, like this, is dangerous. And it was your fault that the Bat escaped from the burial vault plant. It was your stupidity that caused him to find those gems and my laboratory. You must have mentioned something about that room in his hearing. I've been on the verge of ordering your death several times, but when you entered this little game, I promised you'd be provided for and I meant it. You and the boys already have a split from the proceeds of the gems I peddled in Europe and you must admit it was ingenuity that snuggled them out of the country."

"I admit I should have killed the Bat," Blackie said ruefully. "But he must have had help. No man could have lifted the lid off that vault. It takes a crane to move one of those around. Just the same I want to see what's left of the swag right now! Just to prove you haven't been holding out. Show me the stuff and I'll do anything you say."

THE man in the shadows approved. "Good! The Bat did, of course, take about half the loot away from us, damn him. I left it at the burial vault plant so you would know I was not trying to cheat you. You know also that a quarter of the loot has already been sold in Europe. Fortunately, I kept another quarter in a place where the Bat could never locate it. That part is checked at the railroad terminal.

"Here are the checks. You may get the stuff and keep it in your room. Examine it to your heart's content, Blackie. I'm not holding out on you. I may have insisted on saying where the loot was to be kept, but except for this last quarter of it, you knew every moment just where I had it.

"I turn this final portion over to you now so you will have no further suspicions of me, and know that I trust you, too. When you get it, just wait in your room until you hear from me. Is that clear? By the way, you still occupy that room at eleven thirty-nine Riverview Avenue, don't you?"

"Right," Blackie said. "I'll get the stuff and go there to wait. I'll sit on the stuff and nobody gets in. When you come we'll split. But say, Boss, why don't you handle this end of it?"

"You'd suspect me of running out," the man in the shadows answered. "Besides I haven't time to get it. That fool of a police commissioner has called everyone connected with the case to his home. At three o'clock in the morning, less than an hour and a half from now. I must go there to avoid being suspected."

"Maybe he's wise," Blackie said, but he gulped.

"He knows nothing," came the contemptuous reply. "How could he? Every track is covered. The Bat found those other gems through sheer luck. Before dawn I shall be at your room to discuss the final sharing of what we have taken. That is all—except, be very careful. A slip now will mean your death. You understand that should we be captured, you are as guilty as I."

"But I didn't kill nobody," Blackie protested. "I—"

"Wait! Listen!" The mysterious leader held up one hand. "Blackie! There is someone uptairs. Follow closely and if you so much as see a shadow move—open fire."

"Got it, Chief," Blackie raised his gun.

Softly they crept up the staircase. They inspected each room until they reached the last one, the master bedroom. Blackie pointed his gun at a closet door while his killer chief prepared to jerk it open.

"He must be in here," the killer chief growled. "Be ready to shoot,"

But when the door was flung hack, nothing happened. The spacious closet was filled with clothing, but by the light filtering from the bedroom it seemed plain that there was no sign of an intruder.

"I am getting nervous," the killer said, mopping his face. "This has lasted too long and I am glad it is now over with. Follow my orders, Blackie. Before dawn we shall feast our eyes on the greatest collection of gems in existence."

THEY hurried downstairs and Blackie departed. Three minutes after the closet door was closed, a portion of shadow in the farthest corner moved slightly. The door opened a crack. The shadow took on a more substantial form, became a man dressed entirely in black.

The Bat! His dark clothing and the fact that every inch of his face and hands had been covered had made him practically invisible. His eyes could see every move made by the killer and Blackie, but they had not been able to distinguish him from the clothing in the closet. It had been a close call for the Bat.

With a coat draped over one arm, and moving with no more noise than a ghost, the Bat retreated to another room, clambered out a window and vanished into the night. In spite of the darkness and shadows which made the killer chief a blur to Blackie, the Bat had seen the face of the man he sought and listened to his preparations for flight. The Bat's testimony would have convicted the man in a split second. Yet that testimony could never be told before a judge and jury. The Bat worked without thoughts of reward or glory. To him went only the dangerous preparation of a case and the police finished it.

CHAPTER XXII
MURDER'S GUN

REACHING the sidewalk, the Bat got into a car that slid up to the curb and stopped.

"Butch," he said, "we're nearing the finish of this business. Silk is holding down our end at the house. Carol has done her share—and well. You have only one more thing to do. At the next corner you will get out. From behind a hedge of that house, which happens to be unoccupied, watch the brownstone house from which I just emerged. A man will leave it shortly.

"Give him fifteen minutes. Then enter through a rear window which I have left open. In the library there is a large portrait of Cecil Rhodes, the South African diamond king. That portrait is part of a false door. Open it and a wall safe of good dimensions will be revealed. On this slip of paper I'm giving you is the combination of that safe."

Butch took the paper and stuffed it into his vest pocket. "You sure don't miss up on anything, do you, Boss?"

"At this stage of the game there can be no misses," the Bat said firmly. "I watched our killer gloat over his loot. When he put it back in the safe, I used these super-sensitive eyes of mine to good effect to get the combination that will open the safe. As soon as you open it, examine the contents of the valise inside. You will find, among other gems, a diamond necklace with a slight scratch on the underside of the clasp. That necklace is my own and I don't want the police to identify it.

"When you have done that, take the valise of gems to Police Commissioner Warner's home. Sergeant McGrath's car will be in front of the house. Put the valise on the front seat of the car and then run for it. You understand everything?"

"A cinch," Butch said, grinning widely. "Boy, wouldn't I like to see McGrath's pan when he finds that bunch of rocks in his own car!"

BUTCH got out and took up his position behind the hedge. The Bat drove away, parked along a side street on the other side of town and made his stealthy way to the door of a rooming house. With a skeleton key, he opened the door quietly, walked up the stairs and entered one of the rooms. He turned on no lights.

Twenty minutes later the door opened and Blackie entered. He was carrying two suitcases that appeared to be very heavy. Blackie switched on the lights, pulled down the cracked, worn window shade.

"So I'm to sit here and wait for his nibs, am I?" he gloated. "That's what he thinks. There's enough rocks in these suitcases to keep me for life, and am I going to live."

Blackie picked up one suitcase, set it on a table and reached for the lock.

"I wouldn't do that, Blackie," a quiet voice said.

Blackie spun around, and his face drained white. Both hands shot upward. He made no attempt to reach the gun under his arm. Something about the Black Bat warned him that might prove disastrous. Perhaps the .45 automatic trained on his chest had something to do with it.

"Listen"—Blackie licked his lips— "I'll make a deal. You take one of these bags and I'll take the other. I'll scram for good."

"I wouldn't take one of those bags for any kind of a gift, Blackie. You'd be a fool to do it, too. Why? Because all the time you have believed this man for whom you work. You've had faith in him. Tonight you seek to double-cross him but he is more intelligent than you. You are the one who has been tricked."

"You—you're crazy," Blackie managed, but without much assurance now.

The Bat's left hand threw a penknife on the table. "Take that and slit open the side of each of those suitcases. Be most careful how you do it, Blackie. The little gems contained inside won't sparkle. They'll *just* give one mighty roar and hurl you into little pieces. If you opened those bags in the regular way, the contents would be set off."

Blackie's eyes were popping and a slow fury began to fill his soul. Carefully he made an incision in the side of the bag, worried the hole larger and finally he had the whole side open. Within he saw layers of small bits of metal topped by a black tin box which had the set of wires leading to three dry cell batteries and a second set attached to the mechanism that would open the bag.

Blackie sat down weakly.

"You win," he gulped. "He was set to frame me, all right. You saved my life and if I can help in running down that heel, I'll do it. I'll talk in return for a light rap. Anyway, didn't that wise guy try to bump me? All you gotta do is grab—"

"I know his name," the Bat smiled behind the mask. "We're going to see him—now. You'll have your chance to prove there is some spark of manhood in you. And Blackie, remove the gun from your shoulder clip. Throw it on the bed and be careful just how you perform that operation. My automatic is equipped with a hair trigger."

POLICE Commissioner Warner occupied the center of the floor. He spoke quietly, but from time to time he glanced anxiously at a mantel clock. It was fifteen minutes past three and his guests were getting more than a little impatient. Every man who had in any slightest way come into this jewelry robbing and murder case sat before him.

Van den Killan arose.

"This is enough for me," he growled. "Out of my bed you took me and for what? To listen to you talk about things I know already."

"He's right," Clifford Carlyle, Van den Killan's partner, grumbled in acquiescence. "I don't understand your attitude, Commissioner. All of us have been through some particularly trying circumstances these past few days. We need rest—not this tableau you've arranged for us. If there are any vital questions, ask them and let us go."

McFayden arose, drew down the corners of his mouth and headed for the door. Sergeant McGrath intercepted him, put a hand against the jewelry store clerk's chest and shoved him into a chair.

"Next time," he growled, "I'll use my fist on your jaw. What's your hurry? Don't you like the atmosphere?"

McFayden's eyes flashed around the room angrily. "I'm not afraid of anything," he snarled. "I'm innocent."

"Are you quite certain of that, Mr. McFayden?"

The voice came from somewhere among the darker shadows of the room. Velvet drapes moved with a slight swish and the Bat stood before them. Both hands held guns and they covered everyone in the room. McGrath gave a yelp of rage and his hand darted toward a hip pocket. It froze halfway there. Those guns in the hooded man's hands were held steadily. "Sergeant," the Bat called out, "why be so hasty?"

McFayden was on his feet, trembling like a leaf. "You—you can't accuse me!" he yelled. "I haven't done anything."

"You haven't done anything much," the Bat put in mildly. "You're a thief, McFayden. You helped yourself to several baubles from the stock of Graham's store. You figured that possibly they'd be listed as the loot of the brainy character behind all this murder and thievery. You tried to pawn one of those gems a few hours ago."

McFAYDEN groaned and sat down. His chin drooped against his chest. "But I swear I didn't kill anybody!" he quavered. "there were just three diamonds I took."

The Bat nodded. "Quite right. Now we come to the real meaning of our little gathering. Among you, gentlemen, is a man whose brains concocted one of the most heinous crimes in modern history. Because of that warped intellect, men have died. Others have been robbed. The faith in every jewelry house in the nation has been shattered. Gems to the value of millions have been stolen. Men have been murdered ruthlessly."

Commissioner Warner jumped up, waved for silence.

"Wait—I have it! Harriman is the killer. He isn't dead! There are tunnels beneath the vaults of the Graham and Gill stores. There is none beneath the Harriman place. He must have robbed his own stock and used the tunnels to steal the gems from the other two stores."

"Harriman," the Bat said quietly, "is dead. It was his body you found in that burned car. Graham also was murdered. The killer was well known to Graham and came into his office. He forced Graham to phone for McFayden to come after several minutes had passed. That was because the murderer wanted a witness to Graham's apparent suicide. Graham was knocked unconscious. Perhaps you recall now that there was a bump on his head which the coroner said had probably been made when his head hit the desk after he collapsed. But the murderer did that. Then he hid behind the chair in which Graham was seated. When McFayden and the secretary entered the murderer shot Graham, but to them it appeared to be Graham's arm that appeared above the desk, his hand that fired that shot."

McFAYDEN protested shrilly. "It couldn't have been. If anybody was hidden behind that chair, where did he go? I wasn't gone but a minute or two."

"You and the secretary ran out," the Bat said. "During that moment, the killer got away. He went into the vault, through the tunnel beneath the floor and vanished. He wanted both Graham and Harriman to commit suicide so that it would seem as if they had looted their own stores. But things broke a little too fast when Mrs. Van den Killan discovered her tiara was a fake. You will recall that she saw the original of her tiara in Europe. Part of the loot was shipped there, hidden in either the caskets or the cadavers of people who had died here and whose bodies were shipped abroad."

"You informed me, during your visit to my room," Commissioner Warner broke in excitedly, "that I had given you a necessary clue. What was it? How did I give you a lead?"

The Bat chuckled, "Graham, as he talked to his murderer said he knew he was going to die, tried to leave a clue. He drew a certain design on a pad and added a few words to it. The killer recognized the danger and ripped the paper off the pad. But there were indentations on the paper below the one Graham wrote on. I brought out the design and the word 'kill.' I knew Graham had written it.

"The design is that of a famous diamond, cut by a great expert many years ago—when that expert was honest. In assuming that Harriman was the killer because his store had no tunnel, you wrong his memory, Commissioner. Graham and Harriman intended to merge their businesses. They had even drawn up an agreement to that effect.

"The murderer knew this and did his best to destroy that paper. I found the ashes and tonight I entered Harriman's store, looked through his files and came upon the duplicate of that agreement. It gave Graham legal right to send a man over to estimate the value of Harriman's stock. That man is the killer!"

Warner whirled about. "Dr. Wohl!" he cried.

Wohl, his face pale, eyes bulging and lips drawn back into a snarl, retreated a few steps. He blubbered alibis.

"Stop it!" the Bat thundered. "You're the killer."

The Bat flung a coat into the middle of the room.

"When you killed Graham some blood got on your sleeve and you brushed it against the back of the chair. You didn't even know that blood was there. That is your coat, Dr. Wohl. I removed it from your house tonight. You came close to discovering me—remember."

"Madness!" Wohl raged. "Madness and nonsense. I do not know what this masked crook is talking about."

"You cut the great Mogul Diamond," the Bat said evenly. "That was the design which Graham traced on the pad. You are famous for that piece of work and Graham hoped someone might put two and two together and realize that tracing was a clue. Unfortunately for Graham, he also tried to write a message which you spotted and destroyed. Wohl, you went to Harriman's store to estimate the value of his gems. You went there several times and with each visit you switched paste gems for the real thing. That was why no tunnel was necessary for the robbery at Harriman's."

"You can't prove anything!" Wohl yelled. "There is nothing against me."

THE Bat gestured with one arm and Blackie emerged from behind the curtains. Wohl's white face grew ruddy with rage. Despite the guns in the Bat's hands, Wohl took a desperate chance. He reached into his coat pocket and fired without removing the gun he had concealed there. Blackie's shirt front turned crimson. He staggered back a step and clapped a hand to the wound. Then he sank slowly into a chair.

Wohl had no time to shoot again. Like a streak of black lightning, the Bat was across the room. He shoved Wohl back with the flat of his hand, measured him and as Wohl's hidden gun came up to fire again, the Bat hit him on the point of the jaw. Wohl staggered back, banged into a chair and tripped over it. He landed in a heap, shrieking curses at the Black Bat.

"It's Wohl," Blackie was saying weakly. "He hired me to help him. I'll tell everything. He took photographs of jewels that were in for repairs. He made up duplicates and switched them. He did everything—the murder of Graham and Harriman, everything. He robbed their stores. Gill's too! He even tried to double-cross me, the dirty rat. Oh, I'll talk all right! Somebody get me a doctor."

Sergeant McGrath leaped upon Wohl and handcuffs clicked. Warner gave terse orders. "An ambulance for Blackie. McGrath, watch Dr. Wohl."

Warner turned slowly, talking to the Bat as he did so.

"You have my thanks, whoever you are—" he began, then suddenly realized he was talking to thin air.

The Bat was gone!

Sergeant McGrath gave a shout of rage. "He got away! He took the stuff that Wohl swiped with him."

"You're wrong, Sergeant." The Bat's voice came from behind the velvet curtains at the window. "You'll find the swag in the front seat of your car. It's been there for some time."

The curtains moved outwardly as an early morning breeze caught them. For a full minute only an eerie silence held sway. Then Blackie groaned.

"I'll put my finger on that killer!" he moaned. "I'll tell you everybody else who helped, too. Double-cross me, will he—!"

Warner turned to McGrath. "Well, Sergeant, what have you to say about the Black Bat now? Pretty helpful gent, eh?"

"He's against the law," the sergeant growled. "That's all I know. And I'll get him, one of these days"

"Well, at any rate," Warner said, hiding a grin, "I understand you were convinced the Black Bat is not our old friend, Tony Quinn. At least, you won't go around accusing poor blind Tony."

"Oh, yeah?" Sergeant McGrath said, his face reddening. "When I examined that hood that was left in the car, I found some grease stains! That means the Black Bat was in disguise—and it could be Tony Quinn! One of these days—"

Commissioner Warner chuckled silently as he left Sergeant McGrath looking grim and with a faraway look in his eyes.

THE END

A 75ᵗʰ anniversary illustrated classic from Volume 1, Number 1 of *Exciting Comics*

adapted by Raymond Thayer from Norman A. Daniels' novel *Brand of the Black Bat*

A 75th anniversary illustrated classic from Volume 1, Number 1 of *Exciting Comics*

adapted by Raymond Thayer from Norman A. Daniels' novel *Brand of the Black Bat*

A 75th anniversary illustrated classic from Volume 1, Number 1 of *Exciting Comics*

An hour ahead of time, Snate's gangsters pour out of the car and into the bank.

Like clockwork, the bandits perform their murderous task and flee —

adapted by Raymond Thayer from Norman A. Daniels' novel *Brand of the Black Bat*

A 75th anniversary illustrated classic from Volume 1, Number 1 of *Exciting Comics*

adapted by Raymond Thayer from Norman A. Daniels' novel *Brand of the Black Bat*

A 75th anniversary illustrated classic from Volume 1, Number 1 of *Exciting Comics*

adapted by Raymond Thayer from Norman A. Daniels' novel *Brand of the Black Bat*

A 75th anniversary illustrated classic from Volume 1, Number 1 of *Exciting Comics*